FIGHTING FOR THE GUN

Redmond dove at Checker from his saddle, driving the former Ranger backward. The Colt sailed from Checker's weakened right hand. As he leaned, Redmond threw a haymaker at Checker's midsection.

Breath exploded from Checker's body. Dazed, Checker took a second blow to his midsection, taking away any remaining breath.

Checker bent over and Redmond leaned down to grab the fallen gun. Before his fingers could curl around the weapon, Checker's left fist viciously slammed the back of the outlaw's neck. Redmond whimpered and flattened against the ground. His fingers released the gun. Checker's boot followed, driving into his stomach. Redmond's groan echoed through the woodlands. A second kick quickly followed, as fierce as the first.

Checker drew his other Colt with his left hand and placed it against the back of Redmond's head. "Go…ahead…Redmond. Pick it up…please."

BLOOD BROTHERS

COTTON SMITH

LEISURE BOOKS NEW YORK CITY

A LEISURE BOOK®

October 2006

Published by

Dorchester Publishing Co., Inc.
200 Madison Avenue
New York, NY 10016

ISBN 0-8439-5538-4

The name "Leisure Books" and the stylized "L" with design are
trademarks of Dorchester Publishing Co., Inc.

Printed in the United States of America.

Visit us on the web at www.dorchesterpub.com.

BLOOD BROTHERS

CHAPTER ONE

Fresh unshod pony tracks crossed the trail ahead. John Checker's hard face was usually difficult to read. Not this time. The former Texas Ranger knew their trouble had just begun.

His hand curled around the trigger guard of his Winchester resting sideways in a short leather holster attached to his saddle horn. Below the gun, a canteen, with its straps wrapped tightly around the horn to keep it from bouncing, offered a gentle swish of its half-filled contents and belied the tension building within him.

Ahead, a fat jay served as a sentinel without knowing its role. He figured the bird would be alarmed before anyone, including himself, could see the war party.

He was counting on it.

"This is no time for any of your tricks," he muttered to himself, recalling Indian legends involving deceptions played by the jay on the coyote and others. "You must be my brother today." He frowned. His own stepbrothers were the reason for this situation.

Saving his sister's two kidnapped children from a savage band of outlaws, led by one stepbrother, was only the beginning. Getting them home safely through the vast, lawless Indian Territory would be a treacherous trip. Especially when he and his three friends must also bring the herd of horses stolen from his sister's ranch, five captured outlaws, and a medicine wagon with two steers and two saddled horses, shuffling behind it on taut ropes.

A wilderness of hiccupping hills and tree-crowded woodlands greeted the strange caravan. They were headed for Dodge City, Kansas, and were moving along the now-silent trail through the territory that had hosted a brown river of Texas cattle in the spring and summer. A few hours behind them was the outlaws' cabin hidden in a swollen forest, where the two children had been freed. Fresh graves were the only indication the rest of the gang had been left there.

Through the quiet land, the group's own music had a mystical life of its own. The jiggling rows of tiny bells lining the wagon harness, the snorting and blowing of the horse herd, creaking wheels, growling saddle leather, and the occasional cough and curse of men blended into a parade of sound. A sound that Checker knew could be heard for a long way. Too long. He continued watching the jay survey the land from a tall branch.

"Let me know, brother jay," he whispered to himself. "I'm counting on you."

Riding beside him on his right, Checker's eight-year-old nephew, Johnny Hedrickson, watched him curiously. The boy wanted to be as close to his uncle as possible, and Checker felt the same way. But the signs ahead told Checker that he would need to move the boy to a safer location. Maybe the wagon. At least he and his sister would be out of sight.

The tall man remained a glorious mystery to the boy,

only a figure in daydreams until a few months ago when he came riding into their lives for the first time. A man born of the stories told by his mother, Checker's sister. A man who had come out of the night with his friends to rescue him and his little sister. A man feared and respected by many.

Johnny tried to push aside the terrible ache about his parents; he knew his father was dead and his mother, terribly beaten. He stared at his horse's bridle. Maybe she, too, had died by now. He wanted to ask again for reassurance about her, but how could the answer be any different than earlier? Of course, no one knew. Not even his uncle.

Autumn had settled around their tension, painting reds and crimsons on the alder, redbud, and arrowpoint leaves, touching the cottonwoods, scrub oak, and willows with golds, oranges, and bright yellows, and turning the long draws, streambeds, and hillsides into a fury of color. It was beautiful, except for the marks of unshod horses as a reminder of ever-lurking danger.

Even the familiarity of the trail itself seemed oddly unfriendly. The Triple C riders had followed it in great haste days before, trailing the gang. Indian Territory was a world truly unto itself and void of law, except in the civilized tribes' settlements. No federal lawmen attempted to patrol the region, turned away by the vast distances and by good sense. Only a few daring federal marshals ever entered the Nations in pursuit of wrongdoers. Only the best, and luckiest, rode out again. Checker had gone into the Nations as a Ranger, but never in this part of the perilous land.

Somewhere ahead were trails once glutted with almost endless streams of Texas cattle. But these grassworn pathways to Kansas would be ghosts now, longing for the spring that hid behind the coming winter. At least they would provide a roadway to safety. Of course, they were also watched by those who sought only to steal and destroy. The only exception would be the occasional group of returning Texas cowboys, but there were far more direct routes for them to take.

"Checker, ya see them tracks? Them's Injun tracks. What'cha gonna do when they come at us?" O.F. Venner, the black outlaw, hollered from his horse. His wide oval eyes searched the tall man's face for agreement. "You ain't gonna have no time to untie us an' give us iron. You'd better do it now."

Checker didn't respond. Only the arrowhead-shaped scar on his right cheek showed any sign of acknowledgment as it reddened with his renewed desire to lash out at the men who had kidnapped his sister's children, raped and dragged her almost to death, killed her husband, and burned down their young ranch.

Revenge rode close. Very close. Everything in him wanted to lynch the remaining outlaws. The image of his torn and battered sister kept a haunting vigil in his mind. Back at the outlaw hideout, only the words of restraint by Sonny Jones—who lay in the wagon, wounded by outlaw bullets—and by Jackson, who now drove it—had kept Checker from hanging the remaining outlaws after the battle was over. His friends had reminded him of his determination in Dodge to keep those same outlaws from being lynched by Texas cowboys, after Star McCallister and his rustlers were arrested and held in the jail for trial. They had appealed to his years of being a lawman, a Texas Ranger.

But that was before they escaped and brought unforgiving hell to Checker's sister and her family. Everything changed—for Checker—after that. Everything. He forced himself to concentrate on the jay and shut out the clamor of the other outlaws also wanting to be untied and armed. He pushed the torturous picture of his sister back into the corner of his thoughts.

"Come on, Checker," Venner whined again, his eyes even wider on his elongated face. "They could come outta them trees painted an' a-screamin' any time now. Look at them tracks, they're fresh as a new calf. Damn it, they'll kill us all."

"Mister, I think y'all oughta stop right now," Peter Jackson chimed in from the wagon. "I killed one man back there and I reckon I've got a taste for it now."

There was no bluff in the black drover's statement with its liquid southern accent, and the outlaws knew it. Not even the blustery Rebel gunman, Tom Redmond, countered his threat.

Peter Jackson, the steady black cowboy with his ever-present spectacles, drove the brightly colored patent-medicine wagon and the team of matching bays as if he had handled such every day of his life. His thick frame made him appear shorter than his six-feet-one; his quiet way belied an immovable toughness. A former slave with a gift for horses, a love of books, and a savvy for cattle, he only went by "Jackson" and most didn't know if it was a first name or a last. He liked it that way. He'd been called a lot worse. More than anyone, he knew the trails of this land, at least the ones that led to Kansas railheads. But even he had been to Dodge only once, and that was this summer.

Next to him was Checker's sleeping four-and-a-half-year-old niece, still holding a half-eaten apple. Strands of Rebecca Hedrickson's golden hair were limp across his thighs. Lying at his feet was a Winchester. His old, scratched pipe swirled fresh smoke about his dark, round face and wire-rimmed glasses, then slipped past graying hair under a misshapen black hat with a half-inch silk band around the rim. A long, weather-streaked gray coat with big pockets carried a book in the right pocket and a pistol in the left, both usual contents. He ran his hand along his lower back. It had bothered him most of the trail drive, but no one knew that either.

"All we're asking for is a chance against them Injuns," Venner pleaded, hoping their common skin color would have a positive effect. "We have to stick together . . . right now. You an' me."

Checker hadn't taken his eyes off the jay still comfortable in its porch. If he was listening, it didn't show.

"Don't go using 'we' with me, black boy," Jackson responded. "Ya'll an' the rest killed friends o' mine, tore up a mighty good lady, scared two sweet children—an' killed their pappy. Letting Injuns have y'all would be sweet justice. Might be I'll change my mind about thinking it's important to get ya back to Dodge." He patted Rebecca's head lightly and resumed his watch of Checker.

The tall gunfighter had barely slept since the gang escaped from the Dodge City Jail and kidnapped the children. Mostly short naps in the saddle. But Jackson trusted Checker's instincts in battle as he trusted no one else's, not even the fearless Sonny Jones's.

Venner looked down at his tied hands and sighed.

Jackson snapped the reins to keep the medicine wagon horses moving at a pace with the riders. They had long ago quit their parade prance and moved with their heads down. The wagon was a rich red, trimmed in gold and purple. DR. GAMBREE'S PATENTED MEDICINES was presented in large, bold letters on both sides. A smaller block of lettering explained PROVEN CURES FOR THIN BLOOD, COUGHING, RHEUMATISM, BALDNESS, SORES, FEMININE ILLNESS, AND MORE! THRILL TO SALOME AND HER DANCE OF SEVEN VEILS! ENJOY THE WORD OF GOD PREACHED BY DR. GAMBREE, ORDAINED MINISTER OF FAITH. Within the enclosed vehicle were bottled and packaged medicines, a trunk of costumes, a box of presentation props, a small portable table, a valise, three large sacks of grain for their horses, extra weapons and blankets, some food from their own trail supplies and from the cabin—and the wounded Sonny Jones lying on a pallet in the back.

The wagon and medicine show had been a front for Blue McCallister, the younger brother of Star, the outlaw gang's leader, and the key to their escape. Both men were half brothers to Checker and his sister, making their treachery terribly difficult for Checker to accept. Realizing Star had been the mastermind behind a well-organized gang of rustlers had struck at his soul. Then the discovery of Star's savagery at Amelia's horse ranch had brought him close to the same evil that his half brothers possessed, in his thirst for revenge.

Ever since they left the outlaw hideout—and his deadly encounter with Blue McCallister, Checker had been chewing on his undeniable connection to the villainous brothers. No matter how much he churned it over in his mind, Star, Blue, and he were brothers. They had the same father. Half brothers, for sure, but nonetheless, brothers. Some of their blood was the same as his. A part of him kept trying to shift the blame for the Hedrickson atrocity to the gang, and away from Star. Even though he knew in his heart that the vicious attack was all Star's idea. It had to be. Still, this odd feeling remained, like a stray dog that wouldn't go home.

Also weighing heavy on Checker's mind was his killing of the younger McCallister. Blue now lay in an unmarked grave not far from the outlaws' hideout. He and another outlaw recruited for the purpose had tried to ambush the former Ranger. That Checker had no choice but to shoot or die didn't give him much relief.

No one knew where Star might be; he had escaped during the fight with the Triple C riders after they surrounded the cabin. The gritty farm boy, Tyrel Bannon, had been last to see him in a brief standoff.

Checker concentrated on the jay ahead of them, ignoring "Salome," the medicine show main attraction, riding to his left. Of apparent Egyptian linage, she had danced seductively while Blue, pretending to be a "Dr. Gambree," preached about the wonders of his medicines. Most of the wagon's costumes were hers. She now rode in sullen silence, also tied to the saddle. She had tried to kill Checker before they left. Thick ebony hair lay over her shoulders. She wore a gray dress, unbuttoned at the neck and down the front far enough to reveal glimpses of her ample bosom. So far, the only ones that appeared to have noticed were Redmond— and Bannon.

At the point ahead of the herd, and proud of the assignment, rode the young Bannon, trying to be ever alert to danger. Freckles and his slim frame belied his eighteen years and his raw toughness. A new Winchester lay across his saddle. That and a new gun belt and Colt had been gifts from the grateful Triple C trail boss for helping save the rustled herd and his life.

Right now he was munching on a piece of jerky and scratching his fingers on a black mark on his new chaps. It wouldn't go away. He didn't know how it got there and was bothered that the chaps, as well as the new shirt, hat, and spurs he had purchased in Dodge didn't look fresh anymore. More like the old stuff Jackson wore.

Bannon was controlling the herd's lead mare with a rope halter, and the other horses were following dutifully. Nipping at each other, they had earlier jostled for rightful positions of leadership and now were settled into a steady, nonconfrontational pace. The herd was a mixture of mares, geldings, and two handsome, long-legged stallions. In addition to the thirty Hedrickson horses, there were extra outlaw horses and relief mounts that Checker and the others had used to keep close in pursuit.

So far, the trail had given him time to think about home, his mother and sister, when he wasn't thinking about food—or the sensual Salome. His family seemed a lifetime away since he was hired to help drive the Triple C herd north. His daydreaming room was frequently interrupted by his own horse. The sorrel had a habit of throwing its head every now and then, and occasionally going into a jogging trot that rattled Bannon's body. Or a sideways canter that defied logic. He hated this sorrel and was certain the feeling was mutual.

Whispering, Bannon asked, "Can't ya walk jes' like John's black? Come on, please. Damn you, come on." He knew his mother would be displeased to have heard the swearing, but the animal deserved it.

Pulling on the reins didn't seem to help. Neither did spurring. That only triggered laid-back ears on the sorrel's head. He should have ridden his backup horse, instead of letting it run with the herd as Sonny's and Jackson's relief mounts were. He kept thinking the sorrel would finally act the way he wanted, seeing positive signs at the end of every day—but returning the next to the same ornery animal.

When he wasn't worried about the horse's habits, or dreaming about home, or wondering what they were going to eat for supper, the farm boy was thinking about Salome. Concentration didn't come easy as his mind replayed Salome's uncovered bosom. He had seen her dance in town and had been instantly captivated by her swirling rainbow-colored wrap around her sensuously undulating body.

Occasionally, he turned in the saddle as if to check the back of the herd, allowing himself another sweet glimpse of her beauty. It helped to break up the monotony of the trail. But he understood well the danger of their return through the Nations. Only a fool wouldn't. Most of the trail seemed only vaguely familiar, even

though he and Sonny had traveled through it just days
before, as the point men in tracking the gang. The only
definite landmark, so far, had been the great rock over-
hang where he had waited while Sonny scouted ahead
in the rain.

He had heard the stories of outlaws seeking safety after raiding towns in Kansas or Missouri. Or worse,
painted parties of Kiowas and Comanches searching
for anything to strike. He may have been on only one
cattle drive, but he could read sign, and had been involved in a Kiowa attack. Indians were likely near. He
could feel it. The hair along the back of his neck rose as
the thought registered.

CHAPTER TWO

Of course, the farm boy knew they could also be met by mounted police of one of the civilized tribes—Cherokees, Creeks, Seminoles, Choctaws, and Chickasaws. They occupied the Territory legally and often stopped cattle herds and demanded payment for passage through their land. However, they had no real authority, except with other Indians.

"Leas'wise, they wouldn't be goin' after nothin' but money," Bannon muttered to himself and shivered again.

He didn't need to be reminded either of the real possibility that Star McCallister himself might circle back to ambush them. He had left the gang's hideout through an escape tunnel and fled on a hidden horse. It didn't matter to Bannon that the outlaw leader had proclaimed he wouldn't bother them again. Jackson had reminded him quietly that the man would lie as easily as he would speak. Bannon thought that was an obvious statement.

It was McCallister's idea to destroy Amelia's ranch, beat, rape, and drag her behind a horse, and take her two children. He knew it would hurt Checker worse than anything else they might do. Killing her husband just happened. It was his revenge for Checker breaking up his rustling operation. No one in Dodge City had suspected a thing; Star McCallister was something of a community leader before being arrested, tried, and convicted of murder and rustling. As were the entire gang captured by the Triple C riders.

Checker, Jackson, Sonny, and Bannon were part of the Triple C crew who brought a herd of more than four thousand cattle from Texas, lost it to the gang, and recovered it, along with catching the outlaws themselves. Many of their fellow drovers were killed during the raid on their herd and the following jail breakout.

Bannon had an opportunity to stop the outlaw leader as he escaped from the cabin, but couldn't bring himself to shoot him in the back. Right now he was wondering if that had been a good idea.

"Would'a been easier if I'd jes' shot him then an' there," he told himself, recalling the outlaw leader coming upon him accidentally.

Not shooting made sense when one was in town, in the middle of civilization and its protection. He wasn't so sure it did out here. Jackson had quietly assured him that he would have done the same thing. Bannon thought he was just being kind and wondered what Checker or Sonny would have done. Neither had said anything about it.

"Wonder what's fer supper?" he asked himself, forcing a change in thought. "Maybe we could eat one o' them Hedrickson steers. Some beef'd taste mighty fine."

He glanced back, wondering if he could ask Jackson about it, and reached for another piece of jerky in his shirt pocket. His glimpse caught Checker's taut expression, a clear reminder of the treacherous territory they were riding through. Bannon gulped and returned to studying the land, trying to keep both hot beef and Salome's bosom from reentering his thoughts. The dried meat would help, he decided, and pushed it into his mouth.

From under his wide-brimmed black hat, Checker's dark eyes searched the wilderness for movement that shouldn't be there. No one was more aware of the potential of war parties than he was. The Triple C drive to Dodge had dealt with a Kiowa war party this summer. But he still didn't respond to the outlaw's request.

"I know ya don't care if we die, Checker—but ya gotta think about them kids. We kin make the difference. We'll give the guns back afterwards. Honest." Venner's dark forehead was furrowed with concern. Maybe bringing the Hedrickson children into it would change the former Ranger's mind.

Checker's continued silence was easy to translate.

Frustrated, Venner yanked on his tied wrists, but they wouldn't move from the saddle horn. He knew it wouldn't matter, but he had to try something. His chest rose and fell and he was silent himself, letting his body sway with the rhythm of his walking horse. He glanced down at his bare feet. Like the other three outlaws, his boots and socks had been removed to make escape more difficult. He stared at his bare feet in the stirrups, then at his captured companions, and rolled scared eyes.

Tom Redmond, the former Confederate riding on the opposite side of the black man, was angry, his snarl the beginning of a challenge. His suspenders and Rebel trousers were faded and worn. The other outlaws lashed to their saddles were two large men: Iron-Head Ed Wells and Wes Morton, who had guarded the trail to their hideout. Neither was inclined to say anything. Morton was recovering from a pistol blow to his head.

Wells had suffered from a beating by Checker; even his massive mustache was thick with dried blood. All four men were connected by a lariat looped and tied around the four separate saddle horns, a further discouragement to attempts at freedom.

"It's a long ride back to Dodge, Ranger. I swear you'll never git there. Injuns or not." The stocky Redmond glared at Checker and pulled on his fists tied firmly to the saddle horn. The result was the same as Venner's. Redmond's thin lips were pasted against yellowed teeth.

Checker looked over at Redmond. Three rifle lengths separated them. "You'd better hope we can handle anything that comes." His intense stare caught each man. "If we go down, you die or get taken by Indians. The only way you can help is to pray we get through this. If you know how to pray. Do you understand? Say it."

Venner and Morton grumbled their understanding; Wells was quite polite in his agreement, shaking his bruised square jaw to support his statement. "Yes, I do, sir." His sun-blistered mouth was badly cut in two places and swollen, making it difficult to speak clearly.

Redmond didn't respond.

"Redmond, I didn't hear you," Checker growled. "I said, say it."

"I understand, damn you," Redmond growled. "What if it's some o' our friends up ahead somewhar instead . . . waitin' to he'p us?"

Checker half smiled. "You don't have any friends, Redmond."

"McCallister's out there, somewhar."

"I hope he is."

"Give me a fightin' chance—or are you a-feared o' me?"

"Put a stopper in it, Redmond," Checker said. "You got full of yourself beating up on old men and women."

"I did a right good job on your sis, didn't I? She were a fine-lookin' woman."

Seeking reassurance, Johnny turned toward his uncle. He was trying very hard to be brave and was mounted on Checker's backup horse, a long-legged bay. The last few days had been a terrible nightmare. When they were taken by the outlaws, he kept telling his little sister—and himself—that his uncle would come. Yet it was difficult to truly believe help would find them as they were carried out of Kansas and into the wilderness. He had heard the outlaws talk and knew they were going to be traded to Comancheros. Anything to complete McCallister's revenge. He hadn't missed his uncle's remarks to the outlaws either.

Aware of the boy's attention, the tall gunfighter tried to smile. "Johnny, I won't lie to you. We're making lots of noise. We're going to draw some attention. Maybe from a war party. Maybe from other outlaws. There's nothing good in here."

"I—I can shoot. Some." Johnny's missing two teeth were evident in his attempt to look confident.

"Got me a fine knife, too." He patted the beaded sheath and knife at his belt; he had looked at it just a few minutes before. It had been Checker's, before the former Ranger presented the weapon as a gift, a replacement for the boy's pocketknife lost in the ranch fire.

Checker leaned over and patted the boy on the shoulder. "You remind me of your mother."

"Will she be all right, Uncle John?" The question just popped out.

Checker flinched in spite of himself. It wasn't the question. It was the jay. The bird was flying away, screaming.

"She's a strong one, like you." Checker turned toward the boy. "I'm going to need your help, Johnny."

Shoulder-length black hair brushed against the beaded and elk-bone-decorated Comanche leather tunic covering his shoulders and shirt.

"You bet." Johnny straightened in the saddle.

Johnny's enthusiastic eyes went to his uncle's gun belt holding a reverse-draw holster with a double row of cartridge loops—one for his rifle, the other for his pistol. In the formfitting holster was a black-handled, short-barreled Colt .45. Johnny was first drawn to the white elk-bone circular markings in the handles, then the half-removed trigger guard that left only a slender quarter circle nearest the handle. It was a gun unlike any he had ever seen. His father had quietly told him it was a killing gun.

As he blinked away the memory, the boy's gaze strayed to a second long-barreled Colt resting in a holster tied to the saddle, just below the cantle and behind Checker's right leg, and, finally, to the rifle in the sideways saddle horn rig. In his heart, he wanted to be a Texas Ranger and carry weapons like those. He had never been around a man like his uncle. A gunfighter.

"I want you to get in the wagon. Do it now, son, and take Rebecca with you." Checker looked back at Jackson. "Company coming, wearing feathers."

Immediately Jackson woke up little Rebecca.

Johnny frowned as he turned in the saddle toward the gentle black cowboy who was helping the little girl through a curtain that led to the inside of the wagon. She was filled with questions, and Jackson tried to answer them without scaring her. That only brought more questions. Finally, he just told her that Indians were coming.

"Why?" Rebecca asked.

Jackson shook his head. She used the "why" question like a gun. "I'll tell you later, Miss Becky. Here comes Master Johnny. You get in there . . . with him."

The boy rode over to the now-stopped vehicle, tied the reins of his horse to the brake as Jackson directed, and climbed aboard. Starting the team again, Jackson hurried him along and readied his own rifle as the two children disappeared behind the thick, dark red veil. He could hear the boy tell his sister to quit asking questions. That was followed by a single "why?"

"Jackson?" Checker asked, studying the tree line for movement that wasn't there yet. He silently thanked the jay for its early alarm.

"Yes, sir?"

"Wish Sonny was well enough. We could sure use him."

"Yeah, we sure could. I can't see back there. Reckon he's sleeping, though. Want me to find out?" Jackson looked over his shoulder more out of reaction than any possibility he could see into the wagon's belly, or even through the veil, much less past the shelf of medicines that cut the wagon into two parts.

"He's a good man," Checker declared.

"Yes, sir, he is that." Jackson hid his grin and wiped his hand on his battered chaps, then back to his rifle.

That was the former lawman in Checker talking, reaffirming Sonny's staunchness to himself. Jackson knew the two men had once been on the opposite sides of the law in Texas. He knew "Sonny Jones" was a made-up name to hide his past and that Checker had actually arrested him and let him go. On the trail drive to Kansas, the two gun warriors had become close.

"No use trying to run." Jackson relit his pipe and pushed his glasses back on his nose. He often said the obvious, but only Bannon had told him that. "Here's as good a place as any to wait for 'em, I suppose."

"Agree. Let's hold up here—but I don't want to open up on them. Might be friendlies." Checker watched the trees ahead of them. "Might."

"I'll follow your lead, John." Jackson slowly brought

the horse team to a stop. "I'll see about Sonny too. We could use his gun—if he's able at all."

Remembering his medicine pouch, Checker touched the small lump under his shirt and tunic. He had begun the simple tribute during his pursuit of McCallister and the children. The pouch had been a gift from an old Comanche war chief who had become, in a strange way, the father he never had.

He pulled the rifle free of its leather restraint and whispered, "I need your help, my spirit helper. Hear me now."

Somewhere a wolf cry haunted the land, as if his whisper had brought the response. His rational mind told him it was just a coincidence. They had been hearing wolves off and on all day. His late Comanche mentor, Stands-in-Thunder, had told him that the wolf was Checker's spirit helper. Checker wasn't certain how the old man decided this. But there were many things beyond his ability to reason. Many things he didn't understand. This wasn't one to challenge. At least not then—or at this moment either.

The tall man, who had lived with a gun for more years than he could recall, listened. A turkey gobble, or what he thought was one, followed by another wolf cry. He thought both could be Indian signals. If it was a real wolf, it was a single cry. Four in a row was the sign of danger to a Comanche war party, a signal their medicine had gone bad. No warrior would advance after such a warning. He could recall hearing such a repetition only once, on his way to Amelia's ranch, chasing the just-escaped McCallister gang.

A wolf cry sounded much like a human voice, he thought. Stands-in-Thunder had told him that his people believed the mysterious beast had a man's soul. Any connection to the wolf was valued highly, the old war chief had advised, and Checker should assume he was favored by the spirits. He wondered if the Indians headed their way were Comanches or Kiowas.

Whichever, they were mere hateful remains of the great tribes that once had been. The effect of their savage military prowess on the entire Southwest had been felt for many years. Their joy came from fighting. Continuous fighting. Now their strength was broken. Forever. Most were on reservations, like Fort Sill near the Wichita Mountains, where Stands-in-Thunder had resided before passing away the spring before this one. Those still holding out were trying to make up for this awful change to their way of life with mindless attacks on any whites. Anywhere.

"Ty! Hold up where you are. Indians are coming," Checker yelled and kicked his horse into a lope. "I'm headed your way."

Bannon nodded, his mouth filled with the remains of a corn dodger he'd found in his shirt pocket; the rest of the jerky was gone.

CHAPTER THREE

"Give me a gun, Ranger! Please!" Redmond yelled.

This time the others joined in the plea. Checker wasn't listening as he rode toward Bannon. Moving the rifle to his left hand, Checker found the holstered saddle revolver with his right, flipped off the hammer thong, and pulled it free. He shoved it into his belt, returned the rifle to both hands, and slowed his black horse to a walk.

Appearing like ghosts through the far tree line rode a dozen warriors. Their copper bodies and horses were painted for war. No sign of women or children meant this was a rogue band.

"There's twelve ag'in three, Ranger. Come on," Venner pleaded.

"Shut up—or we'll trade you to 'em," Jackson growled. "This wouldn't be a good time to try something," He swung his gun in the direction of the outlaws. "You either, lady."

"I . . . gonna do nothin', mister," Wells whispered and swallowed.

Salome's glare was hateful, but Jackson was already paying attention again to Checker's advance.

Jackson's intensity burst into a loud idea. "John, they might be scared of the wagon—an' me. I'm the great medicine man back from . . . ah, Shadow Land." He waited and yelled again, "John, did you hear me?"

Checker turned in the saddle and nodded his agreement to the idea, then refocused on Bannon. Quickly swallowing the corn dodger, the farm boy had dismounted and held his horse's reins on the ground with his boot. The lead mare's rope was lashed to his saddle horn and the fine horse was calmly searching the ground for any grass that remained. Checker was impressed with the young man's savvy; shooting from the ground was always better than from the back of a horse. He reminded himself that he couldn't worry about the horses for the moment. Nor the arrested outlaws.

"It's Comanches." Checker levered his Winchester into readiness as he pulled up beside Bannon and swung down. "Wish it were a Cherokee Light Horse patrol. I'd pay a toll to pass through. Maybe get some directions." He stepped on his dropped reins and studied the slowly advancing war party.

"Yeah, Dan told me one year a patrol wanted a whole ten cents fer each head of beef," Bannon muttered without looking at Checker. "Ten cents. Can you imagine? Ol' Dan said he up an' paid 'em, though. Thought it was better than having to fight 'em."

Checker put his hand to his head to shelter his vision from the late afternoon rays. "We'll see what they want first. If shooting starts, Ty, take out that lead fella. The one with red on his face."

"I got 'im. Just say when." Bannon glanced at his

horse and whispered for it to be good and not act up.
Not now.

"Jackson?" Checker yelled without turning around

"Yes, sir?"

"The one with the all-black face is yours. First." He
grinned at the obvious connection.

"I got 'im." Jackson hollered back. "Think he's one of
those minstrel boys?" He chuckled, shifted the pipe to the
other side of his mouth, and pushed on his eyeglasses.

"Could be." Checker returned his concentration to
the slowly advancing war party. "You know the Utes are
the ones that named them—'*Komantcia*.' In their language, it means 'enemy who fights me all the time.'"

"I didn't really need to know that right this minute,
John." Bannon tried to smile.

"Yeah. Just act confident. They can see fear."

"Didn't need to be knowin' that neither."

A round-faced, squatty warrior with plucked eyebrows and bloodshot eyes led eleven others. A war shirt
of antelope skin held dangling pieces of tin, glass, and
silver, as well as a line of bear claws. Such a finely decorated war shirt was a sign of leadership, Checker knew.
Flickering in the warrior's great lengths of black hair
were five kill feathers. Checker knew what that meant,
too. Five men killed in battle. The leader's face was
completely covered in red paint; a yellow zigzag line
crossed his right cheek. An earring made of a long, thin
shell dangled from his right earlobe. Long fringe draped
from his leggings and moccasins, a typical sign of Comanche dress.

He rode with his right hand held high. A greeting of
friendship. In his left fist was a lance, shortened for
horseback warfare, a war shield, and the buckskin reins
of his magnificent bay stallion with white forelegs,
painted with the record of many successful battles as

well as spirit medicine. Eagle feathers fluttered from its mane and tail, and a small beaded pouch with a tangling eagle feather rested on its broad chest. Checker noted three fresh scalps dangled from the lance.

The former Ranger had always been impressed by Comanches, even before he met the elderly Stands-in-Thunder. On the ground, they were short and stout with massive chests, almost humorous in their large features. On horses, though, they became the most feared cavalry to ever ride through Texas. Smooth. Graceful. And absolutely fearless. He had seen them do things on horseback no one could match. No one.

"Not that it matters none, but how do you know it's Comanch'?" Bannon asked as calmly as if he had been questioning the weather. His field of vision never left the slowly advancing warriors.

Checker stood with his rifle in his crossed arms. "Lots of signs. Long fringe. Parted hair in the middle with paint down it. Scalp locks. No eyebrows." His gaze took in the war party. "Antelope skins means they're part of the Antelope band. They're the worst. Last to go to the reservation. They love horses, though, like they're members of the family. Give names to their best ones."

"Wouldn't ya know?" Bannon swallowed and wiped his sweating hand on his pants.

Checker wasn't certain if his young friend was responding to the comment about the Antelope band or the Comanches' feelings for horses. It didn't matter. He concentrated on the war party, watching them spread out and stop.

"If they come at us, it won't be like a military charge, Ty," Checker muttered in a low, steady voice. "They fight like they look, as individuals. That'll help us. Maybe."

"Yeah, maybe."

Black paint was the predominant paint among the

copper-hued warriors, a mark of death and war. But a few also were painted with blue, a favorite Comanche color. Their leader was the only one with an emphasis on red. All had their hair parted from the center of the forehead back to the crown, forming a braid on each side, in traditional Comanche fashion. A line of yellow or red paint highlighted each part. The braids were wrapped in various furs and pieces of cloth. Coup feathers shivered from their heads. Each also had a scalp lock braided from the hair at the top of his head. All twelve, including the leader, wore a single black feather in their scalp locks.

"There's a bunch with antelope skins on, John," Bannon observed, shaking his head at its meaning. "Hey, that one fella's got black stripes all over him—even his britches. How come?"

"Don't know, Ty. Why don't you ask him? Maybe he's wondering why I've got on this brand-new white Stetson."

"Maybe so." Bannong gulped. "John, one of 'em is wearin' a dress. A white lady's dress. Don't think it's a woman, though."

"It isn't."

Bannon's horse snorted and pawed the ground. He grabbed the reins and yanked on them, then returned his attention to the war party. His muttered assessment indicated the Indians had four rifles: two Springfields, a Spencer, and one Winchester. The rest were armed with bows and arrows and lances. The lever gun was carried by the warrior with the completely blackened face. If trouble started, Checker wanted him down; that was why he had given the assignment to Jackson. Even if Jackson was preoccupied with his "Shadow Land" idea. Whatever that might become. With only three shooters, it would be important to make their first shots count.

"Don't underrate the boys with bows, Ty. They can put three arrows in a man before he can get off a shot."

Checker noted to himself that another warrior had a long-barreled revolver among the group carrying bows and arrows. He was just as concerned about their shortened lances and war clubs. If the warriors got close enough to use either, they would overrun the Triple C men quickly.

Behind them, Salome let out a wild wail; Bannon glanced that way and jerked back. Part of him wanted to go and comfort her. He managed, instead, to ask Checker if he knew much of the Comanche language. It was more of a hopeful gulp.

"Yeah, I do. Let's hope my old friend taught me enough. They aren't so good at sign."

Bannon nodded, not understanding, but deciding it wasn't the time to question the tall Ranger more. He didn't like the expression of the black-faced warrior at all. It reminded him of someone who was quite hungry.

A leggy bay in the rear of the herd pawed the ground, eager to keep moving. A brown horse agreed and did the same. But the other horses were standing quietly, following the mare's manner; most were grazing. He whispered to his sorrel to pay attention to the others.

"What if the horses break on us?" Bannon asked, focusing once again on the lead warrior and trying to keep from looking at the black-faced one. His horse yanked on the reins. The farm boy gave it a look of disgust and whispered, "Maybe I'll let the Injuns have you."

"Let 'em go. We'll get them later." Checker's total attention was on the war party.

"*Hau!*" The Comanche leader saluted, ending the conversation between Checker and Bannon for the moment.

"*Hau.*" Checker returned the greeting without moving.

"Be careful, John." Bannon hunched his shoulders as a shiver walked across his back. "That black-faced boy looks like he could eat a bear."

"Yeah. Look like *you* could eat two."

Bannon nodded, pulled on his hat brim and squinted into his most formidable face. He was certain that it just made him look like he had a bad stomachache, but it was the best he could do.

A painted warrior wearing part of a U.S. cavalryman's jacket and earrings in both ears moved his horse alongside the leader and introduced him to Checker. The former Ranger knew most of the words and could guess the rest. The warrior said his leader's name was *Ekakwitsee*. Lightning. His war medicine came from the Sky Beings and the Thunder Spirits, and was exceedingly strong.

Lightning could not be killed in battle because the Sky Beings protected him. The name was significant; Comanches were particularly afraid of thunder and lightning. It reminded him of his old friend, Stands-in-Thunder, and the power of his name. Few Comanches would ever challenge the Thunderbird as the old war chief had done—or this warrior facing him.

Once, without bravado, the old man had told Checker, "Do not talk to thunder and lightning. Do not challenge thunder and lightning. There is no pity, no caring, no understanding. I do so as a young man only because my vision showed me the Thunder Beings were there to guide me, not hurt me. Few are so chosen." He had further explained that part of his spiritual connection included never eating any raw meat, to sing a special song during all storms, to always carry white stones and a hard ball from the buffalo's stomach into battle, and to paint his face and body with lightning bolts and hail marks.

Completing his introduction, the warrior started to return to his former position, then stopped and said something to Lightning. Both warriors studied Checker's tunic.

With his shoulders set defiantly, Lightning questioned in a loud voice, "Where you get Comanche leader's shirt?" Pronunciation came slowly, typical of the Stake Plains Antelope band.

Checker understood the implied threat. He cocked his head to the side and replied in his best Comanche, "I take it from Blue Elk. We fight. I win."

Lightning pointed at Checker's arrow-shaped scar.

"Yes, it was remembered fight," Checker responded, touching his cheek, then his shoulder. "We fight in *Llano Estacado* many years back." He described the Staked Plains, once a Comanche stronghold, using its traditional Spanish name.

Lightning spoke again to the warrior who introduced him; Checker couldn't hear what he said. Immediately, the war party leader turned back to the former Ranger and announced that *tuwikaa*, the raven, was no longer telling them where the buffalo had gone, that white soldiers had burned their tipis, and killed their women and children, and that he considered all white men responsible.

The horses and the woman would be taken as payment. Scalps would be ripped away after Checker and his men were dead. The ultimate in annihilation of life, according to the Comanche way. They believed no warrior's spirit would continue in the afterlife if the man was scalped or mutilated after death.

In halting Comanche, supported by sign language, Checker declared, "That is not so. I know of your coming. *Tuhtseena* tells me so. The wolf is my *puhahante*. My spirit helper. Strong *puha*. I am friend of Stands-in-Thunder, a great leader among *Noomah*, the True People. His medicine also came from the Sky Beings—and the great Thunderbird itself. He would disapprove of your threats to me." He hoped the combination of his tribal words and sign would make sense, even if the tribe was typically not adept at sign language. Using the two together couldn't hurt.

Cocking his head to the side, Lightning straightened his back and spat, "You lie. His-name-I-shall-not-say travels to spirit land."

Checker hoped for that response. Using a dead person's name was forbidden by the tribe. The important thing was his late friend was known.

"Yes, he does. I buried him. With his best horse and his finest weapons. I prayed and sang for his spirit passage. I watched his spirit ride toward the great valley of wonder and youth." Checker stared at the war party leader. "He gave me this." He reached inside his shirt and lifted out the medicine pouch and held it in front of him. "It is strong *puha*. The cry of the wolf lives there. He is my spirit helper. So does the Thunderbird's song, a gift from Stands-in-Thunder."

CHAPTER FOUR

Lightning's eyes narrowed and he blustered even more loudly, "His-name-I-shall-not-say was a beaten dog. Lived in white man's dirt cage until he passed. Medicine no good." He snorted and shook his lance. "We take horses. We take woman. Kill all. Your scalp will hang here." He made a short thrust in the air with his lance.

Checker's gaze captured Lightning's eyes and motioned with his arms toward the wagon. "If you try, I will tell the great shadow shaman—in the shadow wagon—to cast a spell on you. He has just returned from the Shadow Land to meet with Stands-in-Thunder. You will shrivel up and die like an old woman. I will watch you and laugh." Checker looked over his shoulder and yelled, "Shadow shaman from the Shadow Land . . . come forth!"

Dramatically, Jackson emerged from the wagon's front curtains. With outstretched arms, he began loudly chanting Bible verses mixed with some nonsensical phrases. Around his head—in place of his old hat—was Salome's long, multicolored veil, draped like a silk turban with long-flowing tails flopping in the air as he gyrated.

Sitting on the wagon seat looking pale but determined was Sonny Jones. He wore no shirt, but did have on his trail-worn, narrow-legged shotgun chaps and his vest with its jammed-full pockets, leather cuffs, and large-roweled Mexican spurs. His bandages showed signs of fresh bleeding. His derby hat sat jauntily on his head. A rifle lay in his lap; his revolver was shoved into his waistband.

Checker wasn't certain which he was most pleased to see, but wondered if Jackson would be able to take out the black-painted Comanche quickly. Then he saw his rifle resting against the far edge of the wagon seat. Checker felt reassured his friend had prepared for his other assignment, if necessary.

"Sonny's there," Bannon half whispered.

"'And bring forth all Glory' . . . na-na-na-hio-oh-be-gah . . . black magic . . . white medicine stone . . . 'do-dah, do-dah, five-mile race track five miles long,'" Jackson warbled loudly. "'And the rain was upon the earth for forty days and forty nights' . . . 'Glory be to the Father' . . . na-na-na-hio-oh-be-gah . . . black magic . . . white medicine stone . . . 'do-dah, do-dah, five-mile race track five miles long' . . . 'God is our refuge and our strength, a very present help in trouble' . . . na-na-na-hio-oh-be-gah . . . black magic . . . white medicine stone . . . 'do-dah, do-dah, five-mile race track five miles long' . . . 'The path of the just is as the shining light, that shineth more and more unto the perfect day' . . . na-na-na-hio-oh-be-gah . . . black magic . . . white medicine stone . . . 'do-dah, do-dah, five-mile race track five miles long.'"

Jackson repeated his incantations several times, waving his arms more with each repetition, occasionally catching the veil tails and spurring them into waves of mystical color.

Sonny moved his head in rhythm to Jackson's chanting. It was Sonny who usually made up songs on the trail. Or new words to old ones. His field of vision took in Redmond and the other outlaws, then came back to Jackson. He couldn't remember ever feeling so weak or so hot. How could it be so warm at this time of the year? He took a deep breath to ease the light-headedness. It didn't help much. His left hand grabbed the wagon seat to help keep him steady. He knew John Checker needed him.

Lightning's face tried to hide his dismay and yelled out, "Black men have no soul."

Checker recognized the tribal belief that black people were soulless creatures.

"His skin is black because he has just come from the spirit world and is still mostly a shadow," Checker yelled in Comanche and glowered at the leader, his eyes grabbing Lightning's own and not letting go.

His supporting sign language would hopefully make up for any gaps in his message. He made the sign for the "Evil Spirit," the opposite of the Great Spirit. Checker always assumed it was the equivalent of the white man's Satan.

Lightning's facial response was as expected: fear. Great fear. Checker said the words—and made the sign again. "He is from the Evil Spirit."

Lightning averted his eyes from Jackson and said something, presumably to himself. Checker guessed he was praying for strength to keep this diabolical spirit from him.

Bannon glanced at the terrified war leader, then back at the crazy-acting Jackson. He couldn't believe what he was seeing. Jackson had been the one who quietly taught him the ways of the trail and tried to steer him from the wilds of Dodge City.

Mutterings followed among the war party. The black-striped warrior shook his rifle in Jackson's direction. The dress-wearing warrior searched frantically for something in a pouch; Checker guessed it was something to keep him safe.

Pointing at the black-striped warrior, Checker pronounced, "Be careful. The one from the Evil Spirit is easily angered. He will turn you into a rabbit."

The war chief looked away, winced slightly, and looked back at Checker. "Lightning has more warriors. We have defeated Utes, Pawnees, Osages, Tonkawas, Apaches, and Navajos." He swallowed and shook his lance for effect. "We have defeated the Yellow Legs. We have killed the whites who live in stick houses. We have killed the bad-smelling men who slaughtered the sacred buffalo."

"All the more to become rabbits—or be strangled, so your souls cannot live. I shall tell the Shadow Man from the Shadow Land." Checker's snarling response startled Lightning into showing his clenched teeth.

Behind him Jackson was dancing back and forth along the wagon seat, waving his arms and chanting loudly with "Camptown Ladies" becoming an increasing part of his presentation, mixed with phrases of Tennyson's "Charge of the Light Brigade," one of his favorite poems. Whenever the words didn't come easily, he used gibberish.

"The great black shaman told us of your coming. He is hungry," Checker pronounced.

"Hungry?" Lightning's question was in Comanche.

"Yes, do you see the four men tied to their horses?" Checker motioned toward the outlaws. "One is a shadow man, like the shaman. He will be spared. The others—and the woman—will be strangled by the shaman, then eaten."

He tried to remember anything he could about Comanche beliefs. He wasn't certain about cannibalism, but it sounded scary. He did know they believed if a warrior was strangled to death, his soul could never be free and would be forever trapped within his body. Any mutilation after death would end his spirit travel as well. Reincarnation couldn't occur either. At least, it would explain the tied-up men. Their captive state would not have been missed by such keen eyes. He had already pushed the Comanches' fear of thunder and lightning—and the Thunderbird—as far as he knew how to do. The wolf was highly respected—and powerful for good, having been involved in many Comanche legends of original creation. And he had made his connection to the wolf clear.

"Jackson just went inside the wagon, John. What's he doin'?" Bannon said in an agitated whisper. He wiped the sweat from each hand on his new chaps, taking turns holding his Winchester with the other.

"Damned if I know."

"Sonny looks mighty pale."

"He'll make it."

Without looking, Checker knew Jackson had returned to the wagon's front seat by the reaction of the warriors. The war chief's bloodshot eyes widened and mutters of fright and concern slid along the other warriors.

"Aiiee!"

Lightning swung his horse around and kicked it hard into a run. The others were only an instant behind, whirling their horses into a mad retreat.

Checker watched them go before finally turning around to see what had made them panic. He chuckled and it became a loud laugh of relief.

Standing in the middle of the wagon seat stood Jackson. Wrapped around his shoulders was one of the veil tails. In one hand was a human skull and in the other, a burning flame, coming right out of his bare hand.

Sonny slid away from him to give Jackson more room; his hand was cupped over his mouth to keep from laughing.

"Would you look at that! How'd he do that?" Bannon hooted and slapped his thigh with his hand. His sorrel jumped sideways, almost freeing the reins from his boot.

"You got me. Let's go see." Checker swung back into the saddle and was loping toward the wagon before the young farm boy could get himself readied.

Bannon's sorrel spun around, making it impossible to for him get his boot in the stirrup. Sputtering, he pulled on the reins so the horse's head was nearly against its chest so he could mount without more agitation.

Jackson grinned at the advancing Checker and threw a hand-sized, thick leather pad, still burning, toward the ground.

"Nice touch, my friend," Checker said as he rode alongside the wagon. "How'd you come up with that?"

"Guess ya'll better thank Dr. Gambree . . . ah, Blue . . . for it. Saw him do this in town," Jackson explained. "Right before he went into his pitch about something. Can't remember what it was."

"Thank you, Blue. At least you were good for something." The corner of Checker's mouth twitched; he uncocked his rifle and shoved it back into the sideways saddle horn holster. "Sonny, you look like hell. What are you doing up here?"

"Good to see you, too, John." Sonny managed a thin smile and touched his hand to his derby's brim. "I wouldn't have missed ol' Jackson's performance for nothin'."

Checker returned the smile. His eyes took in the fresh blood on his friend's bandages. "Thanks for being there, good friend, but you'd better let Jackson take a look at those wounds."

"No big deal. I'm just leaking a little."

Bannon rode up, eager to find out how the trick was done.

Jackson explained that it was a thick pad holding a small, flat candle that could easily be hidden by curling up one's fingers so the effect was a fire being held in the hand. There were several in a box right inside. Blue Mc-Callister, the professional killer posing as Dr. Gambree, used the device to dramatize the wonders of nature as a lead-in to his medicine pitch.

Like the escaped Star McCallister, Blue hated Checker's connection to them. Their father was the late J. D. Mc-Callister, an infamous Dodge City outlaw leader in the town's early buffalo hunting days; the man had never married Checker's mother, nor recognized him and his sister as his children. Their home was a tent; their lives, mostly squalor. His only visits were to rape Checker's mother—or once, to beat up Checker for whipping Star and Blue. No one cared, either way.

"Hey, I liked your version of 'Camptown Ladies,'" Sonny said through gritted teeth. "One of my favorites."

"Don't know how much longer I could've held that thing, though." Jackson shook his hand. "It was getting a bit warm."

"What did . . . ah, Dr. Gambree do with it?" Bannon looked down at the smoldering pad.

"He blew it out, then reached down for a bottle of his stuff." Jackson shook his head. "Dropped it out of sight then, I reckon. He was good at it." He cocked his head to the side. "Of course, most of the menfolk were watching the gal, not him." He winked at Bannon, then changed subjects.

He suggested camping for the night at a spring not far from where they were. It was a good location for cattle and had been used by Triple C on the Ellsworth drive last year. He reminded them that they had passed it coming through, following the outlaws, and thought the grass would be enough for the night. He was comfortable making suggestions to both Checker and Sonny. They were always interested in good judgment and oblivious of skin color, unlike most white people.

Checker straightened himself in the saddle, pulled his second Colt from his belt, and returned the weapon to its saddle holster. "Sounds good to me, oh great shaman."

Jackson grinned.

"I didn't know he could dance like that, did you, John?" Sonny teased. "Hell, I don't think what's-her-name could've done any better."

Bannon started to say something and thought he'd better not.

Sonny exhaled slowly. "You think they'll come back?"

"A smart man never figures he knows what an Indian will do for sure," Checker said. "They won't try again right away, though. Jackson scared 'em good."

Two small heads peeked out of the crack in the wagon curtains.

"Hi, Uncle John, we've been playing in here," Rebecca chirped. "Have the Indians gone?"

"Yes, they have, honey."

"Why?"

Checker looked at Jackson and said, "Jackson asked them to leave—and they did."

"Why did you do that, Uncle Black Jack?"

Jackson smiled at the name she had decided for him and said they weren't nice people.

"Can we come out now?" Johnny asked before his sister could question the men further.

"Sure. We need your help with the horses." Checker jerked his head in the direction of Bannon.

"What about me?" Rebecca's face screwed into a full pout.

Jackson opened the curtains to let them out. "Well,

Miss Becky, I need your help right here—driving this wagon."

"Oh, good. Can I bring Mary with me?"

Jackson looked puzzled.

"That's what she calls that doll you made for her," Johnny explained, rolling his eyes skyward as he scrambled across the seat, toward his tied horse.

"Can Mary handle a team?" Jackson asked, not quite keeping a straight face.

Rebecca giggled. "Yes, but she likes white horses."

Bannon wiped his hand across his mouth and sneaked a glimpse at Salome. From this angle, he could see most of her breasts. His face reddened and he hoped no one noticed. But Checker was watching Johnny remount, while Jackson and Sonny tended to Rebecca's return to the front of the wagon.

And three of the outlaws, Wells, Morton, and Venner, were too busy marveling at Jackson's performance and the fact the Comanches had fled. Redmond's sarcastic remarks about only a black man would have "carried on like that" went unnoticed.

The young farm boy couldn't help stealing another glimpse of the woman's bosom. She looked at him and smiled. Her smile made him tingle all over. He reached into his shirt pocket again and was disappointed to discover it was empty.

CHAPTER FIVE

As dusk lay upon them, the group pulled up near a spring cut from a rock-strewn draw. Sunlight was releasing control of the nearby trees to the dominion of emboldened shadows. A line of young cedars, mixed with miserably shaped mesquite, redbud, and willow, separated the watering hole from a wide, natural pasture. Aging cottonwoods watched over the shorter trees. Autumn breezes nipped at the brown-and-green grassy field that had mostly recovered from the summer's use by passing cattle herds.

The weather had already defeated bent-over, brown willows lining natural stone walls that formed a pocket of crystal-clear water. A dark jagged hole in the pond's center led to a spring whose soul lay deep within the earth. Tracks around the water's edge indicated animals of every kind and from every direction had sought its cool salvation. Dried cattle manure was spread about the area in various stages of decay.

Checker rode alongside Bannon and Johnny. "Ty,

Johnny, we'll let the herd water first. Let 'em have all they want, then move 'em to the grass—over there. I think they'll stay put until we can put up a rope corral." He pointed toward the grassy field.

Behind them, Jackson and Sonny had ordered the outlaws to stop and wait. The black drover held his team of matching bays to keep them from advancing toward the welcomed water.

With a pop of his coiled lariat against his leg, Bannon brought up the Hedrickson herd. Johnny rode with him, confidently helping ease the animals toward the small spring and pointing out the characteristics of his family's horses to the farm boy.

Confident they could handle the horses, Checker wheeled his black around to watch the grumbling outlaws.

Comfortable with the assignment, Johnny guided his horse back and forth along the side of the herd, keeping the animals from all rushing the pond at once. Johnny watched the older boy's every move, even slouching in the saddle the same way. Bannon's attention, though, was mostly on his contrary sorrel. Muttering to himself, he let the lead mare drink and nuzzle the cool wetness; her lead rope was outstretched, lying across the top of the water. He watched the circles spring from the rope's touching and thought briefly of home and his widowed mother and little sister.

Oh, the tales he would be able to tell about his first cattle drive to Kansas. Then he decided against sharing too much; his mother might not let him go on another. She would be happy about the money he had earned, though, including the bonus for helping save the herd from rustlers and saving the trail boss's life. She would be proud of his opportunity to work full-time on the Triple C. It seemed like another lifetime since he had been home, instead of just months. Jackson had helped him write a letter to them, but it wasn't the same as telling.

Realizing Johnny was watching him, Bannon straightened his back and kept an eye on a bay stallion trying to muscle its way through the other horses.

"Yeah, that's Rimfire. Dad always called him that because he was kinda fiery," Johnny explained. Talking about his murdered father brought a jolt of emotion through his body and he bit his lower lip to keep from crying. "He an' Dusty—over thar—they's our two stallions. For breedin', ya know." He pointed at a line-back dun nipping at another horse.

"It's all right to cry, ya know." Bannon rubbed his chin, ignoring the boy's unnecessary information. "I lost my dad a year ago. Still hurts. Real bad."

"I—I'm n-not cryin'."

"I know. But if you wanted to, it's all right."

"I'm not crying. That thar's ol' Frankie. He's young. Gonna be a good roping hoss." Johnny stared at Bannon. "Paw thought he would sell him next year. Course he's a gelding. Cut proud, Paw said. Thinks he's a stud."

Bannon called out authoritatively, "Johnny, watch that mare, she'll kick."

Johnny nodded his understanding and hollered, "Susie's all right. Need to give 'er some room, that's all. Ya know, bein' a mare n' all. Might wanna hold her and that gray mare—the one with the three white stockin's—an' let 'em water alone."

Embarrassed, Bannon muttered, "That's what I were a-gonna say."

He tried to think of farming details to share, anything to show superior knowledge to the Hedrickson boy. The best he could come up with was that the land didn't look too good for crops. Johnny responded that was why cattle were driven across it; the grass was good and thick most of the way. Bannon felt a little silly. Of course that was true. Even the dried grass from autumn would hold nutrition for their horses.

Without warning, Bannon's horse took quick steps into the water, up to its knees, and started to lie down.

"Spur 'im! Spur 'im!" Johnny yelled.

It was too late.

The cantankerous sorrel settled sideways into the cool water. The farm boy only had time to kick free of the stirrups as he disappeared into the water. Gasping for air, he reemerged moments later, shaking his soaked arms and dripping head. The closest horses looked up to see what was happening, then returned to their drinking. His sorrel rolled to its feet and stood quietly in the same place. He grabbed at his hat floating on the pond. Behind him, the guffaws of the outlaws rattled his ego. Smiling, Checker told them to be quiet.

Jackson's voice cleared the laughing. "Y'all all right, Ty-rel?"

Bannon muttered that he was.

"Had me a feelin' that red'un was gonna do that," Johnny said with no trace of a smile. "Think he's a nasty one, I do." He nodded at his own assessment and kicked his horse toward a gray biting at a buckskin horse.

Shoving his hat back on his head, Bannon retrieved the reins resting in the water and swung into the saddle, dripping water as he did. He reined the horse around, kicking it hard. The sorrel responded as if nothing had happened and calmly walked out of the spring.

At the wagon, Sonny pursed his lips. "You teach our young pup that trick, Jackson?"

Jackson grinned. "No, sir, I do believe Master Bannon learned that himself."

Both men laughed.

"Make sure we camp where they didn't put no cows," Sonny said. "Looks like half of Texas had their beeves here." He looked even paler but refused to lie down again.

"I'll swing over there. How's that?" Jackson said, facing a slight basin where remnants of old campfires indicated similar decisions.

Sonny liked Jackson's choice. It was defendable and he was certain the Comanches would return—or another band of Indians discovering their noisy trek. Or roaming outlaws getting interested in what appeared to be an easy looting. The three had already agreed to separate their own horses from the Hedrickson herd at night to make it difficult to steal all the horses, in case of a raid.

"How's our grain?" Sonny asked, studying the dying grass in the open field.

"Got enough for three days—for all o' them." Jackson adjusted his pipe to the other corner of his mouth. "Won't be enough to get us to Dodge, though. I think the grass'll keep the herd happy, don't y'all?"

"Yeah. We'll hold the grain until we need it."

Jackson eased the wagon team to a halt and watched Rebecca play with the doll he had fashioned earlier from some rags and padding made from folded paper. She seemed completely absorbed, chattering to herself something about "Mary riding in a beautiful carriage." He smiled, relit his pipe, and shoved the wagon brake in place. It was a good feeling to see her simple joy, one he had slowly learned to relish. Like a sunset. Or a hot cup of coffee. Or a horse that handled smoothly.

Memories of his childhood kept poking into his mind, but he didn't want them close. Although he remembered finding solace in make-believe, too, it was with sticks and rocks as his imaginary friends.

Probably some of the bond between him and Checker was the result of both having had terrible childhoods. Black and white men rarely were so close.

Jackson's early life had been filled with turmoil and heartache as he helplessly watched his brothers and sister be sent away, never to be heard from again. His mother had been raped repeatedly by their white owner, his father whipped nearly to death when he tried to stop it. Maybe that's why Amelia's awful treatment lay on his mind so bitterly.

Similarly, a fourteen-year-old Checker had been forced to flee Dodge City—leaving his younger sister with neighbors, after their mother died of whooping cough. Neighbors took in Amelia; however, young John Checker posed too much of a threat. Pent-up anger at the way his mother had been treated in life by the merciless J. D. McCallister broke loose after his mother's terrible death. The boy had gone to his uncaring father's saloon to confront him and ended up fighting some of his men, wounding one with a knife. A sympathetic prostitute had helped him escape.

As the two children said their tearful good-byes, Amelia had pulled a button from Checker's shirt as a remembrance, along with his promise to return. Three of McCallister's men went after the fleeing boy, and the returning two men reported him dead. She had assumed it was the truth until years later, a chance overheard conversation between a Texas cowboy and a Dodge City store clerk told her of a Ranger Captain John Checker. Jackson, Sonny, and a few others knew he carried Amelia's letter that had found its way to him in Texas and finally triggered his return to Dodge City and her family.

"Uncle Black Jack?"

Rebecca's reference to Jackson broke him from his troubled reverie. "Yes, Miss Becky?" He smiled widely at the title and returned his gaze toward the horse herd and the outlaws.

"Uncle Black Jack, I want to go." She grabbed for the reins in his hands.

"Oh, we're going to camp here. Let's get these horses unhitched, all right, Miss Becky?"

"Of course. Which one do you like the best?" She beamed. "I like the one on the right. He's my fabe-or-ite."

Jackson nodded. "Well, that's mine, too."

She frowned. "Maybe you should like the other one. He might feel bad."

Lifting her to his left so he could climb down first, Jackson agreed. "You're right. I like the one on the left."

"Oh, good." She leaned over to look at the quiet Sonny. "Uncle Sonny, which one do you like the best?"

The former outlaw tried his best to smile. "Oh my, let's see. Maybe the one on the right. No, maybe the left." He began a singsong tune. "Rebecca likes the pony on the right . . . on the right . . . on the right. Uncle Black Jack likes the pony on the left . . . on the left . . . on the left. Uncle Sonny likes the pony on the left . . . and the right. Left and right. All the live-long day."

Rebecca laughed and so did Jackson.

"Which one does Mary like?" Jackson took the pipe from his mouth and smiled. He couldn't remember feeling so tired.

Rebecca frowned at the simple doll in her little hands and asked, "Mary, which is your fabe-or-ite? Hmmm. All right." She looked up at Jackson. "She's not sure—she wishes they were white."

"That'll be a woman for you," Sonny muttered and took a deep, uneven breath.

Chuckling, Jackson told her to stay on the seat while he set up a rope stand for their own horses, separate from the herd. She wanted to get down and help, but he convinced her that it was important for her to stay there and keep an eye on the wagon team and on Sonny.

Tying a lariat about four feet off the ground from a sturdy cedar tree to the next closest one that looked strong enough, he returned to strip the harness from the team. He reminded himself to cut some long stakes before they left tomorrow. They would come in handy for a remuda string when they stopped where there weren't many trees. He told Rebecca to help him by making certain he didn't forget any of the bridling. She immediately began describing each piece of harness leather and where it was connected, punctuated with a frequent "why?" Jackson's responses to those questions were always gentle and thorough, as if he were talking to another adult.

Sonny appeared to be dozing, leaning against the side of the wagon's entrance frame. Jackson was pleased to see that; he wanted to tell Sonny to lie down in the back, but felt it would insult him. Maybe after the horses were tied, Sonny would respond favorably to the suggestion—if it were worded just right.

He led the freed horses to the newly created rope stand and retied them there, allowing enough slack for the animals to graze. Watering would have to come later. He didn't normally like doing that. It was a good way to cause problems, but there was too much going on at the pond to add to the confusion. Next came his own horse that had been tied to the rear of the wagon, along with Sonny's. Both were unsaddled, wiped down, and added to the remuda string. He gave them grazing room, too. Checker's black would be tied near there, as would the main Triple C mounts, including Johnny's horse.

This time, Rebecca came with him, holding the tail end of the lead rope for his horse, while she walked beside him. He retied the two Hedrickson steers to the farthest cedar, allowing them sufficient rope to graze as well. After the horses were watered, he planned on giving them some of the grain. It was important these animals stayed as strong as possible. Rebecca watched the effort, suggesting that her mother would not be happy if she did that with their steers. Jackson smiled but couldn't think of anything to say.

"Are you gonna milk them tonight, Uncle Black Jack? So we can have some with supper?" she asked.

He pushed his glasses on his nose. "Well, Miss Rebecca, they can't give us any milk. They're steers . . . ah, they used to be . . . ah, he-cows."

"Why can't they?"

"Only mommies can do that."

"Oh. We had a mommy cow at our place. She gave us milk every day. It was very good," Rebecca said. "Why isn't she with us?"

Jackson's shoulders rose and fell. "Don't know, little lady. I just don't know."

"Why?"

Meanwhile, Bannon and Johnny began moving the herd toward the open field to let them graze and Checker ordered the outlaws to move to the spring.

"Let your horses drink. All they want." Checker's command to the outlaws snapped through the gray day. "Then go over there." He pointed toward the waiting cedars.

He told the outlaws that, after their horses were watered, they would be untied and allowed to dismount one at a time to relieve themselves. Each man would be expected to unsaddle his own horse, carry the tack, and lead his horse to the wagon. Jackson would take each horse from there.

"Tyrel, can you keep on an eye on this bunch?" Checker yelled, and the soaking-wet farm boy quickly responded, kicking his horse into a lope and hoping the animal wouldn't do something stupid again, especially in front of Checker.

He reined to a stop and was happy the sorrel responded as if it would never think of doing anything wrong.

"Watch the others while I take care of Wells," Checker said. "Wells, if your horse is through drinking, come on over here."

Bannon swung down from his horse, dropped the reins, and stood on them as he levered his new Winchester. The ominous *click-click* wasn't missed on the outlaws, who had already heard about the farm boy's prowess with a gun.

"If one of them tries something, Ty, put a bullet in all of them," Checker said. "I'll be right close."

Near the pond, Checker untied Iron-Head Wells first, dropping the reins of his black and standing on them.

"Why him, Ranger? I gotta pee bad," Redmond spewed.

"Piss in your pants an' shut up. I've had enough of your caterwaulin'," Wells snapped. His face was bulging with purple and red blotches; his hands were swollen and he rubbed them as if they were breakable.

After the former Ranger removed the rope from Wells's hands and saddle horn, the slow-minded outlaw slid from the saddle and stood without moving for a few seconds. Though his bare feet didn't like the touch of the raw uneven land, he knew better than to say anything about it. He had already met the full rage of this tall lawman in front of him and didn't want to see it again. The stiffness of Wells' movements indicated sore or broken ribs. He looked up at Redmond as if daring him to say anything more, but the Confederate outlaw pretended to be gazing at the herd as it spread out along the grass with the Hedrickson boy watching for strays.

Wells slowly unleashed the cinch and slid the heavy leather and saddle blanket from his tired bay. Checker told him to wipe down the animal's sweating back and flanks with the blanket and handfuls of dried grass and weeds. The battered outlaw complied slowly, but without grumbling.

Waiting for approval and direction, Wells led the animal to the wagon and handed the reins to Jackson. The black cowboy told him to leave the saddle near the front wheels. Wells quietly complied and returned to Checker. The two men walked to a line of cottonwood trees where Wells relieved himself behind them.

From the wagon, Jackson removed the headstall of the outlaw's horse, replaced it with a rope halter, and tied it to the side of the rope stand opposite where he had put the wagon team. The animal would be allowed to graze. He would shorten all of their leads later, after he grained them. It would ensure a quiet group for the night. He handed the bridle to Rebecca to put with the saddle. Her smile at being included brought a return grin from Jackson.

After the battered outlaw's limited freedom, Checker moved Wells to the first cedar tree, looped the reins of his black around a low-hanging branch, and retied him in a sitting position. Wells said something to Checker that the others didn't hear; the former Ranger's nod wasn't understood either. He returned to the other outlaws, walked past Redmond, and untied the black outlaw.

Venner swung down and Checker had him repeat the process of unsaddling his horse, rubbing it down, and leading it to Jackson, before letting him relieve himself behind the trees. Checker retied him to a tree next to Wells and returned to the others, freeing Wes Morton.

Shifting the rifle in his hands, Bannon watched the process with the attention that comes from being given an important assignment. He decided to pat the sorrel on the neck and moved the gun to free his left hand. Maybe if he showed it some affection, the horse would act better, he thought. His first pat was tentative. The horse snorted, then nuzzled his arm. Bannon was surprised and patted it more.

Rubbing his freed hands, the bearded outlaw remained in the saddle and whined, "Ain't ya gonna help me git down? My head's screamin' at me. I'm dizzy from gettin' hit on the head. I can't stand." His high-pitched voice didn't fit his large frame.

Bannon started forward but stopped when he caught Checker's hand motion.

"Don't push it, Wes," Checker said.

"What ya gonna do, Ranger? Kill me?"

Checker drew his Colt.

"No, no, I'll git down. I'll git down," Morton pleaded and slid awkwardly from the saddle. He grimaced and half fell to the ground. His head pounded from being knocked out while guarding the hideout. He looked down at himself and rubbed his hands on his dirty vest, streaked with food grease and trail dust.

Redmond glared at Checker, but the tall gunfighter was reholstering his gun and watching Morton take care of his horse.

"How about me, John Checker?" Salome's eyes invited him closer. "Would you please help a woman?"

CHAPTER SIX

Before Checker could respond, Bannon grabbed the reins of his sorrel and half ran toward her.

"Please, Miss Salome, ma'am, allow me." He helped her down, inhaling the intoxicating scent of lilac and woman.

Standing close to the young rider, she caressed his face with her eyes and held out her hands to be untied. The sorrel bumped against him with its nose; he frowned and pushed its head away.

"Oh, of course, ma'am, of course." Bannon hurried to unlash the ropes, fumbling with the rifle as he did.

As soon as she was free, she took an uneven step, stumbled, and fell into his arms. Without attempting to withdraw from his sudden embrace, she pressed her breasts into his chest and purred, "Thank you."

"Ah, you're welcome . . . Miss Salome."

He was afraid to look down at his waist for the bulge that must be there.

From the wagon came Jackson's stern command. "I'll

walk her into the woods, Tyrel. Y'all go watch the others. Now, Tyrel."

Bannon couldn't hide his disappointment. "Sure. Sure."

She stepped away from him slowly, her eyes never leaving his face. Her freed right hand brushed over his stout manhood pushing against his pants as she retreated.

"I'm glad to see you like me."

His face dawned into crimson.

Jackson lifted Rebecca into his arms and walked Salome to a tight cluster of trees where she could have some privacy.

With her little arms wrapped around Jackson's neck, Rebecca studied his face, her own peering from the tightly tied bonnet. "Can I play with Uncle Sonny?"

"Maybe later, Missy," Jackson said. "He's sleeping right now."

"Why is he sleeping?"

"Because he's been hurt."

"When I'm hurt, my mommy kisses the 'owie' and makes it better." She puckered her lips to imitate the action. "I could kiss Uncle Sonny's 'owie' and make it better."

"That would be very nice, Missy. When Uncle Sonny is awake, we'll visit him. He will be very glad to see you."

Continuing to study his face, the little girl changed subjects and asked if Salome was Jackson's wife. He shook his head negatively and hoped the wagon dancer hadn't heard. Salome's seductive glance in his direction told him otherwise.

With Jackson gone, Checker decided to walk with Morton and his horse to the wagon.

"Sit down. There. Don't move." Checker pointed with his rifle and Morton eased himself to the ground. Leaning his rifle against the wagon, the former Ranger tied the outlaw horse to the wheel. He glanced up at Sonny

Jones sitting asleep on the wagon seat and decided it was best not to comment.

"Get up and let's head for the trees." Checker tossed the bridle on top of the outlaw's saddle.

Morton stood, wiped the back of his pants, and headed toward the area where Wells was now tied. "I never hurt no kids, Ranger. Didn't have nothin' to do with the lady either. Honest." His high-pitched voice made him seem younger than he was.

"You're a real stand-up man," Checker growled. "You rode along, didn't you?"

Morton swallowed and walked on in silence, tiptoeing to keep his feet from being fully exposed to the hard ground. Nearing the tied black outlaw, Morton unbuttoned his pants, weaving sideways as he did.

"Hey, you damn bastard! You're peeing on me!" Venner lifted his left foot away from the stream.

The dazed trail guard stared at Venner in disbelief, then reaimed. "Sorry, I didn't mean—"

"Sorry, my ass." Venner tried to wipe his toes on brown weeds lying around him.

Watching from his tree, Wells laughed and it hurt his ribs so much that he looked away to help stop the response.

Jackson returned with Salome and Checker tied her to a fat cedar that was ten feet farther away from the others. She tried to get his attention with her eyes, throwing back her shoulders to emphasize her chest, but the former Ranger didn't notice as he headed back to give Redmond his turn.

Minutes later, Redmond was lashed to the fifth tree and fully ready to resume his jawboning. "How's ol' Cole doin', Ranger? I shot him, too, ya know. Maybe I can collect the reward. Bet there's a good one for Cole Dillon."

Checker stepped back, withdrew cigarette makings from his shirt pocket, and began preparing a smoke as he walked toward his motionless black waiting where he had left the animal.

"Hey, Ranger! What's the difference between us an' him? He's nothin' but a back-shootin' bank robber. Cole's wanted all over South Texas. Come on, you know that. You were a lawman."

The other outlaws watched Checker walk away, rolling a smoke and lighting it.

Venner shook his head. "You're askin' for it, Redmond. You'd better shut up."

"Aw, hell, he's not gonna do nothin'." Redmond chuckled and yelled, "I thought Rangers were supposed to put bad'uns like Cole Dillon in jail, not take care of him."

Redmond's eyes widened as Checker spun around and returned. In his right fist were the papers and tobacco pouch; his mouth held the cigarette. The former Ranger said nothing, stopping two feet away from the tied and squatting outlaw. With a burst of anger, Checker grabbed him by the hair and yanked his head upward to face him.

"Redmond, the only thing that's keeping you from an awful death are my friends," Checker said. "Be thankful they're here. But if you ever say 'Cole Dillon' again, it won't matter who's around." He released Redmond's hair and the man's head bounced off the tree.

Checker walked past him to the others. "Cole Dillon died in Texas."

A mixture of "I know," "I don't even know a Cole Dillon," and "Yessir," followed in a chorus of scared voices.

Wes Morton inhaled some courage. "I don't care about no dead owl hoot. But ain't ya gonna give us somethin' fer our feet? It's damn cold. An' when we gonna eat? I ain't had nothin' all day."

"I'll let you know about the eating," Checker said. "Your feet are fine."

Wells quietly told Morton not to press his luck, and the bearded outlaw nodded and was silent. Venner volunteered that John Checker acted like a man on the edge. Wells reminded him of what they had done to his sister and her family. Venner shook his head and stared down at his roped body. They watched Checker lead his black horse to the remuda stand.

After the rest of the horses were watered and their canteens refilled, Jackson and Bannon constructed a rope corral to hold the horse herd. It was Johnny's job to watch for any strays; his baby sister was in front of him in the saddle, happy to be close. Jackson insisted on examining each of the young man's knots and each tree-wrap to make certain the double-rope corral was satisfactory. It annoyed Bannon that the black cowboy felt he had to check on his work. Silently he told himself that he tied better knots than anyone on the drive from Texas, except the trail boss. Jackson also insisted on their hobbling the lead mare and three particularly fiery geldings. He left the stallions alone and that surprised Bannon, but he didn't comment.

"I'd think them hosses could push through that real easylike," Bannon offered, watching the black cowboy complete his inspection.

"They could, if they tried. But they won't as long as they don't get scared. They'll see it as a real corral." Jackson stood up. "Let's move the stallions away from the others. They'll just start problems. Tie them to that tree. Leave that extra rope ri't hyar."

At the wagon, Checker unsaddled his own horse, rubbed its back with dry leaves, cleaned its hooves of dirt, and examined its legs for any soreness.

"Tuhupi, you did good today, boy," Checker said softly.

At least their slow travel wasn't hard on their horses. He refused to let his hard use of the fine black horse on the way to finding the children enter his mind. He removed the bridle and tied the big animal to the control rope with enough slack to allow for easy grazing. Unlashing the canteen, he set it aside for refilling later, moved to the wagon, and got a sack of grain, being careful not to wake up Sonny. Using his hat for a container, he began feeding each animal a good amount of grain.

With the familiar work, his mind was free to ride back to the awful sight of his sister after Star McCallister's gang was through with her and her family. In black memory, she leaned against a sagging porch, unseeing, unknowing, as he rode up. All around her was a hell of flame as their house, barn, and outbuildings were swallowed by fire. Even in his mind's recollection, she was barely recognizable through the blood, dirt, and soot. He could see her beaten face with the side of her head blistered with blood and the missing yank of hair from being pulled as she was dragged, her arms and legs skinned and purple, her dress a mere rag of blood. Once more, he could see her holding his childhood button when he arrived at their burning ranch.

He shivered and shook his head to rid it of the claws of that memory. He had discovered a wonderful sweetness in Amelia's family, one he had only felt once before in Texas. Now it had been destroyed by his half brother. What kind of madman could do such a thing? Was it wrong to want to see him hang? Was he really in charge of that atrocity? For an instant, he wanted to walk to the trees and drag one of the outlaws behind his horse.

He clenched his teeth and chose, instead, to wake Sonny and get him to the back of the medicine wagon. It was time. He climbed up to the wagon seat, his spurs clanking against the wheel itself. At first, he wondered if his friend was actually breathing. Maybe he shouldn't try to wake him. He felt Sonny's forehead. It was hot. Damn. The fever had returned.

"Wh-what's the . . . matter?" Sonny fumbled weakly for his vest pocket and removed his watch. Along with it came several cartridges and two pieces of hard candy, some of the usual bounty kept in the filled pockets.

Checker noticed the silver lid of the watch was deeply dented. It hadn't been before. The dent must have come from a bullet. He couldn't think of anything else that would hit with such force. Likely it had happened during the battle with the gang at their hideout. A mental calculation told him the Waltham timepiece had deflected a bullet that would have ripped into Sonny's stomach.

"H-here she is. L-look at her," Sonny mumbled and tried to open the lid by pushing on its stem. The watch wouldn't click open. He frowned and pushed harder, but it only made his hand shake with weakness.

"Let me do it, Sonny." Checker gently took the watch and pried open the lid.

Inside, a spidery crack controlled the glass over the watch face. The hands were stopped at 5:21. A young woman stared back at him from the lid. The faded photograph had a hole in her cheek, matching the bullet blow to the lid.

"Have you seen her today?" Sonny's eyes fluttered. "Come on, my f-friend, where is she?"

Checker smiled. "Yes, I've seen her, Sonny—in your eyes." He closed the lid and returned the watch carefully to Sonny's vest. "There. Now she's right next to you." He hadn't met the woman, but knew it was Sonny's beloved Mary, his late wife.

He encouraged the half-awake Sonny to climb down from the wagon seat, holding him steady as he moved.

"Wh-where's my gun? M-my gun!" The wounded man's voice had a frantic edge.

Checker withdrew the Colt from Sonny's waistband. He held the weapon against Sonny's chest and guided his right hand to it.

"Here. It's right here, Sonny."

Sonny grabbed and held the Colt as it were a priceless jewel.

"There anything else you want?" Checker asked.

"Wh-where are the kids? The kids!"

"They're safe, Sonny. They're safe. You go to sleep now."

Holding him upright, Checker finally returned the wounded drover to the wagon bed and covered him with warm blankets. Sonny didn't hear him; he was asleep with the pistol held tightly with both hands.

Joining him was Jackson. Without a word, he immediately began working on the feverish wounds of the gunfighter, recleaning and dressing them as best he could with torn strips of Sonny's shirttail and salve he had found in the medicine wagon. Jackson had been the one who tended to Amelia before they took her to town to see the doctor. Checker had taken Jackson's earlier recommendation and placed Sonny inside the medicine wagon, so he could rest while they moved toward Dodge, instead of waiting for him to be strong enough to ride.

Quietly, Jackson advised Checker that Sonny was weak from the loss of blood and that his fever had risen again. He noted a lesser man would have died from losing that much blood.

"We need to get those kids back to Dodge, Jackson. An' Sonny needs a doctor. Should we leave the horses?" Checker asked.

"We're moving as fast as we can. They're not slowing us down," Jackson responded. "Besides, Sonny would be furious if he knew we left them—for him."

"Yeah, you're right." Checker looked into Jackson's strained face. "Still think we should take this bunch back? We can hang 'em nice an' legal right here. Lots of good cottonwoods. Save us a lot of trouble."

"You already know the answer to that."

"Yeah." Checker's face rolled into a slow smile. "If you're wondering if I've changed my mind about wanting to drag each one, that hasn't changed. But I know what we need to do, Jackson, I promise."

"I wasn't worried."

"Yeah, you were," Checker said. "And you probably should have been."

Jackson returned the smile. "Why don't you see if Tyrel can scare us up something to eat while I get a fire going?"

CHAPTER SEVEN

Supper was roasted grouse, thanks to some good hunting by Bannon, wild onions, potatoes from the outlaw hideout, and coffee. Jackson did the cooking with special assistance from Rebecca. The outlaws would be fed separately after the Triple C men and the children had eaten.

Shortly after the meal, Checker and Jackson got the children ready for bed, preparing blankets for them in the front part of the enclosed wagon and helping them remove their clothes. Jackson had even remembered to buy new nightwear for them, and they were excited about the apparel. Both men helped them crawl into the vehicle from the front so they wouldn't disturb the sleeping Sonny Jones.

Rebecca insisted on them hearing her prayers. Checker listened on his knees beside both children; Jackson was outside on the wagon seat, watching with one hand holding the entrance curtain against its frame. The black man watched the tall gunfighter with quiet admiration. He knew Checker had barely slept since the jail break and that the hard-to-read man had nearly snapped when he discovered what had happened to his sister and her family. Yet somewhere inside him was a resolve few ever had.

They were a long way from Dodge, Jackson told himself, but he couldn't think of any man he would rather be riding with—or more likely to get them there. He recalled what one of the Triple C riders had said about Checker when he joined their drive to Kansas: "Checker's a man who's seen trouble an' trouble ran like hell to git away." He recalled telling Bannon himself about a saying in Texas: "In order for a man to be a Texas Ranger, he's got to ride like a Mexican, track like a Comanche, shoot like a Kentuckian, and fight like the devil. I think that pretty well describes John Checker from what I hear." But this man was squatting beside two children he dearly loved, looking more like some country minister than a feared gun warrior.

With tiny folded hands, Rebecca closed her eyes. "Thank you, God, for my food. Thank you for Uncle John and Uncle Black Jack and Uncle Tyrel. Help Uncle Sonny get over his hurt. Help Uncle Black Jack not hurt from his black skin. Bless Johnny and me . . . an' Mommy an' Daddy. Amen."

Jackson stared at the darkened sky and sniffed; Checker patted her back and helped her into the covers. "Johnny, how about you? Do you want to say your prayers now?"

"Do you pray, Uncle John? How could God do this to us? How could He take . . ." Johnny drove his head into the rolled shirt used for a pillow.

Checker put his hand on the sobbing boy's shoulder. "Yes, I pray. A lot. I pray for lots of things. Right now, I'm praying for strength and understanding—and your mother to get well—and Sonny to get well—and for us to get home safe."

Johnny's words were muffled as he spoke into the shirt. "I h-hate G-God. I hate Him."

"He loves you, Johnny. God brought us to you." Checker was surprised at his own words.

"Why d-did He let . . . th-this happen?" Sobs were jerking their way through his body.

Checker pulled Johnny to him, holding the boy tightly against his chest. "He didn't, Johnny. He didn't. It was some very bad men that did this."

Johnny's head buried itself against Checker's leather tunic. The boy's sounds were more like from a small injured animal than human. Checker patted his back, uncertain of what to do or say next. He looked over at Jackson, who nodded support.

"Hold me, too, Uncle Black Jack." Rebecca sat up and wobbled over to the front curtain and held out her tiny arms.

"You bet I will, little honey." Jackson lifted her to the wagon seat and held her, humming a trail song, the only one he could think of at the moment.

"I prayed that your black skin wouldn't hurt you," she announced proudly.

"I know you did, that was very nice," Jackson murmured.

Inside the wagon, Checker talked to Johnny with the boy's face pressed against him. "Johnny, you are the head of your family now. You are the man." He stroked the boy's sweating head. "I want you to think hard about your father. Think about how he did things, what he believed in, how much he loved you, your little sis, and your mother. I want you to pray to become a good, fine man just like him. Can you do that—for me?"

"I—I want to be . . . jes' like you, Uncle John."

Checker shook his head. "Your father was a brave, strong man. He built a fine place for all of you to live. He cared for you. He gave everything he had to make you happy. That's more than I've done—for anyone."

"B-but you're . . . a gunfighter. I want to be a gunfighter." Johnny pulled his head back and stared into Checker's still face.

Before Checker could answer, the boy went on to say that there wasn't any home anymore, that it had been destroyed. The former Ranger promised that their horse ranch would be rebuilt, that he would stay until it was—and until Johnny was ready to take over. The tear-streaked boy sat back on his blankets and asked if his mother would be alive when they got to Dodge and if Checker would find Star McCallister and kill him.

"Johnny, I don't know about your mother, not for sure," Checker's shoulders rose and fell. "She was in very bad shape when we left her with Dr. Tremons." He hesitated and knew it was the best approach, the truth. "But he's a mighty good doc—and, like I said before, your mother's a mighty strong woman."

"Why did those men do this . . . to us?" Johnny frowned. "We never did them no wrong."

"They're evil, Johnny. Evil doesn't care about right or wrong, just in taking what it wants. They steal and hurt—and kill. They must be destroyed . . . like a rattlesnake."

"You didn't say if you were going to kill Star McCallister."

"No, I didn't, Johnny." Checker winced.

Checker had avoided the question earlier because he didn't know the answer. How can one kill his own brother, even if he is just a half brother? Hatred for his half brother, his late villainous father—and his younger half brother, Blue—had driven him in recent days. Driven him like he had never known before. It was as if all the pent-up frustration from his childhood had erupted inside his brain and taken over.

"We'll worry about that later. All right?" Checker finally said, squinting back the edges of anger. "Now I want you to say your prayers and ask God to help you grow up to be like your father. All right?"

"Yessir."

Checker gave him a quick hug, listened to the heartfelt recitation, and eased him into the blankets. Rebecca joined them and he helped her into bed as well.

Outside the wagon, Checker looked for Jackson. The black cowboy was already filling plates and coffee cups for the outlaws. Bannon was standing beside him, waiting. When the tall ranger walked over, Jackson said, "That was nicely done, John."

"Don't know about that."

"Maybe tomorrow we'll give 'em the new clothes we brought. What do y'all think?" Jackson scooped meat and potatoes into a plate with his spoon.

"Oh yeah, I forgot." Checker smiled. "Should I remind the kids?"

"Well, I wouldn't. They won't sleep a wink." Jackson handed the plate to Bannon along with a filled cup of coffee. "We can do it at breakfast. If Johnny's not ready to change, so be it."

"Sure."

Bannon brought a tin plate and coffee cup to Wes Morton while Checker took food to Salome. The farm boy wanted it the other way around, but the former Ranger insisted. Both were untied long enough to eat, restrained again, and the rest of the outlaws were fed.

"Thanks, Tyrel, I'm obliged," Morton said. "You know I didn't have nothin' to do with hurtin' that fine woman—or her husband. You know that, don't ya?"

Bannon stared at the young man, easily no more

than four or five years his senior, in spite of his thick beard, and shook his head. "No, I don't. An' I don't know if you killed some of my friends back on the trail. You picked some bad-uns to ride with."

"I—I reckon you're right, Tyrel, I never had no folks, not since I kin remember anyhow." Morton finished the food and sipped the coffee with untied hands. "I wish I'd found men like John Checker to ride with. Things mighta been different, ya know."

"Yeah, they mighta been."

From the campfire, Jackson called, "Tyrel, could y'all give me a hand?"

"Gotta go, they need me. I have to retie you."

"You let a nigger boss you around, Tyrel?" A sneer crossed Morton's face.

"Don't. That's one of my best friends."

"Oh, sorry, I didn't know. Hey, I'm sorry."

"Stand against the tree—and put your arms around it."

"Sure. Sure." Morton stood and hugged the tree as ordered. "I'm not like those others." He winced. "That's awful tight, Tyrel. Please. I ain't goin' nowhere."

At the campfire, Jackson was packing his old pipe with tobacco when Bannon sauntered over.

"What do you need, Jackson?"

"Sit down a minute, beside me, will you?"

"Well, sure, but—"

After Bannon squatted beside the black man, Jackson lit his pipe and let the first smoke encircle his face as he released it. He spoke without looking at Bannon. "Y'all know that man wants ya to feel sorry for him."

"Jackson, he's about my age—and he didn't have nothin' to do with hurtin' Mrs. Hedrickson an' the kids. He tolt me hisse'f."

"What did y'all expect him to tell you, Tyrel?"

The young farm boy squinted at his dark friend.

Sometimes, Jackson could be downright exasperating in his questions.

Jackson didn't wait for him to answer. "This is going to be a long ride, Tyrel. The easier thing would have been to hang that bunch back there. I'm right proud of John for not doing it that way."

"What difference does it make?"

"Lots, Tyrel. We're not the law, even if we want to be," Jackson said. "If this country is going to be anything, it has to be built on laws—not on what somebody thinks is right, whenever he thinks it's right. Understand?"

"Well, I reckon."

"Y'all think on it, and we'll talk some more," Jackson said. "In the meantime, y'all remember something for me, will ya?"

"Sure, what?"

"Remember Wonsen, Harry, Tex, Freddie, Isreal, Old Pete, Jake, Stuart—remember how it felt when ya found the camp after the rustlers hit, and y'all found Dan all shot up. Keep that picture close when y'all are around those bastards. Including that young one."

"But that doesn't mean—"

"An' remember Wes Morton wears two pistols tied down and he was there when our friends went down. Y'all think he didn't shoot at them?"

"Well, I don't—"

"Yeah, Tyrel, ya do know. Y'all know he shot at our friends—and likely killed one. He may be young, Tyrel, but that doesn't make him like y'all."

Bannon stared into the fire for a moment, glanced over at the darkened cottonwood trees where he could barely make out the shapes of the outlaws. Checker was finishing with their dinners.

"And stay away from the woman." Jackson's last statement was a knife.

"Wh-what do you mean?" Bannon's eyes were hot.

Jackson smiled softly and took the pipe from his mouth. "Tyrel, sometimes beautiful things aren't good things. Roses have thorns, ya know. She tried to kill John, and only an empty gun kept her from it."

"I—I wasn't—"

"I saw what she was trying. Earlier." Jackson eased the pipe back into his mouth, pushed on his glasses, and shook his head. "She'll try to make y'all stop thinking, Tyrel—if ya let her."

"I won't."

"Just stay away from her, Tyrel. She's made a lot of men do wrong, I reckon."

Bannon didn't like his older friend's apparent mistrust and shoved his boot heel in the ground, making a long shallow mark, but couldn't think of anything worth saying.

With his Winchester cradled in his arms, Checker returned to the campfire. His mind was on the Comanches and the preparation for their attack. "If" wasn't a question in his thoughts. It was "when."

Standing a few feet from the dying fire, Checker started into the subject without salutation.

"They'll come at first light."

It was understood by Jackson and Bannon that he was referring to the war party.

Timid streaks of yellow light from the weakened fire traveled up Checker's frame to his tanned face, pausing briefly at the double row of cartridges on his belt and produced metallic shimmers.

"They'll go for the herd. First."

"How do you know? Why won't they come now?" The questions popped from Bannon's mouth before he had a chance to think about them.

Checker's response was almost gentle. "If a warrior

dies in the dark, his spirit will never find the way to . . .
Shadow Land . . . to heaven."

Jackson picked up a burning stick from the fire and
relit his pipe. "Y'all think the big boy'll convince 'em
that his medicine is strong enough—to match the black
shaman?"

"Yeah, he's got to—to save face. There was a little
lightning in the sky a while back." Checker looked skyward. "He'll say that's a sign his powers are with him.
Thunder and lightning. Big medicine."

Puffing on his pipe, the black drover asked Checker if
he had ever seen the place along the upper Red River,
where the grass seemed to be permanently burned off
in the shaped of a huge bird with outstretched wings.
The Comanche believed the Thunderbird had been
there once. Lots of thunder and lightning came from
that area. Checker hadn't seen it, but had heard about it
from his late friend, Stands-in-Thunder.

The conversation was easy, like two men sitting in a
barbershop, passing the time. Bannon was amazed at
their apparent calmness. Inside, he was filled with but-
terflies and some of them wanted out.

The two men talked for a few minutes about other
Comanche beliefs—their reverence for the buffalo, that
the owl brought bad news, their belief in reincarnation,
that the wolf gave power to a man to walk barefoot on
cold snow and was always connected to good, about
their fear of strangulation, about the relationship between a warrior and his supernatural power, his
guardian for life, given to him in a vision—and about
the "little men"—*nanapi*—who were a foot tall and
could kill with every shot of their tiny bows.

Jackson wondered if Checker would bring up the
story he had heard several times about the former
Ranger being blessed by some powerful shaman and

how he couldn't be killed, except by his own relations.
It was one of those wild stories that everyone snickered
at, except at times like these. The white elk-bone circular mark embedded on his pistol grips was supposed to
be related to this tale. Jackson shook his head; there
were lots of stories about Checker. Some of them be-
lievable, some the result of much retelling and as much
embellishment. Still, here was one of the gun warriors
who had stood between utter savagery and Texas. And
all of Texas was safer for it.

The black drover knew Checker wouldn't bring it up;
he never did. The only story he ever refuted—when others were present—was that he and Star McCallister
were related.

Bannon thought it was fascinating and scary, especially the part about the "little men." His gaze took in the
silent land now filled with darker images and imagined
what could be lurking in them. He also was concerned
about what they were going to do about the Comanches coming, instead of talking about their crazy
ways. Finally he said so.

"What are we gonna do—to get ready for 'em?" Bannon's question came with widened eyes.

Checker grinned. "Good question."

With an easy simplicity, Checker gave the assignments. Bannon would move to the top of the wagon
and stretch out there for the night. The height would
give him a good field of fire, Checker advised. The former Ranger would take a position near the herd, and
Jackson would remain near their own string of horses.
All three should take their rifles and a box of ammunition. That was it. No statement about everything being
all right—or concern about their safety—or advice on
what to do. Just the assignments.

Checker's face was unreadable. Only pale blue eyes
that could see inside a man carried the dark marks of

little sleep. He shook hands with both men, wished them luck, and headed toward the rear of the wagon. Jackson guessed he wanted to look in on Sonny. The handle of a second handgun was visible above Checker's back waistband. Probably his saddle pistol, the black drover thought to himself.

After Checker left, Jackson told Bannon to hold out his hand. Surprised, the farm boy raised his opened palm and the black drover placed a small white pebble in it.

"John gave this to me before we got to the hideout." Jackson's face was stern and frowned. "Said it was good luck. It reminded him of a pebble his Comanche friend had given him once. I want you to carry it."

Staring at the small rock, Bannon wasn't certain of what to say. "I—I g-guess it worked for you, didn't it?"

"Yes, sir, guess it did. I put a prayer with it, too. Y'all do the same, Tyrel," Jackson added. "You stay steady up there. They'll come like shadows. You'll think they aren't there—and they are. When y'all hit one, shoot him again. Y'all don't want him crawlin' closer when ya think he's done."

"All right." Bannon carefully shoved the pebble into his pocket.

Jackson patted him on the shoulder and walked away.

It took the farm boy several minutes to climb on top of the wagon. The flat wood roof was surrounded by a trim of gold filigree. He laid with his Winchester beside him. Everywhere was quiet and dark. He couldn't tell where Checker or Jackson were. Even the sleeping outlaws were little more than black shapes among the trees. But it made him feel good that Checker and Jackson trusted him with this responsibility. Made him feel like he was truly one of them.

The silence of the night brought rushes of memories and tried to bring back the sense of killing from two days before. He managed to keep the thought away by concentrating on Salome. Her face was gone now, hidden in shadow and sleep. Her body was unclear in his memory, but he continued to let her perform her magic on him anyway, replacing her with the ways of the prostitute from Dodge who had introduced him to the ways of the flesh.

It seemed strange; he'd never been so close to a bunch of bad men before. Not like this anyway. When they rounded up the gang with their herd, it was impersonal. Now they were turning into real people. Like Wes Morton. During the afternoon, he heard them talking back and forth, mostly about the things he and his friends cared about. In many ways, they were the same. They talked about women and mentioned Salome. He had strained to hear what they said about her and wanted to tell them that she had smiled at him. He didn't, certain Jackson wouldn't approve.

On the far side of the camp, John Checker slipped unnoticed toward the horse corral. Something in the eyes of the war party leader had warned him. That and knowing Comanches. Businesslike and practical, they would return and would go for the horses first. So many fine mounts was a worthy prize on any day, especially the two handsome stallions. Their leader, Lightning, would point to the moonless night as a further indication of his power over the black shaman.

Putting his Winchester over his shoulder and chest with a rawhide thong connecting the weapon, Checker climbed an old cottonwood tree just above the horses. Twenty feet off the ground, he chose a level area, created by three thick branches growing close together from the trunk. Sitting cross-legged, he cocked his rifle slowly to keep the sound consistent with the night's music. He didn't think the Comanches were close yet, but it was smart to be careful. Just in case.

Fatigue pushed at the corners of his mind and body.

Sleep had been only fitful rests, always in the saddle, as he had searched for his niece and nephew. He fought to concentrate. When the Comanches came, it would be like the softness of sleep. At least, the night was his ally. He could always see—and track—in the darkness. Stands-in-Thunder said it was because Checker's spirit helper was the wolf. Whatever it was, nighttime withheld no secrets from him. Instead, he always felt he could see more accurately at night than during the day. It was like all the unimportant details and colors faded away from his perception, leaving only whatever he needed to see. His ability to track men at night was legendary among Texas Rangers. Almost as great as his reputation with a gun.

But they wouldn't come until the new day was promising them salvation if they died. The night itself would be long—and filled with memories. He let his tired mind wonder back to Sarah Ann Tremons, daughter of the town doctor. For most of the ride, she had been only a daydream away. Her kiss when he left burned on his lips even now. Could he start over in Dodge? Could he leave behind his reputation and find peace? Would she be interested in a life with him? Would she?

He had promised Johnny that he would rebuild their ranch. Were they just words to calm a boy or was it actually something he longed for? Sonny, too, had offered to stay behind and help. His attachment to Amelia's children was obvious. So were his feelings for her. Would his sister be interested in him—after she recovered? *If* she recovered, his mind corrected. *If she recovered.*

Where had Star McCallister gone? He had told Bannon that he wouldn't be bothering Checker anymore as they rode away. Would Marshal Rand be there when they returned to Dodge or would he have fled from Checker's threat? It was clear the lawman had been involved in the gang's escape. Checker intended to hold him responsible for the death of their two friends help-ing guard the jail. Did he really want to confront Star McCallister again? What if he caught up with his half brother and Star wouldn't surrender? What if it came to a gunfight? He hoped the outlaw leader would head to St. Louis or Kansas City and stay there. It would be the smart move, Checker thought.

His head nodded against his chest and John Checker was asleep. The night drifted through the plains without disturbing him. He stirred. Not aware initially of where he was, he jerked awake as he remembered he was up in a tree. A glance around the darkened land indicated all was well. A faint blush of rose told of a dawn not far behind.

As his eyes began to review the herd below, the dark-ness signaled its concern by becoming noticeably quiet. Too quiet. Something had silenced the night creatures and it wasn't the coming daylight. That was an hour away. He studied the horses in the corral, looking for indications of advancing warriors. He didn't have to wait long.

The lead mare's head came upright, her ears straight up, listening. A glance at the nearby trees told him both stallions were alert and agitated. With ears laid back, the bay began pawing the ground and snorting. The dun struggled against the rope and reared twice, flail-ing its front hooves.

Comanches were sneaking up from that direction, from the south. Three crawling warriors appeared as if manifesting out of the night air. One moment nothing was there and the next, three men were nearing the ropes. They hadn't made a sound. They hadn't dis-turbed the horses, except for the wariness of the mare and stallions. They wouldn't.

Checker eased his rifle into position.

CHAPTER EIGHT

Bannon was suddenly aware of the early morning stillness and remembered what Jackson had said about
learning from the sounds around him. He leaned on his
elbows and looked into the quiet grayness, holding his
Winchester at the ready. Nothing. Nothing. He looked to
see if the outlaws were in place. He counted. One, two,
three, four, five. Yes, there were all there, sleeping. He
tried not to dwell on Salome. Or Wes Morton. Jackson
was right.

Was that a shadow moving? A shadow within a
shadow? Bannon tensed and squinted into the darkness. He wished he could see at night like John
Checker could. Around the campfire, he had heard the
stories that he could track a man at night as well as he
could during daylight.

There. There was the movement again. Dark gray
against gray.

A shot tore into the night, down by the horses; then

three more, as if they were breathing. Bannon heard a wild war cry that ended in a long gasp.

Bursting from the night came a screaming shape flying toward the wagon. Instinctively, he raised his rifle, but the hurdling body was shattered in flight by bullets coming from his right. The dead body thumped to the ground a few feet from him. It was the Comanche warrior in the white woman's dress. A second behind came a brass tomahawk, freed from the Comanche's hand, skidding to a halt ten feet in front of the wagon seat. He stared down at the dead warrior, at first wondering what the Indian had done with his Winchester, then slowly realized what was happening.

From the back of the wagon, he heard a curse followed by several shots. Pistol shots, he thought. Bannon stared into the night and felt, more than saw, another shape running toward the wagon. His Winchester hit his shoulder and he fired. An arrow sang of death as it sailed past his left ear.

Nothing. Had he missed?

He levered the gun and stared into the blackness. Something told him to move and he shifted four feet to his left, nearer the front of the wagon. A minute later, the shape reappeared, this time climbing over the top of the wagon itself. The warrior was surprised to discover Bannon wasn't where he had been, and the difference was enough for the farm boy to have time to shoot. Orange flame reached out and the Indian's painted chest blossomed with crimson.

Wild-eyed, the Comanche stutter-stepped toward him with a scalp knife raised to strike.

Bannon fired three more shots into the warrior's midsection. Stepping back, the farm boy levered another cartridge into the Winchester's chamber and watched the dead Indian stagger and disappear over the side of the wagon. Bannon gulped for air that wouldn't come fast enough, his face and body aflame with nervous energy.

Forcing himself to be steady, he leaned over the top of the wagon and peered below. The warrior was splay-legged on the ground, a black circle spreading under him. *He's dead and I've killed him.* Bannon jumped back and thought he was going to be sick. He remembered the white pebble Jackson had given him and shoved his hand into his pocket to find it. Trembling, he pulled it loose and opened his hand to reveal the tiny rock. It was nothing special, he told himself, just a rock. He started to throw it away but another thought followed. What made him move when he did? Was it this little rock? *Was that what saved my life?* He returned the pebble to his pocket. He would ask Jackson about it all later, when this was over. Would it end with everyone safe? Would he be safe?

To his far right and below, he caught the glimpse of movement and spun his rifle in that direction

"It's me, Tyrel. Are you all right?" The voice was Jackson's. It was urgent.

"Y-yes. I—I k-killed one, I think."

"Reload while you can. They're all around us."

Bannon remembered to move again, bending over and crawling toward the back of the wagon roof and studied the darkness for shapes that shouldn't be there.

"D-did you shoot . . . that first one?" Bannon yelled, slipping fresh cartridges into his rifle.

"Yes, had a good angle."

"Thanks, Jackson."

"You bet. Watch careful, son. There's a bunch left."

A quick glance at the outlaw trees told its own story. Salome was screaming; Venner and Redmond were yelling to be set free; arrows were stuck in their trees. Morton had three arrows in him, one in his heart.

Bannon's gaze was drawn to movement. Morning light

was sliding into place and helping. Wells was furiously kicking at a warrior trying to get close enough to kill and scalp him. The farm boy took careful aim and fired. The warrior straightened his back and took a step backward. Bannon fired again and the warrior collapsed.

"Thanks, kid. Thought I was done fer." Wells hollered. "There ain't any more up this way. If'n I see one, I'll let ya know."

Salome's cries were babble, unintelligible, unstopping. Bannon felt sorry for the woman and, for an instant, thought about going to her. The other two outlaws pleaded for their release. While Bannon thought it wasn't a bad idea, that was for Jackson and Checker to decide.

"Come on, boy, cut us loose. We can help." Redmond growled loudly. "Come on."

Venner's plea was more polite. "Please . . . give us a chance. Remember them two little kids."

Jackson's voice stopped the outlaws' fearful demands. "I'm heading back to our horses, Tyrel. Watch out for them trying to get inside the wagon." Jackson's direction came as Bannon heard the black cowboy's hurried footsteps. It dawned on the farm boy that he had never really seen him. Not really.

Within the corral, a bay horse with its nose full of fear reared and snorted. Another ran against the rope corral and broke free. Three others followed to freedom, whinnying their defiance as they galloped away.

Satisfied no more warriors were near the horses, Checker climbed down. The stallions were troubled, but in no immediate danger of getting loose by themselves. But if the break in the corral ropes wasn't fixed, they would lose all of the horses. He moved quickly to the open part of the corral, laid his rifle on the ground beside him, and tried to quiet the rest of the herd. The horses seemed eager to calm down, or most anyway.

Primarily because there wasn't any more shooting. The lead mare strolled over to Checker, stopping only a few feet away. She was amazingly quiet, but acted like she expected him to advise her of any concern. He talked to her in a low, steady voice to reassure her.

Checker took advantage of the opportunity and began retying the snapped restraints with new lariat. His manner was like that of an elk drinking water with his head constantly coming up to search the land for more trouble or any horses attempting to rush the opening.

Behind him came a faint odor of wood smoke, animal grease, and sweat. So faint he wasn't sure it was there. He didn't move, letting his senses assess the morning. A soft click like that of an injured cricket was ten feet away, or was it the tinkle of tin against a bear claw on a war shirt? Then came the rush of leather against leather. His jump sideways was just enough to avoid most of the thrust of the Comanche leader's lance as he ran at Checker. The steel point slid along the side of Checker's stomach, but only drew a line of blood, then caught the edge of his cartridge belt, making strange metallic music and slicing through two bullet loops as it fiercely passed.

Without turning around, Checker grabbed the spear shaft and yanked it hard toward him. As the war chief stumbled forward off-balance, Checker spun and delivered a left cross into the shorter man's chin. As he released the lance at the same time, Checker's right fist exploded into the Indian's stomach.

A groan from gritted teeth followed. Staggering, the Comanche did not go down. Checker's eyes connected with the wild, bloodshot eyes of Lightning.

The lance clattered on the ground, but Lightning had already drawn a tomahawk and regained his balance. Yellowed teeth sneered through his red-painted face. Checker reached for his Colt and fired. The war chief's grunt was an instant before his tomahawk slammed against Checker's gun fist. The fierce blow drove the weapon from his hand. Breath exploded from Checker's body as the pain reached his mind.

Dazed, he staggered and tried to push away the burning rush of anguish from his bleeding hand. As Lightning's tomahawk rose for a follow-up strike, Checker's left fist caught him again on the chin. A right jab followed, snapping against the Indian's cheek and jarring free his tomahawk. Blood flew from Lightning's mouth and a tooth flew into the air, joining the weapon. Both hung in the grayness for an instant before succumbing to the land. The blow with his injured hand sent shivers of excruciating pain through Checker's entire body. Fighting through the distress, Checker hit him again with his left, a short powerful jab into the Indian's nose. He couldn't bring himself to use his right. His entire right arm was numb.

Checker pushed the stunned Comanche away from him and drew his second Colt from his belt in back with his left hand. The urgent motion was jerky and felt awkward. He thumbed the hammer and fired as it came forward. Lightning jolted upright, hesitated, and tried, this time, to reach a sheathed scalp knife at his waist. Checker fired three times more, using his right hand to fan the Colt. Even the brushing against the hammer tormented his wound.

Lightning collapsed to the ground, his antelope-skin war shirt showing black circles filling with crimson. Three of the Indian's feathers were bent in half; one was completely broken off. His legs were awkwardly curled beneath him. The legging fringe looked like it had frozen in flight.

Checker stared down at the dead Comanche, trying to find his breath. His right hand was numb and a line of red covered his wrist. He rubbed his hand, hoping it would bring relief. A tingling had begun as if he had slept on it. He tried to bend his wrist, and shooting pain stopped him. It wasn't broken, he didn't think. Part of the tomahawk blow had hit his pistol first, taking away some of the force. Shoving the second gun back into his waistband, he looked around, saw the first, and tried to pick it up with his right hand. The ache and stiffness made him switch to his left. He stood shaking for a few minutes before attempting to remove the spent shell from this Colt. The cartridge slid from his numbed fingers and bounced off his boot. He leaned over and retrieved it carefully as if handling something precious.

Clicking open the cylinder lid, he rejected the old and slowly inserted the fresh. His mind reminded him of his other, nearly empty, pistol. Slowly he holstered the first and began reloading the backup gun, forcing the fingers of his right hand to do most of the work. It was slow. The anguish was receding, more of a dull pang now.

At the other end of camp, young Bannon thought he saw movement and fired. Whatever it was, vanished. It might have been his imagination, he decided. He wiped his hands on his pants to get rid of the sweat growing there. He rolled on the roof farther to his right and took a new position.

Announcing his advance, Jackson knelt beside the wagon, pushing his glasses back into place and searching the uneven terrain for any sign of movement. "Wait there for a little longer, Tyrel. I think they've gone, but I'm not sure."

"I—I k-killed two, Jackson."

"You had no choice, Tyrel. It's right that you feel bad about it. That means you value life. But, remember, they were going to take ours." Jackson moved toward the front of the wagon. "I'm going to see about the kids. Johnny, are you and Rebecca all right?"

Silence.

From above, Bannon asked, "Are they there? Are they all right?"

"Johnny? It's me, Jackson. Uncle Black Jack."

"Y-yes, sir. Me an' sis are all right. Is it Injuns?" The voice was trying to sound confident and failing. "I've got my knife . . . ready."

"Yes, it is. I think we've driven them off—but we've got to be sure. Don't come out yet, all right? You stay down."

"Yes, sir, but Rebecca says she wants to be with you."

Rebecca's voice followed, urgent and frail. "Uncle Black Jack . . . I want to be with you. I'm scared, Uncle Black Jack."

Jackson bit his lower lip. "I know, honey, but you stay with your brother. I'll come to you . . . in a little while. All right?"

"But I'm scared."

Jackson wanted to say he was scared too. "It's going to be fine. Just fine. You and your brother just lie down. Please, Rebecca. Please. Uncle Tyrel is watching over you. He's right on top of the wagon."

"Hi, Johnny. Hi, Rebecca. I'm up here. I . . ." Bannon stopped before his own battle actions were recited again, adding to their anxiety.

Sounds of shuffling were an indication of their compliance, so Jackson slipped along the side of the wagon and back to the remuda string, telling Bannon where he was going. He assured himself that the rope ties holding the Triple C and wagon horses remained steadfast. The two steers moaned their dislike of the noise. The horses were alert and agitated. Only Redmond's bay seemed to be frightened, pulling on its rope and snorting. Jackson tried to quiet the horse with easy words of comfort; the animal shook its head and continued an assault on the binding.

From the roof, Bannon watched. His gaze fixed on the black man as if Jackson were the only sanity left in the world. The young man wasn't certain if he wanted to laugh or cry. Part of him wanted to yell out that he was alive. Another part wanted to scream that he had taken away the life of two men. A sad gnawing at this thought swelled in his throat and took away any words of celebration or anguish.

Checker's black pawed the ground and snorted.

"Yeah, I know, Tuhupi, ya want to be free—to fight. Y'all are just like your master." Jackson stroked the horse's head. "I think it's over now. But stand watch, will ya?" After patting the strong mount again, he walked on toward the back of the wagon.

"It's me, Jackson."

There was no response from inside where Sonny would be lying. From the roof came Bannon's soft acknowledgment.

Two dead Comanches lay sprawled next to the back end. He kicked their bodies to assure himself of their condition. His glance at the other side of the wagon told him that Bannon had killed another.

"Sonny, it's me, Jackson. I'm coming in."

After announcing his presence, he parted the curtain. He stared into the black nose of Sonny Jones's Colt in the happy-go-lucky cowboy's left fist.

Weak and trembling, Sonny greeted him. "Good to see you, Jackson. Had some folks drop by earlier. How we doin'? Where's Checker?"

Sonny tried to smile, even as the movement brought a sharp sting through his waist and awakened the dull ache in his right arm. It didn't stop there. A wave of weakness streaked through his body and reached his head, taking away his ability to focus his eyes. He lowered his left hand, still holding the gun, down on the wagon bed to steady himself.

"You shouldn't be up, Sonny," Jackson said. "You're burning with fever."

"I thought maybe I had just slept through to July." His grin was weak but it was pure Sonny.

Even in the makeshift bed, he was still shirtless, but wearing chaps, spurs, cuffs, and his vest with its ever-filled pockets. Neither Checker nor Jackson earlier when dressing his wounds had made an attempt to take them off. Beside him was an assortment of items that had fallen out of his pockets. Five cartridges. A piece of hard candy. A stray nail and a curl of leather thong. Sonny's derby, however, lay next to him. Piled neatly in a corner, thanks to Jackson, were his empty gun belt and the dark leather garters that were usually worn on his upper arms.

Shadow covered most of Sonny's broad nose, flat nose, wiry mustache, and fleshy frame. Fresh bandages covered his right arm and around his right hip. Although Sonny didn't look like it, Jackson knew no one who could fight any fiercer. Unless it was Checker.

Like the former Ranger, Jackson knew Sonny's real name was Cole Dillon. Say the name along the border and watch many draw back in fear. Sonny had become an outlaw after the War of Northern Aggression, finding justification in lawlessness to drive away the bitterness of losing. But a greater loss came when his wife, Mary, died from sickness. And great change. He rode away from her grave, determined to be the man she wanted him to be, and left his name there as well. Jackson knew Checker had accepted that as fact, even though, as a Ranger, he had once tracked him across the windswept Staked Plains of Texas. One night on the trail, Sonny told him that Checker had actually helped him escape, later informing the authorities that Cole Dillon was dead. The former Ranger and former outlaw had become as close as real brothers, perhaps filling the hole in Checker's soul left by his evil half brothers.

A small red circle indicated Sonny had broken open the wound in his arm. Jackson decided not to say anything about it; Sonny would've been angry if he did. Son of a top vaquero for a vast Mexican ranch and a proper Englishwoman, Sonny Jones was darker skinned than most, except Jackson. Sonny's blue eyes and light brown hair covering his ears were physical evidence of the difference between his parents. But even in this poor light, Jackson could see the cowboy was pale.

CHAPTER NINE

"Did John tell you about the Comanches?" Jackson asked. He had never seen anyone who enjoyed the challenge of battle more than Sonny, usually laughing through it. On the trail, Sonny was the one who liked making up funny songs about what was going on, even when it was bad. It was a rare day when the man didn't wake up smiling.

"That he did. Well, it was sort of in passing. You know Checker." Sonny grinned and winced. "He stopped here, mumbled something about wishing I was strong enough to use my gun because Comanches were coming at dawn—and left. I suppose he's out there—showing off how well he can see in the dark."

Jackson shook his head and glanced at the coming dawn in the distance. Full daylight was still a half hour away. Sonny told him that he had decided to keep watch out the back, peeking through the curtain. But he slept most of the night anyway. He chuckled and said that he hadn't heard the two warriors at all, only wakened and seen them when they got close.

"Did I hear the kids up front?" Sonny motioned with his head. A three-foot shelf with a series of drawers containing medicine bottles separated the front of the wagon from the back. The bottom row was opened and jammed with various medicines.

"Can't see through them damn bottles." He pushed at a jar of Hamlin's Wizard Oil that lay free of the others. It careened off a box of Doan's Pills and came to rest against three bottles of Dr. Pepper's Tonic.

"Yes, they're awake. An' Tyrel's on the roof of the wagon. He took out two."

"He'll do to ride the river with. Can I see the kids?" Sonny's eyes met Jackson's. It wasn't a question.

Jackson waved his rifle. "After we're sure this is all settled down. All right?"

"You've got a deal." Sonny inhaled, and the motion brought a long shiver. "Think I'll just rest . . . a little . . . until then." He lay down on his pallet, holding his gun.

"Good, Sonny. That would be good." Jackson patted the man's knee and left, returning the curtains to their proper place. He announced to Bannon his intention to search the rest of the camp. The farm boy answered the statement with a crisp response that hid his desire to go along.

At the corral, Checker greeted Jackson from the shadows.

"Y'all think they're gone?" Jackson turned his head in both directions to emphasize his question.

"Yeah, I think so. They'll be back for their dead, though." Checker kept his right hand at his side. "We'll let them do that. Think I'll move the bodies out away from here."

"I'll help y'all."

"Kids all right?"

Jackson nodded affirmatively.

"Was that Sonny shooting . . . from the wagon?" Checker glanced in that direction.

"Oh, sure. He dropped two of them. They were trying to get to our horses."

"Damn, wouldn't you know he'd be there when we needed him?" Checker's admiration was evident on his tanned face.

"Tyrel took out two himself." Jackson licked his dry lower lip. "He's pretty shook-up about it."

Checker took a deep breath. "Not exactly what he thought a cattle drive would be. Hope he doesn't tell his mother about all this. She'll never let him go on another."

Jackson nodded and asked if the Hedrickson herd was safe. Checker told him of the loss of four horses and fixing the ropes. They walked the perimeter of the corral with both men stopping to stroke the inquisitive noses of two horses and check the retied ropes. The lead mare followed them with her eyes, not moving from her earlier position near the once-broken ropes. They passed over three Indian bodies, then two more ten feet away.

"I see the stallions."

"Yeah, they're fine. Just mad."

"Reckon there's any chance we'll get them back?" Jackson asked.

"You mean the horses that got loose?"

"Yes."

Checker shook his head. "I'm sure whoever is left has them now and will use them to try to salve what he can of his reputation. I figure we took out most. There's three here. Two more by Sonny an' . . ."

"Three more."

"That's eight. That leaves four."

Jackson studied the unmoving shapes, half expecting to see more Indians again. "Unless ol' Lightning picked up a few more braves during the day. Quite a story to tell. All those horses." Sometimes his voice carried a heavier Southern accent than other times. It seemed to depend on who he was talking to. Right now it was smooth, but not laced with emphasized syllables.

"Good point."

Jackson's gaze took in the dead Lightning, and the familiarity of the war shirt registered. "That's Lightning himself."

"Yeah, it is."

For the first time, the black drover noticed the streak of blood on Checker's shirt. His study then took in Checker's bloody right hand.

"John, y'all's bleeding."

"Yeah. It's nothing serious. Really."

Jackson wouldn't accept his observation and insisted on examining Checker's hand and midsection. The stomach wound was a slice of six inches, but not deep. Checker's hand was puffy and red, the cut itself bleeding lightly.

The tall gunfighter explained what had happened as Jackson felt his hand and bent his wrist to see the extent of the damage.

Checker's attempt to hide reaction to the pain didn't go unnoticed.

"Y'all were lucky. Could've taken your whole hand off," the black cowboy finally proclaimed. "Let's get it into the water. At the spring. Might keep the swelling down. Otherwise, ya not goin' to have much use of it for a while. I'm betting there's a bone or two broken in there."

"I'll do that. After we finish looking around."

"If ya don't want McCallister's boys to see your right hand's hurt, y'all better put away the gun—in yur left."

Checker returned the gun to his waistband without comment. That reminded him of the handgun hit by the Comanche leader. He hadn't even thought of examining the weapon before. His glance at the hammer told him all he needed to know. It was bent. A dent in the

handle completed the damage. He realized that he had
reloaded the weapon earlier without being aware of its
condition.

Withdrawing the Colt from his holster as best he
could using his left hand, he turned the weapon barrel
down to study it further. "Looks like Zimmerman's going
to have some business."

"That's what saved your hand." Jackson pointed at the
damage to the gun. "Somebody up there be lookin' out
for y'all, John."

"Yeah." Checker returned the gun to his holster with
his left hand and patted the backup Colt now positioned
to be used by his left hand, resting in his waistband.

For a fleeting moment, his mind scurried away to
what Stands-in-Thunder had said about the power of his
spirit medicine. He took another deep breath and
locked away the thought. Who was he to question
something like that? Who really knew? Maybe it wasn't
just the friendly conversation of an old man who believed in a mysterious bond between himself and the
supernatural powers that controlled his world. Maybe
there was truth in it.

Checker blinked and realized Jackson was quietly
waiting. Attempting to get them moving again, he motioned toward the outlaw trees with his right hand, and
a darting pain stopped the movement. His face paled as
his system absorbed the shock.

Jackson knew better than to push the concern now.
"Better let Tyrel know it's us moving around." He looked
toward the wagon and waved. "Don't shoot, Tyrel. It's us,
John and me."

A responding wave came from the wagon top.

Salome was sobbing, curled into a childlike ball as
best her ropes would let her.

"Ya let Wes git kilt. See?" Redmond snarled as they

walked past, refinding his courage after Checker's threat concerning the use of Sonny's real name. "You an' the nigger."

Checker and Jackson paused in front of the arrow-struck Morton. He was dead.

Kneeling beside the slumped body, Checker said, "You can bury him."

"Not me," Redmond growled.

"Another word, Redmond, and I'll leave you right where you are—for the Comanches." Checker's glare stopped any words entering the outlaw's mind.

"Ranger, the kid done saved my life," Iron-Head Wells blurted. "I thanked him for it. See that Injun? He wanted my hair."

Checker nudged the unmoving Indian, rolling over his body to make certain. One of Bannon's shots had hit the warrior in the head. He made a mental note and decided the outlaws should be aware of the accuracy.

"Damn, that kid can shoot. Hit him in the head. From thirty yards. While it was still dark." Checker walked on, as if talking to himself.

"Is it all over?" Venner asked. His voice was exceptionally polite. He noticed the bloody streak on Checker's shirt, but didn't say anything.

Jackson answered affirmatively.

Without responding to either man, Checker studied the hillside for the possibility of any remaining warriors, wounded or otherwise. He agreed with Jackson's earlier assessment that it would be a mistake to assume more hadn't joined the war party until they were certain. He tried to ignore the throbbing in his hand, holding it as immobile as he could. Lack of movement didn't help much as the fierce throbbing matched his heartbeat.

Bannon came running from the wagon, carrying a

shield in one hand, his rifle in the other. "Hi, Jackson. Hi, John. Are they gone?" He waved his rifle for emphasis. His freckled face was pale, almost green.

"Looks like we took out eight, including their leader," Checker responded, joining Jackson. "I'm going to move their bodies over toward that gulley. Across from the pond."

"Why ya gonna do that?" Bannon asked.

"Comanches come back for their dead. I'd rather not have them too close to camp."

"Oh." Bannon stared at the dead warrior lying near Wells.

"Jackson, when you get a chance, I'd appreciate it if you would make us some coffee. Taste real good, I'm thinking." Checker kept his right hand at his side and away from the outlaws.

"Sure. If you'll take care of that business at the pond." Jackson pushed his glasses back on his nose and headed for the wagon. He wanted to ask how his friend was going to drag bodies without using his right hand, but didn't.

Bannon held up the shield. "Would you look at this?"

Feathers wiggled from the bottom of the war shield as he presented it. On the scraped buffalo bull hide were painted geometric designs and a stylized bear showing large teeth. Bannon noticed three scalps hung from the shield, along with a horse tail.

"There's something in here. Between these two skins. Feels kinda crinkly. Like paper."

"It is paper," Checker said.

"Oh, come on, John, you're spoofin' me."

Checker told him the space between the two hides, about an inch thick, was packed with feathers, horsehair, and paper taken from white men's books, magazines, or newspapers. He said the shield would stop a bullet.

Bannon's expression indicated he wasn't certain if the former Ranger was teasing him or not. Jackson assured him that the description was indeed true, although a buffalo gun, a Sharps, would rip through the protective layers easily.

"Can I keep it?"

"No other warrior will use it, that's for sure," Jackson said. "I'll go get the coffee going. Y'all help John. Would you like me to put the shield in the wagon for safekeeping?"

"Oh, sure." Bannon studied the shield again and handed it to Jackson.

As he walked away, Jackson couldn't recall a time so filled with gloom. Ever. On top of this trek back to Dodge had been the rustling of their Triple C herd, the murder of their friends, and the awfulness at the Hedrickson ranch.

It had taken a toll on all of them, but worse on John Checker, Jackson realized. He knew Checker was a hard man; no one survived being a Texas Ranger any other way. But this had pushed him to an edge that few could understand. Jackson trusted the former Ranger, yet feared him. He had been around other men who were good with a gun, but none quite like Checker. It was almost like he couldn't be killed. Maybe there was something to what Sonny said the old Indian had told Checker. He shivered when he thought about the tall gunfighter handling Lightning's surprise attack.

The black cowboy always figured he knew how Checker would react under pressure. Now he wasn't sure. Sonny was the only one who could have stopped him from hanging the remaining outlaws back at their hideout. And Checker had agreed to the idea. For the time being.

But Checker was a man fighting himself. It was one thing to realize his half brother was a bad man and have to arrest him; it was something else to find that he had tried to destroy much of what Checker thought was beautiful, his sister's family. On the other side of the equation was family blood. Nothing was stronger. When Checker finally dealt with this gnawing pressure within him, the only question in Jackson's mind was whether it would come out for good—or for evil, too. After all, Checker's father was, by all accounts, a thoroughly disreputable man who murdered, stole, and plundered his way in the early days of Dodge City. His blood ran through Checker's veins.

He shrugged off the thought and paused beside the wagon seat and listened. Comforting sounds of sleeping children slid through the curtain. Good, he thought, but climbed up the wagon to see for himself. Both were asleep; Johnny had his arm draped over his little sister. In addition to his nightshirt, he had added his boots. Beside him was his beaded sheath knife. Jackson laid the shield against the seat, climbed down, and walked past the now quiet horses. Opening the back curtain, he saw Sonny was also asleep as he expected. Jackson felt the wounded cowboy's forehead. Fever was gone. He shook his head. How typical of Sonny to feel better after a fight. Satisfied, Jackson went to his saddlebags made from old boot tops and withdrew a small bag of coffee.

After Checker and Bannon completed their tour of the area, ensuring that they were once again alone, Bannon found the courage to speak. "You were sure ri't 'bout them Injuns comin' back."

Behind Checker, Redmond snickered. "How come ya never tolt us 'bout 'em, Checker? Hopin' they'd do the job for ya?"

"Not a bad idea, Redmond," Checker said over his shoulder. "Who knows? They might try again."

Redmond shook his head and looked away.

Bannon stared down at his feet. A clump of dirt had

attached itself to his boot toe. He wiped it against his leg, and the clod broke into pieces. He wanted to tell the tall gunfighter about the gnawing in his stomach that wanted release.

Rubbing his right hand with his left, Checker walked on, toward the wagon. "I'm going to look in on the kids." He paused. "Can you keep an eye on the horses in the corral for a while? Better look at the ropes on the stallions. They were working 'em hard."

"Sure."

"How 'bout some coffee for us, Ranger?" Redmond growled. "Could use a little whiskey to settle us down, too."

Checker didn't respond and headed down the incline. He met Jackson with an armful of branches and the sack of coffee.

"When are y'all goin' to the water hole?" Jackson asked.

"Think I'll look in on the kids, then start carrying bodies. I'll get to the pond after that," Checker said in passing. "How's Sonny?"

"He's asleep. Fever broke." Jackson smiled. "The kids are, too."

"What if . . . their mother . . . Amelia . . . doesn't . . . make it?" Checker's face looked ten years older.

Jackson tried to meet Checker's gaze but knew he couldn't. "Keep praying she does, John. That's all we can do. She's a tough lady, yessuh. Got a lot to live for. They're in that wagon." He looked up and his mouth was a narrow strip. "Y'all do, too, John. They need ya."

"What can I do, Jackson? I don't know how to handle kids. I know men and whether they'll stand and, likely, how they'll fight—and a little about horses. And guns. But not kids." He shook his head.

"Y'all can love them, John. Just like they were ya own. Just love 'em. That's all they want."

CHAPTER TEN

When Jackson next saw John Checker, he was sitting on a log beside the stream, his right hand immersed in the cool water. The back of his hand was streaked with purple and red; the bleeding had stopped. Soreness was throughout the hand and he was less certain no bones had been broken than earlier.

"Well, John, how are y'all doing?" Jackson stretched as he advanced; his entire body felt stiff and abused from the trauma of the battle. Energy had wafted away as the adrenaline from fighting slowly disappeared. The black drover wanted badly to sleep, even though he knew he couldn't.

Checker looked up and slowly smiled. "The Comanches came back . . . an hour ago, I suppose. Hauled away their dead."

Jackson nodded. "Any more problems with the horses?"

"No. I heard them picking up the bodies and yelled out that the black shaman was watching them—and to ride away while they had the chance. Only saw four."

Jackson withdrew his pipe from his coat pocket, shoved it in his mouth, and snapped a match to life. Smoke caressed his dark face as he pushed on his spectacles. "Didn't know y'all knew that much Comanche."

"Well, who knows? I might've said something about picking flowers—but it sounded right to me. Didn't hear anybody laughing anyway."

"Where's Tyrel?" Jackson looked around the chilled camp.

"Last I saw him he was eating something—under that tree. Over by the horses."

Jackson took several steps to gain a better angle and saw the sleeping farm boy.

"I asked him to keep watch. He did. Lasted a half hour or so." Checker pushed his hat back from his head. "He's going to be a good one—if we can keep him away from Salome."

He laughed and Jackson nodded. The black man asked to see Checker's hand, and the former Ranger withdrew it dripping from the water and wiped it on his pants. Jackson's examination was methodical and slow.

"John, I'll bet there's a bone cracked in there. Maybe more."

"Yeah, I think so. Right here." He pressed on his hand about midway between his wrist and his forefinger and winced. "Yeah, right there."

"I'll wrap it with some bandages from the wagon."

"No. I don't want Redmond and the others to know." Checker tried to squeeze his hand into a fist, stopping the attempt as the pain gathered force.

"John—"

"We'll wrap it at night. All right?"

Removing his pipe, Jackson smiled. "Guess it'll have to be. How's y'all's stomach?"

"Sore. Nothing serious."

"I've got some coffee ready. Sound good?" Jackson said. "I'll get workin' on some breakfast too."

"Sure enough. Let's go."

They walked to a sleeping Bannon and watched him.

Quietly, Jackson muttered, "Killing takes a lot out of a man. No matter what. Probably took away his appetite."

Checker reached into his shirt pocket, under his tunic, and withdrew cigarette makings. "Yeah. One moment the man facing you has all kinds of hopes, and dreams, and loves, and cares. The next, he's . . . a mound of dirt." He completed the line of shredded tobacco, rolled the paper into a smoke, and ran the open end across his tongue. "Let him sleep a little longer." He ran his finger across the wetness, sealing it. His right hand was stiff but there was no pang with the movement.

"Good idea." Jackson wheeled away and Checker followed.

"When are we gonna eat?" Redmond yelled. "An' I gotta pee."

"Do it in your pants, Redmond. I haven't decided if you will eat. Again." Checker's face was contorted with hate.

"Easy, John. He's just a loud fool," Jackson said.

Checker's continued expression made Jackson wonder if he should have kept quiet.

"Yeah, you're right. I just . . ."

"I know."

As they neared the wagon, from inside came a stirring, then a jumble of shouted words.

"Becky, ya done peed in our bed."

Jackson shook his head. "Looks like we had a little nighttime accident."

"I'll take care of it—if you'll see to some breakfast." Checker waved at the fire. "Don't figure anybody would want to take on my cooking."

"Sure, I'm going to see how Sonny's doing first."

While the black drover walked to the back of the

wagon, Checker climbed into the front seat and lifted the curtain. His stomach wound reminded him of its existence as he moved. Using his left hand was awkward as he tried to keep the other as immovable as possible. Maybe that would help it heal.

"Good morning. How are you two?" It was his cheeriest voice.

Johnny was crouched over at the far edge of the wagon, looking absolutely petrified. Little Rebecca sat cross-legged and crying among the blankets. Her nightshirt was wet, matching a part of the blankets themselves.

"Uncle John, Becky wet our bed." Johnny repeated, his face squeezing into a frown.

"I—I d-didn't mean to." Rebecca's cheeks were flooded in tears.

"Of course you didn't." Checker bit his lower lip and held out his hands. "No big deal. We'll get you all cleaned up—and we've got a surprise for both of you."

"A surprise? What is it?" Her eyes widened and the tears stopped.

"Oh, then it wouldn't be a surprise. Let's get washed first. You too, Johnny."

"What about all this wet stuff?" Johnny grabbed at the damp blankets.

Checker frowned at the boy. "They'll be fine after we wash them in the pond and let them dry out."

"Are we staying here today?" Johnny asked, sliding toward the front of the wagon, then remembered what had happened during the night. "Are all them Injuns gone? Did ya kill 'em?"

"They went away, Johnny, so we're going to keep going. But we'll have a good breakfast first."

"Could we go on a walk? Mommy always takes us on walks. So we can see the leaves change color." Rebecca slid into Checker's arms. The bottom of her shirt was soaking wet.

"Let's get washed up first, all right?"

"Of course, Uncle John. I'm hungry."

"Good. We'll see if . . . Uncle Black Jack can help us in that department."

With Johnny walking happily at his side, Checker headed back toward the fire, now growing stronger with Jackson's added wood. A large pot of water was already warming at the edge of the fire. Two towels lay folded nearby. One was from his own saddlebags, the other from the wagon supplies. To himself, Jackson thanked Checker's late younger half brother for carrying such a complete store of goods and materials with him. A smart way for the late killer to travel, he thought.

Rebecca was in Checker's arms, chirping about everything she saw. Her wet undergarment rested against his arm. Unmindful of the growing dampness on his shirt, the tall Ranger smiled at the liveliness of her patter. It was music to his soul.

"Good morning, Uncle Black Jack. Uncle John says you're going to make breakfast. Is that right?" Rebecca's bright eyes sought Jackson's face.

Withdrawing the pipe from his mouth, Jackson smiled. "I sure am, Miss Becky. Just as soon as you two get yourself ready for the day."

Washing a little girl was a new experience for Checker and Jackson. Neither was sure what he should or shouldn't do. She made the decision for them, pulling off her nightshirt and underclothes and handing them to Checker. It happened so fast, he didn't have time to tell her that it was cold out.

She shivered in her nakedness. "Oh, I'm cold, Uncle John, Uncle Black Jack."

"I'll bet you are, honey." Jackson removed his long coat and wrapped it around her. At his suggestion, Checker dipped a corner of the towel in the warm pot water and began washing her as best he could.

She giggled when he touched her stomach with the wet towel.

Johnny followed her lead, removing his nightshirt and washing quickly.

"Are you going to take off your clothes too, Uncle John?" she asked, studying the beadwork on his Comanche tunic.

"Not this time, Rebecca." He chuckled.

"Why?"

Jackson bit his lip and looked away.

Checker hadn't expected the question. "Ah . . . because . . . because I have to take care of the horses next."

"Oh. Then will you wash?"

"Maybe so, if we have time."

"What about you, Uncle Black Jack?" Rebecca's wide eyes sought the black cowboy.

Jackson told her that he had already cleaned up; Checker muttered he wished he had thought of that answer, and the black man chuckled again.

After washing, Checker gave them brown-paper-wrapped packages, which they eagerly opened to reveal new clothes and a coat for each. Checker helped Rebecca into her new underclothes, socks, a dress of blue gingham, a warm bonnet, and a buttoned coat. More blue ribbons for her were there too. Although the coat was too big, it would be warm and the autumn chill was carrying more bite than before. Unlike when they left the hideout, Johnny hurried into new underclothes, dungarees, flannel shirt, coat, and woolen cap. His coat fit well.

"I wish Mommy an' Daddy could see us right now!" she exclaimed and spun around to let her dress swing.

Checker wasn't sure of what to say.

Johnny's response was harsh. "Don't be silly, Becky. Paw is dead—an' Mama's prob'ly, too." His eyes blinked to hold away new tears and he tugged on the brim on his cap. "An' our old clothes is good, too. They're from home."

A look came over Rebecca and everyone expected her to cry. Checker froze and Jackson stepped over to console Johnny.

"Uncle John . . . Uncle Black Jack . . . I have to . . . poo-poo." Her expression was total worry.

Checker's mouth opened and remained there. Jackson responded first, patting Johnny on the back as the boy held around him. "John, why don't you take her behind there?" He pointed toward a circle of tall weeds. "Should be some dry leaves around there. Or there's some paper if you want it—where Sonny is. Down to the right. For writing, I suppose. Some kind of catalog there, too." He smiled gently. "Better take along that towel. The wet one."

The tall Ranger's face was uncertain and Jackson thought it was one of the few times anyone would ever see that expression on him.

"She'll do just fine, won't you, Miss Rebecca?" Jackson said.

"I know how to poo-poo," she declared defiantly.

With that, Checker led Rebecca away, holding her little hand. She was eager to talk, sharing her thoughts on virtually everything they passed. Or asking questions to follow his responses.

Bannon sat up, awakened by a particularly loud whinny. He was disoriented and unsure of where he was. His first thought was that he was late for his milking chores at home. That notion flickered and ran, and he gradually put together the day's reality. His mouth tasted awful as if something bad had been resting there all night. He would need to use the bark-peeled stick he kept in his saddlebags for brushing his teeth as soon as he could. If Jackson had some baking soda, he would put that on it, too.

He couldn't resist looking for Salome. She was slumped against the tree and from the movement of her bosom, she was still sleeping. He watched her breasts and glanced away, feeling the red crawling up his neck. Looking around for something to do, he saw his rifle on the ground. As he leaned over to pick up the weapon, he heard Redmond griping to Venner and Wells about their boss, Star McCallister. Bannon wiped the morning dew from the gun with his shirtsleeve. He was miffed at himself for letting it lie on the ground.

"Star knew these bastards were ri't behind us. He knew Checker was comin'," Redmond growled. He shook his head and wished he hadn't as the throbbing increased. "Can you believe that sumbitch? He done rode off and left us. Left us. What a bunch of crap." He spat a thin stream of saliva. "If I ever see him again, I'm gonna—"

" 'Bout the onliest place you're gonna see him is in hell," Wells interrupted, trying to relieve the catch in his right shoulder. His entire body ached from the beating Checker had given him.

"Oh, he'll be coming," Venner muttered. "Been lookin' for him since we headed out. Where do ya think he is?"

"Shut up, Venner. The devil hisself be hearin' you," Redmond snapped.

Venner chuckled. "You talkin' about Star—or Checker?" Then he looked at Bannon and said, "Hey, kid, when we gonna eat? I gotta pee somethin' fierce too."

The black outlaw was unnerved by the intensity in the farm boy's eyes and the lack of response. Bannon's gaze took in the unmoving shape of Wes Morton and he wiped his nose with his left hand.

Redmond whispered something to Wells that Bannon didn't hear.

Shrugging his shoulders to rid them of stiffness and the sight of the dead young outlaw, Bannon started down the hill toward the campfire. His Winchester was cradled in his arms. Smells of frying salt pork and boiling coffee were inviting. Checker was returning with Rebecca at his side. She wasn't happy with the way he had tied on her new blue ribbon in her hair, because her bonnet covered most of it, and she immediately asked Jackson if he could retie it. She also wanted a mirror.

Jackson looked up from adding chunks of cut-up potatoes to the frying pan. Johnny was at his side. "Sure, Miss Rebecca. Sure. Let me get this cookin' done first."

Leaving Checker's hand, she waddled over next to the black cowboy. "Are we having jam? Mommy gives us jam sometimes. When it's a special day. Is it a special day?"

Johnny frowned at her as he wiped his knife on his pants He had finished cutting up the potatoes, proud to be asked to help. "Becky, we don't have no jam."

Her face became a pout and Checker quickly assured her that they would get some when they got home. Satisfied, her pout vanishing, she asked if Jackson would be able to fix her ribbon now. Jackson chuckled, wiped his hands on his long coat, and retied the hair decoration to her satisfaction. This time he managed to keep the bow in front of her bonnet by pushing it back far enough to let the front curls be presented.

Shaking his head, Checker asked Bannon to help him water the horses and they left for the corral.

"Did the Injuns come back—fer their dead?" Bannon asked as they headed toward the milling herd. He shifted his rifle to his right and held it at his side.

"Yeah, it took them a while to carry them away. Just four braves were left." Checker rolled a cigarette and lit it as they walked.

"Will they try again?"

"That's a good question." Checker inhaled the fresh

smoke and let the white stream find the pale sky. "One of them might feel he's got to do something to gain face. But I figure they can tell a good story—with the four horses that got out. Got a feeling they don't come together much with other Comanches, like the old days. Just renegades left. No big gatherings to tell stories and count coup."

"You sound like you feel sorry for them."

"Guess I do, sorta. Their way of life is gone. Forever. Makes me think of an old friend." Checker held out his hand for the lead mare to smell his familiarity before stepping through the ropes.

"Do ya think McCallister will swing around an' . . ."

Without turning around, Checker said, "He might. I think he's long gone, though. Plenty of other desperadoes along this stretch. You remember the Kiowas that hit us this summer. Some of them around, too. Could run into another bunch of Comanches, for that matter. It's not my favorite place to ride, that's for sure. Not with all we're bringing with us."

Bannon walked a few feet along the taut rope. A big-chested gray pawed and whinnied.

"That big gray lay down in the pond yesterday. Had us a bad time gittin' him up," Bannon observed.

Checker nodded. "Like your sorrel? Some horses aren't real smart. An' some are just plain ornery. Kinda like people."

Fibbing that he liked his red horse, Bannon watched the tall man ease inside the rope corral, talking gently to the swirling horses. He felt safe with this strange man. Home seemed like a whole other world. Would he ever see his mother and sister again? The thought hit him like a blow to his stomach. He looked around at the trees, the hillside, the pond; suddenly everything seemed wicked. He squinted. Was that an Indian hiding behind that huge rock? He swung his rifle into his hands.

Behind him, Checker spun around, a cocked Colt in his left fist. His cigarette went flying. "What is it, Tyrel?"

"Not sure. Thought I saw somethin'."

"Where?" Checker ducked under the rope.

Bannon felt foolish. He hadn't really seen anything. Should he tell Checker what had happened? That he had a sudden thought about not seeing his family again. What would this great gunfighter say? Would he laugh?

"I—I didn't see anything. Not really," Bannon stuttered. "My imagination, I reckon." He lowered his gun and lowered his eyes. "I—I had a worry. Kinda hit me outta nowhere."

"I know how that can be." Checker's voice was low, almost gentle.

Bannon stared at him. Did this legendary Ranger actually get afraid? Did killing another man ever bother him? He wanted to ask, but couldn't.

"Only a fool never gets scared, Tyrel." Checker uncocked his Colt and returned it to his waistband. "We've got a ways to go before any of us can rest easy. A man who rides without fear will likely ride into trouble."

"Yeah, I guess so."

Checker guessed something else was bothering the young man. "You know, I'd hate to be around a man who didn't feel something bad about killing. No matter how bad the other fella needed it—or how close you were to being killed yourself." He pushed up the brim of his hat with his left hand, and his voice carried an ache. "How could a man want to kill one of his own . . . a sister . . . his own brother? That's way beyond me, Tyrel. I just don't understand."

For the first time, Bannon realized Checker had been hurt. "Y-you've been hurt. Your shirt. You used your left hand, did—"

"Yeah. Should've been more careful." Checker raised

his right hand to show the angry cut and the ugly purple welt dominating the back of his hand. "Hit it against a tree last night. During the fight. It'll be fine. Just bruised some."

"Looks mighty nasty to me."

"Yeah, guess it does." Checker glanced toward the farthest cottonwood and saw a jay light on a low branch. Was it the same one? He decided it might be and muttered thanks for its help. Far away, a wolf declared its loneliness and he thanked it too. He would be sure to leave some scraps for both to eat when they left. Maybe he should leave some tobacco, too, as a tribute to the spirits. Stands-in-Thunder would have.

Watching him, Bannon said, "I'm sorry. Didn't hear you."

Checker patted him on the back. "Oh, I said, I can't think of any men I'd rather have riding with me than you, Jackson, and Sonny. I owe you men a lot for helping my family like this. It isn't your fight."

Bannon's widening smile was cut short by the last statement and he managed to stutter, "I—I think it is."

CHAPTER ELEVEN

Star McCallister stared into the mirror. He leaned to the right to let his face clear the crack that ran all the way down the reflection. His eyelids fluttered for a long breath, an uncontrollable impulse triggered by his brain.

He smiled, liking what he saw. A bath, fresh shave, and new clothes did wonders to a man. His dark blue pin-striped suit set off his light blue eyes and blond hair. It was new, bought just yesterday in town. The tailoring fit well on his short, frail frame. He readjusted his suit coat to help hide the shoulder-holstered pistol. He took another sip of the whiskey in his glass; the bottle had come from his saddlebags. Tahlequah didn't allow whiskey to be sold in town. His admiring field of vision took in his saddlebags resting on the floor. They contained the money he always kept hidden in his Indian Nations hideout and the proceeds from his gang's robbery of a general store when they left Dodge. This ill-gotten gain came after his younger brother freed them with the help of the town marshal. That money would come in handy today.

It had always bothered him that he looked younger than he was. Unlike his half brother, John Checker, he didn't present a powerful physical appearance. Although both McCallister brothers were blond-haired, he wasn't as striking as the younger Blue, either. And unlike Checker, neither of them looked much like their father.

"But I got all the brains, John Checker." He laughed into the mirror. "I got all the brains." His voice was thin, yet velvety.

He was staying in Tahlequah's best hotel, a sturdily built brick structure. Tahlequah served as the capital of the Cherokee Nation, the most civilized of the Five Civilized Tribes legally occupying Indian Territory. The town was nestled within hills eight miles south of the Kansas border and truly the heart of Indian progress.

It wasn't McCallister's first time to stay in Tahlequah. He had discovered it to be a good jumping-off point, if needed, usually when his rustling operation had required his personal attendance along the cattle trails. The Cherokees didn't like white men, but they didn't ask many questions either—as long as the white men weren't federal marshals or cavalry. They had long ago lost trust in any representative of the federal government or white man's law, for good reason.

As far as the tribe was concerned, the Cherokee Nation was an independent republic. Their treaty with the United States agreed. Their governing structure was built along the lines of the United States federal body with two houses of legislature and a principal chief who was the acting head of state. However, wealthy Indians among the Cherokees, as well as all five of the so-called Civilized Tribes, had owned many black slaves and had sided with the Confederacy. That allegiance had already cost them a large chunk of their western lands—supposedly theirs forever—taken by an angered Congress.

After one last look, he placed the short-brimmed Stetson on his head, grinned, and started to walk out of his hotel room. He shoved his hand into his coat pocket and felt the small sack of gold coins there, then remembered the brown-paper-wrapped book on the bed stand and went back to get it.

"The only thing bad about this town is no whiskey." He laughed as he strolled along the gas-lighted hallway with the package at his side.

Then his mind brought up John Checker. After the rigged jail break, he knew his half brother would be coming after him and his gang, and coming with all the vengeance of an archangel. Shaking his head in amusement, McCallister wondered how the battle with his gang came out. It wasn't a thought of concern about his men, only the curiosity of a strategist determining his next move.

He was certain, though, Checker would prevail. After all, that was why the outlaw leader left when he did, through a hidden passageway to where a fast horse waited. A smart man always left himself an option. He could still see the questioning eyes of his younger brother, Blue.

"Why couldn't that fool stay in Texas—and leave me alone? I never bothered him any." McCallister felt his cravat to make certain it was straightened. "It was bad enough having his sister around—without that fool." He paused in midstride, remembering an earlier exchange. "Why in hell does he have to look like my father?" He shook his head and his eye twitched again. "I should've listened to Seals and not tried to take the Triple C herd." A snarl reached his thin lips. "Then that bastard had the nerve to testify against me. Someday, I'll find that son of a bitch. . . ."

If his men were successful, Checker and anybody with him would be dead by now. The hot-headed Blue had dramatically claimed the right to kill Checker. McCallister hadn't tried to warn him about how good the former Ranger was with a gun, but it wouldn't have made any difference. The fake medicine show doctor needed the victory for his ego. McCallister told himself that he wouldn't want to live on the difference between the skills of the two. But Checker might hesitate; the Ranger had a funny sense of obligation to his half brothers. Blue wouldn't; he was a pure killer. Even so, McCallister just knew Checker was alive. And Blue was dead. He could feel it in his gut.

Checker was like his late father, gifted with the instinct of survival. McCallister's eye twitched a third time, but he didn't notice. He rarely did. "I got the same gift, Checker . . . dear brother."

McCallister paused at the top of the stairway and looked down. The lobby was nearly empty, except for two top-hatted Cherokees wearing black swallow-tailed coats and starched white shirts at the main desk. With them were two Cherokee women in white women's dresses. He assumed they were checking in.

He shook his head. Seeing Indians dressed as white gentlemen and ladies was a sight he always found hard to get used to. But the Cherokees were unlike any other Indian tribe. They even had their own alphabet, and their language had been transformed into books and newspapers. An effective school system had been in place for more than two decades. There were two seminaries, separating boys and girls; McCallister had passed them a few miles south of the town itself.

The children were taught, among other subjects,

Latin and algebra, grammar and science. He heard that some of the best students were sent to eastern universities for completion of their training. He grinned to himself; *the foolish Cherokees think they will be accepted by the white man with all their hard work and planning. Just wait. Just wait.* He had heard the stories about Washington trying to find ways to wrest the Cherokee Outlet away from the tribe. The westward finger of land was originally supposed to give them access to the buffalo lands. But they couldn't settle on it and now the Texas cattle drives had used it to fatten their herds before the final push into Kansas. He shook his head. It wouldn't be long before the homesteaders made the decision for everyone.

McCallister knew that many Dodge businessmen didn't believe he was guilty of the rustling and murder convictions and thought it was simply a way for Texas cattlemen to shove their weight around. Burning the homestead and kidnapping the children could be explained away by letting the word get around that he, Star McCallister, had been forced to ride with the gang after they broke out. That he wasn't a part of them and had managed to escape finally. The matter could be handled in court as well—at the right time. With the right town temperament. That was easily created with a little time and the proper placement of the idea. Bribing the mayor wouldn't hurt either; he had found the man could be swayed in this way before. Several councilmen could also be similarly influenced.

As he walked down the winding staircase, he tried to remember "good morning" in Cherokee. *Tibo* was the only word he could recall and that was the name for a white man.

Osiyo gradually came to his mind as some kind of greeting, and he touched the brim of his hat to the group, muttered the phrase, and headed outside. Both

Cherokee men responded with "Good morning" greetings in perfect English.

His pale eyes squinted against the sudden sunlight. They had always been sensitive. He tugged on his hat brim and headed for the restaurant. His right eye twitched again. A planned meeting with the two mysterious Cherokee killers-for-hire, Do'tsi and Kana'ti, would be significant. If the brothers agreed, they would ride together back to Dodge. He had already wired Alfred Diverrouve, the Frenchman who had managed his saloon and was purchasing it. His message advised him to hold the next payment and not send it to the Kansas City post office box as planned. Someone would pick it up instead. The message was signed "M." Diverrouve would understand the intent of the message, as well as the name; the telegrapher wouldn't.

If things went as he planned, he would be positioned to regain his rightful place in Dodge before Checker and his bunch showed up. And he was certain they would. Do'tsi and Kana'ti would make the situation easier. Much easier. If he could convince the two that it would be good for them—and their reputation. Ah, that would be the key for Do'tsi; more important than the money involved. For the other brother, Kana'ti, it would only be about the money—and the money would be very good.

Their names were all about reputation. Although to most Cherokees, a name was something to keep secret. Both brothers had chosen to let their names become known. An old Cherokee had told McCallister about the two brothers—and the meaning of their names— several years ago

*Do'ts*i, the snake, was a name the younger—and more cunning—brother had chosen for himself. For a snake strikes from anywhere. Deadly. Unpredictable. Coiled energy. A snake was an unexplainable ancient force that knew more than it gave away, or so the Cherokees thought. In ancient Cherokee legend, the serpent family had been Sky Beings who came to earth to give knowledge to the People. The serpent was an ancient spirit of resurrection because the snake often sheds its skin and is reborn over and over again. It fit the killing brother well, for he believed in reincarnation, born of his grandmother's influence.

It fascinated McCallister that Do'tsi was inclined toward various religions and their varying treatments of death and the afterlife. He should have been a preacher or an undertaker or a sociology professor, the outlaw leader chuckled to himself. A foolish waste of time for an otherwise efficient killer.

Kana'ti was the older and far stronger brother's chosen name. Wolf. A wolf was thought to be the "true brother," an ancient force, going back in time before all memory. Emotionally connected to the moon, he loves freedom and struggles against rules. Kana'ti was a dual personality in Cherokee legend; warm to his kind, vicious to any outsiders. The wolf is a totally wild creature living within the mystical line between all darkness and dawn, the rebirth of light, between symbolic birth and death. To the ancient Cherokees, Kana'ti provided the connection between the netherworld and Mother Earth.

The older brother had considered naming himself Bear, but his younger brother had convinced him of the mystical power of the wolf. Kana'ti consented, even though most observers would agree with the older brother that his strength was more like that of a bear. Stories of his brutally beating victims were repeated in hushed voices throughout the region.

A bright autumn day greeted McCallister as he reached the boardwalk. Across the street was a stately, two-story brick building with a large, majestic portico, serving as the capitol of the Cherokee Nation. McCallister had seen the Texas capitol building in Austin, and it wasn't much more impressive. At least not to his eyes. Although activity was heavy around the building, he wasn't interested; other than the mild curiosity that came from seeing Indians dressed in formal white man's attire.

He walked along the boardwalk, greeting Cherokee men and women with a fiendly nod of his head. As expected, a white man was noted with a suspicious graciousness. He passed the clanging music of a busy blacksmith, several merchants, and the *Cherokee Advocate* newspaper office. Behind the commercial buildings, he glimpsed several huge estates highlighted with antebellum porches and massive columns reminiscent of fine Greek architecture.

It was a glimpse of the old South, before the War. Like a transplanted picture of yesterday. That made sense, he thought, since the Cherokees had come from there, before they were forced to move to this Territory. Of course, most of the homes were small framed structures; however, the wealthy Cherokees lived well.

As he approached the restaurant, he eyed a large black dog sprawled out across the planked sideway, forcing passersby to walk around it. The animal belonged to the brothers, or McCallister thought it did. The last time he had been with the Cherokee killers, they had showed off the savage animal, telling him that it would attack at either twin's command. He couldn't remember the dog's name at first, then recalled it was related to some religion. Zoroastrianism? That was it. Zoro? Yes, that was the dog's silly name, he muttered. He glanced at the beast to assure himself it hadn't heard.

He recalled Do'tsi telling him that ancient Zoroastrian priests brought a dog to a person's deathbed to guard the "Bridge of Judgment" from demons as the soul departs. According to Do'tsi, the dog's stare drives them away. McCallister thought the Cherokee brothers' dog could do that easily. With his hand resting against his hidden pistol, he tiptoed around the dog, watching it carefully. The beast was apparently sleeping; at least it hadn't moved.

McCallister let out a breath of relief, dropped his hand to his side, and hurried on. Aware that suspicious eyes followed him—as they followed any white man in town—he entered the restaurant, paused, and let his squinting eyes adjust to the gray interior. The small, tidy establishment was filled with mostly Cherokee men, but here and there were couples dining.

He knew the two killers from a previous engagement; they had proved to be an effective force, even though an expensive one—and, sometimes, most difficult men to locate. Luckily, they were in Tahlequah, instead of away on an assignment. It was about time his luck changed, McCallister thought, smiling to himself. The two brothers had nothing to do with the Cherokee tribe, and they had nothing to do with them. Even the tribal Light Horse Police avoided them. But they never caused any problems in Tahlequah, and the city's authorities never paid any attention to the fact that federal marshals wanted them for murder. Why should they?

And everyone knew they always worked together. Always. Usually with one in the front and one somewhere behind. They were careful, though; few had ever actually seen them kill a man—or, at least, any willing to testify to that fact, or alive to do so. In the case of Kana'ti's beatings, witnesses would be quick to support his claim of self-defense. Or actually, his brother's claim. Kana'ti never spoke to anyone except Do'tsi—and then only in Cherokee.

McCallister shivered in spite of himself as the details

of the two brothers swept through his mind. He stood in the doorway, pretending to look for them as he gave himself time to resettle his composure.

The professional killers would be dressed as they always were. Totally different from each other. Do'tsi would be wearing a black, gabardine frock coat with a velvet collar. High boots, whose curving tops covered the knees, were encircled at the upper edge by a small decorative band of inlaid red serpents. His hat was flat in brim and its crown was banded by inch-wide, flame-red silk. In his lapel was a red flower. It was a certain kind; McCallister couldn't recall what it was. Part of the Cherokee serpent mystique, he thought.

As usual, the bigger brother would be wearing a dark gray business suit coat, a starched white shirt with a paper collar, and a brown silk cravat. But no pants. Only a long, plain breechcloth and knee-high Apache boots. A trail-beaten top hat with an eagle feather dangling from it made him look even taller. The white man's clothing—and the boots—were supposedly taken from victims. A funny-looking sight, for certain, McCallister thought, but no one ever said so. At least, no one who was around.

No matter how well he prepared himself, meeting with this pair of intimidating, self-possessed men made him ill at ease. He got the same sensation when he was around John Checker. A queasiness born of a lack of confidence. He hated the emotional response—and the reason for it. Neither Checker nor Do'tsi—and certainly not Kana'ti—could match his mind. Or his leadership skills. None of them. It annoyed him greatly that they had not recognized this innate superiority as so many others did. All three would come to realize it soon enough, he reminded himself.

The two Indians were somewhat alike in facial appearance with triangular heads, anchored by long pointed chins that balanced widely set, dark eyes, pencil noses, and massive ears. Overall, though, they were quite different. Their physical being was as completely different as their manner of dress. Do'tsi was thin, almost emaciated; Kana'ti was huge, powerfully built in his arms and chest, and outweighing his younger brother by fifty pounds. Their thinking was similarly different. Do'tsi was deep into religions, death, and immortality. As far as anyone knew, Kana'ti had no deep thoughts at all; his only known interests were money and women. They had one thing in common, though: Both were cruel, enjoyed killing, and were good at it.

Do'tsi and Kana'ti would be sitting at the seventh table as usual. Do'tsi's decision as always. In the back of the room, a pair of narrow, dark eyes caught his attention first. Then a second pair. They seemed to be illuminated by some strange light and were fixed on him from under black hats.

McCallister shivered again at the sight of the men in spite of himself. Truly sinister, he thought to himself. Immediately he stopped the thought, hoping neither could somehow read his mind. He straightened his vest, trying to get mentally comfortable, and walked casually toward them.

McCallister nodded as he approached, catching only Do'tsi's attention. He chose not to repeat his earlier Cherokee greeting, in case it wasn't correct. Across Do'tsi's vest hung a gold chain attached to his pocket watch; dangling from its middle was a gold-encased fire opal, a sign of the snake. A gold ring on his right pinky finger contained a similar stone. A gunbelt carrying a long-barreled, open-top Merwin & Hulbert revolver was strapped outside his coat. The holster rested on his front left hip for easy right-hand use. Black handles were inlaid with a fire opal on each side. McCallister knew the thin brother also carried a derringer strapped to his left wrist, beneath his shirt cuff.

"You're late," Do'tsi said without standing. "We were about to leave."

Kana'ti grunted something in Cherokee and his brother chuckled.

Paying no attention to his brother's comments, Do'tsi continued, "We have another place to be. By tomorrow night."

CHAPTER TWELVE

Dot'si's words were measured, ominous in what they didn't say, as if counting them to make sure they added up to a desired number.

"My instructions—from your associate—were to meet at twelve thirty." McCallister met their cold gaze. His eye twitched, but it was unrelated to the encounter.

What passed for a smile slid along Do'tsi's slit of a mouth. "Hmm, that is so, come to think of it. Sit down. The beef stew is rumored to be quite good today." He waved his hand in dismissal and continued the motion to indicate McCallister should sit.

McCallister knew this was the younger brother's form of a game, trying to get the person he was talking to off-balance, or better yet, intimidated.

Do'tsi's thin smile became a condescending leer. "You know what the great challenge is for all religions?"

"Getting the collection plated filled."

Do'tsi chuckled. "Ah, I should have expected that from you—or my brother." With his chin raised, he declared, "It is the problem of deciding that if their main God is all-powerful, why does He allow all the evil and nastiness in the world? Or if he's weak or uncaring, why should He be worshipped?"

"Never thought of it that way before." McCallister removed his hat and placed it on a nearby hat rack and pulled on the offered chair. He nodded a greeting at Kana'ti, who only stared at him.

"Of course not. Take Zoroastrianism. They decided God—they call Him *Ohrmazd*—was all good—and that all the bad came from the devil." Do'tsi licked his lower lip as he continued.

"Sounds familiar." McCallister scooted into the chair across from Do'tsi, feigning interest in the subject while he carefully cleared his suit coat of any wrinkles.

He glanced over at the other brother and was surprised to see Kana'ti seemed to be listening and understanding. The big man's machete, carried in a quiver on his back, clanged against the chair as he shifted his weight to lean his elbows on the table. McCallister couldn't see it, but knew Kana'ti also kept a scalping knife hidden in his right boot.

Turning toward Do'tsi, the powerfully built brother asked a question in Cherokee; a glare took in McCallister, before his gaze returned to his brother.

Do'tsi repeated his brother's concern. "Was Zoro outside?"

"Yes. Asleep."

"Good. She obeys me well. Remind me to order her a steak before I leave."

"Of course."

Do'tsi spoke in Cherokee to his brother, who responded in a single short sentence, ending it with a glimpse of broken yellowed teeth.

A long-stemmed pipe lay on the table beside Do'tsi's plate, next to a leather-bound book about Eastern religions. McCallister smiled. His own gift for this brother was a good choice. Something for Kana'ti had been easy to decide: gold.

"You know, McCallister, I've been restudying Hinduism. Interesting." Do'tsi stared unblinking at the blond outlaw leader. "Lots of gods. Lots of demons, too." His eyes sparkled and the crow's-feet at their corners danced. "Looks to me like the only difference between their gods and plain folks is they don't sweat or blink or get dirty—and their feet don't touch the ground." He snickered at his observations. "Of course, it looks like all these Hindu gods are usually thought of as part of a single, all-great one. Like a lot of Indian religions."

"Sounds fascinating. I guess I don't qualify as a god, then. My eye twitches every now and then." McCallister chuckled at his self-analysis.

For an instant, he had the foolish, unrelated fear the gift book he carried for Do'tsi was just a schoolbook for children. His mind quietly assured him it was a learned edition about Japan. A bead of nervous sweat toyed with his forehead. He wiped it off, making the motion appear as if he were scratching his forehead with his fingers.

"Here. I thought you might find this interesting to read." McCallister laid the brown paper package on the table. "I brought a gift for your brother too. Something I thought he would favor." He withdrew the small sack of gold coins from his coat pocket and laid it on the table in front of the other brother.

Do'tsi stared at the wrapped book and the sack, told his brother in Cherokee that they were gifts, then slowly retook McCallister's face. "How very thoughtful. I would not have imagined you would have had time for such things, running as you did. From Captain John Checker."

McCallister's face couldn't hold back the surprise.

How did this man know of his situation? He had told no one. He tried to keep from watching Kana'ti slowly take out each coin, study it, and return it to the sack.

"Don't be surprised, McCallister. I know many things—about you," Do'tsi said methodically, "and your little brother. Blue, isn't he called? It's my business to know things. You definitely feel much insecurity around this Captain John Checker, don't you? Yet you are drawn to him. Why is that? Is your eye twitching like that a habit or a weakness you can't control?" He unwrapped the paper and examined the book, holding it in his left hand.

McCallister noticed Do'tsi's right hand wasn't visible. He assumed it was near his gun. Kana'ti was stacking the coins, knocking them down, and restacking them.

"You believe I have an interest in the ways of the Japanese, I see."

"You said so yourself—at our last meeting." McCallister motioned toward the book. "I found this in Dodge some time ago. This summer, I think it was. Came into Bob Wright's place with a shipment of other books. Mostly Bibles. I bought it for . . . you."

It was a lie. Actually, the book was one of several Iron-Head Ed Wells had taken from their general store break-in, along with a coffeepot and a set of false teeth. Other than the coffeepot, none of the gang understood why he took the things; Wells couldn't read and had reasonably good teeth. McCallister had taken the book with him when he decided to ride for Tahlequah and the Cherokee killers. No one in his band would ever read it, that's for certain. Especially Wells. A faint smile was allowed as he took satisfaction in his ability to think and plan, even when the worst was happening around him. Like taking the time to read enough of this book to impress Do'tsi, or so he hoped.

McCallister declared, "I never realized how complex

the funerals are for the Japanese. Sikh is their religion—
or Buddhism."

Do'tsi's eyes widened in surprise as McCallister's
words tumbled from his mouth as if they couldn't get
out fast enough. "They believe a dead man loses his
own identity and becomes a part of a grand ancestral
spirit, made up of all his dead relatives. This big family
spirit, it's responsible for the birth of new children.
Sometimes the dead one is reborn—in another body.
Reincarnation shows up everywhere, doesn't it?" His
eyes sought the Cherokee killer's face with renewed
confidence.

"Of course." Do'tsi nodded. "I shall enjoy this." He
glanced at his brother, returning the coins to the sack.
"My brother is equally pleased." He laid the book back
within its opened shell of paper. "I assume our meeting
was more than about gifts—or a discussion of the ways
of gods."

Tucking the coin sack into his coat pocket, Kana'ti
said something to his brother in Cherokee.

Do'tsi acknowledged it in their language.

Confidently, McCallister proclaimed, "Yes, I have a
proposition for you, one that will make you known—
and feared—by all the Texas cattlemen and Kansas
merchants. One that will make you known for all time."

"That will be for me to decide."

"Of course it will."

"Is Captain John Checker I have heard so much
about . . . dead?"

McCallister's eyes twitched. "I don't know for certain,
of course—but I believe he is alive. That is what my
meeting is about. Killing him will make your name live
forever."

There was no advantage in stressing a possible victory by Blue, he told himself. He didn't want to give
away the fact that his brother intended to kill Checker

after McCallister left their hideout. He figured one of them was now dead. Maybe both.

"Hmmm. Let's hope for my sake—and yours—that he is alive."

Smiling, McCallister summoned the waiter with a casually raised toss of his hand. "Of course."

Quietly, the outlaw leader told Do'tsi that they would return to Dodge, that the Cherokee killers would become deputies of the city marshal there—Marshal Jubal Rand—and that McCallister himself would remain in hiding near Dodge until certain things occurred.

Do'tsi couldn't hide his surprise. "Assistants? Should the great Do'tsi be someone's assistant? How does that make me important?"

McCallister had prepared for that response. "It is the perfect situation—for you, and for me. Rand can appoint his own deputies. That avoids a confrontation with the city council. Faster, too. His other deputies were . . . ah, killed in a jail break, so there is an opening."

"Your jail break."

"Yes. Checker knows Rand was involved in the escape and will come after him. Rand will be quite happy to have you two at his side—and leave Checker to you."

Do'tsi smiled. "A lawman going after another lawman. How nice."

"Checker isn't a lawman . . . anymore." The envious statement came out of McCallister's mouth before he realized its possible implications.

"Ah, so, but he is one of Texas's great ones," Do'tsi purred.

McCallister wasn't about to make another mistake. "Yes, one of the great ones."

Turning to his bigger brother, Do'tsi repeated the situation in Cherokee. Kana'ti listened intently, asked one question, and his brother nodded agreement. McCallister guessed Do'tsi's words in Cherokee to his brother were along the same line. However, the lack of reaction by Kana'ti made it impossible to tell.

McCallister couldn't help remembering stories told of Kana'ti killing eight men by breaking their backs or necks. Depending on the teller, four or five more were cut down by knife. One bloody tale told of his sticking a man's cut-off head on the tip of his machete and riding around some border town with it held high. To remove the terrible thoughts, he waved again, more aggressively this time, and, across the room, the bald-headed waiter grumpily acknowledged his presence.

The thinner brother ran his fingers along his book. "How will the good citizens take having two . . . Indians as deputies? Won't there be an outcry?"

"Who are they going to complain to?" McCallister grinned. "Rand? I already own the mayor—and several councilmen. And, besides, the mayor will be given a nice gift to look the other way." He inhaled his confidence. "A few townsmen may grumble, but they won't have the guts to challenge you, will they?" He looked down at the table and straightened a spoon. "Soon they will be stirred up about something else. The arrest of John Checker for the murder . . . of Dr. Gambree." He shook his head at the brilliance of his idea. "We will take over Dodge before anyone realizes it." To himself, he acknowledged that if Checker was already dead when they reached Dodge, he would proceed immediately to the second part of his strategy, reestablishing his innocence.

Kana'ti's eyes flickered and he asked his brother a question that drew a chuckle. This time, Do'tsi made no attempt to explain.

Instead, he said, "McCallister, how can you do all this? Have not you been convicted of rustling and murder? Are you not scheduled to hang? A wretched demise, I must say. The Comanches believe strangling to death keeps the soul from leaving."

"Don't worry about it," McCallister said. "I plan to have that conviction set aside. At the right time, of course."

"You are a chess player, aren't you, Star?" Do'tsi looked up and was pleased to see the waiter headed their way. "Wouldn't it be easier just to set up in another town? What's so special about Dodge? I hear it's nothing more than dust and wind—and, sometimes, Texas cows."

McCallister smirked. "Thought about that. On my ride here. I know the way it works and thinks. I've got investments there. And people waiting to help. You'll see. It will be easy—for you and me." His smile turned richly confident. "Besides, no one will be expecting my return—especially John Checker."

"My brother wants to know what the money is," Do'tsi said.

"Five hundred dollars now. Another five hundred when the job is finished."

A wicked smile popped onto the bigger brother's face as Do'tsi related the offer.

Mirroring the smile, Do'tsi responded, "All right. I've never been a lawman before. Neither has my brother. I look forward to it. He looks forward to the money."

McCallister returned the grin. "Dodge will be mine again. I deserve it."

"And Captain John Checker will be mine. I deserve immortality." Do'tsi paused as Kana'ti said something more. "My brother wants to know *where* the money is."

"As soon as we finish eating, we'll go to my hotel room. It is there."

Do'tsi repeated the statement to Kana'ti, who reached over and patted McCallister's arm. The same yellowed, broken teeth appeared again.

They stopped talking as the waiter came to take their order. Do'tsi ordered the beef stew for the three of them, without asking McCallister for his opinion. McCallister added that he would like a loaf of bread as well. The bored waiter listened to their requests without comment and left.

"Tell me about your men, McCallister. Where are they?" Do'tsi's question came like the strike of a snake. Swift and unexpected. "Are they now dead? Arrested?"

McCallister knew he must answer carefully and accurately. "I don't know. They could all be dead—or arrested, I suppose. Or Checker and his friends left lying in the dirt." He inhaled to gain control of his emotions. "I left before the encounter. There was nothing left for me to gain."

"You ran out on your men."

"There is a time to fight and a time to get away so one can fight more effectively another day."

Do'tsi rubbed his narrow chin. "Seems to me, that's always said by generals, not their troops."

"Perhaps." McCallister liked the reference to "generals."

"How much do you know about the Cherokee religion?" Do'tsi changed the subject as abruptly as he had started the previous one.

"Not much, I suppose. I would like to, though." McCallister wasn't interested in the subject but knew it was best to act interested. He was relieved to get past his escape from Checker and the leaving of his men. Out of the corner of his eye, he could see Kana'ti studying the salt and pepper shakers, as if he had never encountered the like before.

Unaware of his brother's curiosity or the reason for it, Do'tsi explained that the Cherokees believed that every single thing in the world was an earth reflection of a star. "People, animals, rivers, stones, trees, flowers. Everything. We're just shadows of the real thing."

"Interesting. What's that got to do with me?"

"You use that word, interesting, often. I think it's a polite way of saying you're *not* interested," Do'tsi said.

"Oh, I'm sorry I gave that impression. I am very interested," McCallister said hurriedly. "Please go on."

Twisting his head to the side, Do'tsi continued, "Your name. Star. I have wondered if there was any Cherokee blood in your background."

McCallister smiled, in spite of his concern about offending the gunmen. "Well, my pappy was pretty loose with his seed—but no. My full name is Starrett. My mother's maiden name."

Do'tsi pursed his lips. "Is Blue your brother's real name?"

"Yeah. My mother was a real romantic."

The killer chuckled. "You know, we met him once in Santa Fe. We were . . . on assignment. So was he. Where is he now? Out with his medicine wagon, selling salvation in a bottle?"

McCallister crossed his arms. Trying not to show, it, he didn't like the direction of the coversation. He forced a smile.

"He wasn't at your hideout with the gang? I thought he was the key to your jail break."

The waiter returned with three steaming bowls of stew and slid away to get the bread and a small bowl of butter.

"We're going to need coffee." McCallister's order stopped the man in midstride. The sharpness of the command was due to Do'tsi's concentration on his own brother.

The waiter nodded and continued his mission.

Eyeing the man's retreat, Do'tsi said, "I have the feeling you're not telling me the truth about Blue. Did he stay to kill John Checker?"

"That's what he said he was going to do."

"Why didn't you tell me this before?" A certain madness dawned in Do'tsi's eyes.

As if connected, the same expression appeared in Kana'ti's face.

"I did. Remember? I told you I didn't know for certain if Checker was alive or not." McCallister picked up a spoon and withdrew some of his stew, acting as nonchalantly as he could manage. "However, I strongly believe he is. That's why I've come to you. That's why I'm willing to pay so much."

Saying nothing, Do'tsi reached for his spoon as well. After swallowing the hot broth, he said, "I won't charge you for killing Captain John Checker. That's like getting paid twice. You will pay us the five hundred for two others that you choose." He sneered. "Plus the five hundred in advance."

"I agree. As I said, the money is in my hotel room. We can go there from here."

"Trusting sort."

McCallister laughed and both brothers joined him and he wondered if Kana'ti could actually understand English. The waiter returned with a loaf of bread and a plate of butter and hurried away to get the forgotten coffee.

"If Blue did kill him, our cost doubles," Do'tsi added as he brought another spoonful to his mouth.

"Fair enough." McCallister smiled. "How soon can you leave? You mentioned another commitment."

Do'tsi mirrored the outlaw leader's grin. "To kill Captain John Checker, we can leave anytime."

"Don't forget the steak for your dog." McCallister smiled again.

"I never forget anything." Do'tsi waved at the waiter.

CHAPTER THIRTEEN

A long day later, Checker led the weary group northward through a maze of interlocking creeks and lush bottomland. Everything once green now wore a coat of autumn-brown. Wildlife was abundant. Everywhere they looked were turkey, grouse, plover, and an occasional deer.

Excited, Bannon recalled passing through the area when he and Sonny were in pursuit of the gang. The two riders had taken after the outlaws while Jackson and Checker took his sister back to town and the doctor, before following the trail.

"I 'member all them birds a-roostin' in them trees over yonder." Bannon pointed. His voice carried over the stillness from his usual position near the front of the herd.

Riding drag, young Johnny nodded, pulled on his cap brim, and excitedly pointed at a deer. "Look there! Ain't he a pretty one?"

"Hey, some deer meat sounds mighty tasty. Maybe John'll let us do some huntin'." Bannon made a make-believe gun with his fingers and tracked the antlered animal as it darted into the trees. He saw a stack of three rocks that Sonny had left for Checker and Jackson to follow when they were trailing the gang. Quietly, he told Johnny what it meant and the boy bit his lower lip.

At the wagon, Checker rode up next to the front wheel. "Where's Rebecca?"

Jackson shook his head and grinned. "Oh, she's back there with Sonny. I can hear them. He's making up songs."

"Good—for both," Checker said. "Do I recollect an old trail camp on the other side of these creeks? What do you think about stopping there for the night?"

Jackson rubbed his chin and pulled on the reins to keep the team from trotting. They smelled water. "You're right. It's a good place to stop. No use pushing farther." Squinting toward a wide creek twenty yards ahead, he shifted the pipe in his mouth. "Can I take the wagon east of that fat creek? Looks like there's a shelf of higher ground across the two main ones. Should be able to snake through all that, don't you think?"

Standing in his stirrups, Checker studied the suggested route. "Why don't I just head that way? I'll give you a signal if it looks all right."

With an easy wave of his hand, Checker galloped away, pausing to say something to Johnny near the back of the herd and then again to Bannon at the front with the lead mare beside him. Checker stopped at the first stream to let his horse drink, then looped to his right and examined the soft ground between two creeks as they rode through. Ten yards from the tree line, he looked up, waved a "come ahead" to Jackson.

The black drover glanced to his left, reassuring himself that the four outlaws were where they were supposed to be. Venner looked his way and smiled sheepishly. Jackson frowned and eased his horses to the right. As he did, he shoved himself deeper into the seat until he was nearly unseen because of the wagon's wide decorative side panels. It had become a habit on this journey, making himself less of a target for anyone watching them. Neither he nor Checker spoke of it, but neither thought they were out of danger.

As he turned away, he saw Salome glance to their left, toward a parallel line of blackjack and brush. She was riding on the far side of the three men as usual. Had she seen something that shouldn't be there? Or just wildlife? His own sideways review of the heavy tree line told him nothing.

After a moment of contemplation, Jackson yelled toward the rear of the wagon. "Sonny? Can you hear me?"

Muffled singing continued for a phrase, then stopped.

"Sonny? Can you hear me?"

"Yeah, Becky an' me were playin' an' singin'. Everythin' all right?" Sonny's voice was thinner than usual. Jackson figured it was like the joyful cowboy to act better than he felt. He was definitely better, healing faster than Jackson expected—and he expected Sonny to heal fast. No matter what the easygoing cowboy said or how he acted, though, Sonny was a long way from feeling himself again.

Jackson spoke over his shoulder, cupping his hand to his mouth to help direct the words. "Gonna cross the creek up ahead. Could get bumpy for a piece."

"Just a minute, Becky. Where do you want me? I can walk."

"No, y'all stay put."

"Naah, I'll get out. With Becky. We need a little stroll. It'll be good for me," Sonny yelled. "Might be enough to keep you from gettin' stuck."

Jackson smiled and held the horses; there was no use arguing with Sonny. After seeing him skip away holding

Rebecca's little hand, Jackson let the two-horse team move ahead to the first creek and drink.

All four outlaws were astride their horses at the next creek over; the stretched-out rope connecting their saddle horns keeping them close together as usual. Checker was on the far side watching them.

Redmond turned to Bannon. "Come an' get me down, boy. I gotta pee."

"I'm busy. Do it in your pants." Bannon's eyes glinted with disgust as he repeated Checker's response from the day before.

The answer brought chuckles from the other outlaws.

"Oh, come on now. I ain't gonna try nothin'." Redmond's whine sounded sincere. "You got them hosses trained now. They ain't goin' nowhere."

Bannon's expression softened as his gaze strayed toward Salome, who was leaning over her horse's neck. Her bosom was nearly exposed by the position as her blouse fell away from her chest. Coyly, she looked up at Bannon to make certain he had noticed. Her smile was both victory and come-on.

The farm boy swallowed and knew his neck was shouting crimson embarrassment. He forced himself to look at the wagon as it skirted the edges of the first two streams and rolled toward the trees.

"Are we campin' soon, Jackson? I'm gittin' hungry," Bannon yelled.

"Soon enough," Jackson replied loudly. "I'll go across first and hold up when I get to hard land." His voice rattled through the late afternoon with little of its usual syrup.

"Sure."

"Make Redmond and the rest go next," Jackson directed. "Give the horses all the water they want. Water 'em for the night."

Bannon's mouth tilted to the right. "Of course." Didn't

Jackson think he had a brain? His attention, though, wandered back to Salome. She was talking to Redmond and didn't notice. A twinge of jealousy snapped through him at their exchange.

"Tyrel, y'all still have that pebble?" Jackson yelled again.

Bannon ran his right hand along the outside of his pants pocket, under his chaps, and indicated that he did. He wished Jackson hadn't asked in front of everyone. His mind assured him that no one knew what it meant.

"Good. Ya keep it handy—along with your rifle."

"I will." Bannon didn't see that it was a concern important enough to yell about, but Jackson had always guided him well during the trail drive and in Dodge itself.

"Hey, boy, still takin' orders from a nigra?" Redmond growled loudly at Bannon. He grinned at Salome and his hands strained at the rope burning into his wrists.

Bannon sat up straight in his saddle and turned back toward Redmond. "Wha'd you jes' say?" The farm boy's angry eyes were hidden by the shadow of his hat brim. He was a bit ashamed that most of his anger was the result of Redmond talking with Salome, not because of his reference to Jackson.

"Ye best be a-watchin' yourself, Tom," Wells whispered. "That boy's just likely to have at ya with that gun o' his. He rates that black fella high."

"Ah, oh, nothin'. Nothin' at all," Redmond responded and winked at Salome.

Her only response was to look straight ahead.

Bannon stared at him a moment longer, tugged hard on his already-bent hat brim, and returned his attention to the herd. He led the mare to the first creek and let out the rope so the horse could drink easily.

From behind, Johnny eased the herd forward; the boy was always pleased about being given this responsibility and eager to show his capability. He glanced often toward his uncle, hoping his efforts would be seen and appreciated. Smoothly, he moved his own horse into position alongside the slurping horses. He had grown up around horses and was very comfortable handling them—and aware of any changes in their actions.

Some of the mounts seemed nervous and on edge. That surprised him; they hadn't acted this way before, even when the Comanches were around. The two stallions were particularly agitated, pawing the water and snorting with their ears laid back. Neither had showed any bad disposition before. Quietly, he attributed that to his father's training. Maybe there was a wolf close by, he thought. Or, maybe, it was just seeing the streams. Who knew with horses?

Five horses to his right, a line-back dun began nipping the horses on either side of him, stirring them up even more. Johnny pulled up his horse's head and reined it toward the offending mount. A slap of his coiled lariat on its rump was enough to stop the play, but not the herd's overall nervousness. Youthful eyes journeyed across the brown and tan mass to the outlaws downstream, then again to the horses. His uncle had made it clear that part of his responsibility was keeping away from the bad men. A sadness sneaked into his mind and he tightened his mouth to keep the thought about his mother and father from taking over. He shivered even though his new coat was warm.

Watching both the outlaws and the wagon, Checker tried to ignore the throbbing in his right hand; waving it had triggered new pain. As bad as it felt, he had been lucky and touched the small pouch around his neck. It hadn't been the only gift from Stands-in-Thunder; the aging war leader had presented him with a war club and a white pebble that could sing.

Although the pebble and weapon had long been lost, he always wore the pouch in remembrance of their friendship. And, sometimes, he acknowledged to himself that it just might bring him luck. He had found a similar-looking pebble on their way to the outlaw camp and had given it to Jackson more out of sweet memory of his late Comanche friend than any belief in its power. Jackson had accepted it graciously.

To his left, the medicine wagon deftly maneuvered around the first creek, avoiding its soft bank and deceiving depth. One struggling cottonwood was coupled with this finger of the stream and its life-giving water. Several birds were gathered in the tree, discussing their next journey for the coming winter.

Flapping wings made Checker reach for his holstered Colt before his mind assured him of the reason for the sound. Or the uselessness of that gun. Or the soreness of his hand. He silently gave thanks for forcing him to remember his own situation; a reassuring pat of the gun in his waistband with his left hand followed. His mind returned to the herd and he motioned for Bannon and Johnny to hold the horses after they were watered.

"So far, so good," Jackson muttered to himself, bit down hard on his pipe, and reined in the team so he could study the next part of the crossing. He, too, had observed the uneasiness among the horses, but expected them to settle down after watering. If not, they were being followed.

Sonny was a few feet to his right now, no longer skipping. He was breathing hard as he watched the wagon's progress. If he had noticed the horses' agitation, he hadn't said anything.

Yanking on his hand, Rebecca giggled and said, "That was fun, Uncle Sonny. Let's skip again."

"Maybe in a little while, honey," Sonny said, feeling light-headed from the movement; his breath was short and jerky. "I need to . . . help Uncle Black Jack." To make his point, he called out, "Looks like . . . pure mud . . . to the left there."

"Yeah, I see it," Jackson replied, trying to decide if the horses would be able to pull the wagon through. "Better untie the cows—and your saddle horse. Can ya do it?"

Checker announced that he would get the animals and Sonny was glad to not have to move just yet. The tall gunfighter told Bannon to keep an eye on the outlaws and let Johnny watch the herd. Immediately the farm boy reined his horse to face them, yanked free his rifle, and smoothly cocked it. Without waiting to see if his order had been obeyed, Checker loped over to the wagon, splashing water as he came.

"It looked to me like you could squeeze through there without getting into anything deep. Did I guess wrong?" Checker asked as he untied the animals behind the wagon without dismounting.

Jackson didn't respond as he mentally gauged the width of the vehicle against the narrow land bridge that separated one creek from the other. He pulled on the reins to keep the horses still. "If I can stay straight, I'll be all right. It's that edge . . . right there . . . that could hang me up." He wondered if the former Ranger had noticed anything wrong with the herd as well.

His breath returning to normal, Sonny yelled, "These three clowns can lean against that closest side, keep it from sliding down. That should be enough."

"Good idea," Checker said and Jackson agreed.

Leading the cows and Sonny's horse, Checker trotted his black over to where the outlaws waited and swung down, avoiding the use of his right hand. It dawned on him that Redmond, for certain, would realize how badly hurt his good hand was when he attempted to release them to help. With his back to the outlaws so they couldn't see he was using mainly his left hand, Checker

secured the animals, and his black, to scrub brush lining the elbow of the nearest creek.

The only thing that made sense was to keep a Colt in
his right hand and make it appear he was being vigi-
lant. Before turning around, he pulled the gun from his
waistband with his right hand. He wasn't sure he could
hold it upright and decided on just carrying it at his
side. The effect would be casual, yet ready. He tested
the weight in his damaged hand and felt he could hold
the weapon at least long enough to get the men untied.

"Redmond. Wells. Venner. You three are going to help
keep the wagon from getting in the mud." Checker
headed toward them.

"Hell, I don't care if you get stuck. Let that nigra do
it," Redmond spat.

"Yessuh, Captain Checker, I'll help." Wells's response
was polite.

Nodding excessively, Venner said, "Me too."

Redmond glared at the other two. "We're gonna git all
muddy—jes' so that nigra can sit high an' mighty."

"Shut up, Tom. You ain't helpin' us none." Venner surprised himself at his statement.

Checker untied Wells first, using only his good left
hand, and the big outlaw eased down from the saddle,
rubbing his hands. "Head toward the wagon, Wells."

"Yessuh."

Without waiting or asking, Sonny retreated to the
wagon and gave Rebecca to Jackson and retrieved his
Winchester. Immediately, she began asking the black
drover questions about the creeks. Cradling the gun in
his crossed arms, Sonny walked back toward Checker
and the outlaws. He made no attempt to jump the narrow expanse of water, simply wading through it. Water
snuggled around his boots and flirted with the bottom
of his flaired pants. His derby was cocked sideways on
his head, giving him a rather debonair look. Anyone not

knowing the situation would assume he was quite healthy. Only the paleness of his face gave away his remaining weakness. While Checker knew most men injured like Sonny would not be walking, he was selfishly glad to see his friend anyway.

Venner was quickly released and walked toward the wagon without hesitation, hoping his cooperation might end in something other than a hanging. His glance at Sonny showed surprise at the cowboy's rapid recovery as Sonny stepped forward to take the reins of both outlaw horses.

"Glad to see you're up . . . Co . . . Sonny." Venner smiled his best smile.

"Me too." Sonny touched the brim of his derby with the barrel of his Winchester in his right hand, the reins in his left, and returned the gun to the cradled position.

"What can I do . . . for you?" Salome asked as Checker unleashed Redmond from his horse.

"Nothing."

Redmond dove at him from his saddle, driving the former Ranger backward. The Colt sailed from his weakened right hand. As he landed, Redmond threw a haymaker at Checker's midsection.

Breath exploded from Checker's body. Dazed, Checker took a second blow to his midsection, taking away any remaining breath.

Checker bent over and Redmond leaned down to grab the fallen gun. Before his fingers could curl around the weapon, Checker's left fist viciously slammed the back of the outlaw's neck. Redmond whimpered and flattened against the ground. His fingers released the gun. Checker's boot followed, driving into his stomach. Redmond's groan echoed through the woodlands. A second kick quickly followed, as fierce as the first.

From behind him, Checker heard Sonny order the

other two outlaws to drop to the ground; he also warned Salome not to attempt escape. The wounded cowboy's Winchester was pushed against his thigh for rapid firing. Reins of the horses fluttered to the ground; none of the animals moved, more interested in the grass at the water's edge.

Bannon raised his readied rifle, his eyes wide with concern. Balancing the weapon in his right hand, he grabbed the loose reins of Redmond's mount with his freed left as the horse strolled past him, eyeing better grazing. It felt good to do something, instead of just watching. The lead mare spun around to meet the approaching horse, then settled into drinking again.

Jackson's rifle was already in his hands; he tried to distract Rebecca by asking her to see if there were any fish in the creeks.

At the herd, Johnny's face was white and he fought to hold back the cry that wanted out. All the terror of the past days ran at him from the corners of his mind.

Checker drew his holstered Colt with his left hand and placed it against the back of Redmond's head. "Go . . . ahead . . . Redmond. Pick it up . . . please." Checker's breath was returning in huge eager gasps. He made no attempt to cock the unusable gun, knowing it wouldn't.

Redmond's fingers jumped away from the Colt beneath them as if the weapon were a red-hot poker. Checker leaned over and retrieved it, after shifting the broken gun to his right hand. It took all of his strength to hold the gun steady. As soon as he held the second Colt in his left hand, he holstered the first, hoping no one noticed his right hand wasn't well.

Checker's words weren't about Redmond's attack, they were about his abusive name for Jackson. Everyone close enough to hear was surprised, except Sonny. "You . . . call my friend that again . . . an' I'll leave you here. Staked down. With bullets in your legs and arms. For the wolves and the Comanches. You'll wish you were dead long before you are."

The nose of the second gun was an inch from Redmond's ear. "He and Sonny are the only reason you're alive, you sorry son of a bitch." Fury spilled all over Checker's mind, and Redmond thought he was going to shoot. "I wanted to drag your ass until there was nothing left but a hank of hair."

"Puleese, don't kill me. Puleese. I—I'm sorry. I'm sorry, Captain. I'll be good. I promise. Puleese." Redmond's southern accent drooled with fear.

Checker stepped back, letting his nearly useless right hand return to his side and fighting to control the rage within him. Shaking with anger, he waved the pistol at Redmond. "Get to the wagon before I change my mind."

Slowly, the big outlaw staggered to his feet. The blow to his neck had made him dizzy and his stomach was screaming pain. He rubbed his neck with both hands and shut his eyes for a moment, then simply started walking toward the wagon. Wet mud squished between his bare toes.

At the wagon, Jackson was struggling to explain to Rebecca what had happened without making it sound scary. She had already advised him that there weren't any fish in the water because it was too cold, and wondered why her uncle was so angry.

Checker watched Redmond, returned the Colt to his waistband, and tried to hide the weakness rolling through him. Redmond's blows to his stomach had delivered their own kind of agony, and his right hand was burning with pain. He climbed slowly into the saddle, keeping his right hand at his side. He looked at Sonny, if as seeing him for the first time, and nodded. Sonny returned the silent greeting.

Dropping the lead rope beside the lead mare, Bannon rode over and handed him the leathers of Redmond's mount, holding them in one hand, his rifle in the other. Sonny saw the look on the farm boy's face and quietly told him it was all right.

Without being told, Bannon reined his horse toward the waiting lead mare. He uncocked and returned his rifle to its scabbard. Sweat dribbled down his face as he reached in his shirt pocket for a piece of hardtack. Sighing at the lack of something to eat, he retrieved the mare's lead rope and headed toward the rest of the herd.

"Come along and watch," Checker said as he passed the mounted Salome and headed toward the wagon.

For the first time, Salome looked frightened.

Checker glanced in the direction of his young nephew, hesitated, and waved with his left hand. Tearfully, Johnny waved back and turned away so no one could see the released anguish. Tormenting scenes of his father being shot, his mother beaten, and their ranch burned controlled his young mind. He swung in the saddle and vomited, barely missing the front left leg of his horse.

Checker tersely positioned the three outlaws on the left rear of the wagon, telling them what their objective was in one short sentence. His eyes burned hate and they knew it. Wells and Venner went quickly to the vehicle, leaned their shoulders against its side, and grabbed hold of the undercarriage. Redmond was a few steps behind; wobbling in the heavier mud, but trying to get in place before Checker erupted again.

With Checker's okay, Jackson started the wagon again, urging the horses forward with a quick pop of the reins and a hearty "Let's go." Rebecca leaned forward and repeated the order. The heavy wagon wheels spun in the thick mud, then grabbed hold of firmer ground.

"Push . . . now!" Checker yelled and his voice was deep and searing.

All three outlaws grunted in their attempts to keep
the rear of the wagon from cutting the corner too sharp
and ending up slicing into the bank. After telling Rebecca to sit back and hold on, Jackson snapped the
reins again hard and yelled for the team to run. The
sweating animals reacted with matched determination
and broke into a thundering run that took them across
the remaining water in seconds, sending waves out on
both sides of the vehicle.

As one animal, the horse herd froze. Ears were alert,
mirroring arched backs and tensed bodies. They were
already on edge. Snorts of nervousness and jittery
hooves filled them. Bannon and Johnny were jerked
into action, working fast to keep them from bolting.
With the lead mare close at his side, the farm boy began
singing what he thought was a trail song as he rode in a
wide circle around the agitated horses. Johnny saw
what he was doing and began imitating the action.
Both stallions resisted their attempts to calm them, rear-
ing and stomping their hooves in a desire to fight something. Anything.

Bannon avoided their distress and concentrated on
the rest of the herd. The lack of continuing noise, the reassuring presence of the two riders, and the appearance of well-watered grass, gradually overtook their
natural desire to run. In minutes, even the stallions had
returned to grazing.

"Hey, Johnny, we did it," Bannon yelled. For himself,
he was pleased that neither Checker nor Sonny rushed
to help. They were obviously confident that he would
handle the situation.

Johnny smiled weakly and held up his fist in a victory sign.

At the end of the woods, Jackson began returning the
wagon team to a walk. Neither horse wanted to stop,
both jerking their heads and pulling on the reins. His

steady pressure soon convinced them to slow down. He decided their friskiness was due to the unseen problem in the woods and not the trek through the water.

"That was fun, Uncle Black Jack! Can we do it again?" Rebecca laughed and shouted.

"Oh, I think that's enough for one day, Miss Becky."

CHAPTER FOURTEEN

At their new evening camp, the horse herd was comfortably grazing in the area to be surrounded by their rope corral, their earlier agitation now forgotten. Bannon and Johnny remained mounted near the rear of the herd; the farm boy was munching something he had found in his chaps pocket and the younger boy seemed unusually quiet. Checker and Sonny were going to use the long stakes Jackson had prepared a few days ago for three corral corners. Only one tree had cooperated in its placement to their need.

The former Ranger's choice of camp was short on trees, even though the trail had been quite heavy with bushes, cottonwoods, oaks, and even a few elms. Cattlemen liked this stopping place for its closeness to water, ample grass, and level terrain. Checker liked it because it provided an easy view from a long way in all directions, making it difficult for anyone to get close without being noticed.

With only three trees of sufficient size, the outlaws had been tied to the same one. Even Redmond was silent and seemed eager to show he was cooperating. Salome was tied to a second tree eight feet away; she appeared to be sleeping, her head resting against her chest.

"So, what happened to your right hand, John?" Sonny quietly asked as they drove in the first stake for the corral. "How bad is it?"

"What? Oh, that. I banged it against a tree the night the Comanches came back. No big deal."

"You're talkin' to me, John. Looked like you couldn'a barely hold a gun. Lemme see." Sonny turned so the outlaws wouldn't be able to view the inspection.

Checker looked up at Sonny, shook his head, and held out his right hand, telling him what had happened in his fight with Lightning and that there might be some broken bones in his hand.

Sonny listened and finally said, "None of them hootowls have picked up on it. I'm sure of that." He looped a rope around the first stake and tested its steadiness. "Thought somethin' was wrong the way you handled Redmond."

"Why didn't you shoot him?" Checker picked up the rope and a second stake and headed toward what would be the next corner fifteen feet away.

"I was gonna, but you pulled your fancy Colt before I could fire." Sonny trailed after him, picking up his Winchester from the ground. "That gun's broke, ain't it?"

"Yeah, hammer's going to have to be replaced. How'd you know that?"

"Didn't—till I looked at it when you passed. So, you challenged Redmond with a damn gun that wouldn't shoot."

"Didn't have any better ideas at the time. Got the

other soon as I could." Checker jammed the second stake in the ground and stepped back for Sonny to pound it in place with the butt of his rifle.

"You didn't want no help, John," Sonny said between pounds. "You wanted him to try something."

"Maybe I did."

Sonny pulled the rope into place and looped it tight. They would add a second rope after the holding pen was in place.

"I wouldn't have stopped you." Sonny attempted to smile and couldn't quite make it happen. "Jackson would've."

Checker stared at him without responding, and headed for the lone tree they intended to use as a corner.

From the center of camp came Jackson's friendly call. "Hey, boys, come ahead when you're through. Miss Becky an' I got supper almost ready."

Behind it came Rebecca's tiny command. "Wash your hands."

Both men laughed and walked toward the small cooking fire, joined by Bannon and Johnny.

Checker watched silently as Johnny walked beside Bannon, keeping his distance from the tall gunfighter. Uncertain of what to do, or what to say to the boy, Checker remained silent as the foursome walked down the hill to the campfire.

"Where's the little miss?" Sonny asked.

Looking up from his cooking, Jackson motioned toward the wagon. "She went over to get a can of peaches."

Sonny immediately headed that way, singing loudly, "Suppertime, suppertime. Come and get it. Suppertime, suppertime. Jackson and Becky got suppertime."

Rebecca's infectious giggle followed as she came bouncing toward Sonny, carrying a can of peaches in both hands as if it were a royal presentation.

"Rebecca, are you taking good care of Uncle Sonny?" Checker knelt to be closer to her height.

She stopped, handed the can to Sonny, looked up at Checker, and cocked her head to the side. "Uncle Sonny's my bestest friend in the whole world."

Glancing away from the sizzling meat, Sonny said, "I think we should take a walk before it gets too dark. Don't you?"

"Oh, I would like that, Uncle Sonny."

"Maybe we'll let Johnny an' Uncle John go with us," Sonny said. "We'll walk over to that little stream and . . . ah, maybe put a leaf in it to see what happens."

Rebecca began telling him about the big orange leaf she had found this morning and put in the wagon for safekeeping.

"Well, it sure smells good, Jackson." Sonny lifted Rebecca into his arms. "Doesn't it, darlin'?"

She smiled. "Yes, but I was hoping Uncle Black Jack might make some dumplings. Mommy makes them for us sometimes."

"Well, what about that . . . Uncle Black Jack?" Sonny laughed as he asked. "Where are the dumplings?"

Jackson pushed a curl away from Rebecca's cheek. "If I can scare up enough flour and such, we can have some tomorrow night. How's that?"

"Oh, that would be wonderful," Rebecca said. "You're my bestest friend too, Uncle Black Jack."

CHAPTER FIFTEEN

Dusk was shoving its way into the trees and urging all the shadows to come out. With dinner over and the outlaws fed, Sonny kept his promise about going to the nearby stream. It was a tiny remnant of the creeks they had crossed earlier and probably didn't hold water most of the year.

Sonny fashioned two boats by adding a leaf to a short stick and then a second one from a bit fatter stick. He and Rebecca carefully placed them in the barely moving water and Sonny declared the race was on.

"Come on, stick! Come on!" Sonny laughed and motioned for his larger stick to catch up as the smaller one immediately took the lead.

"Oh, hurry. Hurry," Rebecca encouraged and knelt on her knees to watch.

"What are you doing?" Johnny asked as he and Checker followed awkwardly, after Jackson's suggestion.

Rebecca stood, bothered by the dangling end of the ribbon so close to her bonnet, and pointed at the sticks in the water. "We are having a race . . . between our boats. Mine is winning."

"Well, I reckon you know more about boats than Uncle Sonny," Checker said.

"Uncle Sonny made both boats," she declared, kneeling again.

"I can make a faster boat than anybody." Johnny whirled to find a suitable piece of wood.

He hurried away and returned with a foot-long branch with a small Y at one end. "This'll be the best ever."

Sonny picked up a leaf among the scattered autumn harvest. "Here's your sail."

"I can do it myself." Johnny took the leaf, then put it back on the ground and selected another.

"I just bet you can." Sonny glanced at Checker and smiled, then concentrated on adjusting Rebecca's ribbon after she told him about it.

Seconds later, Johnny's boat entered the water but immediately got stopped on a rock by one side of its Y.

"Better give it a little shove," Sonny suggested. "Mine got hung up the same way." He splashed some water at Johnny's stick and freed it to sail once again. "It'll be good to get . . . home. To Dodge. Won't it, John?"

Rebecca was jabbering about how her boat was going to float around the world.

"Yeah, it will," Checker responded.

Johnny tugged on his cap and studied his uncle before blurting, "My paw was the best at trainin' hosses."

Cocking his head to the side, Checker said, "Yes, he was."

"He's gone." The statement was presented without tears. Just a straightforward sentence of fact.

"Yes, it'll be up to us to carry on what he started." Checker picked up a stick and dragged it in the water.

"Ever'time I see those hosses, I think . . ." This time the

idea wouldn't let the boy finish. His eyes filled and he looked away.

Sonny noted the twitch in the Ranger's face at the last statement. "You know that's the way it should be, Johnny," Sonny said. "Ever'time you see horses, you can be reminded of your father. Good way to be remembered. I think horses are beautiful things." He looked up as if to examine the distant shapes in the rope corral.

"Y-yes . . . but . . ."

"We're gonna help you make your ranch something your father would be proud of," Sonny continued.

"Y-you're not goin' back . . . to Texas?"

"There's nothing for me in Texas—except shadows."

An unstoppable tear rolled down Johnny's cheek.

Checker stood, more slowly than usual, using his left hand for balance. "Join me, will you, Johnny?"

"Sure thing, Uncle John." The boy and his uncle walked away toward the lone cottonwood.

Sonny returned his attention to Rebecca and her flow of questions about where they were going, why the water was cool, making sailboats, his derby hat, his bullet wounds, and why Johnny had cried. Sonny answered all of them gently, especially the last. He told her that her big brother was crying because he was worried about their parents since both had been hurt. He didn't think it made any sense to tell her more.

Rebecca's eyes were restless and in need of the release that more questions brought.

He explained, as simply as he could, that bad men had burned their home and hurt their parents. He couldn't bring himself to tell her that their father was dead; that awful truth would come later. But she needed to have some idea of what they faced when they returned. Her questions continued and he tried to push her mind toward the fun of rebuilding their ranch and what she might want it to look like.

At a silent tree, Checker stopped. The words came jerkily as if ripped from the innermost corner of his soul. "Johnny, there's nothing easy about losing someone you love. I won't tell you that the hurt will go away, either. It won't. But you can use it to help you learn and grow. You can use it to become the man your father wanted you to be." His shoulders rose and fell. "I reckon that's what life is about, learning to deal with hard things, learning how to be happy, no matter what."

Johnny listened quietly. He loved being with his uncle. For the first time, he noticed the dark bruises and swelling in Checker's right hand. He started to ask about the injury, but Checker leaned over and picked up a small stone, examined it, and tossed the pebble into the darkness.

The motion sent a shiver of pain from Checker's fingers to his shoulder. He stood with his arms at his sides, hoping it would pass. Realizing the boy was watching and waiting, he forced himself to continue.

"I sure liked your father. Wish I'd gotten to know him better." He picked up another small nearly white pebble, this time with his left hand, and squeezed his fist around it. "Never knew mine—and my mother died when your mother and I were young. She was about your age when it happened." Gripping the stone, he wiped the back of his left hand across his mouth to remove the sting of hard memories.

"Mama said my gran'pa owned a saloon in town." Johnny watched his uncle, then picked up a small stone himself and tossed it. "Said he had him a lot of money too. Lots o' folks liked him. He died a long time ago. I never knew him a-tall. I knowed Uncle Thomas and Aunt Henrietta, though. They raised Mama—after you left."

Quietly, Checker asked, "What did she tell you—about your grandma?"

Johnny nodded his head in anticipation and jerked

on his cap to keep it in place. "She used to talk about her a lot. Not as much as about you, but a lot. Said she was real purty. Real nice. Worked real hard, Mama said—an' that you lived in town. The place is gone now, though." As an afterthought, he added, "Showed me that picture of you."

Checker wasn't sure he wanted his mind to return there. To a dingy yesterday that smelled of laundry soap and sickness. To a tent that was their home. He had already decided it wasn't necessary the boy be told the truth about J.D. McCallister; his mother's description was good enough. At least for now. Telling him about the man's evil ways would not help Johnny deal with his grief; only make him wonder if anything in his world was true. Checker told himself that it also added nothing to tell him that Star and Blue McCallister were actually related to his mother and him.

"And what about your grandparents on your father's side?" Checker asked gently.

"Don't know 'em neither. They live a long way away—in Sweden. That's across the ocean, ya know." Johnny twisted his face to deal with the grief that wanted to consume him once more. "Paw said my gran'pa were a lumberjack. Paw only had a little tin image of 'em. From their weddin', he said. Got a letter from 'em oncest. I'll bet the fire got both."

"We'll look when we get home."

Johnny looked up at Checker and reached out to take his hand. "I'm scared, Uncle John. I'm real scared . . . I'm sorry." He choked and continued, "I was scared . . . when that awful man . . . came at you. I—I . . ."

Immediately, the tall gunfighter knelt beside his nephew and looked into his crumpled face. "That's all right, son. Everyone gets scared. It's part of living."

"But you ain't never scared . . . an' Sonny ain't. I don't think Jackson neither."

GET
4 FREE BOOKS!

You can have the best Westerns delivered to your door for less than what you'd pay in a bookstore or online. Sign up for one of our book clubs today, and we'll send you **4 FREE* BOOKS**, worth $23.96, just for trying it out...**with no obligation to buy, ever!**

Authors include classic writers such as
LOUIS L'AMOUR, MAX BRAND, ZANE GREY
and more; PLUS new authors such as
COTTON SMITH, TIM CHAMPLIN, JOHNNY D. BOGGS
and others.

As a book club member you also receive the following special benefits:

- **30% OFF** all orders through our website & telecenter!
- **Exclusive access to** special discounts!
- **Convenient** home delivery **and 10 days to return any books you don't want to keep.**

There is no minimum number of books to buy,
and you may cancel membership at any time.
See back to sign up!

*Please include $2.00 for shipping and handling.

YES!

Sign me up for the Leisure Western Book Club and send my FOUR FREE BOOKS! If I choose to stay in the club, I will pay only $14.00* each month, a savings of $9.96!

NAME: _____

ADDRESS: _____

_____

TELEPHONE: _____

E-MAIL: _____

☐ **I WANT TO PAY BY CREDIT CARD.**

☐ VISA   ☐ MasterCard   ☐ DISCOVER

ACCOUNT #: _____

EXPIRATION DATE: _____

SIGNATURE: _____

Send this card along with $2.00 shipping & handling to:

Leisure Western Book Club
20 Academy Street
Norwalk, CT 06850-4032

Or fax (must include credit card information!) to: 610.995.9274.
You can also sign up online at www.dorchesterpub.com.

*Plus $2.00 for shipping. Offer open to residents of the U.S. and Canada only.
Canadian residents please call 1.800.481.9191 for pricing information.

If under 18, a parent or guardian must sign. Terms, prices and conditions subject to change. Subscription subject
to acceptance. Dorchester Publishing reserves the right to reject any order or cancel any subscription.

JOIN NOW!

Checker stared at the ground for a moment. "That's not so, Johnny. We're all scared. Being scared helps make you sharper, work harder, be ready. If a man tells you he's never scared, he's either a fool or doesn't know what's going on. How you act when you're scared makes the difference."

He started to place his left hand on Johnny's shoulder and realized he held the small white rock in his fist. He withdrew his arm and opened his hand in front of the boy to reveal its contents.

"Well, isn't this something?" Checker smiled.

"What? You mean that lil' rock?"

"Yeah, that little rock." Checker tilted his head to the side for a moment. "A good friend gave me one just like it once. Said it could sing. To him. He's gone now. Stands-in-Thunder. He was an old man when we met." Checker tossed the pebble easily in his hand, watching it as he spoke. "I guess a lot of people were surprised we became good friends. A Comanche war chief and a Texas Ranger. But we enjoyed each other's company. He gave me this, too." He held up the small medicine pouch around his neck and explained its meaning.

"So, wolves are your . . . friends?" Johnny's tone was a puzzle.

"According to Stands-in-Thunder, they are."

"D-do you believe that, Uncle John?" Johnny asked, staring into his uncle's eyes.

"That's a good question, Johnny." Checker tossed the pebble in his hand and caught it several times. "Let's just say I try to honor my friend's belief. Most Indians see themselves as a part of a great big circle of all life. A circle of animals, trees, everything. They see everything as being connected to everything else. So they look to things, like wolves, for strength and guidance. That's why circles are sacred to them."

"They didn't believe in God? Go to church?"

"Oh yes, they definitely believe in God. The Great Spirit, they call him," Checker said. "And their church is the land. Everywhere is sacred. You know, he told me once that every step we take on Mother Earth is sacred. Each step is a prayer. Guess that means all of the land is their church. Hard to live up to—but it really stuck with me."

"Is that why you leave stuff behind every day?" Johnny rubbed his eyes to remove the last tear that wanted release. "I seen you leave some tobacco by a tree or somethin'—when we leave camp each mornin'."

Checker pushed his hat back from his forehead. "You're going to make a good scout some day, young man. Yeah, that's why. It's just a thank-you for letting us be safe there." He explained that Stands-in-Thunder would bury a bite of meat before each meal as a tribute to the Great Spirit.

"I think you like the Comanches."

"Well, one Comanche, I did. That's for sure," Checker said. "And I respect their way of life. In some ways, I've lived it, too."

Johnny stared at the small rock and touched it gingerly as if expecting it to do something. "What do you mean . . . Stands-in-Thunder . . . said it could sing?"

Checker squeezed his hand over the pebble and opened it again. "Don't know for sure. A lot of Indians thought that rocks were the oldest . . . things. That they were alive and could offer wisdom to the man who listened."

"Did yours ever sing to you?"

Checker smiled. "Nope, but I reckon I didn't give it a chance to." He looked up into the darkening sky. "My guess is that if a man stayed quiet long enough, looking at this pebble, thoughts would come to him. That would be the singing."

The boy wasn't certain of what to think, so he changed the subject. "This war chief, is he why you know so many Injun words?"

"Yes, I wanted to learn as much as I could from him."

Johnny stared at the pebble, then back to his uncle. Checker's tanned face was calm and comforting.

"Lost that pebble a long time ago. Guess I didn't put much store in it. Just thought it was an old man wanting to give me something. I don't know." Checker closed his fist over the stone. "Hadn't even thought about it until . . . on the trail after you and Rebecca, I found one just like it. Rain was coming down something awful—and I was scared that we hadn't found you."

Slowly, he reopened his fist. "I picked up that white rock and threw it. Hard as I could. Then ol' Stands-in-Thunder's words came leaping at me. I went and found it—and shortly after that we found you. Gave it to Jackson for luck."

"Does he still have it?"

"No, he gave it to Tyrel—just before the Comanches hit us."

Johnny's eyes widened as he examined the pebble again.

"Here, I want you to have this." Checker handed him the rock. "Don't know why, just tell yourself that your uncle's a little crazy sometimes."

Johnny lifted the stone from Checker's hand as if it were a precious jewel. "Is this kinda like Mama takin' one of your shirt buttons when you two was kids—an' you left?"

"Well, sort of, I guess." Checker bit his lower lip. "She wanted something to remember me by—and that was all I had." His mind slipped to his sister at their burning ranch and showing him the button kept all those years before she collapsed in his arms. He let his mind shift to Sarah Ann Tremons, who had heard the story and pulled off one of his shirt buttons when he left town, as a reminder for him to keep his promise to return to her.

"Why did you leave, Uncle John?"

The question stung.

"I didn't have any choice, Johnny. Some . . . bad men were after me—and I couldn't stay or your mother would've been hurt. Your uncle Thomas and aunt Henrietta, too."

Johnny shoved the pebble into his pocket.

"There's one more thing I want you to do for me, Johnny."

"Sure."

"Close your eyes." Checker's command was soft. "Now . . . I want you to see a happy time when you and your father were doing something together. Can you see it?"

Johnny swallowed and shut his eyes. "Yes. Paw and me . . . we're fishin' . . . down at the creek. It's early in the mornin'. Just him an' me. He said we could wait to do our chores. An' I caught me a fish." He squeezed his eyelids tighter. "Paw said it was the biggest we'd ever caught."

Checker smiled. "You can go there any time you want, Johnny. Your father will always be waiting for you. There."

Johnny jumped into Checker's chest, almost knocking him over. He hugged the tall gunfighter tightly and Checker held him close. Silence wrapped itself around them.

Without releasing him, Checker said, "Should we go see how Uncle Sonny and Becky are doing?"

CHAPTER SIXTEEN

Checker stood, hoping there would no more questions about the past.

"You bet, Uncle John." Johnny hesitated. "I—I l-love you, Uncle John."

"Well . . . I love you, too, Johnny. We're going to be partners, right?"

"Right!"

"Let's find a white rock for your sister, too, what do you say?" Checker smiled. "We want her to have good luck, too."

"Sure, Uncle John."

After a few minutes of energetic searching, they had selected three stones and Johnny decided on the whitest one. Checker agreed and stuck it in his pocket, beneath his shell belt. They walked hand in hand to the stream and were joined by Sonny carrying Rebecca back to camp. Immediately, Rebecca started a flow of questions about what Checker and Johnny had been doing.

Johnny felt in his pocket for the pebble, then decided not to tell her about it. He looked at Checker, who winked. The tall gunfighter told her a simpler version of the Comanche white pebble story, asked her to shut her eyes and hold out her hand. He placed the white rock in her little hand.

"That's a good luck rock. You put it in your pocket until we get home, all right?" Checker said.

"How does it work, Uncle John?" Her soft eyes sought his for assurance.

Checker chuckled. "Well, that's a good question. I don't know how it works. I just thought it was a fun thing to do. What do you think?"

Sonny asked to see the pebble, leaning over her shoulder. "Hey, that's pretty neat, sweetheart. A Comanche white magic rock."

"A Comanche white . . . magic . . . rock?"

"You bet." Sonny sang into her ear, "Comanche magic. White rock magic. Comanche magic. White rock magic."

She giggled. "Oh, Uncle Sonny, you're so silly."

"That I am, honey, that I am." He grimaced and straightened his back.

Only Checker noticed.

Johnny pulled his rock from his pocket and held it up for Sonny to see. "I got one, too!"

"Oh, that's great. Which one is bigger?"

Before Rebecca could ask another question, Sonny deflected her curiosity by getting her to sing a song they had made up about stick boats.

"Stick boat . . . stick boat . . . carry me away, carry me away. All the way to San Antone. Carry me away." Sonny sang in rhythm to their steps with Rebecca joining in.

Night brought a rich coolness and the men added blankets of their own to the children's bedding inside the wagon. After listening to their prayers, insisted upon by Rebecca, the two men turned to walk away.

"Uncle John . . . Uncle Sonny, do you say prayers?" Rebecca's question stopped them.

Checker spun around more quickly than Sonny. His eyes caught the questioning look in Johnny's gaze first, then the happy sparkle of his little sister's.

"Yes, Becky, we do. Both of us."

Sonny glanced at him. "Sure 'nuff, little darlin'. Sure 'nuff."

"Oh, good."

"You two go to sleep now. We've got a long day ahead."

Smiling, Johnny held up the white pebble and Rebecca quickly did the same. Checker grinned and the two men resumed their exit.

As they strode into the darkness, Sonny said, "Glad to hear you're talkin' to the big fella. Been doin' that some myself lately."

"Yeah. It was hard . . . for me. I couldn't . . ."

"I know. Got a smoke?"

"Sure." Checker handed him a tobacco sack and papers from his shirt pocket.

As he rolled a cigarette, Sonny said, "When I rode away . . . when you let me ride away . . . after Mary died, I was black as all hell. Rode alone for days. Came to a little town. Can't even tell you what it was called. Nor far from the Rio. Sorta in a valley." He accepted Checker's lit match and inhaled. "Wouldn'a stopped there, but my horse had thrown a shoe. Went to what looked like a blacksmith's place. Probably lucky I didn't run into anybody. Would'a shot anyone who said somethin' I didn't like."

Checker rolled one for himself, using mostly his left hand. He cupped his hands around a new match and brought his own smoke to life. They continued walking to the back of the wagon and retrieved their Winchesters from where they lay beside Sonny's makeshift bed.

"Saw this fella behind the workin' fire. Thought he was kneelin', I guess." Sonny watched the smoke from his cigarette dance in the night air. "Anyway, he shouts out somethin' real happy like—an' I grunt back about my horse. Halfway mad that he would act so damn happy."

Sonny glanced at Checker. "Never told anybody about this before. Seems kinda funny to do."

"Don't, if you don't want to." Checker levered his rifle left-handed into a cocked position and eased the hammer back down.

"Nope. I want to." Sonny took another puff, repeated the same procedure with his gun, and continued. When the blacksmith came around the fire in a wheelchair, Sonny saw that both of his legs were gone. A result of cannon fire at Shiloh. The sight had jolted Sonny from his blackness. How could this wretched excuse for a man be so happy? Why?

"Well, I guess he figured out what I was thinkin'," Sonny said, "an' ups an' tells me that a man has to make a stand on just how happy he's gonna be. Don't matter what cards he's dealt. You can't toss 'em in, you have to play 'em. He told me that he wakes up every mornin' givin' thanks for the day and just for the joy of being alive—an' being able to work as a smithy."

"Sounds like quite a man."

"He was. Been tryin' to be like him ever since."

"He'd be proud to know that."

Sonny looked embarrassed and changed the subject. "Where do you think Star's headed?"

They walked toward the now-darkened campfire without Checker answering. Jackson and Bannon were sitting on logs, talking quietly while the farm boy speared peach halves from a can with his pocketknife.

A few feet from them, the former Ranger finally answered. "I wish I knew, Sonny. My guess would be some place where he could disappear. Kansas City, maybe. St. Louis. Maybe Santa Fe."

"You're not worried that he'll double back on us?"

"I'm always worried," Checker said and turned his attention to their sitting friends. "Evenin', Jackson, Tyrel. I see you like sittin' in the dark."

"Say, who is it that doesn't like sitting in the dark? Is it me?" Sonny chuckled.

Bannon was the first to respond, his mouth full of chewed peach. "It were Jackson's idea. Safer, he be sayin'. Told me it weren't smart to stare into a fire neither. If somethin' happens, a man is blinded for an instant when he turns toward the dark. Might make the difference." The farm boy's presentation sought confirmation of the black drover's advice.

Sonny walked over and put his left hand on Jackson's shoulder; his right hand carried his rifle at his side. "You know, Jackson, you talk like a man who's either worn a badge—or been chased by one. That's good savvy you're puttin' in the kid's head."

Jackson nodded his appreciation and pushed on his eyeglasses.

"Sorry." Sonny squeezed Jackson's shoulder for a moment. "Didn't mean to sound like I was pushin' along your back trail."

Jackson looked up and grinned. "I know y'all weren't. Say, where'd you get that shirt?"

Checker stared at Sonny as if he hadn't seen him in days. "Well, hey, that's right. I've never seen that before."

"Some tracker." Sonny snorted as he moved to an open spot on the log where Jackson sat. "Been talkin' with this here Ranger fella all night an' he doesn't notice I'm wearin' one o' that quack doctor's shirts. Found it in the back. Fits real nice, I'd say." He peered down at the white, collarless shirt, noticed a blood spot on the side of his stomach wound, and turned away so the others wouldn't see it.

But Jackson already had, so had Checker. The former Ranger was also aware Sonny had referred to Checker's half brother as "that quack doctor" when he knew Blue was related to him. That would be Sonny, sensitive without appearing to be.

"Y'all are bleeding. Again." Jackson pointed. "I told ya that y'all shouldn't be up an' around so soon. Y'all need quiet. Let your body heal proper."

"Yeah, I know. I know. I'll be fine. Not my shirt anyway." Sonny stood quickly to reinforce his readiness. "I'll take the first watch, and then I'll sleep." He motioned toward Bannon. "Them peaches look good."

"Yeah, mighty good."

"I'll come an' get you at midnight," Jackson said, knowing further expressions of concern would only aggravate his friend. "Tyrel, you come about three—an', John, you've got the rest of the night. All right?"

"Sounds good to me." Checker stretched and yawned. "I believe some shut-eye would be real good."

Jackson glanced at Sonny, and the looks exchanged the understanding that both thought the former Ranger's statement was a good one. His lack of sleep during this entire endeavor was wearing on him, even if Checker wouldn't admit it.

Sonny turned to walk away and Jackson stopped him with a comment. "I was a state policeman—under Governor Davis. Part of the Reconstruction hell. They hired some of us coloreds." He shook his head. "Didn't go over well, believe me. I figured it might be a good way to track down my brothers and sisters. It wasn't. They let us all go when the Rangers came back."

With a new bite of peach halfway to his mouth, Bannon froze.

"Ain't that somethin'? I'm surrounded by lawmen." Sonny threw back his head. "No wonder I've been so good." He walked away into the darkness, singing to himself. The tune was "The Old Chisholm Trail" and the words were about riding with two lawmen.

Checker and Jackson talked a few minutes longer about the postwar days in Texas while Bannon listened eagerly. Bannon asked several questions, mostly about Jackson's siblings, and the black drover politely answered them, stating that he didn't figure on ever seeing them again "this side of the Pearly Gates."

"Found something interesting, John." Jackson changed the subject and reached into his big coat pocket, withdrawing several folded papers. "In the wagon, when I was tendin' to Sonny."

"What is it?" Checker was immediately interested.

"Well, there's all kinds of papers, receipts, and letters in a box—from the Nebraska town of Lincoln. I brought a few to show you. A woman did the letter writing," Jackson explained as he held out the crumpled discovery. "She writes to a fella she calls 'Dr. January'—but, according to the envelopes, his real name's Janiskowski. Ivan Janiskowski. That's her name too. Hezbela Janiskowski. Wife or sister, I reckon."

Checker took the materials and began to read. "You think he was Blue's partner? Another gun-for-hire?"

"No, looks like Dr. January owned that wagon and was a real medicine peddler," Jackson said. "Hired Blue to be his assistant."

"How do you know that?"

"Well, she mentions Blue—by name—a couple of

times. Asking if the doctor's new assistant is working out. Reads likes she met Blue when he started working with her husband."

"Wonder what happened to . . . Ivan." Checker looked up.

"That's easy to figure. There's a wanted bulletin for Blue McCallister for the murder of Dr. January, Ivan Janiskowski." Jackson pointed in the direction of the lower portion of the papers. "I looked close at the wagon paint. Scratched on it some. Under 'Dr. Gambree' in two places on both sides, there's 'Dr. January.' "

"Should've guessed."

"Blue went by some other names too. Besides his real one—and Dr. Gambree. The reward poster lists Billy Frederick and William Frisco. There's another bulletin in there, wanting him for a different murder. Extortion. Fraud."

Checker shook his head and flipped through the sheets to find the reward posters.

"There's a poster for Salome, too. Want her for murder and extortion too. In Chicago." Jackson glanced at Bannon. "Her real name is Alice Dundle. Well, I shouldn't say that. There are two names listed. That, an' Helen Mae Beidler."

"Wonder why Blue kept all this stuff." Checker handed the papers back to Jackson. "Seems strange to me."

"Wondered about that myself." Jackson pushed on his eyeglasses and looked again at Bannon, who only seemed sleepy. "Could be he wanted to know what he was up against. Trophies, sort of. He was a strange one—an' real particular. Everything is stacked neatlike in the box. Got all kinds of receipts and business notes. Even a couple of recipes—for medicine."

"Trophies? I can see that, I guess. But why keep letters to a man he's killed?"

"Well, letters are scarce. Any kind—out here. You've

been carryin' one from your sister a long time." Jackson poked at the dead fire with a handy stick and returned the folded letters to his pocket. "Maybe he just couldn't bring himself to destroy 'em."

Checker patted the shirt pocket where he kept Amelia's letter. "Maybe he thought they might come in handy if anyone asked about Dr. January." He pushed back his hat from his forehead. "He could show a letter an' say the man sold out an' headed home."

"Bet there's a made-up receipt for buyin' the wagon."

"You think like a crook," Checker said. "Or a lawman."

Jackson smiled. "I'll put 'em back. When we get to Dodge, we can wire the marshal up there, wire her too. She deserves to know that her husband's killer . . . got justice."

"Justice," Checker repeated. "I didn't want that, Jackson. I didn't want to kill him. He gave me no choice."

"I know."

"He was my brother."

"That didn't make him a good man." Jackson was surprised that he declared the relationship in front of Bannon.

A quick look at the farm boy showed he was more interested in picking the last peach from the can with his pocketknife than the conversation.

Checker said nothing more.

Jackson knew Checker needed to rid his mind of the guilt of killing his half brother, but he also knew the man wouldn't say any more about it. He just wouldn't— and no amount of prying would change it.

The former Ranger studied the quiet shapes of the outlaws as if transitioning his mind to the present. "Everything's quiet. We'd better get some rest. You got the watch after Sonny, right?"

"Right."

Checker excused himself and left. Bannon yawned

and returned his knife to his pocket. He didn't want to be asked what he thought about Salome's real name being something else. It didn't matter. She was still a beautiful woman. Just because her name was on a wanted poster didn't mean she did it.

Jackson told the young farm boy to get some rest and he, too, walked away to his usual place of sleeping under the wagon. Not even Jackson knew where Checker slept; he told Bannon he thought the gunfighter usually found some place away from camp and difficult to access without making noise.

Jackson took over for Sonny a little before midnight, and the happy cowboy was definitely weary. Jackson's turn at guard came and went and the camp was silent. Bannon took his turn with a rifle and a cup of coffee. It made him feel good that Checker and the others trusted him with the responsibility. It made him feel like he was truly one of them.

The silence of the night brought rushes of memories and tried to bring back the sense of killing from two days before. He managed to keep the thought away by concentrating on Salome. Her face was gone now, unclear in his memory, but he continued to let her perform her magic on him anyway, replacing her with the ways of the prostitute from Dodge. Around him the night was quiet. Suddenly, he remembered what Jackson had said about learning from the sounds around him. He jumped to his feet and looked around. Nothing. Nothing. He walked toward the outlaws. He counted. One, two, three, four. Yes, they were all there, sleeping. His gaze headed toward the shape that was Salome.

In the dark, he heard her unmistakable voice, although it was barely a whisper. "Tyrel, is that you? Would you please come here?"

He knew he shouldn't. Jackson had told him to stay

away from her. More than once. But how could it hurt to be polite? He walked over to her with no further regret; his rifle was in his right hand at his side.

"Oh, thank you, Tyrel. You are a real gentleman." Even in the dark, he could see her eyes settle amorously on him. He found it hard to breathe and tried to swallow.

"What do you . . . need, ma'am?"

"I'm so embarrassed to ask." She looked away. "I . . . ah, I need to . . . you know."

Bannon understood she needed to relieve herself. "Yes, ma'am."

"I know you shouldn't—but could you possibly find it within yourself—to untie me so I could, you know? I would be so grateful." Her long eyelashes fluttered over soulful eyes.

Before he realized what he was doing, the farm boy laid down his rifle and began loosening her ropes. When he was finished, he stepped back and she stood. Slowly. Without hesitation, she came to him with her arms outstretched.

"Oh, Tyrel. I've wanted to be with you—for so long." Her mouth found his; her body pressed against his; and he was lost in lust.

He felt the barrel of a gun in his stomach before he realized its significance. His mind told him what had happened and his hand rushed toward his empty holster. The next thing he knew was a bright light, then nothing.

"Tyrel . . . Tyrel . . . wake up, boy." The voice coming from somewhere in the trees was Jackson's. "He's coming around. Got a cut on his head, though."

Bannon wasn't certain what was going on. He thought he heard Checker say something about rounding up the loose horses, but that didn't make sense; they were inside the rope corral. He thought he heard Sonny agree. His eyes tried to focus and gradually he saw Jackson leaning over him with a wet bandanna in his hand.

"Wh-what happened, Jackson? Did the cattle stampede? Do we have to cross the river now?" Bannon jabbered.

"Everything is fine, Tyrel. You rest."

"She went this way," Checker yelled from the tiny creek. "Got a half-hour lead. Ridin' that dun mare from the corral." Checker's voice was softer. "Doesn't look like any of the horses got loose, though."

Sonny's voice came from somewhere near the corral. "Let her go, John We've got better things to do than trailin' some lady in the dark."

CHAPTER SEVENTEEN

It had been a week since the Comanche attack as the weary group of Triple C riders, two children, three outlaws, a medicine wagon, a small herd of horses, and two steers cleared the last ridge separating Kansas from the Arkansas River and Dodge City.

The sun was high in the sky, not yet releasing control to the shadows. Brisk winds whipped at the edges of cottonwoods, struggling elders, and tired willows along the riverbank. In the long brown buffalo grass where the land stretched out again like a flatiron, the Triple C chuck wagon and trail remuda were settled. Waiting for the return of their friends, hopefully with good news.

From the distance, Checker could only make out the shape of Randy Reilman, the drive's horse wrangler. The other two Triple C men left in camp weren't in sight: Tug Jamison, their cook; and Dan Mitchell, the trail boss who had been wounded when their herd was rustled. The drive to Kansas, and the subsequent arrest of the rustlers and their breakout, had taken a deadly toll on the Triple C crew. Of the twelve drovers, plus a cook, wrangler, calf wagon driver, and Mitchell, who left Texas with the herd, only seven remained, including Checker, Bannon, Jackson, and Sonny.

Whinnies from the Hedrickson mounts were quickly answered by the grazing Triple C horses.

"Hey, I can see our camp! Randy's wavin' at us," Bannon yelled back from the head of the Hedrickson herd. "Bet they're gittin' supper ready!"

Johnny waved from the other side of the herd.

Bannon hadn't recovered from his embarrassing situation with Salome, at least not emotionally. The cut on his head was mostly healed, however; it was his ego that remained bruised. None of the men had talked about the escape other than to decide they couldn't afford to take the time to track her down. The closest thing to any criticism had been a disappointed look on Jackson's face that was burned into the farm boy's mind.

Checker cupped his hand to his mouth. "Tyrel, Johnny, hold the herd. I'll join you." He nudged his black into a lope.

In the wagon, Jackson grinned and puffed on his pipe. "Well, we did it, Sonny. We did it."

Riding in back of the outlaws, Sonny nodded and sang, "Yippee ti yi yo, yippee ti yi yum, back to Dodge we come. Back to Dodge we come." He had been riding every day since Salome escaped and daring anyone to say anything about it.

Jackson had given up trying to examine his wounds; Sonny assured him that he had been hurt worse. A brown streak on his shirt indicated he hadn't bled any for several days.

Little Rebecca stirred from her sleeping position against Jackson's shoulder, cradled in his left arm. He whispered into her ear, "Look there, Miss Becky, here comes Randy. See the chuck wagon? We're almost there."

She stirred, rubbed her eyes, and looked out at the dark shapes ahead. She turned to him and said, "Will Mommy an' Daddy be there too?"

Jackson swallowed. "No, Miss Becky. But you remember Tug an' Randy, they were out at your . . ." He stopped when the image of the burned-out ranch caught up with his words, and he changed the subject. "Look at all those horses over there. Those are Triple C horses, aren't they pretty?" He pointed at the Triple C remuda.

"Are they as pretty as my daddy's horses?"

"Well, no, I reckon they aren't," Jackson answered. He turned to Checker for support, but the tall Ranger was already gone.

"Why won't Mommy and Daddy be there, Uncle Black Jack?" Her wide eyes sought his for clarification.

Jackson hesitated. "Here, Miss Becky, y'all help me with these reins, will you? We don't want these horses to start running."

Her smile was what he had hoped for as she enthusiastically put her tiny hands around the leather straps in his right fist.

Checker rode alongside Bannon and reined to a stop. Bannon's horse stutter-stepped and turned sideways with the approach and the young farm boy frowned.

Johnny wheeled his horse over to join them.

"Well, that's a sight for sore eyes." Checker waved at their waiting friends.

"Wonder if'n Tug's got anythin' to eat," Bannon said, relieved he didn't comment on his horse's action.

"Wonder if they'll know about Mama." Johnny frowned, in recognition of a truth soon to be facing them.

"I'll bet they do, Johnny." Checker's voice was reassuring; his insides weren't.

The boy's countenance was split between anticipation and fear.

Checker tried to help him concentrate on something else. "Work the herd alongside the camp horses. Let 'em get acquainted. All except the two stallions. Keep them separated."

The boy tugged on his cap and nudged his horse into a lope.

Afternoon sun blistered the chuck wagon bright bronze and orange and turned the hundred trail horses into a bright mosaic of browns, blacks, and tans. The Triple C camp was settled on the flatland on the far side of the Arkansas River. Just across the toll bridge and onto Bridge Street was Dodge's South Side gathering of saloons, dance halls, pleasure houses, and gambling casinos. The town was strangely quiet now, even from this distance. Hibernation from cattle and cowboys had settled throughout this wicked wonderland of trails-end merriment. All of the Texans had finally left for home, instead of waiting for the possible return of Checker and the other Triple C riders with the kidnapped children. Where raucous noise and boisterous laughter had held the South Side captive all summer long, now only murmurs and faint music lingered, like disembodied ghosts. To the relief of many townspeople, Dodge was theirs once more.

From behind them, they heard Sonny bellow, "I wouldn't be thinking we're not paying attention back hyar, boys. Me an' my Winchester are just waitin' for somethin' to do."

Sonny's challenge set off an easing of their herd toward the camp, now eager to meet the strange horses in front of them. The trail remuda accepted the Hedrickson horses with customary bites and kicks to protect the long brown grass they grazed in. Soon, the two Hedrickson stallions and lead mare were in control of both groups.

Randy Reilman came loping toward them and reined up beside Checker and the boys. "Well, hog-tie me down an' spit in my goddamn ear if'n ya ain't a sumbitchin' sight fer these hyar sore eyes!" He reined his horse to a quick stop and appeared pleased with its response. "We done been mighty worried. Damn, if we ain't."

Bannon couldn't help smiling at the greeting. He couldn't remember many sentences coming out of the lanky wrangler's mouth that weren't sprinkled with a wild array of cusswords, some common and some quite unusual. Randy was the Triple C wrangler for their trail drives. The farm boy glanced at the wrangler's forehead and saw the sun hadn't quite erased the red streak where a rustler's bullet had creased it. He touched his own scalp where Salome had coldcocked him with his own Colt. He stared down at the empty holster and wondered if he should buy another. It would only take a little bit from the money he had set aside to give to his mother.

Randy's own smile split his lean face and he yanked off his weathered hat, and slapped it excitedly against his thigh. Pushing the hat back on his head, he jerked the reins to keep his horse quiet; the movement was more an expression of joy than anything the animal was doing.

"Goddamnsumbitch, it's 'bout goddamn time, too, boys," Randy said. "Ol' Tug, Dan, n' myse'f, we'uns done wore out all our silly-ass, goddamn stories. Got to swappin' each other's and lettin' the other'n do the tellin', jes' to have something goddamn different to do." He rubbed his gloved hands together at his observation. "'Ceptin' when we was a-workin' at the Hedrickson place. Damn,

if'n that Tremons gal didn'a make ever'body around
work on it. Hellfire, she be a tough one." He slapped his
thighs again.

"Good to see you, you ol' hoss roper," Checker said
and added, "Remember now, we're ridin' in with some
young ears, ol' friend."

"Oh, hell, I done fergot! Goddammit, I'm sorry, I won't
say another go . . . word."

"That'll be the day." Checker grinned and held out his
hand, unsure of what Randy was talking about concerning Sarah Ann and the Hedrickson ranch.

Pulling off his glove, Randy shook the former
Ranger's hand enthusiastically. The removal was a sign
of genuine friendship and respect. His callused, rope-
burned grip sent a jolt of pain through Checker. His
face gave no indication of discomfort, only the warmth
of seeing an old friend again.

"Where's Tug? How's Dan doing?" Checker asked,
glad to be releasing his hand from the pressure of the
wrangler's handshake.

Randy looked in the direction of the chuck wagon.
"Hell, they's back thar, other side o' the chuck. Tug
wouldn't hear nothin'—an' Mr. Mitchell might be a-nap-
pin'." He slapped the glove in his hand against his thigh.
"The boss'll tell ya he's as good as a fancy colt, but he
ain't. Yet. Still a mite weak. Hell, don't tell him I said so,
though."

"Count on it," Checker said. "Look over our herd, will
you, Randy? We've tried to keep them from getting run-
down."

"Sure will. My first eyeballin' says they be ri't fierce
fine. They be the Hedrickson hosses, I reckon." Randy
studied the new animals with appreciation. "There be a
lot to like in them two studs too. How many jes' hosses?"

Checker knew "jes' hosses" meant geldings. "Six
mares. The rest, geldings."

"Green-broke?" Randy cupped a hand above his eyes to see better.

"Better'n that, Randy."

"Mercy. Be they skittish?" Randy glanced back at Checker.

"Haven't come across one yet," Checker said. "Orville Hedrickson was good, Randy, real good."

"I'd say."

Checker introduced Johnny to Randy. "Now, here's a fine young horseman, Randy. Just like his dad. This is Johnny Hedrickson."

"Well, howdy, son. I'm ri't glad to see ya again." Randy extended his hand.

"Thank you, sir. It's good to be back." Johnny shook the wrangler's hand. "Have you heard anythin' 'bout my mama?"

Randy's eyes shot toward Checker and back to the boy. "Matter fact, we have. That purty Miss Tremons was out at your place two days ago, when we done finished." He looked again at Checker and smiled. "She be askin' 'bout ya ever'day. Either she done come out hyar—or catches us when we was a-helpin'. Yessir."

He returned his attention to Johnny. "Anyway's, she be tellin' us that your ma, well, she was doin' good. Mighty weak, mind you. Been through hell . . . ah, through a heap o' trouble." He rubbed his unshaved chin. "Seems like, well, quite a while back, they done moved her from the hotel to the Tremons' place. Said it would be better. Yessuh, that's what she said." He finished with a nod of his head to emphasis the point.

Johnny's face was a sunrise. "Oh, thank you, sir!"

Checker's own countenance reflected the same relief.

"You bet, son, but I ain't no 'sir. Jes' plain Randy."

"Yes, si . . . Randy. Thank you." Johnny nudged his horse and rode back to the herd, repeating, " 'She was doin' fine.' 'She was doin' fine. She was doin' fine.' "

"Tell me about my sister's place," Checker said, watching the boy. "Sounds like some of our work might be done."

"Hell, that Miss Tremons, she done had all the damn neighbors a-workin' on it. Day after ya rode out." Randy waved his hand to reinforce his recollection. "Most folks didn't think you'd make it. Your sis neither. No, sir, not Miss Tremons, she kept at 'em. Had us a-workin' thar, too. Sunup to sundown, seems like."

He explained the house, barn, and a main corral were rebuilt. "Yessir, that ranch's jes' a-waitin' for ya. Mighty fine lookin', I'd say. Dan an' me he'ped with the damn roofs. Got it all finished two days back. Tug did some cookin'." He shook his head in appreciation. "Thar be a neighbor, Nathaniel Brode be his name, now he were some kind o' carpenter, I tell you. Miss Tremons, she wanted it done right. Damn."

Licking his chapped lips, the wrangler changed subjects. "Captain, there's trouble a-brewin' in Dodge, I reckon. Glad we'll be leavin' hyar—now that you're back an' all. That Marshal Rand done hired hisself two new deputies. Injuns, they is." Randy fiddled with his reins as he talked.

Checker's eyebrows arched and Bannon finally greeted Randy warmly. The foulmouthed wrangler had more to tell and was eager to do so.

"They be strangers. Rode in a week or so back. One wears a gun like he enjoys usin' it. Other'n is bigger'n a barn. Carries one o' them machetes. Scary bastards. Do'tsi is one's name. Don't 'member the other'n. You know 'em?"

"Yeah, I've heard of Do'tsi. He's Cherokee. A killer— for money." Checker lit his cigarette. "Heard he had a brother. Big an' strong. Likes to fight. Heard he broke someone's back in a brawl."

"Well, godammit, that figgers. Don't know why they'd

pick fellas like that. Ain't got nothin' ag'in Injuns, mind ya—but they's killers, looks to me."

Bannon ventured a guess. "Probably nobody'd take the job."

"Don't know 'bout that. This hyar Do'tsi, he done already kilt a Texas boy. One o' that Lazy R bunch. The Injun said he tried to kill him. None o' us knew the rider. Benson were his name," Randy said, only occasionally taking his eyes off the Hedrickson horses. "The Lazy R bunch buried him out on the prairie and headed home the same day. They were the last to go, 'ceptin' us, o' course. We've been a-keepin' to ourselves. Out hyar. A-waitin'. Or workin' on the Hedrickson place. Done got our supplies fer headin' home." He cocked his head and remembered something. "Say, Tyrel, how'd that red hoss do fer ya? Were a mite green."

"Oh, he was fine. Just fine." Bannon decided it would be better to keep his dislike of the animal to himself.

"Well, that's damn good to hear." Randy turned his attention to Checker's black. "An' I reckon ol' Tuhupi did ya proud. That's some good-lookin' piece o' hossflesh."

Checker patted the horse's neck. "Yeah. He did good."

Without waiting, Randy explained that *tuhupi* was the Comanche word for "black." Bannon smiled; Jackson had told him that a dozen times.

"Damn it to hell, you been hurt, John." Randy saw Checker's swollen hand. "What the hell happened? Did I hurt ya . . . when we shook hands? Goddammit! Why didn't—"

Checker dismissed his injury as minor and explained that Sonny had been wounded and so had Bannon. He didn't say how Bannon was hurt. Randy's response was to shake his head and lament how many good men they had lost on this drive. Checker agreed.

"You boys better git on over to the chuck. Tug an' Mr.

Mitchell'll be wantin' to see you. I'll be along—after I see to these hosses."

As Checker, Johnny, and Bannon rode toward the chuck wagon, Captain, the camp's three-legged cow dog, barked his affection and Bannon jumped down to receive the animal's eager greeting. Johnny dismounted and joined Bannon in the dog's welcoming. A few steps behind the dog came Dan Mitchell, the Triple C trail boss. His manner indicated he had mostly recovered from the bullet wounds inflicted by McCallister's rustlers. His weathered face, though, was several shades lighter than its normal year-around brown.

His heavily bowed legs made walking look like the earth was substantially uneven. He might have been a bit paler than usual, but his grin made up for it. His brown war map of a face framed a thick, graying mustache and a chin that was shoved out to make it clear who was boss. The crease along his right ear, from a rustler's bullet, was only a dull red mark.

Checker guessed that the bullet wounds in Mitchell's lower right arm and shoulder were progressing as well. The tough cowman had wanted badly to go with them after the children and Star McCallister; Checker had refused to let him. There was no way Mitchell's body could have kept up with his will.

The big-eared cowman spat a long stream of tobacco juice, resettled a large chaw on the other side of his mouth, and bellowed, "Mighty good to see you boys. Mighty good. Climb down an' try on some of Tug's coffee. It ain't changed any. Hot an' thick."

"Good to see you're lookin' strong again, Dan." Checker dismounted and held out his hand.

Mitchell shook it heartily and ignored Checker's observation. "I see you brought back quite a crowd. Don't see that bastard McCallister in that bunch, though."

Managing to keep the grasp, Checker winced and

said, "No, wish he were. He got away. Left his men to do the fighting. An' his brother."

Mitchell didn't notice Checker's reaction. "From the looks of it, some of 'em didn't make it." He squinted at the slowly advancing three outlaws, then waved at Sonny and Jackson. "What's with that thar medicine wagon?"

Checker told him about the fake doctor being his younger half brother, his role in breaking out the Mc-Callister gang, and his subsequent death at Checker's hands. He planned on leaving the wagon and its team at the town livery, then wire the U.S. marshal in Nebraska, so they could notify the widow of the real doctor and wagon owner. He figured to pay for the livery keep until the federal lawmen advised them of what to do with the property. At some point, it was the law's concern, he observed.

"That's a might more'n fair," Mitchell said and returned to Checker's first comments. "Mighty sorry 'bout your lil' brother. Ain't your fault he were a skunk." He spat for emphasis. "A man ain't got no choice pickin' kin. Judge 'im by his friends."

Mitchell studied the tall man without speaking, spat another brown stream, and held out his hand for Johnny, then for Bannon, greeting both warmly. He repeated Randy's observation that all the Texas drovers had left Dodge. Spitting again, he said that included the six Circle J drovers, the men who had been wrongly arrested of breaking out the McCallister gang to lynch them. The other Texans in town made sure they weren't harmed, thanks to Checker's declaration of their innocence before he left to find the children.

With a sly grin, the grizzled trail boss repeated Randy's good news about the Hedrickson homestead, patting Johnny on the shoulder as he spoke. "The house, corral, an' the barn's back up at your sister's place. Finished it all two days back. 'Bout dusk, it were. Folks out that way weren't so sure anybody'd ever be needin' the place again. Miss Sarah convinced 'em otherwise." He stopped long enough to spit a thick stream of tobacco juice. "She was like a wolf after a calf. Determined as can be. Reckon they didn't know you an' your sister being tough an' all. But she did. Said you'd be comin' back an' your sis would make it. Us an' some o' the Texas boys done helped. A'fore they left fer home. That Ham fella, the stable man, was there too." He spat again and chewed aggressively. "Even got it fixed up inside, real nice an' purtylike. Miss Sarah did a lot of the cleaning herself. Think folks done brought some chairs an' such. Worked over some other stuff that weren't burned too bad. Yes, sir, looked real purty, I thought."

Checker's face was a mixture of joy and surprise. "Well, I'll be . . . that's more than I could have . . ."

Johnny's face was lit up and Bannon slapped him on the shoulder.

"There's more to do, I reckon." Mitchell splattered brown saliva against the rear wagon wheel. "Winter's probably gonna come too fast to do 'er now, though." He advised Checker they had found three loose Hedrickson horses that were now in the new barn, along with a good amount of hay. Several neighbors had helped cut the Hedrickson hay and stored it. Some of the corn crop was burned; the remaining acres had also been harvested and sold to pay for lumber.

Johnny was quiet with a strange twisted look painted on his face.

Looking up from scratching Captain's ears, Bannon asked, "Ya got anythan' to eat?"

Mitchell laughed. "Tug's workin' on some chow. Prob'ly didn't hear ya ride in." He turned and yelled, "Hey, Tug, our boys are back. They want to know if there's anythin' worth eatin'!"

With a bowl of biscuit dough in his fat hands, Tug waddled around the wagon tongue. He was a man of spare parts, it seemed. His walk was as though his right leg was shorter than the left. Stumpy, permanently tanned, and bald-headed, his beard filled with colors of red, gray, black, and splatters of dough. To make things worse, he couldn't hear well.

"Wha'd ya say?" He stopped midway crossing the tongue and almost fell over as he realized who had just ridden in. "Well, why didn't ya tell me the boys was back, Mr. Mitchell? Are ya hungry? Gonna have biscuits and stew in a bit."

The grizzled trail boss started to tell the cook that he had just told him, but spat again, instead. Repeating sentences for Tug was an everyday thing and had been for years. After the greetings, Tug told them that supper would be a little longer since he would be cooking for more.

Checker told them that he wanted to deliver the outlaws right away. He asked Bannon to stay with the children and went to tell Jackson and Sonny what he planned to do. He asked Johnny to stay and help with the horses, and the boy eagerly agreed.

Checker didn't want the children to go along when they moved the outlaws into the jail and confronted Marshal Rand, or his new deputies, if necessary. After that was done, he would come back and take them to see their mother. They would leave the medicine wagon at the livery on the way. He figured the Triple C crew would be eager to head for Texas now that they had returned.

Before greeting their trail friends, Jackson had pulled the medicine wagon a few yards from the mingling horses while Sonny watched the outlaws. Randy offered to move the two steers, tied to the wagon, while Jackson saddled his own horse. The wagon team would remain harnessed for the trip to town. Randy led the stubborn animals to a grassy area and retied their lead ropes to heavy rocks. They quickly began to graze as if this was an everyday occurrence.

Jackson didn't need to be told to be ready. Rebecca walked with him, hand in hand, toward the others, leading his readied horse. As soon as he introduced her to Mitchell and Tug, her questions began about the chuck wagon. Smiling, he swung into the saddle and pushed on his glasses

"Better hunker down, boys. She's not going to run out of questions soon. I'll be back before she does." Checker laughed and motioned to Jackson and Sonny to bring the outlaws as he remounted.

Although he was tired, his mind was working on the news from Randy and Mitchell. Checker wasn't surprised to hear the town marshal was still there, even though he had told Rand to leave once he realized the corrupt lawman had been involved in the McCallister gang breakout. Checker had told Rand that he would come after him for being a part of the killing of the two Triple C riders who had helped guard the jail. But the marshal would have logically assumed that Checker wouldn't make it.

But why would Do'tsi and his brother come to Dodge? They were killers for hire. That was all he knew about them. He knew little about the bigger brother, except of his reputation for fighting. Had Rand hired them just in case Checker did return? Maybe it was just a coincidence—and the Cherokee brothers were just passing through and needed cash. Maybe.

Sonny rode up beside him. "What's with these Indian deputies? You know 'em?"

"Heard of them, that's all. Do'tsi's a bad man with a gun. Likes killing. Really likes it. His brother broke a man's back in a bear hug—or so I heard."

"Why are they all of a sudden in Dodge? Thought you told Rand to leave." Sonny looked over his shoulder to make certain none of the outlaws tried anything. Their being this close to being imprisoned again, the urge might well grow stronger.

"Reckon Rand didn't figure we'd make it. Maybe they were just passing through and needed the money."

"You don't believe that," Sonny said. "Jackson thinks Star's in the wood pile."

"Good reason to ride ready."

Sonny wheeled his horse and returned to where Jackson trailed the outlaws.

CHAPTER EIGHTEEN

Late afternoon sun blistered the false-fronted buildings as they advanced toward the main intersection of Bridge and Front streets, and to the city jail, riding parallel to the shining railroad tracks cutting Front Street in two and stretching as far as the horizon allowed. The clinking of billiard balls and saloon laughter accompanied them for a few yards, then stayed behind. A shout of gambling achievement burst from a saloon, and all three swung their rifles in the direction of the noise. A woman's forced laugh from inside released them from the distraction.

The Great Western Hotel watched them silently from farther away on the south side of Front Street and First Avenue. Checker glanced at it; he had left his sister there near death. He looked back at Sonny and saw that he, too, was gazing there. Her battered face shot through Checker's mind, and his broad shoulders rose and fell with its passing. Seeing her like that had been raw on his thoughts for most of the trip. His fear of what they would find upon returning had worked his stomach like nothing he could recall, even though he continued to tell her children that she would recover.

He had willed himself to think she would. Checker's mind should have been dancing with joy. Amelia was alive. She was getting better. Her kids were safe. Hearing about the resurrected homestead was more good news. He had shared it with Sonny and Jackson on their ride to town; they were both surprised and pleased.

Yet there was no sense of victory. Only the dullness that came with knowing Star McCallister had not yet answered for his brutal crimes against his friends—and his family. Looming in his mental shadows was Star's connection to him. A strange thread of new concern about Do'tsi and his brother had settled in his thoughts, too. Could his half brother have sent them to Dodge as revenge?

"Hard to believe, Dodge looks like a real town, don't it?" Sonny observed. "Maybe there's a reason these Kansas folks don't like Texans comin' to visit."

"They like Texas money," Jackson said.

"Yeah, they do. Got a lot of mine, that's for damn sure." Sonny shook his head.

Several saloons were heavily boarded, suggesting they wouldn't be among the spring blossoms that came with the return of the Texas cattle drives and with them, the flocks of cattle buyers and speculators. Townsmen with a more dignified air—and fewer numbers—had replaced the raucous cowboys in other saloons. Most of the dance halls were sullen and empty. At the far end of the eastern section of merchants and saloons, however, the Dog Kelly Saloon appeared to be going as strong as ever.

From an upper window, he saw Thunder Alice, the whore who had introduced Bannon to the ways of the flesh. She smiled warmly and leaned far forward so her enormous breasts could be well viewed as her low-cut blouse fell away. Sonny's face reddened and he looked at his horse's ears as she called to him. He dared not look at any of his friends, but no one apparently heard her or didn't care.

The sound of a piano chuckling to itself could be heard as Checker, Jackson, and Sonny with the outlaws rode past a mostly empty Varieties Dance Hall on one side of the street and the quiet Lady Gay Dance Hall on the other.

With Checker's warning locked in their heads, the other two Triple C riders paid little attention to the changed atmosphere but, instead, were alert to any signs that Star McCallister might be in town, waiting to spoil their return. Across their saddles were readied Winchesters. Every window and building rooftop was examined from under their wide-brimmed hats. Instead of a sense of completion, each tingled with the edgy fear of riding into a trap.

Townspeople stopped their tasks to watch the silent riders with their grim outlaw bounty. Several men hollered their congratulations. The only drunken cowboy on the street was dressed in a suit of blue velveteen, now crusted with dirt and dried vomit, and a bell-crowned hat with the top crushed inward. As they rode by, he raised his half-filled glass of beer in tribute, burped, then stumbled and sat down hard on the planked sidewalk. He looked around to see who had yanked him. Seeing no one, he drank the rest of his beer from his sitting position.

From the alleyway came a rattling farm wagon loaded with supplies and five laughing kids. Checker and the others reined up to let it pass. The gray-headed farmer realized who he had just cut in front of and apologized loudly. His haggard wife looked at them, but didn't care.

Checker nodded. A part of the former Ranger half expected, half hoped, to see Sarah Ann Tremons standing on one of the wood-planked sidewalks to welcome him. But the rational side of his mind knew that didn't make any sense. She had no idea they were in town. Besides, no matter what Randy Reilman had told him, by now she had probably found a more worthy beau anyway, he told himself. Some townsman with accomplishment and money, he guessed. But he couldn't bring himself to ignore the earnest faces as they rode.

His Winchester lay easily in front of him, free of its saddle horn holster. Cocked. His face wasn't readable to anyone except those who knew him well. His left hand held it steady. He planned to use it left-handed, if need be. Using a pistol with his left hand was one thing; firing a rifle that way was quite another. He held the reins loosely in his right; the damaged hand was tingling and sore, but it was better than trying to handle a gun with it. As he rode, he squeezed and loosened his fist as if it would magically be well again. Each tension brought new pain.

His backup Colt remained in his waistband for use by his left, in case. It would be handier than the saddle pistol behind his right leg. He didn't really expect trouble, not even from Marshal Rand, but being ready was just a smart way to keep living.

Barely a whisper, the black outlaw Venner whispered to Jackson, "Big Tom did it, ya know. Honest, like I told you before. The rest o' us didn't wanna hurt them folks. We didn't wanna take them kids neither. Most o' us, anyhow. Honest, we didn't. I sneaked 'em extra food when Star n' Big Tom weren't watchin'. Star shot that Swede— an' he an' Redmond did the burnin' an' took them kids.

I didn't do no takin' of the lady neither. That were Tom. All I done was round up the hosses. I'm a hoss thief. I ain't no killer—an' no lady beater, nohow."

Jackson tilted his head to the side. "You should have told that to the judge."

Overhearing most of Venner's plea, Redmond snorted his disgust. "Ain't that jes' like a couple o' niggers? Whining back an' forth." His eyes sought Jackson's dark face. "Ya gonna step in an' try to save his dark ass, huh? Figgers."

Pushing his glasses back on his nose, Jackson turned toward Sonny. "It's hard to believe we're almost done with this awfulness. It'll be good to get back to handling beef again—and bitching about the weather."

Sonny nodded in agreement.

"Ya notice anythin' missin'?" Redmond carved a half smile on his unshaven face. "Ain't no hangin' stand up there no more." He chuckled. "Reckon these folks didn't rate you boys too high—'bout catchin' up with us."

Without looking at him, Checker said, "They expected us to leave you facedown in the Nations."

Wells growled at Redmond to be quiet.

Recognizing the significance of the approaching riders, a goateed man in a green brocade vest, string tie, and boiled white shirt burst through the hand-carved door of the Nueces Saloon, hurried down the street, and disappeared into the city marshal's office.

As the Triple C riders and their captives pulled up in front of the small jail building on the opposite side of the railroad tracks, a thin man in a black swallow-tailed coat, high boots, and flat-brimmed hat appeared in the doorway. A double-barreled shotgun was cradled in his arms. Clenched teeth created a strange reptilian smile. From under his frock coat, part of a deputy marshal's badge partially revealed itself pinned to his black vest. Confidence oozed from every part of him.

Checker's eyes went quickly from the shotgun to the gun belt strapped over his coat. A long-barreled pistol in a short holster rested on his left thigh for a right-hand draw. A reddish jewel glistened within the black handle. It matched the gleaming opal on his pinky finger ring.

So this was Do'tsi. It had to be.

Do'tsi spoke and it looked like a snake opening its jaws. "You must be Captain John Checker, the great Texas Ranger. Glad to see the gods thought we should meet in this world." He examined the faces of the outlaws and asked, "I assume this is some of the McCallister gang you went after—or so I was advised. Where are the rest? Where is this notorious Star McCallister I've heard about? Did you have to kill him?"

Checker swung down from his black horse and held the Winchester in his left hand at his side. "Didn't find him. The others didn't want to come. Where's Rand?" To himself, he asked where the other brother was.

"That is most unfortunate. I hear Star McCallister is one mean bastard," Do'tsi said, not taking his eyes off Checker. "An evil god." His following laugh was a trill and it made Jackson shiver in spite of himself. He couldn't remember seeing a more evil man.

Sonny seemed to be paying more attention to the large black dog that had stepped to Do'tsi's side and bared white fangs. He mimicked the dog's expression with an exaggerated toothy stare and chuckled. "Now, there's a real Kansas welcome. He looks like some of the store owners I've met in this town."

Jackson glanced at him but didn't smile. A black Texas cowboy was even less thought of than a Texas cowboy, except for his money. He was drawn to Do'tsi, then studied the rooftops of nearby buildings. This had to be Star McCallister's doing. Nothing else made sense. Did Checker and Sonny see it that way? It had to mean the outlaw leader had returned—and not gone to another town, as Checker thought.

With his rifle leaning against his leg, Checker took a bag of tobacco from his shirt pocket and rolled a cigarette, taking time to smooth the paper's ends carefully before placing it in his mouth. His right hand didn't want to cooperate so he tried to make the preparation look deliberately slow. Finally, he popped a match alive from his belt buckle and inhaled the new smoke. He didn't want the cigarette but he wanted the time—and the opportunity—to see how much agility his right hand would provide. The answer wasn't the one he wanted.

To the Cherokee gunman, it seemed like the cigarette assembly took an hour. To himself, he counted the various steps Checker took. Thirteen. A magical number in ancient Cherokee religion. World without end, it represented. Reincarnation. Patting the black beast's head, he waited, enjoying his adversary's approach. He sucked on his pipe between clenched teeth, letting it hide his eagerness.

"Do'tsi, isn't it?" The words came like a rattlesnake striking, wrapped within the first strand of white smoke from Checker's cigarette.

"Ah, the great Captain John Checker has heard of me. That is, indeed, satisfying."

"I know lots of people." Checker cocked his head to the side and retrieved his rifle with his right hand.

Pain shot through the back of his hand when he gripped the Winchester, and he grabbed the weapon with his left as well, to take away the pressure. His grimace was masked by looking down at the gun and checking to see if it was cocked. He knew it was. Carefully, he eased the hammer and trigger back into a safety position and shoved it into his saddle horn sleeve. The activity gave him time to let the pain pass without anyone, except his friends, noticing.

"This is what's left of McCallister's gang," Checker said, speaking slowly to hide the loss of breath taken by the throbbing from his damaged hand. "You can add kidnapping, arson, robbery, murder, and attempted murder as new charges." He didn't mention rape; his sister didn't need that stigma. That thought triggered more anger. "I asked you a question—where's Rand?" It was a throaty snarl.

"They've been busy lads, it would seem." Do'tsi didn't react to the question or the tone and lowered the shotgun to his right side with his right hand. "I take it you have proof of these accusations. Marshal Rand will need that." He patted the dog's head again. "It was my understanding that eight prisoners escaped, including Star McCallister. What happened to the others?"

"Don't know. We just went to get my sister's children."

"What happened to their boots? And their socks?"

"Guess they lost them."

"How many of you Triple C men are there . . . now?" Do'tsi enjoyed the last word.

Shoulder-length black hair brushed against Checker's shoulders as he positioned himself a step below the planked sidewalk. The arrowhead-shaped scar on his right cheek was redder than usual. He took the cigarette from his mouth.

"Enough to handle most trouble, I suppose." He laid his right hand gently on his holstered pistol butt. "Look, Do'tsi, I'm in no mood for games. We've been on a long ride to find two kidnapped children and return these men to justice." Checker's eyes locked with the Cherokee gunman's. "Better talk real straight real fast. I asked where Rand is." He paused. "While I'm at it, where is your brother?"

"My, my. A bit testy, aren't we?" Do'tsi said. "Bring these men inside and put them in the open cells." His upper lip curled against his teeth as he enjoyed the observation. "Marshal Rand is out of town—on business. He will be sorry to have missed you." His forefinger rested against his thin nose and slid down it. "My brother is inside. He will be happy to meet you. He's heard a lot about your Indian fighting ways."

Two businessmen in slouch hats and gray greatcoats, walking together, stopped to watch the proceedings. They stood at the edge of the planked sidewalk next to the alley separating the last building from the jail itself.

Out of earshot, the larger man said to his associate, "I can't tell which ones are the outlaws, can you? They all look like ruffians to me. I'll be glad when the day comes that we don't need those Texas herds."

The squatty, older man squinted toward the busy group. "Me too. Especially the black ones. You know, that tall fella reminds me of somebody. I just can't place who, though."

"Well, if it's anybody who used to live in Dodge, you'd be the one to know." The taller businessman pulled a gold watch with its dangling chain from his broadcloth vest pocket and clicked open the lid. "He doesn't look like anyone I know—or want to know. I think the whole bunch of them railroaded Star. There's no way he had anything to do with their precious cattle being stolen. No way."

The older man withdrew two cigars from his coat pocket and handed one to his talkative friend.

"Can you believe the marshal hired two redskins as deputies! What in the world possessed his mind to do that?" The taller businessman received the cigar and drew it to his nose to savor the aroma. "I've a good mind to talk with Judge Buchanan about it."

"Yes, I would agree. Completely out of line. I've told the

mayor what I think—and that the town council needs to take charge. What will other cities think of us? Dodge has Indian lawmen. My word! We'll be a laughingstock."

"Don't say it so loud, Henry."

"Oh. Of course."

CHAPTER NINETEEN

Outside the jail, Checker, Sonny, and Jackson untied the outlaws, and the various ropes were recoiled and laid over their saddles. Like Checker, Sonny had re-booted his rifle and drawn his pistol. Jackson kept his Winchester and took a position several feet from the jail entrance. Holding his gun at the ready, the black drover stood facing Do'tsi, who remained on the other side of the door.

The only reaction from Do'tsi was a nearly imperceptible, yet condescending, sneer.

With a wave of his pistol, Sonny marched the three barefooted outlaws toward the marshal's office with Venner in the lead. Tossing his cigarette into the street, Checker followed a step behind the three outlaws. Sonny brought up the rear.

After a long, exaggerated bow, Do'tsi stepped aside, telling his dog to do as well. The animal reluctantly obeyed, slipping directly behind him and growling at the approaching men. Venner appeared especially nervous about the large beast.

"You gonna keep that thing away . . . from us?"

"Of course. Zoro is quite gentle. Unless."

"Unless what?" Venner's eyes were wide as he hesitated at the doorway.

"Unless you don't do as you are told."

" 'Zoro? What kinda name is that?" Venner asked as he walked sideways.

Do'tsi's face twisted into a cruel mask. "You wouldn't understand. Ah, let's say it means man-eater . . . and he's developed a taste for dark meat."

Venner hopped inside. There was no sign of the man who had alerted Do'tsi; evidently he had exited through the rear door. Standing along the front wall was a powerfully built Cherokee dressed strangely in a suit coat, paper collar, and white shirt, a rumpled cravat and an old top hat, but no pants, only a breechcloth and knee-high moccasins. A deputy badge was hung lopsided from his coat lapel.

Venner started to laugh, but decided against it as he glimpsed a machete handle from a quiver slung over his shoulder.

Kana'ti stared at the black outlaw through slitted eyes, and Venner gulped and hurried toward the opened cells.

Sonny nodded jauntily at the black-attired deputy as he nudged Redmond along with the nose of his pistol. Do'tsi returned the greeting by touching the brim of his hat with his gun. As he passed, Sonny again mimicked the dog's threatening grimace. Wells quietly told him not to agitate the animal.

"Git along, big black doggie, git along," Sonny sang and laughed.

Inside, nothing had changed in the office since the

gang's breakout, except the bodies of the two dead
deputies and two Triple C guards had been removed
long ago. Scattered papers occupied the majority of the
marshal's scarred desk. A blackened coffeepot continued its lonely vigil on the overworked and stammering
stove in the corner. A lopsided rack of rifles and one
shotgun took most of one wall. Two wall lamps cast a
sallow light across the cramped room.

The row of six cells along the farthest wall completed
the area; only one was currently occupied by a man
sleeping deeply, if the heavy snoring meant anything. A
small back door, heavily padlocked, was almost hidden
by the large iron frames.

Do'tsi trailed them, telling his dog to remain on the
sidewalk. He glanced at Jackson in passing. "Won't Captain John Checker let you come in?"

Jackson's dark face was stone.

Do'tsi laughed. "Looks like Captain John Checker
trains his coloreds well."

"Leave the door open," Jackson spat.

"Certainly." Stepping inside, Do'tsi commanded in a
confident voice, "Put him in the farthest one." He
pointed at Venner and said something to his brother in
Cherokee. Kana'ti grinned.

"Captain John Checker, this is my brother, Kana'ti."

The string of outlaws—accompanied by Checker and
Sonny—tramped by the strangely dressed Cherokee.
Kana'ti made no attempt to greet them; his silent eyes
stayed on Checker as he walked behind the others. He
muttered something that made Do'tsi shake his head.

"*Osiyo,*" Checker said without stopping. "*Kana'ti.* The
wolf."

"Ah, so you speak the language of the Cherokee,"
Do'tsi said.

Checker stopped beside the cell where Redmond
was entering and turned toward the bigger brother.

"Only a little." He pushed the brim of his hat back with his left hand, as he often did when concerned.

"*Siyo*," Do'tsi responded.

Checker recognized the Cherokee word for "of course." With his chin raised, he said, "My Comanche friends call me *Tuhtseena Maa Tatsinuupi*, Wolf with Star. The wolf is my spirit helper. I wear a medicine pouch of wolf medicine. It is strong." He repeated the statement in Comanche, staring at Kana'ti.

"*Wado*. It is good, Captain. Your Comanche is good," Do'tsi said, his eyes wide with appreciation as he spoke in Cherokee to his brother.

Kana'ti stepped forward from the wall; his face was a question. His words came in a guttural string.

"My brother wants to know, how strong is this wolf medicine?" Do'tsi smiled and his whole face was bright.

Without glancing at Do'tsi, Checker said to Kana'ti in Cherokee, "Strong enough to handle him."

"Ah, the great Captain John Checker does know Cherokee."

Kana'ti's hands became tight fists. His response was in his native tongue. Checker knew from the way it was spoken that it was a challenge to him.

"Tell your brother I have more important things to do than mess with his silliness." Checker's gaze alternated between the two Cherokee killers as he slammed shut Redmond's cell door.

Amused, Do'tsi repeated the statement and Kana'ti's eyebrows rose and he grunted a response.

"My brother says your medicine is from the wolf's cousin, the whining coyote." Do'tsi snickered.

"Where are the keys?" Checker said, motioning for Wells to enter the cell beside Redmond.

"I have them." Do'tsi cradled his shotgun in his left arm and patted his coat pocket with his right.

"Lock them up."

"I take it you accept my brother's assessment of your spirit medicine." Do'tsi cocked his head to the side as he pulled a ring of keys from his coat pocket.

"Your brother is quite the wit. Or is he the fool? Ask him."

Do'tsi's eyes flickered hatred.

"I said, 'Ask him.'"

His eyes narrowing, the Cherokee gunman spat Checker's response in Cherokee.

The big man took a step forward, his fists coming up, his face black with anger.

Without looking away from closing Wells's cell door, Checker said, "Tell your brother to settle down or I'll put a bullet in his brain. I'm tired and don't need any more of this crap." His right hand settled lightly on the broken gun in his holster.

"The second bullet comes from me." Sonny's challenge caused Do'tsi to whirl his head in the cowboy's direction. Sonny touched the brim of his hat with his pistol barrel, imitating Do'tsi's earlier gesture.

Turning to his brother, Do'tsi told Kana'ti to step back and be quiet. Shaking his head, the big Cherokee obliged, but his eyes never left Checker.

Sonny moved back to the side of the door, looked outside, and waved at Jackson, like a kid waving at a classmate. Holding his Winchester at the ready, Jackson had returned to their horses, standing where he could see both sides of the jail and in either direction. The black drover shook his head and waved at Sonny. It had been his idea to stand guard outside. Who knew what else Star McCallister might have in store for them?

Checker walked over to the marshal's desk and leaned against it, watching Do'tsi lock each cell and noting the gunman kept the shotgun balanced in his left arm. He glanced at the stack of papers dominating the desk. Next to it lay a current edition of the *Dodge City Gazette*, folded into reading position. A ten-bit Fairchild ink pen sat in its holder. A long-stemmed pipe was still smoking. A leather-bound book about the mysterious land of Japan lay on top of one pile of warrants. A little out of Rand's class, Checker thought.

Why did that book seem familiar? Checker knew he had seen it—or one like it—before. Maybe just in passing. He read the upside-down title, *History of Japan*. His mind wouldn't release the location, so he returned his attention to the locking of the cells. Bone-tired, the former Ranger knew he must stay alert for any tricks by the Cherokees. He wasn't worried about anything happening outside with Jackson there. A hot bath and a good sleep sounded mighty tempting.

Everything was progressing without incident, other than the expected cursing. As Do'tsi locked Wells's cell, Redmond grunted a string of obscenities; Wells muttered something no one could hear. Do'tsi dropped his right hand to the trigger guard of the cradled shotgun and both men were quiet. He completed the lockup and stepped away.

Redmond spat, "This ain't over, Cole."

From the doorway, Sonny smiled. "Just about . . . for you, Big Tom. Just about."

"Hey, lawdawg, this hyar's Cole Dillon. Wanted in Texas." Redmond pointed at Sonny through the bars. "Ya kin become a big man if'n you bring him in."

Do'tsi's showed he didn't like the reference to his not already being well known.

Sonny started to respond, but Checker blurted, "Well, whadda ya know? All this time I thought you were Clay Allison."

Sonny shook his head and laughed. "Hey, I thought you were."

Do'tsi snorted at the joke and Kana'ti joined in, his eyes never leaving Checker.

"You should've told me when we were in Texas, Sonny, I could have used the reward," Checker added to the banter.

"Well, I should've. We could'a split it." Sonny bit his lower lip and stepped into the doorway.

"That's the truth, lawdawg." Redmond slammed his fist against the bars.

Do'tsi sneered. "Shut up. You are bothering me."

Wells pushed through the bars at Redmond to get him to stop talking and said politely, "Officer, we could sure use some chow. Boots an' socks'd be nice too."

"Food will come later. Boots are for men."

Redmond snarled a threat under his breath. Only Wells heard him and told him to shut up.

Checker's gaze finally sought the wood floor and the darkened spots there. Blood spots. Some from the blood of two Triple C friends who had been helping guard the jail. When he looked up, Sonny was staring at the same thing from the doorway.

"Lots of stories about Captain John Checker. Big ones." Do'tsi's view took in the jail weapon rack.

He counted the number of weapons to himself without thinking about it. Eight. Six rifles and two shotguns, counting the one he held. The number that represents starting over, repeating the octave. Reincarnation. He smiled. Eight was his favorite number.

"Like you crossing the Rio Grande right behind some Mexican outlaws. You killed four in the water and captured the other six." He continued his presentation through clenched teeth. "Of course, there's that wild one about you becoming friends with some old Comanche war chief. Now, that's a tall one."

"It was two and three," Checker said, breaking away

from his review of the bloodstained floor. "And Stands-in-Thunder was his name."

Do'tsi appeared amused. He said something in Cherokee that no one understood except his brother, who grunted.

Checker responded in Comanche and no one understood that either.

Do'tsi laughed. "I like you, Captain John Checker. It's going to be a real honor to kill you. Not now, of course." From his vest pocket, he deftly took a match and snapped it along the edge of his shotgun, still carried in his left arm. The movement was swift and designed to make it appear he was going for his gun.

In response, Sonny's fist came up from his side with his own Colt cocked.

Kana'ti started to reach for his machete, stopping as he saw Sonny's gun was now pointed at his stomach.

Do'tsi's gleeful expression at seeing Sonny react was almost childlike. His eyes playfully rose from watching the match flame to catch the cowboy's reddened face.

"Hard way to keep living, Do'tsi. Playing games with real men." Checker motioned for Sonny to lower the weapon. "Tell Rand I'm looking for him."

"I understand you made a threat upon the life of a peace officer." Do'tsi's eyes brightened.

"He will answer for the murder of our two friends."

"My, my. That's for the law to decide, isn't it?" Do'tsi folded his arms. "And I am the law, I and my brother."

"For now." Checker's response was less than the gunman desired. And more. The threat was there. Unspoken but clear.

"There is the smell of death in this room," Do'tsi said. "Your eyes tell me it was blood you cared about."

"Some belonged to our friends," Checker said. "But you already knew that."

Do'tsi changed the subject and asked the former Ranger if he had ever heard about an ancient Persian religion that told of a wise man who was given the life span of seven vultures. He fed and cared for them, and died at the same moment as the seventh vulture died.

"Can't say as I have, Do'tsi. Sounds like quite a story." Checker glanced again at the book as he straightened himself to leave. "Does your dog like eating vultures too?"

Stepping away from the wall, Do'tsi cocked his head to the side. "All religions are about the same when it comes to death. It's the journey afterward that's different." He waited for a response; none came. "The Comanches believe in reincarnation, don't they? Do you think you'll come back, Captain John Checker?"

"Hadn't given it much thought, Do'tsi. Too busy staying alive." Checker straightened a stack of papers on the desk, hoping it would help him recall where he had seen the book. Of course. He had seen it at the outlaws' hideout when he sneaked in to get the children. That was hours before McCallister escaped. Was it just an interesting coincidence?

Do'tsi's eyes flashed, but he changed the subject. "You know, the Comanches would have made up songs for great warriors like us." His smile was broad. "Can you imagine how great one of us will be—when he kills the other?"

Sonny purposely stepped forward from the doorway, stopping between Checker, standing next to the desk, and the black-clothed killer, essentially blocking Do'tsi's view of Checker. The tenseness in Sonny's face was obvious; he didn't like this Cherokee deputy or his manner.

The snake-faced man's nostrils flared in anger. "Get out of the way, whatever your name is, I'm talking to Captain John Checker."

"*Mr.* Jones to you, pecker head."

Do'tsi snickered. "Move out of the way, cowboy. You're not that good."

Sonny smiled. "Really? You know, I wouldn't be so loose with my mouth around folks I didn't know. We ain't in the Nations no more." His right hand held the readied Colt at his side.

"I know enough. You've already taken lead." He pointed at the dried bloodstains on Sonny's shirt and grinned.

"That I did—and the man that gave it to me is dead."

Checker moved toward the door and patted Sonny on the back with his right as he passed. "Let's go, Sonny. We'll be back, Do'tsi, to see how the prisoners are doing. Their horses are now city property. I assume you will see that they get properly watered and fed."

"When do you think your right hand will be able to hold a gun again, Captain John Checker?"

CHAPTER TWENTY

Silence rode with the three riders as they headed toward the Triple C camp along Front Street, riding parallel to the railroad tracks, and turned south between the blocks that separated the Varieties and the Lady Gay dance halls. Each man was drawn inward to his thoughts about what had just happened as the wonders of Dodge became mere backdrops of shadow and sound.

A teenaged girl in boiled bonnet, shirtwaist, overgaiters, and a tie-string purse, strolled across the street in front of them, oblivious of their approach. They reined to a halt to let her pass. She looked up, smiled, and continued, hoping the men would watch her exaggerated exit. The interruption served to break their individual reveries.

Patting the Colt in the pocket of his long coat, Jackson said, "John, if you stay in this town, you're going to have to kill both of those men." He pushed back his wandering eyeglasses. "They're here to kill you. It's Star McCallister's doing, I can feel it."

Neither Sonny nor Checker responded as they resumed their ride. The girl glanced back at them, disappointed to see they weren't watching her. The easy thud of their horses took them past the last buildings. Ahead was the river, the Triple C camp, and an unending horizon. A wagonload of prostitutes rattled past them on the way to Fort Dodge, headed for a new market now that the Texas cowboys had left. Several of the girls waved. None of the riders paid any attention; their thoughts had blanked out any distractions.

"Or do you think Rand decided to buy some courage?" Checker asked, not mentioning the book he'd seen and deciding it was just coincidence after all.

Neither man answered the question.

"You need the doc to look at your hand, John. I'm sure there are broken bones in there," Jackson advised. "You need to have him check you, too, Sonny. Those wounds are a long way from healed."

Checker frowned.

"What I need is a good cigar and a tall glass of rye." Sonny grinned widely.

Jackson's dark forehead wrinkled. "Do'tsi isn't funny. He's a killer. So's that big brother of his. Biggest Indian I ever saw. He likes to kill—with his hands. They're here for a reason, John."

"Look, this is supposed to be a happy day. We've got Amelia's kids back safe—and it sounds like she's gonna be all right." Sonny twisted in the saddle to face first Checker on his right, then Jackson on his left. "Let's forget those two bastards for now, damn it—and get to being happy that those little folks are gonna see their mother. We can worry later."

The immediate response was for Checker to nudge

his black into a lope, and his friends followed. The tall former Ranger glanced over at them. "For once, Jackson, Sonny is right. It's time to be happy."

The clatter of hoofbeats across the Arkansas River Bridge was a song, and Sonny began to sing along with the rhythm. Ahead of them was a sprawling, windswept land broken only by the Triple C chuck wagon and a fat group of horses.

"Oh, John Checker, don't you cry for me. I'm goin' to see Amelia with her kids next to me," Sonny bellowed into the dusky air.

Jackson shook his head.

Checker leaned his head back and howled like a wolf.

Johnny saw them coming and started running toward the three men. A half dozen steps behind came a determined Rebecca. Dan Mitchell, Tug, Randy, and Tyrel Bannon stood, each with a coffee cup in his hand.

"Can we go see Mama now? Can we?" Johnny asked excitedly as they reined up.

"Just as soon as you get washed and into clean clothes," Checker announced as he swung down. "Get your horse. Becky, come on and ride with me."

Placing her hands on her hips, the little girl pursed her lips. "Can I ride with Uncle Sonny?"

Checker laughed. "Of course you can."

Sonny jumped down and knelt to receive her enthusiastic approach.

Rebecca quickly announced that she, Johnny, and "Uncle Tyrel" had been given honey and biscuits to eat, and that it was the "best she ever had." Captain happily followed them for attention—and an occasional bite of biscuit.

The chuck wagon had definitely been readied for travel since they left for town, Checker noted to himself. Tied-on water barrels were dripping through their lids. Wheels were freshly greased. The big toolbox hanging on the side of the wagon, opposite the water barrel, was repacked and tied in place. It contained a shovel, ax, branding irons, horseshoeing equipment, hobbles, rods for the pot rack, and extra skillets.

Sturdily built, the wide-beamed wagon, with its bent-wood bows holding protective canvas, had been previously loaded with foodstuff for the return trip—sacks of green coffee beans, flour, sugar, salt, dried apples, pinto beans, and cornmeal, as well as boxes of soda, canned goods, and wraps of salt pork and bacon.

A box of tobacco squares, papers, cigars, and tobacco sacks was shoved in there, too, along with two bottles of King Bee whiskey, one of Rebel Yell bourbon, one of Jameson's Irish whiskey, and a jug of Old Bison straight rye. They walked to the open end of the chuck wagon so that Mitchell could show them their preparation for the trip home. In addition to food supplies, a book of Tennyson poems, a new deck of cards, and three *Harper's Bazaar* magazines were shoved into the corner.

There were also several bars of John H. Woodbury's facial soap that Tug had discovered and grown fond of. A store of medicines had been packed away, including Coltsfoot Ague pills, Saint-John's-wort, and calamine lotion. The trip home wouldn't take anywhere nearly as long as the drive north. Riders and a wagon could go a lot farther in a day than a bunch of grazing beef. Still, the supplies would be needed.

Without any preamble, Mitchell said he would like to buy the twelve Hedrickson geldings to take back to Texas; Randy was quite high on the well-broken mounts. He offered forty dollars a head; Checker said he wanted to keep four of them to give to the neighbors for their help in rebuilding the ranch. Mitchell readily agreed.

There was no advantage in keeping all the geldings

through the winter. Checker had already planned on adding more mares and another stallion at some point. Only the best would be kept for breeding; the idea of creating a successful horse ranch was growing within him. Maybe this was the place to hang up his gun and reputation.

Quietly, Sonny told the trail boss that he was staying to help his friend, and Mitchell indicated he wasn't surprised.

White-faced and visibly torn, Bannon listened and wished he could say the same.

"Tyrel, I'd like you to go with us to see my sister," Checker said. "Dan, would that be all right with you?"

"You bet." Mitchell winked and spat.

Bannon's mouth twisted. "I . . . ah, want to—"

"Your mother and sister will be right glad to see you," Checker interrupted, anticipating what was on the young farm boy's mind.

Sonny glanced at Jackson, preoccupied with adding a bow to Rebecca's hair. No one else could do it well enough to suit her, not even Checker.

Spitting a thick stream of tobacco juice, Mitchell told the three men that the chuck wagon and horses would pull out for Texas in the morning since they had returned. He hoped to make it to the ranch before cold weather set in. Checker thanked him for staying until they returned.

"We'll come back and take the Hedrickson herd on to their place." Checker rubbed his unshaven chin. "Steers too. Maybe we'd better do it now. Before we lose daylight."

"Do it in the mornin' if'n ya want to. They ain't goin' nowhere," Mitchell said. "Weren't ya gonna haul that fancy wagon into town?"

"Yes, I was."

"You're gonna need a good milk cow for them young'uns, John," Mitchell advised. "Wish I had one to give ya."

"Been thinking about that," Checker said. "Figure a neighbor might sell us one."

Mitchell spat. "Don't let 'em be too proud 'bout it."

"I'll try not to." Checker grinned.

Johnny's face was a scowl. "Do we have to take a bath before we see Mama?"

Checker patted his shoulder and smiled. "I think we all do."

"I reckon you'll find that new barn to your likin', son," Mitchell observed.

Leaning against the chuck wagon, Randy drank deeply from his coffee cup. "I'll keep an eye on your herd." He threw the remainder of the brew toward the open ground. "Need to see how that roan o' our'n's doin'. A mite heady. 'Fraid o' his shadow. He were one o' Woodman's string, 'member?"

"We'll trade 'im for some milk an' eggs an' sech on the way. We got eight good'uns to take its place." Mitchell nodded support of his own declaration and added, "Sure hope you'll come an' have supper with us. Tug's already workin' on somethin' special, he says. 'Sumbitch Stew' from the looks of it." He glanced around to make certain the children hadn't heard his description.

"Sounds good to me," Checker said.

"Sure 'nuff." Mitchell spat and his eye caught Bannon's empty holster for the first time. "Hey, Tryel, what happened to your Colt? Did ya lose it already?"

Checker answered before the farm boy could. "He lost it in the fight—with the Comanches. Got two of them while they were sneaking up on our wagon."

Mitchell nodded appreciatively.

Self-consciously, Bannon unbuckled the useless gun belt and shoved it into the back of the chuck wagon where the men kept their bedrolls and extra clothes. Silently, he thanked Checker for lying about what had really happened—and was thankful Mitchell couldn't see the cut on his head, for that would have brought more questions.

An hour later, after baths and clean clothes, the five men and two children left the medicine wagon and its horses at Ham's Livery. The small, but sturdy, stable operator greeted them warmly, especially Checker. The former Ranger explained the situation, including the death of Blue McCallister masquerading as a medicine peddler and being the key to the gang's escape.

Surprisingly, Ham expressed his suspicion of the man the day he came to town; he volunteered his own assessment of Marshal Rand and his likely involvement. It matched that of the riders. Checker offered to pay in advance and Ham told him it wasn't necessary.

Pointing to two stalls near the far side of the cavernous stable, Ham asked if they were ready for the gray mare and brown gelding Jackson had left for fresh horses when they set out after the McCallister gang and the kidnapped children. Ham volunteered that both animals were superior to the ones taken, the only horses he had available at the time. Checker told him to keep them as a thank-you for coming through when they were in bad need of new mounts, as payment for taking care of them, and for helping at the ranch. Ham reluctantly agreed and pledged his help whenever they needed it.

It wasn't long afterward that the group pulled up in front of a small, one-story frame house shoved into the residential section of Dodge City. Both men and children were excited; especially the children, jabbering to each other. A comfortable side porch and a gravel walkway to the street beckoned. Yellow glow from room lights was inviting and letting the dusk know it wouldn't be allowed inside.

Dismounting, Sonny lifted Rebecca from her place at the front of his saddle. "You look absolutely beautiful, little lady."

She smiled demurely and looked down at her just-purchased dress. "Do you think Mommy will like this? I don't know if she likes blue."

"She'll like it, sugar. More important, she'll be mighty happy to see you two. It's just the kinda medicine she needs." Sonny looped the reins over the hitching rack.

"Are my mommy and daddy staying here? Why aren't they at our house?" she asked, her bright eyes searching Sonny's.

"Ah, your mommy is here. Remember, she was . . . ah, hurt real bad. She's staying here to get well," Sonny stammered. "She will be very happy to see you and Johnny." He couldn't tell her the rest of the story.

"Does she know where we've been?"

"Yes, she does."

"Did the fire go away—from our home?" Rebecca's eyes were bright and wide.

"Some, I think," Sonny said. "We'll go there tomorrow and see."

"Will Daddy be there?"

Sonny looked away. Couldn't someone else deal with this? Why should he have to be the one? Or should he let Checker or Amelia? Anyone?

"Uncle Sonny, did you hear me? Will Daddy be at our house when we go there tomorrow?" Rebecca's voice was urgent and indignant.

"No. No, he won't, honey." Sonny swallowed. "Your daddy . . . is in heaven. It's real nice an' pretty there. He's real happy."

"Will he come back? Doesn't he want to see us?"

Jackson overheard the conversation and knew his friend was dealing with something neither Checker nor he had wanted to do. He leaned over in the saddle and touched her troubled face.

"Miss Becky, y'all remember your mother and father taking ya to Sunday meetings?" Jackson's voice was soft.

"I think so."

Sonny was relieved to have help with this discussion. He glanced over at Checker, who was talking to Johnny and Bannon.

Jackson continued, "Miss Becky, your father was killed by those evil men we got you away from. He died trying to save you and your mother—and your brother. He was very brave. Now he's in heaven with God."

Her face disappeared into a ball of tears.

Checker looked over and Sonny mouthed, "We told her about her dad."

CHAPTER TWENTY-ONE

Nodding, the former Ranger swung down from the saddle, looped the reins over the hitching rack, and walked over. Without saying anything, he lifted the sobbing girl into his arms and began whispering that they were going to see her mother and she wouldn't want to be crying. He wiped at her wet cheeks with his fingers.

"Uncle John, I want to see my daddy." She pulled back in his arms and put her tiny hand on his freshly shaved chin.

"I know you do. I'd like to, too," Checker said, amazed at his own calmness. "Sometimes, we don't get our wishes, no matter how much we want them. Right now, though, we are going to see your mother."

"Does she know about my daddy?"

"Yes, she does. She misses him a lot, just like you."

His hair slicked into place, Johnny jumped down from his horse and joined them. Like Rebecca's apparel, Johnny's clothes were new, just purchased. The boy's face was strained with a mixture of worry and joy.

"Becky, you quit that. I tolt you a'fore about Paw. You quit your cryin', we're gonna see Mama. You quit it now, you hear?"

A sniffle followed, but Rebecca didn't cry again. "Mommy will be glad to see me, won't she?"

"Oh my, yes, she certainly will," Checker said and hugged Johnny with his other arm. The movement brought pain to his right hand. "She'll be very happy to see you—and her fine son."

Johnny's smile was part pride and part grief. He was flushed with the need to be strong, to be the man of the household.

Rebecca was silent and staring at her big brother. Checker was clearly relieved and fatigued.

The three men swung down from their horses, their faces painted with a range of emotions. Sonny looked like he was going to be sick; Tyrel Bannon's expression was the same as when he had a stomachache; and Jackson appeared uneasy. But all were bathed, shaved, and in fresh clothes. And all were drained by the emotion of finally dealing with telling the little girl about her dead father.

The door of the house swung open and a tall man with spectacles, a skinny mustache and graying hair appeared. Dr. Tremons waved enthusiastically and began walking toward them, limping as always. Sonny caught Checker's attention and both grinned at the thought of hearing again of the doctor's participation at Little Round Top during the Battle of Gettysburg and how two Confederate rifle bullets had stiffened his left leg.

"By all that's holy, it is you!" Dr. Tremons exclaimed as he scooted down the rock-strewn pathway. "I knew you boys'd make it, I just knew it." In combination came two of his more visual habits; he pushed his spectacles into place, wet two fingers of his right hand in his mouth, and attempted to lock a straying lock of hair back into place on his graying pompadour.

"Howdy, Doc, it's mighty good to see you, too," Checker said. "How's Amelia?"

Tremons stopped, inhaled, and stroked the lock once more. "She's a mighty strong woman. Mighty strong. Took us a week before she'd let me take that button out of her hand. Kept mumbling that it was a promise."

Carrying Rebecca in his left arm, Checker held out his hand and Tremons shook it warmly. The tall gunfighter grimaced as the handshake brought a jolt of pain.

"Hey, what's the matter?" Dr. Tremons slid his hand away, holding Checker's fingers to examine them. "Damn, how'd you do this, John? There's broken bones in there."

"We had some trouble coming through the Territory."

Jackson immediately told the doctor about the fight with Comanches, about Sonny being wounded at the gang's hideout, and Bannon's blow on the head. He didn't mention how it happened, instead told about bringing in three outlaws, about Star McCallister escaping, and Star's younger brother posing as a medicine show peddler and being killed.

"I'll need to look at the three of you," Dr. Tremons declared, glancing first at Checker, then at Sonny and the farm boy. Satisfied, he greeted the others with the same enthusiasm as he did Checker, talking all the while that he hoped Checker didn't mind his moving Amelia to his house. He thought it was a better place for her to heal.

"Can I go see Mama now?" Johnny asked.

"Of course you can, son. Of course." Dr. Tremons motioned for the boy to follow him as he fingered his glasses and played with his hair.

Sonny walked over to Checker, who was responding to a question from Rebecca, nestling in his arms. "You go with the kids. Jackson, Tyrel, and me'll stay here."

She looked at Sonny and frowned. "Uncle Sonny, aren't you going with us?"

"You go on. I've . . . we've got good feelings about her . . . her gettin' well." Sonny's neck reddened.

Checker bobbed his head and turned toward the house with Johnny at his side and Rebbeca holding tight around his neck. He heard Sonny tease Jackson that he and the doctor must be related because both were always fiddling with their eyeglasses. Jackson denied that he did it that often.

As they walked, Dr. Tremons told Checker that his daughter, Sarah Ann, wasn't home at the moment. She had gone for groceries and should be back soon.

He winked at the tall Ranger, wet-stroked the disobedient lock of hair, and added, "She's been worrying about you something fierce, John. Rode out to the Triple C camp every day, I think. When she wasn't there, she was out at the Hedrickson place, makin' sure it got all fixed up real fine. Hear tell she wouldn't take 'maybe' for an answer. They finished out there, oh, about three days back. No, it was two. Yeah, two."

Checker smiled. "Heard that from the boys. That's mighty fine of everybody, expecially Sarah Ann. Sure didn't expect that. We owe some serious thanking."

"Well, it wouldn't have happened 'ceptin' for my Sarah Ann," Dr. Tremons said. "She was bound an' determined you—and those kids—would have something good to come back to. Started on it the day ya left, yessir, that very day."

The tall gunfighter's mind wasn't on the rebuilt ranch. It was on Sarah Ann. How good it would be to see her again. How good to hold her in his arms, to kiss her soft lips. He could barely hope that she felt the way she had when he had ridden out, when she told him that his shirt button had worked to bring him back to his sister and had pulled one from his shirt. He looked down at himself; it was a new shirt, purchased at the general store with their other clothes, and he wished he had thought of that earlier. The button-shy garment was wadded up in his saddlebags, but he couldn't return to the street for it. Not now. Besides, she wasn't home.

"Your mama's sleeping," Dr. Tremons said. "So we need to be real quiet when we go into her room. It's here, on the other side of my office."

He led them through a short hallway, then through an oblong room overgrown with counters and cabinets with a table controlling the middle of the floor. On the farthest wall, a Columbia Regulator Clock with a brass pendulum declared the time. Everywhere they looked were bottles, packaged medicines, surgical instruments, and boxes of bandages and wraps. Checker noticed some branded names he'd seen in Blue's medicine wagon: Bromo-Seltzer, Dr. Pepper's Tonic, Castoria, and Lydia Pinkham's Compound for Female Weakness. He wondered if the good doctor had purchased them from his fiendish half brother when he came to town for the purpose of freeing Star McCallister.

That seemed like another age ago.

With a careful twist of the doorknob, Dr. Tremons opened the far door, held his finger up to his mouth to remind them of the need to be quiet, and stepped into the darkened bedroom, then moistened it and a second finger to complete his habitual task. Small, but clean, the room's natural light was limited by heavy curtains pulled over the single large window. A small table with a pitcher and bowl sat next to the wrought-iron bed. A dresser of questionable age and condition slunk in the far corner. This room was used by the doctor as a hospital of sorts since the town didn't have a formal hospital.

Lying in the large bed, under several blankets and a boiled sheet, was Amelia Hedrickson. Asleep. Checker immediately thought she looked smaller. Of course, she would be thinner, he told himself. He couldn't see much of her face. What he could see of it appeared to be in the final stages of healing. The swelling was gone, leaving only swirls of purple and yellow about her cheeks and mouth and under both eyes. Her once-ballooning right eyelid had retreated to normal.

Raw places on her face from being dragged and burned had turned dark with scabbing. A gash on her lower lip was healing nicely and a wicked-looking cut on her forehead had definitely lost its fire. Although the bruising around her nose was extensive, the break wasn't apparent—thanks to Jackson straightening it; he had been the first to treat her, right at their burning homestead.

He couldn't tell if the awful wound in Amelia's head was better where someone had grabbed her hair and dragged her, eventually yanking it from her scalp. Her pillow covered that part of her head. Her broken left arm was held in a sling. Her right arm lay partially exposed on top of the covers, heavily bandaged from her wrist to her elbow.

His mind ran back to the horrible sight of their ravaged home and Amelia standing behind a stone well near the burning house as he rode up. Her tall frame was bloody and half naked. Somehow she retained the will to keep her trembling body from collapsing. Purple and swollen, her face was a distortion. Little was left of her dress and long, blood-raw bands on her arms and legs told of being dragged. A thick lock of hair had been yanked from her scalp, leaving a knot of blood and dirt. It was like looking at someone he didn't know, and the sight of her tore into his mind, looking for the image of his dying mother. In her blood-streaked fist was a button, the one she had taken from his shirt years ago when they were separated.

"Mommy! It's Mommy!" Rebecca yelled and ran toward the bed.

The exclamation snapped Checker back from the agonizing recollection as he watched the little girl scurry into the room. Amelia stirred, reacting at first as if she were dreaming. Her shoulders rose slowly and Checker saw the white bandage covering her head wound. Her hair was down, lying on slightly humped shoulders. Although old, the boiled, whitish gown was definitely clean.

"Wh-what? I—I'm coming. I'm coming, Becky," she mouthed.

In the uneven light, Checker thought it looked like her loosened teeth had firmed themselves as Jackson said they would.

Trying to hide his aggravation at the little girl, Dr. Tremons stepped farther into the gray room and announced, "Amelia, my lady—you have visitors. It's your son and daughter—and Captain Checker. They're all safe."

A smile cutting his face in half, Johnny hesitated to enter.

With a soft pat on his arm, Dr. Tremons said, "Go on ahead, boy. Be better'n any medicine I can give her. She's mighty weak, though."

The words were barely out of his mouth before Johnny was alongside the bed, reaching for his mother. She held out her right hand stiffly and he squeezed it. Checker followed. He lifted Rebecca onto the bed next to Amelia's pillow, close enough for the little girl to give her mother a giddy hug. The movement drove a sharp pain through his right hand; it was difficult to hide his reaction.

"Why not go around and climb up on the other side?" Checker motioned to Johnny.

This time without hesitation, the boy half jumped,

half ran to the far side of the bed and leaped onto it. The gathering of mother and children in a huge, one-armed hug made both men blink away the impact. Amelia kissed her children on their cheeks and fore-heads as best she could with her cut lip. Tears slid down her face and soon covered her pale cheeks. "Oh, I love you. I missed you two so much."

"Maybe we should leave them alone for a bit," Checker said and stepped back.

The doctor nodded agreement and they slipped into his surgical room

"How is Amelia really doing?" Checker asked.

After playing with his hair, Dr. Tremons said he thought her internal bleeding had stopped on its own, that it had mostly come from three cracked ribs. Checker asked him what he owed for this special lodging and treatment.

"You owe me nothin'. That reminds me, though, thar's what was left over from the hotel money—and the Hedrickson's corn crop." Dr. Tremons pointed toward a small sack of gold coins laying on the counter. It was Checker's, left with the hotel to cover their expenses. "You already paid me—before you rode out, boy, remember?" The doctor shook his head to reinforce the fact that nothing more was due.

Checker pressed the matter further, certain that he had not paid the doctor earlier.

Flaring slightly, Dr. Tremons said, "Damn it, man, I said there wasn't any cost. You take that sack o' gold. Sarah used most o' the corn money to buy lumber for your place. An' a chair or two, I think. That's all that's missing." He cocked his head to the side and grinned. "Rode out with my Sarah Ann yesterday to see it. Except for a tree burned on one side, you'd never know there'd been a fire. You'll be pleased, I reckon."

"I'm sure I will. That was mighty nice of her—and

Amelia's neighbors." Checker ran his tongue across his lower lip. "How is she doing—with the other . . . thing?"

Staring at the cabinets, Dr. Tremons knew the tall man was talking about her being raped. He cleared his throat. "I can heal bruises an' cuts an' such about as good as anybody—but I can't cure thinking. Wish I could. She doesn't talk about it. At least, not to me. Talked to Sarah Ann a little. At first, she was out of her head, mumbling all kinds of stuff. Gradual, though, she started worrying about those kids. Got to be something awful. Having those bastards take 'em an' all. Damn."

Checker's chest rose and fell as a black anguish rushed into his soul.

Dr. Tremons walked over to the counter and straightened a row of instruments. "Wasn't much I could tell her. Except that you an' your friends had gone after 'em. My God, it seemed forever that we waited." He wiped his nose with his hand. "My Sarah Ann, she kept telling her that you'd bring 'em back. Yessir, she did. Never wavered. Not once. Wouldn't let any of the folks stop work on their place neither. Stubborn as her mother, she is."

He took great pride in telling about her tough negotiations with the lumberyard manager. Dodge was growing, and lumber, shipped by rail and wagon, had been plentiful during the building season. However, as winter approached, lumber was getting scarce and the man had tried to raise his prices. She had even threatened to order a ready-made structure from Lyman Bridges of Chicago. The doctor chuckled at the idea, something she had read about, and said that had turned the trick.

One neighbor, Nathaniel Brode, came in for special praise from Dr. Tremons. A skilled carpenter, the man had done much of the finish work and wouldn't accept a cent. He said Orville Hedrickson had helped build his house several years earlier. The doctor thought it was three neighbors, plus Brode, who did the work, along with a few leftover Texas drovers and the Triple C men, all of them working under Sarah Ann's direction.

Checker said, "I'm mighty grateful to her for caring that way."

The doctor grinned and pushed on his hair. "I reckon it has a lot more to do with caring about you than anything else."

His face reddening, Checker changed the subject and told him about the rescue, bringing in three outlaws alive, Star McCallister escaping, the role of Blue McCallister, disguised as Dr. Gambree, and of Marshal Rand's involvement.

"Ya know Rand's gone an' hired hisself two guns. Injuns. Cherokee tribe, I think," Dr. Tremons related. "Already killed a Texas drover. Hard to believe why they're here. I complained to Stanton, he's the mayor, ya know. Like talkin' to a wall."

"Yeah, we met them."

"I thought you told Rand to get out of town."

"I did."

Dr. Tremons was quiet for a moment, waiting for more from Checker that didn't come, then said, "Better let me take a look at your hand, John." He held out his hands to receive Checker's right hand.

"After you take a look at the kids, Doc. They've had a rough go of it," Checker said quietly without moving his hand toward the doctor's. "Jackson's been tending to them, so I reckon they're doing fine, but . . ."

"I know, son. I'll give 'em a goin'-over after they get through makin' their mama feel alive." Dr. Tremons dropped his left hand and let his right seek the comfort of his hair. "But it ain't gonna do them a lick o' good to have you act like you're not hurt."

CHAPTER TWENTY-TWO

"Johnny? Oh, John?" Amelia's weak voice broke into their conversation.

Dr. Tremons studied John Checker for a moment, his face filled with a mixture of admiration and fear. "Your sis wants to see you, my friend. Afterwards, I want to see your hand."

"All right, Doc."

"Did Jackson look at it?"

"Yes, sort of. He wanted to wrap it, but I—"

"You didn't want them damn outlaws to know you were hurt, I know," Dr. Tremons interrupted. "That colored man would make a fine doctor." He rubbed his chin. "Wonder if there are any colored doctors."

Checker shook his head. "Don't know. There damn well should be. Jackson's a mighty good friend. Just found out that he carried a Texas law badge once."

Dr. Tremons's expression was a question mark.

"Right after the War. Governor Davis got rid of the Rangers and had state police. There were some Negroes in it. Mostly clerks. Not all, though. Jackson would've been a good one, that's for sure."

Amelia called out again. Her voice was louder this time. More urgent.

"You go to her—an' I'll see to your friends," Dr. Tremons said. "What's his name—Sonny, yeah, Sonny Jones needs lookin' at, too. Reckon he'll be as hard to handle as you."

"Couldn't have saved those kids without him—or Jackson. Or Tyrel, for that matter." Checker shook his head to emphasize their importance. "Better take a look at Tyrel's head while you're at it. Got coldcocked in a fight."

"That reminds me, I got your wagon out in the back." Dr. Tremons motioned with his hand, then returned it to his straying lock of hair.

He was referring to the Hedrickson buckboard Jackson and Checker had used to bring Amelia from the ranch to town. One of the wagon horses was actually Jackson's mount; the other was one of the few Hedrickson horses they had found remaining at the ranch. Both had been traded at the livery for fresh saddle horses to search for the children.

Removing his hat, Checker entered the room. It seemed brighter than before as giggles bounced off the drab walls. Johnny and Rebecca were cuddled next to their mother as she stroked their heads alternately with her right hand. Her smile was enough payment for Checker as his own tiredness vanished.

"Good afternoon, Amelia."

"Oh, Johnny, my Johnny," she said, referring to Checker by his childhood name. "Sarah Ann kept telling me that you would find them. She was my rock, Johnny. You should marry that girl." Amelia's thin, bruised face was alight.

Without responding, Checker stepped closer, his hat in his left hand at his side.

She hugged the children as tightly as she could with one arm, first young Johnny, then Rebecca. "Look what they gave me." She opened her fist and revealed two small white pebbles. "They said you gave these to them—for luck. An Indian story, it sounded like."

Checker's head bobbed. "Yeah, one night something reminded me of what an old friend gave me once. Stands-in-Thunder was his name. Taught me a lot of things. Mostly about dignity, I reckon." He smiled. "I was, ah, feeling close to him—an' them—when I . . . sorta silly, I guess."

"I think they are the most beautiful things I've ever seen—next to these two." Single tears worked their way down her face, racing over previous wetness.

He walked to the bed, sat edgewise on it, and laid his hat at its foot, suddenly feeling very tired, almost drained.

Removing her arms from around the children, Amelia reached out to him with both hands, her slinged left arm not stretching as far as her right.

He stood again and got close enough so they could hug. In spite of the many years that had separated them during much of their childhoods—and as young adults—there remained a strong connection. Maybe because of them.

As he released her embrace, Amelia took his right hand in both of hers. "How can I ever thank you, Johnny? You've been through the fires of hell—for my family."

Her eyes sought his face, studying it carefully. She reached up and touched the arrowhead scar on his cheek. "Mr. Mitchell told me about Star's brother breaking them out of jail—and killing two of your friends."

She patted Rebecca's arm as the little girl kept trying to interrupt with questions. "Just a minute, Becky, I'm talking with your uncle." She looked up again at Checker. "I'd forgotten all about Blue, had you?"

"Yes, he didn't fall far from the tree," Checker said, straightening his back. "Looks like he killed the real owner of that medicine wagon somewhere on his back trail. We're going to wire the U.S. marshal's office in Nebraska so they can notify his widow." He paused. "Blue won't bother anyone anymore."

"What about Star?" Her face drew tight and the corner of her mouth twitched.

Checker touched the medicine pouch under his shirt and tunic. "Wish I knew. He's as smart as he is bad. I'm hoping he's headed for Kansas City or some place like that. Some place where he won't hurt us anymore." He pursed his lips and added, "He's our brother, you know. I keep trying to forget that—but I can't. I can't forgive him for what he did to you either."

"I know. Sarah Ann told me some of the town's businessmen don't believe he's even guilty of running that rustling operation," she said, apologetically. "They say it was just the Texans trying to show the town who's the real boss."

Examining his hat at the end of the bed as if seeing it for the first time, he knew Jackson thought the hiring of the Cherokee brothers was Star's doing. Now wasn't the time to share that concern, however. He didn't respond. What did it matter if a handful of townspeople thought Star was innocent?

Into the quiet came Rebecca's renewed quest. "Is Daddy living in this house too? Can I see him?"

Young Johnny's eyes flashed and blurred with anguish.

"Orville . . ." The name was a choked sob bursting from Amelia's soul.

Checker's expression was shattered china.

"Becky, I told you . . . Paw's dead." Johnny's mouth hung open after the words left, wishing his words weren't true.

"Thank you . . . for bury . . ." Amelia couldn't finish and a fresh round of tears took control. She held Rebecca to her and pulled her son into the hug. Her whispers to them made Johnny wince and Rebecca whimper.

"He was a good man, Amelia. A good father," Checker said. "He was the kind of man I would have wished for you. Mom would've liked him too." He reached over to grab his hat, mostly to have something to do.

Frowning, the boy slid off the bed, deciding he should appear more mature. It fascinated him to hear his mother call his uncle "Johnny," and reinforced the fact he was named after this tall, mysterious man. Rebecca asked why her mother's arms were in a sling and bandaged, and how the bruises got on her face.

With a few deep breaths, Amelia swallowed back the gnawing emotion. "My Johnny has been telling me of your troubles. The fight with the outlaws. Indians. That girl escaping." She shook her head. "I guess I should start calling you John." She smiled faintly. "And dear Sonny Jones. How badly is he hurt? And Tyrel, he's just a boy."

"I reckon it will take a lot more bullets to slow Sonny down. And Tyrel's a man, by anyone's measuring stick."

"Are they here? Your friends?"

"Yeah, they're waiting outside with the horses."

"Oh, I would like to see them—and thank them. Please." Amelia's eyes were bright.

Checker turned to leave.

"How could Star do this? He's our blood. Our brother. Half brother, anyway. Star let them take me, John. They took me. They took me. He laughed when they grabbed me and dragged me. I can still hear his laugh."

The words were bullets.

She stared at him for several seconds, not even aware of Johnny and Rebecca crawling around on the bed.

"I don't know, Amelia. I don't know." Checker rubbed his chin and returned his hat to his head. "Maybe he came by it naturally. J.D. wasn't much to stand beside."

"You look like him, John. You look like . . . our father."

"Wish I didn't."

She bit her lower lip. "What am I going to do, John? I can't . . ."

"I'm staying." His eyes were bright with determination. "At least until you're up and going again." He cocked his head to the side. "And your place is going well."

She pursed her lips. "I'll have Mr. Whitaker draw up papers. He's an attorney in town. Helped us before. The ranch should be half yours now. More than half."

"That isn't necessary, Amelia."

"It's what I want, big brother." She tried to smile. "But what about the children . . ."

"Don't worry about it, sis. Just get well. The kids an' me'll do fine. An' Sonny's going to stay to help."

"Sarah has been giving me . . . reports. She got the neighbors to . . . rebuild . . . everything. She asked me if she could use the corn money to buy lumber. I told her she could." Tears flowed again from Amelia's battered face. "Isn't that wonderful? Did I tell you that you should marry that girl . . . John?"

"We'll head out there tomorrow—with your herd."

"But . . ."

"Sis, this is your big brother, remember? The one whose button you took. I said I'd come back—and I did." Checker forced a confident smile.

"Johnny . . . thank you."

"You're welcome, sis."

He heard familiar voices in the doctor's office behind

him and headed there. One voice he longed to hear wasn't among them, but his friends were chatting with Dr. Tremons. Actually the doctor was doing most of the talking, telling them in detail about his Civil War wound. But he could also hear Sonny declaring his wounds were healed and Jackson being equally adamant that they needed attention. Jackson had been reluctant to go inside the doctor's home, but Dr. Tremons had insisted. In fact, he wanted to show the black drover his office, telling him that he should consider becoming a doctor.

Checker entered the room and the conversation stopped, except for the doctor's description of Gettysburg and his wounds.

"Hey, John, how is . . . Mrs. Hedrickson?" Sonny asked, turning toward him.

"Boys, my sister would like to see you. Come on in. Please."

"Remember, she's still mighty weak. Just a few minutes," Dr. Tremons advised.

Bouncing off the bed, Rebecca skipped toward the incoming men and headed for Sonny. The happy-go-lucky cowboy knelt and lifted her into his arms.

Johnny slid alongside Bannon and the young farm boy grinned his approval.

Looking wan but pleased, Amelia held out her bandaged right hand, asking Bannon to come closer. He looked over at Checker, who nodded.

"Mr. Bannon, thank you so much," she said. "I understand you were in charge of our horses—and helped keep my children safe."

Rubbing his nose in embarrassment, Bannon pulled off his hat, stepped to the bed, and grasped her hand gently. As he did, he hoped the dried cut in his head wouldn't be seen. He tried not to look at her bed gown. "You're most welcome, ma'am." He gulped and released her handshake. "Johnny, here, he's gonna be quite a hossman." He stepped back awkwardly to allow Jackson to be greeted, relieved to be out of the limelight—and without his wound being noticed.

"Oh, Mr. Jackson, Dr. Tremons said your care was the key to my recovery. You fixed my nose. My arm. My . . . thank you, thank you. And for going after my children. How can I ever repay you?" She held out her hand for Jackson.

His hat at his side, the black drover pushed back the eyeglasses on the bridge of his nose. He sounded more like a doctor than Dr. Tremons as he accepted her hand. "Mrs. Hedrickson, y'all are definitely John Checker's sister. Begging your pardon, ma'am, but y'all be one tough lady."

She smiled warmly as their handshake released. He folded his arms and listened as she told him that her cracked ribs were healing nicely, according to Dr. Tremons. And that the skin on her legs would not likely heal for a long time but they didn't hurt as much. Jackson wanted to suggest letting her legs be open to the air, but didn't think he should. Dr. Tremons walked next to him and spoke quietly. It appeared to Checker that the old doctor was conferring with the black drover on treatment. Both men pushed on their spectacles and Dr. Tremons worked his pompadour. Checker smiled at the similarity in habits.

As the black drover and Dr. Tremons talked, Checker glanced at Sonny and was surprised at the strange look on his friend's face. When Jackson formally excused himself from the doctor, Checker watched his friend retreat to the doorway; the black man's lips were moving slightly and Checker guessed it was a prayer of thanks.

Dr. Tremons held a hand to her forehead, pursed his lips, and stepped away.

"My dear Mr. Jones, please come closer and let me

thank you." Amelia beckoned stiffly with her right arm. "I see my youngest is already smitten."

Checker couldn't remember Sonny looking so red-faced or being so slow-tongued.

"It's Sonny . . . Mrs. Hedrickson," Sonny said as he kissed Rebecca on the cheek and walked bedside. "It's my real pleasure to be with your children."

She smiled and outstretched her hand. "Amelia, please."

He shifted Rebecca to his left arm and accepted her greeting. His eyes connected with hers, then fled to the far corner of the room. He released her hand. Quickly.

"You are so brave—and so good." Her throat was hoarse. "Johnny . . . John . . . told me you were shot. My God, how awful."

Sonny smiled. *What an amazing woman*, he thought, *to be worrying about me when she has been dragged through hell.* "Amelia, they only nicked me. It was nothing."

"I guess you an' the others will be headed for Texas soon," she said, awkwardly smoothing the covers on the bed to rid them of wrinkles. She looked up into his face and brushed her hair back with her freed hand.

"Yeah, everyone's headed back tomorrow." Sonny swallowed. "I figured on stayin'—to help John, you know. Ain't got nothin' waitin' for me in Texas."

"Oh, how wonderful." She winked. "I know Rebecca will love that."

Rebecca stared at Sonny's face, cocked her head to the side, and announced, "Mommy, can Uncle Sonny come live with us?"

Sonny coughed and nearly choked. No words could break through his surprise, but Amelia only laughed. "I'm sure he will come an' visit, won't you?"

"Yes, ma'am, I'd like that."

"Well, boys, I think the little lady's had enough of a parade for one day," Dr. Tremons announced with a swift touch to his glasses and a follow-up sweep of his hair.

Immediately the men retreated from the room, saying their good-byes. Checker told Johnny to tell his mother good-bye and Sonny said the same to Rebecca. He told them the doctor wanted to give them an examination and then they would head for the Triple C camp where Tug's stew would be waiting.

With the Triple C men waiting quietly, Dr. Tremons studied the children's eyes, tongues, and ears. He listened to their hearts beat with his stethoscope, which brought several questions from Rebecca about what he heard. After declaring them fit, he turned to Sonny and Bannon, ignoring their protestations. Dabs of a yellow medicine were placed on their healing wounds, but both successfully resisted having bandages.

Checker watched and smiled. He had originally planned on staying in the hotel with the children, but both had been excited about sleeping out with the chuck wagon. That would make it easier in the morning, when they would move the Hedrickson herd to the ranch and determine what needed to be done next.

His mind had been shifting from the idea of getting a place in town to obtaining the proper furniture for the rebuilt ranch house. The great news about the ranch being ready was truly sinking in. He had figured on construction, most likely not beginning until spring and, therefore, keeping the children—and later, Amelia—in the town house. How long before Amelia became truly well again was anyone's guess.

He wasn't wealthy, by a long shot, but his savings from Ranger pay, except for one major exception, were intact—and he had secured a handsome reward for the capture of the bank robber Harry Steely after leaving the state's service. That was a few weeks before joining up with the Triple C drive and more of a happenstance than a plan. Steely had tried to rob the bank where he kept his money, and Checker was there at the time of the attempt.

The lone exception to using his savings was his purchase of a small house for a destitute widow with two youngsters. He had no particular caring for the woman or the children, but they reminded him of his own childhood.

Combined with his Triple C pay, he had planned on buying something in town worth living in—and still having some money for lumber. Maybe hiring a carpenter to handle things he didn't do well. He had assumed the money left behind for hotel expenses would be gone, or nearly so. Dr. Tremons's generous takeover of Amelia's hospitalization had surprised and pleased him. But he still planned on giving the good man money for this care.

If more work was needed at the ranch—and he expected there would be—it sounded like this Nathaniel Brode would be the one to hire. Selling some of the Hedrickson horses to the Triple C might come in handy. He had forgotten to tell Amelia of the proposed sale and get her permission, as well as approval to give a horse to each neighbor, too.

After Dr. Tremons declared the children fit, he turned to Checker. "Now you. You're not getting out of here before I take a look at your hand, John Checker," Dr. Tremons insisted as they crossed through his office.

A smile crossed Jackson's face. "Thanks, Doc. It needs tending."

With his friends watching, Dr. Tremons began wrapping Checker's right hand. He said the bones had to be held in place or they would never heal correctly and he wouldn't be able to use it effectively again.

"Can you wrap it—so I can use it some?" Checker asked, watching patiently as the doctor alternated between wrapping, pushing back his glasses, and stroking his wayward hair. Although he hoped dearly that Sarah Ann would return before they left, he knew they should be leaving so the children could eat.

"Have you met the new deputies in town?" Jackson asked Dr. Tremons.

The older man looked up at the black drover and repeated his facial ritual before responding. "Yeah, saw one struttin' peacock a few days ago. Just after he shot up some poor cowboy. Only heard about the other. Big thing with a machete, I hear. Not sure why they're here in Dodge." He turned his attention to Checker and an earlier subject. "Ya figure hirin' them is Rand's answer to your tellin' him to git?"

A fleeting look at Jackson preceded Checker's response. "Could be."

"If you leave 'em alone, maybe they'll leave."

"Maybe so."

Dr. Tremons finished and patted Checker's bandaged hand. "I know you were asking about holding a gun—not a hammer. Best you did neither." He licked his fingers and stroked his hair lock. "This hand has got to be real still for a long time. A long time. If you don't do that, it'll never heal right. You hear me, son?"

Rebecca broke the unspoken tension by asking if she could have some wrap on her hand and the doctor gladly complied. It gave him something to do.

"Rand will have to wait—and I have no quarrel with Do'tsi or his brother." Checker's face was taut; his dark eyes were black rock. "Got kids to take care of—and a ranch. Thanks to . . . your daughter."

Jackson's worried eyes sought Sonny's, and the cowboy shrugged his shoulders.

"Let's go eat. Miss Becky and me are hungry." Bannon's statement broke the moment.

Sonny laughed and slapped Jackson on the back. "Sounds mighty fine to me."

CHAPTER TWENTY-THREE

As the four men returned to the Triple C camp with Amelia's children, none noticed Alfred Diverrouve watching from the shadowed alley of his saloon. Satisfied with what he observed, the goateed Frenchman walked to his saddled horse tied to a hitching rack at the rear of the building. Over his white shirt, vest, and tie, he wore a Billy Yank greatcoat with the collar turned up and a dark bowler.

He didn't normally carry a gun. However, he was armed now; a shoulder holster held a French Le Faucheux pin-fire revolver. The wheel gun was old, but he felt comfortable with the weapon as he untied the reins. A double-barreled shotgun rested in his saddle sheath as well. Next to his mount was a packhorse carrying food and supplies.

If asked, he was to say the load was for friends near the fort. Actually, they were for the hidden Star McCallister.

Cautiously, Diverrouve stopped beside the saddle horse and listened. His extended upper teeth, with one made of gold, bit into his lower lip. An inebriated businessman staggered through the back door, cursing his luck at the faro table. His arm was tightly holding a one-armed woman. The Frenchman recognized her as "One's-Good Martha," a longtime whore from the Lady Gay. Annoyed by the interruption, Diverrouve decided to stand silently and let the man and his mischief for the moment find their way up the alley and toward the street.

Muttering an obscenity in French, the saloon manager watched the man bump into the side of the building, apologize to the wall and not the woman, and finally make it to the sidewalk. Diverrouve's mouth quivered as if foreshadowing a smile. The impulse vanished as quickly as it came; he hadn't cracked one in probably ten years. The pairing wasn't an unfamiliar sight. At any time of the day or night.

He turned to more important matters, double-checking his wares to make certain he had everything his boss had asked for. His loyalty to McCallister was deep—and with good reason, he felt. Diverrouve was an order-taker, not a thinker. Morals were for others. He believed in making money; he believed in Star McCallister. The outlaw leader had rewarded him handsomely for his profitable management of the Nueces Saloon and had given him the opportunity to buy the place after McCallister was jailed.

It didn't matter to the practical Frenchman that the establishment would eventually have been sold by the city, after McCallister was hanged, since he had no known family, nor any will. McCallister had arranged for Diverrouve to purchase the saloon over time with payments from profits. This was completed on the day before the scheduled breakout of the gang. For McCallister, it was the best of a bad situation.

It didn't matter either that McCallister's return meant

the Frenchman wouldn't get to buy the saloon; he was genuinely pleased to have him in control again. His confidence in McCallister knew few bounds. It never occurred to him to question why he had returned, instead of going elsewhere.

Diverrouve didn't think anyone in town realized the Lady Gay Dance Hall, with its back bedrooms and stable of prostitutes, was actually also owned by McCallister. The establishment was managed by the notorious madam Winchester Sally Sachim. She reported to Diverrouve and the profits were under his control as well. Before Checker's interference—and the arrests over the stolen Triple C herd—McCallister was in the process of purchasing the other dance hall, the one with all black dancers, and the Williams Haberdashery and Men's Tailoring Store. He still coveted them.

McCallister had even contemplated ending the cattle rustling operation, as effective as it was, to concentrate on other growth developments. Or so he had told Diverrouve. Becoming mayor was definitely a target. Checker had ended that strategy. For now.

Satisfied no one else was near, he climbed awkwardly onto his horse, wrapped the lead rope of the pack animal around the saddle horn, and eased away toward the west.

"*Lentement. Lentement,*" he said, urging the animal to go slowly.

He didn't like horses; they were unpredictable. He much preferred French wines. Or French whores.

As directed by the outlaw leader, he had been planting the idea with selected community leaders that McCallister was innocent, a victim of vindictive Texans. The awful Hedrickson homestead violence was attributed solely to the gang, who had forced McCallister to ride with them. The story had already found a reasonably good reception. Most Dodge citizens liked the cattlemen's money, not the men or their actions. McCallister's reputation among many was well established, respected for his growing wealth and business acumen.

Keeping his horse at a walk, in spite of its desire to trot, Diverrouve disappeared into the heavy dusk. Occasionally, his thick French accent would break into the growing dusk, cursing the need to ride. The wind was gaining strength as darkness gave it permission.

From the jail, Deputy Sheriff Do'tsi ambled outside, said something to his resting dog, and headed for Ham's Livery. Kana'ti had agreed to watch the jail tonight. A bottle of whiskey and a new cigar were his special company.

At the livery, Do'tsi found his mule saddled as requested earlier. The stable boy tending to the evening operation was eager to be helpful. Partly out of fear of this strange man, and partly out of the generous tips he gave.

Do'tsi swung easily into the saddle, flipped the boy two bits, and rode away. After a quick growl in the direction of the frightened boy, Zoro thundered after its master. The Cherokee killer loped to a shallow embankment northwest of Dodge, pulled up behind its clay ridges, and listened. An old habit. One that came naturally to men who lived by the gun and their wits. The weathered dirt reminded him of a horse's teeth, only crumbling around the gums. He studied the dark shapes of the buildings, searching for anything out of place. His pipe would taste good, but he didn't dare strike a match; even the bowl's small orange fire could be seen by a knowing man from a distance. He would wait until he was satisfied that he hadn't been followed.

He and Diverrouve were headed to the same place—McCallister's hideout—but they would arrive separately. Any chance meeting by someone else would be more easily explained and dismissed if they weren't together. If asked, Do'tsi was to say that he was checking on a rumor about a band of Indians nearby.

Purposely, he stared into the sky. But it was too early to see the Milky Way or "the "Pathway of Souls" as the Cherokee and other tribes envisioned the starry mass. Each soul had to travel along the Milky Way; the Lakota thought its stars were the fires of dead souls waiting to pass by an old woman who judged them. The good were allowed to pass on to a bountiful place; the bad were pushed over a cliff and their evil spirits left to roam the earth. He chuckled to himself, *I would shoot the old witch and go on.*

Night brought strange feelings. When the images came to haunt him, he usually pushed them away with a pipe-bowl of opium and tobacco. That wouldn't be tonight, and the cruel pictures rushed forward without worry about being thwarted. His earliest memories were of Owl Watcher, his grandmother who raised both brothers. He had no memories of his parents, although Kana'ti said he did. Feared as a "raven mocker," their grandmother was ostracized by the Cherokee as one of the legendary life-stealing creatures who sought immortality by sucking life from its victims. Because of her reputation, the medicine woman and her young grandsons were forced to move often.

Do'tsi's childhood name was Yellow Pony; Kana'ti's, Red Rock. Serpent and Wolf would come much later, long after they had killed the white men who murdered and scalped their grandmother. Years before, both young grandsons had been forced to watch the horrible event, tied and gagged.

The magical powers of his grandmother had never passed to him, although his interest in death rites and beliefs among religions—and, more so, in immortality—had been ignited by her ways. Owl Watcher believed she had lived many lives. At least once as a raven. An image of seeing her drink the blood of a young dead woman was always lodged in his head.

Every time he killed, it was in his grandmother's honor. At least that's what he told himself. Whenever possible, he left a raven feather near his dead victim. A tribute to her. However, he had never tried drinking anyone's blood. That was nonsense, he had decided. But he fully expected to meet her again—at some time—in his life. The trick was to recognize her.

He, too, had lived other lives. Of such he was certain. Like the Hindus, the Comanches, and others, he was destined to come again and again. It had taken away the fear of death, the real gift from his grandmother. That and the drive for immortality. He had studied religions as long as he could remember to learn how best to seek it.

A part of him looked forward to coming back and hearing about himself as Do'tsi. The immortal Do'tsi. Killing John Checker would guarantee this magical position. Learning Checker actually had a friendship with a Comanche war chief stirred fresh fire into the Cherokee killer's strange childhood memories. Before the great Ranger died, he would ask Checker what the war chief told him about death. Was it possible they had met before—in another life? Had one killed the other before? Did that explain the twinge in his shoulder when Checker walked close?

He had talked about immortality and reincarnation with his brother many times before. Kana'ti told him once that he was certain he had seen their grandmother; she was now a white soldier. It was the only time he had mentioned this, and Do'tsi didn't think the subject was anything his brother really believed in or cared about. Kana'ti did care about being paid to kill John Checker—or anyone else in Dodge. Do'tsi had told

Kana'ti that he would give him his share of McCallister's payment if he helped kill the former Ranger. Kana'ti was eager. Too eager. His younger brother had needed to remind him that the timing must be right. It must appear they were acting in their capacity as lawmen.

The growing darkness reminded him of a story he had heard several times about John Checker. The Ranger captain was supposed to have uncanny night vision and had brought a number of outlaws to justice by surprising them when they thought the darkness was their friend. He shook his head at the notion. Killing Checker would truly immortalize him. His Cherokee brethren would say the Ranger was a bright star in the night sky. Do'tsi didn't want McCallister to know that he would have come for nothing just to have this opportunity.

He kicked the mule into a ground-eating lope, savoring the knowledge that Checker's right hand was injured. He didn't know the extent yet—or the reason for it—but he knew Checker would be forced to fight with his left hand. That was the reason the former Ranger had a second revolver in his belt, set for left-handed use. Of course, he had no intention of facing him directly. That was fool's play. He and his brother would ambush him, of course.

So far, McCallister's strategy was working well; everyone in town was afraid of them, except the magistrate. Judge Buchanan appeared to be a man afraid of little and not inclined to intimidation—or bribery. At least that was Do'tsi's first impression. He had offered to kill the man—at night, assuring McCallister that no one would know who did it. The outlaw leader wanted to wait; such a murder would likely bring the U.S. marshal and he didn't want that kind of interference. If Judge Buchanan proved to be a problem, they would deal with the situation later.

Nightfall found Do'tsi and the saloon manager arriving within twenty minutes of each other at the outlaw leader's cabin three miles west of the city. Marshal Rand was already there, nervous and on edge. He had been staying at his home as soon as he heard Checker had returned. Diverrouve arrived before Do'tsi at the tiny, run-down shack shoved against a treeless ridge. It had once been owned by a buffalo hunter and now stood empty, or at least everyone thought it was.

Since few rarely rode in that direction anymore, the place was a perfect location for Star McCallister to hide. And wait. Wait for his plans to turn into victory. Wait for John Checker to slip into his trap. Wait for community leaders to be swayed to his claim of innocence. Wait for a return to even greater power in Dodge.

A small, smokeless fire of dry cedar and cottonwood root glittered in the blackened fireplace. A well-placed branch over the top of the chimney made certain any smoke would be dissipated into nothing. Inside, the fire's glow was screened off by a tipped-over table, so the flames wouldn't give away the cabin's use either. The solitary window was planked over so the lone lantern could also work its best secretly within the cramped quarters. McCallister was a very careful man, Do'tsi noted to himself. Would he have the nerve necessary to achieve his scheme when it really got going? The Cherokee killer wondered as he entered to McCallister's welcome.

"Come in, Do'tsi, come in." McCallister's tone was warm and friendly. "There's no place like home, right?" He snickered and his eye twitched.

"Evening, Star. Evening, Rand, Diverrouve."

Even in the oily light, it was clear McCallister had swept the floors vigorously and removed cobwebs and other remains of disuse. To himself, Diverrouve decided his own apartment in town wasn't nearly as clean.

"No one followed you, I presume," McCallister said.

"You may presume."

Around a second table, they sat, sharing a bottle of burgundy the Frenchman had brought along. Finding a level place to set the bottle was difficult as the table was warped from long exposure to the weather. Especially where the roof had broken through. McCallister had covered the hole in the roof with a tied-down tarp. Diverrouve had brought it from town on a previous trip.

McCallister was dressed formally as if he intended to stroll down the streets of Dodge at any moment. Only the soiled paper collar distracted from his tailored appearance. His gray herringbone suit fit him well. It, too, had been brought by the Frenchman from McCallister's closet in the saloon office. The outlaw leader smiled through the report of the day's events that included the jailed members of his gang asserting Blue's death and the attack by a Comanche war party.

"We'll let those Triple C fools take off for Texas—and John Checker will be all alone." His laughter raced around the room and finally hid in a shadowy corner.

Diverrouve reminded him that the Hedrickson ranch had been reconstructed—house and barn—by neighbors, so Checker would likely be there most of the time.

Marshal Jubal Rand visibly shivered at the mention of Checker's name. His narrow face was cut in half by a thick handlebar mustache. Unlike with McCallister's attire, Rand looked like he had been sleeping in his gray business suit for days.

Do'tsi noticed the fearful response, glanced at McCallister, and grinned savagely. "So my brother and I are going to arrest him—for the murder of Dr. Gambree, your brother." Do'tsi's face was yellow and streaked in the uneven light, as he waited for a response and leered at the lawman. "Rand, you need to be there."

The mustachioed lawman nodded affirmatively, although he didn't want to think about the idea.

"Yes, many in Dodge will remember Dr. Gambree from his visit. A godly young man with golden hair and a caring manner." McCallister raised his own glass as if in tribute. "Alfred says they brought back the wagon. Fools. That will hang Checker." He sipped the wine and continued, "Do you know what happened to the . . . lady with him? The dancer. Salome, I believe she was called."

"No one's said anything about her. I can ask your bunch in jail."

"Yeah, do. Checker and his boys might've killed her, too."

"What if Captain Checker resists? Do I get to kill him then?" Do'tsi asked keenly.

Rand started to respond, but McCallister's orders took over.

"Take Mayor Stanton and Judge Buchanan with you. Wait until he comes to town to see his sister. She's at that fool Dr. Tremons's place. Checker won't resist with them there." McCallister poured himself more wine.

"You think I can't handle him?" Do'tsi's eyes slitted with barely concealed anger.

McCallister's left eye twitched. "My point is that he respects you as a professional, not as a lawman." He paused for effect. "Or do you not mind him shooting first?"

"Wh-what about me?" Rand asked timidly.

"He doesn't respect you. Period."

"I'm not afraid of . . . Checker," Rand blurted.

McCallister blinked and cocked his head to the side. "Of course you aren't." His face hardened. "Remember, you take your orders from Do'tsi. Understand?"

Rand swallowed, nodded, and asked, his voice quavering slightly, "Why can't we leave the judge out of it? He's—"

"You think Checker's going to do what you—or that clown mayor—want?" McCallister's face transformed into crimson. He took a breath and his face lightened. "Besides, we need Buchanan to make it look legal. Right, Do'tsi?"

Do'tsi smiled his approval.

Rand showed a surprising amount of courage by countering, "Wouldn't it be easier to get him at the Hedrickson ranch?" He twisted his face into a long frown. "You know, when he's—"

"If you want to try," McCallister snapped, "I'll see that you get a decent burial."

"Ah . . . I was thinking more of . . . sneaking up—"

"You want Do'tsi to shoot Checker from long range," McCallister interrupted. "Or do you intend to try?"

"Well, ah, yeah, him." Rand stared at the screen in front of the fire, not at either McCallister or Do'tsi.

"Sounds fine to me." Do'tsi placed his eldows on the table and folded his hands together in front of his face, as if in prayer.

Straightening his back, McCallister went on to a long presentation of Checker's abilities and his younger brother's. "Here's a man who has earned a reputation in Texas—with his gun. With his gun, Rand." His face was reddening. "Do you think he's not expecting something like that?" He turned toward the Cherokee killer. "Do'tsi, I'm disappointed. I thought you—of all men—would expect more from John Checker. Didn't you listen when my men told you about the Indian fight on the way back? This man thinks like an Indian and fights like . . . some kind of wild animal." He almost said "like his father," but didn't think the two would understand.

"I am an Indian—or have you forgotten?"

"Of course not. Have you forgotten how difficult this man is to kill?"

Do'tsi studied McCallister's face for a long, tense moment. His hands dropped beneath the table. When the Cherokee killer spoke, a different concern was addressed. "You're . . . we're . . . going to let that southern loudmouth live so he can testify that Checker did the deed, right?"

"Right. Tom Redmond. He'll jump at the chance." Star's eye twitched more. "But don't talk with him in front of the others."

"You think I'm stupid?"

"Of course not. I was merely reminding you."

"Do'tsi does not need reminding."

"Sorry. I didn't mean to suggest that you did." McCallister held his sharp tongue. This wasn't the time to argue—or the man to argue with. He had pushed his own thoughts far enough.

"Excellent." McCallister smiled and turned to Rand. "Jubal, you go to the *Times* and suggest the same thing. Tell Allen one of the rustlers admitted it. Make the suggestion that he interview him."

"Redmond again," Do'tsi said.

"Yes."

Rand's response was immediate. "What if Redmond won't talk to him?"

"He will—if he thinks you're going to let him go free after all this is over."

"What if this editor doesn't see it . . . as a story?" Do'tsi's words hissed from the unreadable red line of his mouth.

"Let me worry about that, if it happens—and it won't."

It was Diverrouve's turn to speak—and to lessen the tension. "*Quartre. Oui*, I have spoken with many men of Dodge. Important men of commerce, *certainement*. I tell them Star McCallister is wronged. He is not a part of the gang of rustlers. *Oui*, he was kidnapped when they . . . broke out of the jail. *Non*, he is not one of them—and the Texians want to punish them for high prices." His recital was laced with exaggerated hand motions, his round face void of any sign of excitement.

"Well done, my friend." McCallister smiled.

"*Sacre bleu*, a grand day that will be—when you are back where you belong—as the king of Dodge." Diverrouve held up his wineglass in tribute.

Taking a small leather pouch from the pocket of his black broadcloth coat, Do'tsi retrieved his pipe from the table and packed new tobacco shreds into the bowl from the pouch. After lighting the new bowl, he considered adding some opium powder kept in a small case, then decided against it. That didn't keep him from mouthing "king" and leering at Diverrouve.

McCallister and Diverrouve watched him without speaking. If the Frenchman feared the new deputy, it didn't show in his eyes. McCallister silently praised himself for selecting a worthy business partner.

Through a series of white circles of smoke, Do'tsi finally spoke. "And when Redmond's through talking, I am to kill him."

"Well, yes, but I will tell you when," McCallister said. "I will want him to testify at my new trial too—when I am freed from any association with the rustlers. Don't let your brother do anything without my word either."

"Kana'ti will wait for my orders." Do'tsi gave him a look of disdain.

McCallister either didn't see it or ignored the visual comment.

The four men clinked their glasses and drank.

Putting down his empty glass, McCallister stood and paced around the small, cramped room. A long, rambling dissertation on the strategy to return him to a place of respect in Dodge followed. Right away, the Frenchman was to start a rumor about Checker killing the medicine wagon doctor. Sheer public pressure would be a factor in forcing a quick arrest. He thought telling Violet Kensington first should ensure rapid spreading of the story. The fat lady was well known for her need to know what was going on in town, and telling everyone she could find about anything she heard. She would embrace the story eagerly. It was also much faster than any newspaper story; whatever editorial support they got would act as reinforcement to what the town had already heard and decided.

McCallister continued with his strategy. A healthy bribe to Mayor Eklin Stanton would ensure his wholehearted cooperation in the arrest and the spreading of the murder rumor. That would be Rand's job. McCallister wanted it done first thing tomorrow. Diverrouve kept close track of the handsome mayor's gambling losses and knew he was in financial trouble. The restaurateur-turned-politician would help balance the well-known honesty of Judge Buchanan with his presence.

McCallister made it a point to remind the three men to not attempt to influence the stout magistrate, Judge Buchanan, in any way. Such efforts would backfire badly. He also warned them to keep away from Ham Bell; he was a councilman who couldn't be influenced—and was likely to take sides against him, if he had the chance.

Breaking into his presentation without thinking, Diverrouve reminded him, "*Capitan* Checker, he took ze medicine wagon and ze horses to Ham's stable."

"Yes, I know," McCallister said. Only a slight frown gave away his annoyance at being interrupted. "If Ham gives us any trouble, we'll make it look like he was Checker's accomplice."

Returning to his strategy, McCallister declared Checker would be arrested for the murder of Dr. Gambree, when he gave the word. Redmond would testify at Checker's trial that he saw the act. The mere appearance of Checker having returned with the medicine wagon would be the final piece of evidence. Except for Redmond, the remaining outlaws would be hanged.

After Checker was out of the way, Judge Hiram Buchanan would be petitioned to set aside the verdict against Star McCallister as new evidence would emerge showing he wasn't involved in the rustling ring and was taken by the gang when they escaped. If the judge appeared at all reluctant to do so, he would just disappear one day and a more helpful jurist put in his place with the mayor's help.

"Won't those kids and their mother tell a different story?" Rand's voice had a thin vibration, a warning sound.

"What kids? What mother?" McCallister burst into laughter.

Do'tsi chuckled. Even Diverrouve joined in the evil mirth by nodding; his expression didn't change, however.

McCallister's face twitched. "Now, I don't want to be misunderstood on this." His head swiveled from Diverrouve to Rand to Do'tsi. "I don't want them touched until I give the word. You got that? Stay away from those kids and their mother."

Only Rand responded, "Well, I guess that's another reason not to try something at the Hedrickson's. Them kids'll be there."

"Good point, Marshal," McCallister said with only a trace of condescension in his voice. "I don't want anything to muddy the water. There's no reason it should. Checker's arrest—and death—is the first step. The *only* step right now." He stared at the lawman. "Rand, you make sure there aren't any posters on Blue—or that woman—around the jail." He smiled. "Checker will try to prove Blue was wanted." He shook his head and giggled. "Say, your brother won't do anything to my men while you're gone, will he?"

"He wanted to. He won't," Do'tsi answered almost softly. "I promised him something else."

McCallister licked his lower lip and a twitch of his eye followed. "Be patient. Checker will visit his sister at that fool doctor's house in a few days. That'll be perfect."

Rand's eyes widened in a prideful glow. "I want to see that bastard dead."

Do'tsi laughed. "So it shall be."

CHAPTER TWENTY-FOUR

Miles away, a shivering night found Checker and the others sitting around a small campfire, drinking coffee laced with whiskey. Bannon was finishing his third plate of stew. Johnny and Rebecca had gone to bed shortly after supper. Worn out from the day's excitement, both were sleeping soundly under the chuck wagon. Sonny and Checker had placed another blanket over them after they were asleep. Captain had curled up next to the wagon as if to guard their sleep.

As they walked back to the campfire, Checker said, "Never asked before, Sonny, but do you have any brothers or sisters?"

"No, never did." Sonny glanced over at the tall Ranger. "Leastwise, none that I know 'bout. Hear tell that Pappy swung a wide loop a time or two, though." He chuckled and imitated throwing a lariat. "Reckon that's why my folks went separate ways."

"I wasn't riding your back trail. I . . . well, I just can't quite come down on my feelings about Star." Checker hesitated and stopped walking. "One minute I want to be the one that stops him. The next, I'm hoping he's escaped—and never comes back. There's no way I can forgive him for what he did to Amelia. No way. Yet . . . he's my brother. Well, sort of."

Sonny pushed his derby back on his head. "Yeah, I can tell when you're chewing on the problem. Don't blame you none. Who the hell can deal with somethin' like that? It's just plain awful. Ol' Jackson'd give his right arm to find his kin—an' you find your sister—an' find out your half brothers are pure bad—at the same time."

"That sums it up pretty good."

"Seems to me—if you're askin' for my advice—Star gave up his rights to being your kin when he tore up Amelia's family. He only had half to begin with." Sonny's shoulders rose and fell. "I'll tell you this, if I get the chance, I'm gonna shoot the sumbitch an' walk away whistlin'." He looked away at the small gathering around the small fire, avoiding eye contact with the former Ranger.

Checker resumed walking. "Yeah, I probably will too."

As he listened, Sonny realized his friend didn't really want to catch Star again. He didn't want the irony of facing him in a life-or-death situation. Checker wasn't afraid of dying; he was afraid of having to kill his own brother, no matter how evil Star might be. Checker had already been forced to kill Blue, and that weighed heavily on him. Maybe he had purposely let Star escape at their hideout. No, that couldn't be, Sonny refuted his own thought.

Yet, it was Checker who let Cole Dillon ride away to become Sonny Jones, instead of bringing him to justice. It was Checker who alone had decided the border outlaw, who would become his close friend, deserved a second chance and had even told his fellow Rangers that Cole Dillon was dead. What was the difference between Cole Dillon and Star McCallister when it came down to it?

Their conversation about the matter ended as they approached the small campfire and joined in the talk of cattlemen. Topics swung a wide circle from cattle and horses, to the Hedrickson ranch being rebuilt and the skills needed to accomplish such work, to women and kids, to the ride back to Texas, to the dangers of the Indian Territory, to the comparison of Dodge and Ellsworth, Triple C's trail destination in the past, and finally landed on the subject of the new town deputies.

Mitchell had heard about Do'tsi and Kana'ti being suspected of killing a cattleman near the Red. According to the rumor, a drover who worked for the murdered rancher had bought the dead man's spread. There was no proof he had arranged for the murder. Randy Reilman loosed a long string of cusswords upon hearing the story and Tug asked to have it repeated, thinking it was a joke about "a bed and a roomer."

Pushing on the small fire with a stick, Checker didn't want to talk about the Cherokee killers or their possible reasons for being in Dodge; his mind was on his sister's home and wondering if it truly would look right, or if the buildings would only be something temporary. He was anxious to see them, and those thoughts kept circling back to Sarah Ann Tremons. Maybe he could ride to the doctor's house in the morning, first thing, on the pretense of seeing how his sister was doing.

Jackson repeated his assertion that Star McCallister was behind the move and had to be hiding somewhere nearby, but Checker wasn't listening.

Young Tyrel Bannon sat cross-legged and quiet, not reacting to any subject, only staring into the fire as he continued to eat.

With his hands behind his head, Sonny seemed more interested in talking about the children and how glad

Amelia was to see them. His assessment of their reunion was presented with a smile that never left his face.

Only Jackson noticed the happy cowboy sat awkwardly due to the bullet wound in his side. Jackson decided not to bring it up because Sonny would only be angered by the attention; he told himself to check it in the morning before leaving. Sonny would be less likely to be annoyed and, anyway, they wouldn't be seeing each other for a long time after that.

Sonny's wounds made the black man think of Checker's injury, and his attention swung to the tall gunfighter's wrapped hand. How would the former Ranger be able to face these awful Cherokee killers? Where was Star McCallister? They had to be his doing. They had to be. Jackson's mind chewed on the situation. The confrontation was coming, he knew. It was only a matter of where and when. Did Checker know that, too? How could he not know? But if he did, his face showed no signs of worry, only enjoyment at listening to Sonny. And how about Sonny? Surely he recognized the extent of the threat. Surely.

Jackson's mind swirled with indecision as he tried to focus on his friend's comments. How could he walk away from two men who saw him only as a trusted friend, not as a black man? Silently, the black drover chewed on the situation, not wanting to put it yet into words. He had earned a position of respect with the Triple C ranch. Beyond that of most Negroes in the South or anywhere. It had taken years to do so, hiring on initially for practically no pay and no assurance of a job beyond riding drag on his first trail drive.

His parents had been slaves; he had been freed by the War. Fatherly advice to learn from everything and everyone—and leave hate to others—had stuck with him, along with the insight that a skilled man would be welcome anywhere, no matter his color. Jackson didn't know what had happened to his two brothers and a sister. Even his brief stint as a state peace officer had yielded no trace. His father and mother had passed away years before. Only in his memories was his family alive. He had made himself indispensable with his skills at handling horses and cattle, providing medical aid, and even cooking. How could he dismiss this effort to stay behind in Dodge?

Sonny's highlights of the day continued. ". . . I'll tell you, her face lit up somethin' special when those two came march—"

Hoofbeats in the darkness interrupted him. Standing where he had lain, Captain's growl was immediate.

"Now who in the hell would be comin' thisaway in the damn dark?" Randy asked.

Checker stood without speaking, his Colt filling his left hand.

Sonny grinned. "It's all right, Captain. I reckon it's a little lady."

The dog's growl lost its intensity and he returned to his resting position, muttering.

Reining up a few feet from the chuck wagon, Sarah Ann Tremons announced, "Dad said we had some visitors today." Her voice held a tremor as she dismounted.

Checker was standing next to her before she could say anything else, his gun returned to his belt. Nervously, she pulled on the lapels of the woolen coat worn over her high-collared, calico blouse and leather riding skirt. Her hat lay against her back, held by its leather tie. Moonlight was drawn to her hair tied in a bun, caressing the rich cinnamon. White teeth flashed a wide, but nervous, smile. Her bosom moved as her breath sought new air and left a fragile trail of breath-smoke. The gold of the fire discovered a few freckles on her perky nose.

"I missed you." She put her hand on his chest, holding the reins with her other.

Checker took her hand in his left. "Not as much as I did you, Sarah."

Her smile widened, but her eyes took in his bandaged right hand now holding hers. "Dad said you were hurt. Said it was bad. He said—"

Raising his left hand quickly, Checker's fingers touched her lips. "Sh-h-h. It's all right. It's all right. Now that you're here, everything's all right." His mind was awash with her soft scent of ginger and freshness like sunshine on newly washed clothes.

Her smile returned to her face and she reached into her coat pocket and brought out a button. Displaying it in her opened palm, she said softly, "See? It brought you back. Just like before."

"I would always come back . . . to you," he whispered.

"That's what I kept telling your button."

"I wasn't sure—"

It was her turn to touch his lips with her fingers. "I'm here."

Without a need for more words, they walked behind the chuck wagon with him leading her horse. Ten minutes later, the sounds of horses riding away brought chuckles from the men at the campfire. Moonlight glimpsed both riders trailing second horses taken from the Hedrickson herd.

"Now that's the first time I've seen John Checker tamed—by anything." Sonny stoked the fire with a bent branch. "Half of Texas would swear it couldn't be done. The other half would just swear." He laughed and slapped Bannon vigorously on the back.

The farm boy swallowed and choked.

"Whoa there, didn't mean to push up your supper, Ty." Sonny's voice became gentle.

Bannon coughed to regain his composure. "That's all right." *Cough.* "Just surprised me, that's all." *Cough.*

"Where're they goin'—an' why they be takin' them extra hosses?"

"Don't know, Ty. Guess we'll know if an' when he tells us." Sonny twisted his body to give relief to the returning ache at his side.

Slowly, the talk resumed about the ride back to Texas. Mitchell was eager to get moving, noting the colder nights were warning them of bad weather coming. He dismissed any comments about his still being weak from the rustlers' attack.

Randy expanded on the thought of the coming coolness, saying their horses would have winter coats by the time they got home. He wasn't worried even though this was, by far, the latest they had ever left Kansas. A few choice swearwords punctuated his affirmation. He didn't mention any concern about Mitchell's state of health.

More to himself than anyone else, Jackson said he planned to remind Checker to wire the marshal in Omaha and the late medicine doctor's widow; she deserved to know her husband's killer had been brought to justice.

Sonny nodded agreement and yawned. With that yawn came the realization that morning would come soon enough and the men drifted away to their bedrolls.

Only Bannon stayed behind, fixed on the dying fire.

Jackson watched him from under his blanket. He knew what was bothering the young man: leaving. The black drover was feeling the same emotion.

CHAPTER TWENTY-FIVE

A crisp dawn brought smells of hot coffee, fresh bacon, and eggs scrambled in bacon grease, one of Tug's specialties, as the Triple C camp came alive with tasks to begin the return trip to Texas. It wasn't an early awakening, not at all like the rugged mornings on the trail drive. Mitchell said the later start was to give the children plenty of time to rest. Jackson figured the trail boss wasn't yet up to moving around as quickly as he once did.

Randy, Sonny, Bannon, and Johnny worked to separate the two herds and keep them apart, with the Hedrickson geldings mixed in with the Triple C horses. The Hedrickson stallions remained tied to ground stakes.

Mitchell checked the chuck wagon one more time to assure himself of its contents while Captain barked and encircled the camp with the energy of a young dog.

After helping Rebecca wash up and dress, Jackson held her hand as they watched Tug finish the breakfast cooking. He should be helping with the herd, but it would be his last chance to be close to the little girl who had stolen the hearts of all the Triple C riders. And his.

"Uncle Black Jack, tell me again about the time when we were taken away," she said innocently.

Frowning, Jackson wasn't sure how to respond. He looked at Tug, who was concentrating on meal preparation and packing away anything he didn't need at the same time, or didn't hear enough of the words to understand their significance.

"Tell me about my mommy being hurt—and my daddy . . . going away." She continued, "And you finding me."

Reluctantly, Jackson began an answer that focused on the positive outcome. "Well, missy, we prayed a lot and God led us right to y'all and your brother. Kinda like with Moses in the Good Book. On the ride back, we saw lots of animals. Remember—"

Checker's return to the camp interrupted their conversation and gave Jackson a reprieve. The tall Ranger was driving the Hedrickson buckboard now loaded with supplies. His saddled black horse trailed the wagon with the reins tied to the rear. His morning had already been a busy one, sending wires, receiving responses, and buying two new Colts. Responses to his telegrams were now folded in his pocket. His new gun was holstered for a left-handed draw, sitting backward in the leather sheath. His backup gun had been returned to his saddlebags.

The Nebraska lawmen had thanked him for his action and the news that Blue McCallister's killing ways had finally been stopped. A reward would be forthcoming. The wire also included a promise to inform the local authorities in Lincoln and to locate Dr. Janiskowski's widow to see what she wanted to do about the recovered wagon and team. His communication to the U.S. marshal in Kansas had also yielded good news.

Jackson pointed toward the incoming wagon. "Well, looky who's here. It's Uncle John with your buckboard."

His thoughts ran to Orville Hedrickson and the thorough way he had trained. It was no surprise the horses took easily to a wagon. After the fire, he and Checker had used one, along with Jackson's own mount, to bring Amelia to town in that wagon. Seeing it again made him take a deep breath.

"Where has he been, Uncle Black Jack?"

With a smile, Jackson said, "Looks like he's got all kinds of good things for your home. See all that stuff in the wagon?" He pushed up the spectacles on his nose with a freed hand and hoped he wouldn't be asked more about their family's tragic time.

Near the herd, Sonny told Bannon that, most likely, Checker had spent the night talking with Dr. Tremons, Amelia, and Sarah. He was proud of the fact that he had managed to keep a straight face as he did, adding that Checker must've bought supplies for the Hedrickson place.

Breakfast was swift and mostly quiet as the riders collected their thoughts for the separation and ate in silence as western men did anyway. Saddled horses for Sonny and Johnny were each tied to one of a series of scrawny bushes that had taken up residence on the grassy plain. Checker's filled wagon and his saddled black were left a few feet from the waiting stallions. Reins of the Triple C mounts were wrapped around the chuck wagon wheels. The two Hedrickson steers had been moved to another grazing spot just after dawn.

Captain watched the herd as ordered by Mitchell; the three-legged dog had already eaten heartily, thanks to both Tug and Mitchell, who each didn't know the other had done so, or didn't want to acknowledge it.

Johnny ate next to Bannon, and Rebecca sat with Jackson. The black man was relieved that, so far, she hadn't brought up the same concern again. His mind was on whether he should stay or go. He had prayed hard during the night for guidance, but so far didn't feel he had an answer. Watching Dan Mitchell head for his bedroll last night reminded him that the trail boss was very weak. Besides Mitchell, no one knew the trail home as well as he did. Randy and Tug were good at their jobs, not necessarily at following a trail that would, at times, be nothing but a direction. They also might need help tending to the tough cowman. They might run into the kinds of trouble they had faced returning from the gang's hideout, and he would be the only one good with a gun. On the other hand, he knew Checker and Sonny would be facing new trouble, very serious trouble. It was a difficult decision. He would leave the matter up to John Checker and would ask him when he had the chance.

As they finished eating, Tug's curiosity couldn't be restrained and he asked Checker what the packed wagon was for. Checker explained he had stopped at the general store for food and supplies to take to his sister's place. He told them about wiring the U.S. marshal in Omaha and his reply and stopping at Zimmerman's for a new Colt. He didn't mention the other wire. Both Sonny and Jackson had already noticed the gun in his holster was new.

"We don't need sech, Captain. My chuck's all filled up. Got tobacco an' whiskey too."

Irritated, Mitchell loudly and slowly restated what Checker had said. "Tug, the supplies are for them . . . to take to the Hedrickson ranch . . . not us."

Tug studied the trail boss and asked, "Did he remember baking powder? Who's going to cook for 'em?"

"Yes, I did, Tug. Thanks for asking." Checker stabbed

his fork at a remaining piece of egg. "Guess I'll be the cook for a while. Won't be anything as good as yours."

Sonny shook his head, chuckled, and said, "Lordy be, that's for sure. We'll be lucky to get anything besides beans and coffee. Might have to take up cookin' again myself." His laugh was deep but forced.

When Tug started to ask another question, Mitchell stopped him by standing, leaving his emptied plate, coffee cup, and utensils at his feet. "Well, there's no gettin' around it anymore, boys. Time to ride south." He held out his hand to Checker. "Ride easy, John. We'll see you come next summer. God willin' and the creeks don't rise."

"Thanks for all your help." Checker held out his bandaged right hand, then switched to his left.

Grasping it with his own left hand, Mitchell began talking about the trail drive and the men they had lost; his voice was gravelly. Their handshake ended and the trail boss mumbled something about wishing they could stay. Checker quietly advised him to take it easy on the way back and to let Jackson lead.

Tug interrupted several times to make certain he had heard correctly, shook Checker's right hand, without realizing it was bandaged, and hurriedly began wiping off the plates and utensils with ashes from the gray fire and packing away the cooking gear.

As if knowing the time would get no better, Mitchell walked over to his saddled horse. "Let's ride, boys."

The raw-faced trail boss grabbed the mane of his horse and climbed into the saddle, trying to hide the weakness in his body. He rode out without looking back, shoving a freshly cut corner of his tobacco square into his mouth as he loped away.

Randy's good-bye was short and the wrangler managed to do it without swearing. His main focus was on the Hedrickson horses, making the observation that they would be what every cowhand was looking for—and that the two stallions would create a herd of great mounts. From him, it was the ultimate compliment.

As soon as Randy left to take over the Triple C remuda, Jackson stepped up to Checker, carrying Rebecca. He held out his left hand to the former Ranger. With his good hand, Checker pulled it toward him and gave the black drover a hearty hug with the little girl in the middle.

"Is this a game, Uncle John?" she asked.

Checker laughed. "No, honey, just good-bye to a good friend that I owe so much." He took Rebecca in his arms as Jackson held her out.

Jackson pushed his spectacles back and blinked away the emotion that was headed into his face. "Good-bye, Miss Becky, I . . . will miss y'all."

Rebecca's face twisted into tears. "Y-you can't go, Uncle Black Jack." Twin tears raced down her rosey cheeks. "Who will take me on walks . . . an' tell me things?"

The black cowboy shook his head and made no attempt to hide the wetness welling in his eyes. "M-Miss B-Becky . . . I will . . ." No words came, only more head shaking. He reached out, tugged on her bonnet straps as if to make certain they were properly tied, then ran his hand softly along her cheek. "Y'all take good care of your uncle John and uncle Sonny."

Rebecca turned into Checker's chest and sobbed.

Biting his lower lip, Jackson said, "Remember. Star's around here, John."

"Yeah, I know."

"I can stay," Jackson finally blurted. "This isn't over. Y'all might need me . . . to help with the horses . . . ah, to cook . . . ya know. I'm a pretty good hand with a gun, too, if need be."

"Jackson, everything in me wants you to stay, but

they're going to need your savvy. And maybe your gun, too, I reckon." Checker patted the crying girl. "Dan's nowhere near ready to ride. You'll have to lead them. You could get into some bad weather."

"This is hard . . . leaving."

"Yeah, I know." Checker's mouth was tight, barely a line on his face. "But it's the right thing." Tension rippled along his cheek and bounced off the arrow-shaped scar.

"Y'all have to let that hand heal, John. If y'all don't, it'll be stiff . . . forever."

"Yeah, I know."

Jackson nodded, touched Rebecca's hand once more, and strode away, knowing distance was the only answer for his sadness. He would find Sonny next and ask to check his wounds one last time.

Watching the exchange, Bannon stood beside the busy Tug. Johnny was helping carry gear to the chuck wagon as he was supposed to be doing as well. The farm boy's eyes were narrow and his mouth, dry. He wasn't hungry either; breakfast hadn't looked good at all. After rubbing his boots against the back of his pants, he took a long, jagged breath and walked over to Checker.

"Ah, John?"

Checker read the young lad's face, saying nothing. Rebecca remained huddled against his shoulder. Wetness from her eyes had dampened his Comanche tunic.

"I wanna stay. With you and Sonny."

The tall man smiled. "Nothing would please me more . . ."

Bannon's face brightened.

". . . but your mother needs you the most, Ty."

Bannon's face sank.

Checker put his left hand on Bannon's shoulder, cradling Rebecca in his right arm. "Ty, you're a man to ride the river with. Already." He patted twice and withdrew his hand. "Thank you for all you did to save Amelia's kids. We couldn't have done it without you."

"But . . ." Bannon couldn't find the words to refute this man whom he had grown to respect so much.

"You've got a great opportunity with Mr. Carlson, riding for the brand," Checker completed. "Your mother will be very proud of you. We all are. Stay close to Jackson—and learn."

Bannon swallowed, knowing there was no way to argue. He knew Checker was right. His face contorted to hold back the tears pushing against his eyes.

"Hey, I almost forgot," Checker said. "Got something for you. It's in the wagon." Without waiting for a response, he walked over to the buckboard, carrying Rebecca, reached over the side with his left hand, and returned with a brown-paper-wrapped package.

"This is for you, Ty. Figured you might be needing one." Checker handed the package to the farm boy.

With a mixture of surprise wallowing in his eyes, Bannon ripped open the paper, knowing before he saw it that it was a revolver. "A Colt! Thanks! I got money . . . I can pay you." He reached underneath his chaps for his pants pockets.

"No, that's my thanks for all you've done. Your mother should be very proud."

Shifting the gun in his hand and studying it, Bannon said, "It's just like yours, only without the, ah, changes."

"Yeah, that all right?"

Bannon's expression was a muddle of joy and sorrow. Words wouldn't come, so he nodded.

From around the front of the chuck wagon, Sonny appeared and moved toward the boy, thanking him and reinforcing Checker's insistence that Bannon should return to Texas. To assist his decision, Sonny was leading the boy's sorrel. Bannon checked the cinch, more to delay leaving than any concern about its tightness.

"Better get your bullet belt from the wagon, Ty," Sonny said matter-of-factly. "There's a cartridge box real close, if you need 'em."

As if also worried about the boy, Captain bounded over from the herd, his tongue already flopping from his mouth. Bannon ignored his arrival and Captain barked eagerly until the farm boy acknowledged him. No one enjoyed the trail drive as much as the ugly beast did. Missing one leg had never slowed him down.

"I know, boy, I know." Bannon shoved his new gun into his belt and leaned over to scratch Captain's ears. "I'll be all right. Yeah, I'm glad to be goin' with you." He led the horse toward the chuck wagon to retrieve his holster.

Jackson advanced with his gathered bedroll, leading his saddled horse, and tossed the tied-up gear into the back of the wagon. With a quick pat on Bannon's shoulder, he walked away, pushing on his spectacles. "Sonny, let me see those bullet holes."

Sonny frowned. "They're fine, Jackson. Really. You plugged me up real good. I'm mighty thankful."

Jackson didn't hesitate and tugged on Sonny's shirt with one hand, holding the reins with the other. "Let me see, Sonny."

Laughing, the stout cowboy raised his shirt so Jackson could briefly examine the wounds, then dropped the shirttail, letting it hang down, as it often did on its own.

"See, *compadre*, no more holes."

"Well, that's not so, Sonny. Y'all are healing, but ya have to keep them cared for—with that stuff from Doc Tremons—and ya can't be twisting and turning."

"All right, Dr. Jackson. I promise."

The two men shook hands. Sonny patted Jackson on the back and the black cowboy swung into the saddle

Captain stood at the rear of the chuck wagon, waiting while Bannon buckled on his bullet belt and placed the

Colt into the holster. He lifted the gun, held it, then remembered it wasn't loaded and began slipping cartridges into the cylinder.

"Come on, Ty," Jackson said and loped to catch up with the string of Triple C horses, pushed along by Randy and Wilson.

Bannon's gaze followed Jackson, then drifted toward Johnny standing next to the chuck wagon, watching him. It was the farm boy's turn to be strong in leaving and he knew it the moment their eyes met. With a hitch of his returned gun belt, Bannon suddenly felt older.

Captain barked.

"Just a minute, Captain. Got somethin' to do first," he yelled over his shoulder.

He walked toward the younger boy, leading the sorrel. Captain wagged his tail and followed.

"Johnny, I sure enjoyed gettin' to know ya." Bannon held out his hand as he came closer. "Wish I didn't have to go—but I do. We'll be back with a new herd come summer. It'll go fast." His mouth curved down at the corner at the last statement, not believing it himself.

Johnny's lower lip quivered and his eyes sought solace in the ground at his feet, and then he pulled off his cap and held it at his side in his left hand.

"'Member, you have to be the man now—in your family."

The boy's head nodded in agreement; his eyes told a different story. He blinked to hold back tears and inhaled deeply to bring new resolve. When he looked up again, Bannon was standing next to him, his hand still extended.

"Wh-when Uncle John left my mama, sh-she took a button from his shirt," Johnny said softly. "H-he promised to come back." Both hands remained at his sides.

Bannon stared at the boy, not comprehending what

the statement meant. He had never heard the story about the button exchange between the two.

"W-would ya give me one o' your buttons? To keep till ya come back?" Johnny mumbled, his gaze searching Bannon's face for agreement.

He started to say it was a new shirt, bought in Dodge after he returned, but thought better of it. With a hard yank, the small white button came free in Bannon's hand and he held it out to Johnny. Captain barked as if enjoying the game. Behind the farm boy, the sorrel nudged him in the back and Bannon jerked on the reins with his other hand.

"Here's my promise."

Johnny studied the button in Bannon's outstretched hand as if not believing it was being offered to him. His right hand rose, stopped, then yanked a button from his own shirt. Trying to smile, he placed his button in Bannon's hand and took the farm boy's.

"Well, thar ya go," Bannon declared and closed his fist over the tiny circle. "I'll miss ya, Johnny."

The boy rushed into Bannon and hugged him, holding the button tightly in one hand and his cap in the other. Bannon hugged back, hoping no one would see the tears that blossomed in the corners of his eyes.

Captain barked until both bent down to pat him.

"Grab leather, Ty. Texas is a-callin'." Tug appeared from the back of the wagon and climbed aboard.

CHAPTER TWENTY-SIX

At the herd, Jackson yelled and waved at Bannon, pointing at the left flank of the herd where two Hedrickson mares were drifting toward the Triple C group.

The farm boy froze; his eyes sucked in the horizon. As if everything depended on his next move, he muttered, "Good-bye" and climbed into the saddle. His spurs against the sorrel made it hunch and leap forward. Bannon's head jerked backward.

Captain yipped and raced beside them, and then ahead. Immediately, the cow dog began weaving through the moving horse herd, taking charge.

In three strides, the young rider was in position, his hat pulled low. The two Hedrickson horses were cut off and returned to the others. He dared not look up to wave. Instead, he adjusted his holstered gun and checked to make certain the hammer thong was well in place.

Tug slapped the reins and urged his team to follow the herd, and the wagon creaked into obedience.

"Good-bye, Tyrel," Johnny yelled, holding up the button in his fist.

"Why aren't we going with them?" Rebecca's tiny voice broke into the moment.

Checker glanced at Sonny, who tugged on his derby.

"We've got to get your home ready for your mother, Miss Becky," Sonny said.

"Why?"

Sonny ran his fingers along his closed mouth. "Why do you think?"

Checker looked amused.

The little girl looked like someone had slapped her face, and then she frowned. "Because Mommy won't come if we don't."

Johnny walked toward them, deliberately not looking at the riders leaving. Checker had seen the exchange and decided it was best not to comment. That was between two friends. The significance of the buttons tried to bring up images of Amelia at her burned-out house. The gunfighter wouldn't let them in.

Turning away from the Triple C riders leaving, Checker said, "Johnny, Becky, we're going to your place. We'll take the horses there, all right?" He tugged on the front brim of his hat; he hated bringing this up. "Now, your house . . . is rebuilt, but we don't know how nice it is. Your neighbors came and did it. Mighty good of them." He glanced at Rebecca in his arms, studying the scar on his cheek. "Says a lot about your mother and father that people would want to help that way." He ran his tongue along his lower lip and patted her cheek. "But we shouldn't expect too much. Right? We've got a lot of work to do. You understand?"

"Sure," Johnny said. "I heard you and Mr. Wilson talking about it. An' Mama told us some yesterday. She said Miss Tremons had seen to it herself." He squeezed the button in his hand and wondered if he should show the gift to his uncle.

"Right."

Rebecca cocked her head to the side. "Where are we going to live, Uncle John? Are we going to the house where Mommy is?"

Checker rubbed his hand across his mouth. "No, we're going to live at your house. We'll have to make do until we get it fixed the way we want. I've got food and things for us—in your wagon. Grain for the horses, too. To go with our hay."

"And, after a while, your pretty house will be all ready again," Sonny chimed in, sounding as enthusiastic as he could.

"Will that be tomorrow?" the little girl asked and held out her arms for him.

With a nod from Checker, Sonny stepped closer and lifted her to his chest. "No, sweetheart. That'll be next spring, I reckon."

Checker raised his hand at the waving Jackson with the vanishing herd.

"Hey, what about the steers?" Sonny asked.

"Oh, I forgot all about them. We'll tie them to the wagon," Checker said.

Johnny couldn't wait any longer. He opened his hand and told about the button exchange, explaining it meant Tyrel Bannon would be coming back for sure, just like Checker had returned to see his mother.

Checker was unsure of what to say.

"It's a good thing Ty didn't give one to all of us. He would've ridden to Texas with his shirt a-floppin' open," Sonny said and chuckled.

"It was just between us." Johnny's reply was matched by the hurt look on his face.

"Whoa now, son. I were jes' a-funnin'." Sonny held out

his hand as a stopping signal. "I didn't mean nothin'. He's a good'un, he is."

"I didn't get a button." Rebecca's mouth was a full pout.

"Well, sure you did." Sonny yanked on his shirt with his free hand and handed her a button from his shirt. "There. How's that?"

Without a word, she took the button, examined it, and asked if she could see her brother's trophy.

Johnny hesitated, but showed her the button in his opened palm.

"I like mine better," she said.

Johnny twisted his face to respond, caught the expression of his uncle, and just smiled.

"I think it's time we rode," Checker said. "Sonny, if you'll take the wagon—and Rebecca—Johnny and I will handle the herd."

"Sure thing. Believe I got the best end of that deal." Sonny studied his friend, wondering why he had made that offer.

Johnny ran toward his horse, pulled free the reins from the bush, and sprang into the saddle. Sonny kissed Rebecca on the top of her head and walked to the wagon with Checker.

"Nice-lookin' Colt, John," Sonny said. "Zimmerman fixed you up good, huh?"

"Yeah, he didn't think mine would ever work right again." He pulled off the tie-down and drew the weapon from its holster with his left hand and handed it to Sonny. "Take a look."

Sonny shifted Rebecca into his left arm and took the gun with his right hand. He held the gleaming Colt easily in his fist, sensing its balance, and returned it. "Looks just like your old one."

Remembering his other news, Checker took the two wires from his shirt pocket and handed them to Sonny.

He read both, returned them, and said, "Think you're gonna need that Kansas one?"

"Hope not."

Johnny yipped, waved his cap, and pushed his own horse against two bays wanting more bites of grass. The closest animal kicked one-legged in Johnny's direction, but the boy had already steered his mount away.

Minutes later, they were riding toward the Hedrickson homestead with the steers and Sonny's horse trotting behind the supply wagon. Even the two straying horses were caught up in the movement. Led by the brown mare, the rest of the horses were only partially agreeable to leaving the good grazing. With heads erect, the two Hedrickson stallions were already dancing proudly, one on each side of the gathered mares. Checker slapped his thigh with his coiled lariat, and a buckskin horse popped up its ears and slowly complied.

Out of long habit, he checked to make certain his Winchester was firmly in place in the sideways saddle horn holster. Only inserted this time for left-handed use. His eyes followed to the saddle Colt holstered just below the cantle and behind his right leg on the saddle skirt. Before he touched the gun, the bandages on his right hand reminded him of his injury and he left it alone. With his left hand, however, he double-checked his new Colt situated on his belt for use by that hand. He told himself that there would be plenty of time for his hand to heal; his only concerns would be getting his sister's ranch up and running again—and taking care of her children.

With Rebecca beside him, Sonny kept a safe distance from the herd; close enough, however, on the left side to help keep them moving. Rebecca unleashed a stream of questions about the horses, their colors and their actions. The happy-go-lucky cowboy was fascinated by her curiosity, instead of being annoyed.

Could Amelia ever grow to care for me? The question
shot through his mind and rattled around in his head,
bringing images of her lying beside him. That soft impression transformed into his late wife. He jumped in
the seat.

"What's the matter, Uncle Sonny?" Rebecca looked
up into his strained face.

"Ah . . . oh, nothin', honey. Nothin'." His forehead
rolled into narrow lines. "I, ah, was watching a horse."

"Which one?"

Sonny nodded at the closest bay. "Ah . . . that one."

"Oh. What was he doing?"

Sonny snorted. Of course she would ask that, he told
himself. "I thought he was going to kick at us."

Rebecca was silent and Sonny whistled and slapped
his thigh to encourage the horses to keep moving. His
own horse was tied to the rear.

"He couldn't reach us up here. My daddy wouldn't let
it kick at us, though."

"I'm sure he wouldn't." Sonny let the statement remind him of the reality of the situation and clicked his
reins to keep the wagon horses moving at a brisk trot.

They rode across the hills as a late autumn sprinkle
decided to meet them. From the dark clouds assem-
bling to the west, it was apparent this was the foreshadowing of a heavy rain, likely hours away. The horse herd
was allowed to spread out, but not graze as they moved
across the dampening land.

From the far right flank, Checker yelled, "Sonny!
Johnny! Looks like it'll be wet soon. Shall we push 'em
some?"

Johnny's face was pleased to be considered in the ap-
praisal, and he quickly yelled back his approval and
pulled on the front of his cap.

"Yeah, keep 'em movin'. But, you know, might not be
anything there for keepin' us dry," Sonny boomed and

began to sing made-up lyrics to "O Susanna." "O Rebecca, don't you cry for me. I come from Triple C with horses at my knee."

The little girl giggled and asked him to sing more, so he did.

Checker glanced upward at the advancing clouds and responded that he expected the new house would, at least, give them protection. They might not get there before it rained, he mused to himself and wiped away the sprinkles gathering on his face. Whether or not a storm came, the only other option was to leave the herd here and head for town. That would likely mean spending days rounding them up again.

He pulled on his Stetson and slapped his lariat again against his thigh. Fresh memories of the delicious night with Sarah Ann settled against his mind and he took a quick look over at Sonny, embarrassed about his daydreaming.

In spite of Rebecca's continuing questions, Sonny was concentrating on keeping the herd moving. Checker was relieved he hadn't seen him. The subject would have been obvious.

They rode on, each lost in thought and in maintaining the horses' advance. A sense of loss was heavy on the two men and the boy from having good friends ride away. Good times rushed through their minds to make the separation harder. Rebecca asked Sonny when they would see "Uncle Tyrel" and "Uncle Black Jack" again, and that made the cowboy even sadder.

As Checker cleared a short rise, he shuddered. A memory long forgotten jerked back into his mind as fresh as if it were yesterday. It was here—beside this tiny pond—that he and Star McCallister had actually played together once as children. They had sneaked out of town together; he was nine and McCallister was eight. The pond had seemed bigger then—and farther from town—when they had tried to fish. Three stray dogs had attacked them and the boys had successfully fought them off, except for a few minor scrapes and bites. After it was over, they had laughed. Together. But the younger Blue had joined them and a fight soon broke out, pitting the young Checker against the two young McCallisters. It was always to be so. Later that day, J.D. McCallister charged into the Checker family's tent and beat both his mother and the boy.

A bright reality followed that his life had been shaped—in an odd way—by this brutal man, leading him eventually into the responsibilities of a lawman. Would he need to take on this responsibility once more? Was his dream to become a successful horse rancher not one that fit the path already set for him?

Checker shook his head and examined the sky to bring him back to the moment.

Clouds strutted across the sky, full of themselves, but the spitting rain stopped and a timid sun attempted to retake control. Hooves padding against the moist earth and the creaking of the wagon were soothing and reassuring. As a group, they cleared a long line of hills, broken only by a sometime stream and an outcropping of yellow rock.

The trail was a familiar one to Checker, as well as Johnny. The former Ranger had come this way on his initial reunion with Amelia, leaving the cattle with the rest of the Triple C crew not far from Dodge. That night, Star McCallister's gang had attacked, killing several men and running off the herd.

Down through a crooked arroyo they went and into a thick wooded area. Checker paused beside a big tree with twin trunks that had grown together long ago. It had been one of the landmarks Amelia had drawn on the map for him to follow. Remains of a long-ago campfire lay close by. He put his hand against the tree as a flood of memories rushed into his mind. Checker's black rubbed its nose against the trunk and he nudged it into moving again.

Johnny yelled out that their place was only two miles away.

CHAPTER TWENTY-SEVEN

Checker's hand went to his shirt pocket to find Amelia's letter. It wasn't there. He remembered he had finally placed it in his saddlebags. His mind wouldn't let go of the worry that the children might be frightened by seeing the ranch again and it looking strange or inadequate—especially with their father's grave not far away—but the scene was one they must accept. He had tried to cushion their anxiety by telling them what to expect. Well-meaning neighbors had probably constructed simple structures at best.

Sarah Ann had been enthusiastic; however, she might have been trying to convince herself as well. Maybe the house wouldn't be fit to live in, he told himself. If so, they would move to town as he first planned. Regardless of the situation, it would be necessary to build a second house, of some kind, for him and Sonny to live in—once Amelia joined them. It wouldn't look right otherwise. This would be a bunkhouse for hands that would come later.

In their young lives, the children had seen too much that was evil and he wanted to make certain this wasn't a big disappointment. He swore to himself that Star Mc-Callister would pay for what he had done, wherever he might be, regardless of their blood connection—but, first, he must care for his sister's family.

Without making it obvious, he slid over to the side of the herd where Johnny was riding and told him again that they shouldn't expect too much from the neighbors' rebuilding efforts; in fact, they might have to stay in town for the winter. The boy nodded his understanding without taking his attention from the horses. If he was concerned, it didn't show.

Mostly brown now, a lake of grama grass awaited them and they eased through it, letting the horses eat as they passed. Everyone was alert. The Hedrickson ranch was just beyond the next rise. It stood alone in the shadows of a long valley.

"There it is!" Johnny yelled. "Look! It's . . . it's . . . home. It really is!"

The brown lead mare's head came up as if she, too, was pleased. She snorted, whinnied loud, and galloped toward the homestead. Johnny kicked his horse into a hard lope as the herd began to rush after the mare. Tossing its grand head, the Hedrickson bay stallion gathered itself and was in a full run in five strides. Two strides behind came the dun.

"They've smelled our home! They're headin' there!" Johnny yelled.

Checker tried not to be too excited. From a distance, the homestead did, indeed, look fully restored. Just like it had appeared when he saw it for the first time months ago. In his mind, it seemed like another world.

So much had happened since that grand reunion with his sister and her family. The Triple C herd was rustled and good drovers killed. He had discovered that his half brother, whom he hadn't seen in years either, was the leader of a sophisticated rustling operation. McCallister and his gang were brought to justice and the herd recovered. Checker had defended them against a lynching.

Star's young brother, disguised as a medicine peddler, broke out the gang with Marshal Rand's paid-for assistance. Upon escaping, Star led a night assault on the Hedrickson ranch that ended in Orville Hedrickson killed, Amelia raped, dragged, and beaten, and the children taken into Indian Territory to be sold to Comancheros. The four Triple C riders rescued the children and killed or recaptured the gang, except for Star McCallister himself.

Checker shot Blue McCallister in a face-down Checker had wanted to avoid. They had faced the terrible return through Indian Territory with prisoners, children, a herd of horses, and a medicine wagon. And now they were back. Truly back.

With another glance at Sonny, Checker spurred Tuhupi into action and the great mount was quickly alongside the now-racing herd.

Sonny held the team to a slower lope to keep Rebecca safe. She screamed her delight and jumped up and down in the wagon, "Look, Uncle Sonny! It's our house! The fire went away!"

Blinking back a swell of emotion, Sonny gulped. "Well, how about that? Now sit down, honey, or you'll fall out. We're gonna go a little faster."

He had been at their ranch only twice; the first at a gathering Amelia and her husband had held for the Triple C riders after their herd was retaken and McCallister's gang arrested; the second, when its smoldering remains told the awful story of McCallister's evil revenge. It was a time when he thought his friend, John Checker, was close to snapping.

Under his breath, Sonny muttered, "Thank you, Sarah Ann."

"What did you say, Uncle Sonny?" Rebecca turned in the saddle toward him.

Sonny grinned. "Won't this be fun, honey?"

"Who's going to cook for us?"

He shook his head. "Well, I think your uncle John is." He watched the herd thunder toward the ranch, marveling at their collective speed.

"Mommy lets me help with the cooking." Her big eyes sought his. "Will she be there?"

Sonny weaved the wagon around a large bush and urged a slow brown and a slower white horse with a sharp whistle. It gave him time to think about his answer. Unsatisfied with the horses' response and happy to have a different subject, he said, "Becky, we've got to get these hosses a-movin'."

"Daddy wouldn't let them do that."

"I reckon not. What would your daddy do?"

She twisted her mouth. "Daddy would tell them that they needed to be with the others." Her pushed-out chin declared confirmation of her thought.

Sonny cocked his head to the side. "Well, baby sister, let's give it a try." In a loud, demanding voice, he yelled, "You there, Brownie and Whitey—you catch up with the others. Do it now." He chuckled to himself as the two horses raised their heads and began to trot.

"See?" She pointed. "That's how Daddy did it."

"Well, I'll sure remember that." He slapped the reins against the wagon horses and they slipped into a lope that encouraged the two straggling horses to keep pace.

Ahead of them, a blur of brown, black, and dun raced onto a level plain dotted with long grasses of green and brown. In the distance was the rebuilt ranch.

The lead mare directed the spread-out string of horses past a trio of young cottonwoods, one barely more than a fat stick, and into the center of the familiar land. Shaking her head, the mare trotted and came to a stop as the closest group of horses encircled her. She sniffed the air, before whinnying her approval for the stallions and the rest to come. As if leading a parade, the two he-mounts strutted into the pasture and snorted their own approvals. Immediately, the first part of the herd began to graze. A few happy whinnies accompanied their return as the others trotted forward.

Excited, Johnny eased his mount alongside the edge of the gathering herd. Checker whooped and encouraged the rest of the strung-out horses to join them. Johnny pulled his horse back and joined Checker at the rear. Sonny and Rebecca in the wagon soon joined them, with two mares—a brown and a white—only a few yards in front.

"These gals liked it on the hillside," Sonny yelled.

"We gonna leave 'em here, Uncle John?" Johnny asked.

"Looks good to me, Johnny. What do you think?"

"Yeah, me an' Paw would always start 'em here—an' move 'em to the south pasture durin' winter. Lots of trees for shelter there. A purty good pond, most of the time, too," Johnny explained.

"Let 'em settle in while we go look at your house. All right?" Checker asked.

Loping toward the buildings, Checker and Johnny rode past an aging elm in the front yard with the side closest to the house scorched. Past their well, unhurt by the fire, and the small stone shed for storing butter and milk, also free of damage, and the rebuilt barn and toward a poled corral.

Johnny pointed toward the house. "Look at that, Uncle John! Our house. There's no fire anymore. But it's . . . it's . . . different."

And so it was. At least on the outside. In place of the

original split-log framed house was a planked wood home with a sturdy-looking, flat roof made of split-cedar covered with a dozen inches of earth. Two string-latched and sashed windows with real glass and molded battens set upright, flanking the doorway. They overlooked a rebuilt porch that ran the length of the building. Two support beams held the extended roof, giving the house a southern feel. Appearing solid as ever, the original front door stood tall and proud with a solitary black streak near the top corner serving as a reminder of its past. From the outside, the only other thing that was the same was the stone chimney, unhurt by the fire, except for a black mark here and there.

Actually it was better built than the first home, Checker thought. No disrespect to Orville Hedrickson, all of the buildings appeared to have been constructed by skilled men working with better materials. And with a determined woman in Sarah Ann directing them. To-gether, they had done quite a job. Checker couldn't hold back a wide grin; she had not exaggerated.

He planned a ride over to the carpenter's house to pay him for his work. Clearly, the house was beyond be-ing neighborly. Sarah Ann had given Checker the names of the three other generous neighbors; he planned to give them a horse each for their efforts. That was the least he could do. He was certain Amelia would agree. Sarah Ann was excited about what had been accom-plished and proud of the people who had helped. Ear-lier, he wasn't sure if her assessments were realistic; now he was certain they were—and was very pleased. However, they had been too consumed with each other during the night to spend much time on the subject of rebuilding.

"Oh, our tree is hurt, Uncle John. All its branches are done gone—on this side." Johnny dismounted and flipped the reins over and around the second corral pole.

Centered in the front yard, a snarled elm had spread gentleness as far as the porch. Now the side of the tree closest to the house was charred and the few remaining stubs of branches frozen black. Instinctively, Johnny looked over the area. His face told of his relief that the shallow creek on the backside of the yard was still there, as if the fire might have destroyed it as well. It was his favorite place to play. His study slid to the west where an open field had produced corn and now lay open. The row of hedge trees protecting the crops was unharmed too. Except for the two downed trees at the far end. Beyond that field was another where hay had been cut. His widening smile, displaying the missing teeth, sharply disappeared.

"Whar did ya bury my paw?" The question hurt him as the words bolted from his heart.

Checker dismounted, swung his reins around the same corral pole, walked over to the boy, and put his arm around his shoulder. "We thought he would . . . like being . . . there." He pointed at the grove of trees. "He planted them to help you." His eyes became slits to hold back the emotion that was mostly packed with hate for the men who had murdered this good man. "Good shade there. There's a wood cross, but we'll need to get a nice headstone."

"May I go there?" Johnny's cheeks were being divided by long strings of tears.

"Yes. Stay there as long as you want." Checker patted him on the back.

Sonny had climbed down, tied the reins to the brake stick, and was lifting Rebecca from the seat. For once, she was quiet and it bothered him more than her usual Gatling gun of questions. She was certain she was about to cry. Her gaze was on Johnny as he returned to his horse, climbed into the saddle, and galloped westward.

Tuhupi raised his glistening black head from of the corral and whinnied after them.

Sonny knew exactly where the boy was headed. His father's grave. The four Triple C riders had buried him there. He watched, saw Rebecca from the corner of his eye, and steadied himself for the question coming next.

"Is Johnny going to see my daddy?"

It wasn't what he expected. Did she grasp the idea of her father's death?

"Ah, reckon so, little missy." Sonny didn't look down. "He's going to the grave where we, ah, laid him."

"My daddy isn't coming back, is he?"

Sonny's eyes tightened. "No, honey, he isn't. Would you like to see . . . ah, where he's buried?"

The nod of her head was definite.

Sonny lifted her back onto the wagon seat and eased himself beside her. As he unwrapped the reins, he yelled to Checker, "We're going to the grave, better join us."

Checker returned to his black and stood there, unsure of how to handle the situation. He had buried men before. Too many. Good friends and fellow Rangers. He had even buried his friend, Stands-in-Thunder, in the traditional Comanche way. But none of that was the same as this. What could he say that would take away the agony these children felt? He wished Jackson were here to sing and read from his Bible. He glanced at the house as he swung into the saddle.

By the time he reached the grave site, a renewed mist was settling over the land. He dismounted near the wagon and stopped. The ground remained humped where Orville was buried. The wooden cross had slipped to the side, nearly touching the land. Sonny was singing and holding hands with both Johnny and Rebecca. His voice was a trumpet within the trees.

The song itself was pure Sonny, a mixture of six

songs: "Sweet Hour of Prayer," "Bury Me Not on the Lone Prairie," "You Are My Sunshine," "Battle Hymn of the Republic," and two other Civil War songs, "The Volunteer Song" and "The Faded Coat of Blue." His voice slid without pausing from one part of a song to another, incorporating what he could remember of each. To the children, though, it was the most beautiful hymn. Ever.

" 'Sweet hour of prayer, sweet hour of prayer, oh how I long for, sweet hour of prayer' . . . 'For you are my sunshine, my only sunshine, You made us happy when skies were gray. You'll never know, Dad, how much we love you' . . . 'Oh, bury me not on the lone prairie, where the owl all night hoots mournfully,' . . . and this land blows free and you rest peacefully' . . . 'Oh how I cling to sweet hour of prayer, sweet hour of prayer.' . . . 'Mine eyes have seen the glory of the coming of the Lord: He is trampling out the vintage where the grapes of wrath are stored' . . . 'Your cause is good, 'tis honor bright, 'Tis virtue, country, home, and right, then should you die for love of these, We'll waft your name upon the breeze, The waves will sing your lullaby, Your country mourn your latest sigh.' . . . 'No more the bugle calls the weary one, Rest, noble spirit, in thy grave unknown. I'll find you and know you, among the good and true, When a robe of white is giv'n for the faded coat of blue.' " With his eyes closed and his chin held upward, Sonny went immediately into his version of the 23rd Psalm:

" 'The Lord is my shepherd, I shall not want for nothin'; He brings me to green pastures and cool waters, an' makes me feel good. He be leadin' me along the right path, so I can walk through the valley of the shadow of death, and not fear nothin' or nobody as I pass; For Thou art with me, givin' me comfort an' such, even preparin' a table full o' food for me. Never mind my enemies. My cup runs over it's so full. Surely goodness and mercy shall follow me all the days of my life; and I'll be livin' in the fine house of the Lord's forever.' Amen."

Checker studied the children's glowing faces. Tears were corralled and their eyes were clear. After Sonny finished, he asked them both to pray out loud whatever they wanted to say. It hit Checker like a fist: Sonny would make an excellent father—for these children. How obviously he cared for them and they adored him. Was it wrong to think of such things with their real father only months in the grave? And what about Amelia? His stomach jerked with the painful thought of her situation. Would she ever want to be with a man again?

"God, please take good care of . . . Paw. He was always good to us." Johnny's thin voice broke into Checker's thoughts. "If ya have any horses up there, my paw's the best at trainin' 'em. I sure do miss you, Paw. Amen."

Sonny nodded at Rebecca and she folded her hands together and shut her eyes. "Now I lay me down to sleep, I pray the Lord my soul to keep. If I should die before I wake, I pray the Lord my soul to keep. Amen."

The happy cowboy sniffed back a tear and gazed upward, letting the mist decorate his face. Checker held his own medicine pouch around his neck and prayed to himself. It felt good. There was a lot to be thankful for; there was much to ask for, too.

Rhythmically touching the autumn-browned tree leaves, the sprinkle was as if a gentle answer from above. A minute passed before anyone realized it was doing anything at all.

"Will Daddy get wet out here?" Rebecca stared at the tiny drops barely reaching the grave's rearranged earth.

"No, he won't." Sonny's head snapped back, his voice emphatic. "God'll see to that."

"How does he do that, Uncle Sonny?"

Sonny smiled and picked her up. "Don't know how He does it—but He does." The cowboy had asked himself almost the same question years before at the graves of his wife and child. "Why don't you two go an' see your new house with your uncle John? And I'll take care of our horses."

Overhead a jay screamed its presence and landed on a branch overhanging the grave as the light drizzle began to gave way to a struggling sun. Checker wondered if the bird was related, in some way, to thunder and lightning or the weather. He tried to recall if Comanches thought the jay was a forecaster of storms. Could this be the spirit of his old friend looking out for them? Jay feathers had once adorned the old man's head, along with an eagle feather. He shook his head; that was foolish thinking.

CHAPTER TWENTY-EIGHT

Two days later, as Checker, Sonny, and Johnny were hitching up the buckboard, a familiar figure rode into view. Sarah Ann Tremons galloped toward them, waving.

She reined up alongside the corral. "I just couldn't stay away any longer. How do you like the place?" Her smile was forced, her manner more upbeat than her eyes.

Leaving the wagon, Checker lifted her from the horse and took the reins. "How can I ever thank you for all this? It's quite a fine job, Sarah. You weren't exaggerating one bit. The house is, well, better than it was." He glanced around to make certain neither child heard him.

"Did you think I was?" Her eyes danced as she spun into his arms.

Checker grinned. "Of course not." He stared into her face. "What's wrong?"

"I'll tell you later." She kissed him lightly on the cheek. "I missed you."

"Not as much as I did you." He returned the kiss and

his smile pushed against both sides of his face. "It's been cold at night."

With a squeeze of his left hand, she walked over to greet Sonny and Johnny who had finished the harnessing. Checker looped her reins around the middle rail.

With Sonny's quiet urging, Johnny thanked her. "Ah, thank you, Miss Tremons—for our . . . place. It'll make Mama real happy." Johnny stiffly motioned toward the house. "Paw, too, if'n . . ."

"Thank you, Mr. Hedrickson, I hope you are all happy here."

Rebecca skipped over from where she was feeding the chickens, thanked her with a curtsey, and asked, "Do you know what happened to our chickens?"

"Quit that, Becky." Johnny pushed on her shoulder. "She don't know 'bout no chickens."

Sarah Ann's eyes widened. "I'm sorry . . . aren't those . . . ?"

"We just bought them," Checker said. "From the Johnsons."

Sonny grinned and added, "Got us a fine milkin' cow, too." He waved enthusiastically toward the barn. "Her name's Milky. Right, Miss Becky?"

"Oh, I see," Sarah Ann said as Rebecca nodded.

Johnny stared at his younger sister. "She built this whole house—for us."

"Thank you, Mr. Hedrickson, but I had a lot of help—from your neighbors. The Johnsons, you know them. Mr. Brode. We couldn't have done it without him. An' Mr. McKinsey. And the Faulkners." Her vision swung back to Checker and stayed there. "And don't forget your Triple C friends. They were wonderful, too. And Mr. Bell from town came out several times to help."

"I know'd 'em all. We took round hosses to each of 'em. Yesterday," Johnny said proudly. "Well, to the neighbors anyhow."

"Oh, how nice," she said. "And, you know, it's quite all right to ask about chickens. I like them too."

"You do?" Rebbeca's face brightened. "What do you like best about them? I like their soft feathers."

Again Sarah Ann forced a smile and pushed a wayward curl from her face as she knelt beside her.

"How is my Mama? We are going to see her today," Rebecca declared. "After we finish our chores." She touched her cheek with her stubby finger. "I've done my chore. The chickens are fed. Johnny, have you done yours?"

Sarah Ann's expression became more and more pained until she abruptly stood and halted the sweet talk to explain her second reason for coming.

"Excuse me, children, but I've got some news from town your . . . uncles . . . need to know," she finally said, glancing at Johnny and Rebecca. Her eyebrows tightened in a long worry.

Without hesitation, Sonny suggested that he and the kids make sure there was water for the animals in the barn. Rebecca noted that was one of Johnny's daily tasks.

"You need to see this, too. Please," she urged.

"Oh. Johnny, can you and Becky handle that alone?" Sonny asked. "I need to stay here for a piece."

"Sure. Come on, Becky," Johnny declared.

The three adults watched the two run toward the barn to get a bucket for the rain barrel.

"Aren't they wonderful!" Sarah Ann said. "They've been through so much. It isn't fair." She wiped moistness gathering in the corner of her eyes.

Checker ran his left hand along the closest side of the wagon bed; Sonny rubbed the toe of his right boot against the hard ground and rechecked the harness to keep his eyes from her examination.

As the children disappeared inside, she retrieved a

folded newspaper from her saddlebags. It was the morning edition of the *Dodge City Times* and the headline read: TRAVELING MEDICINE DOCTOR MAY HAVE BEEN MURDERED. While Sarah Ann waited, Checker and Sonny read the accompanying story.

Convicted rustler Tom Redmond was quoted as saying Dr. Gambree, described as a traveling medicine wagon doctor and ordained minister, was murdered by John Checker, following an argument at the McCallister gang's hideout. He said the doctor had followed the gang and successfully secured the children's release, before Checker and his men appeared. Upon their arrival, the outlaws surrendered; Checker grew angry and demanded that the doctor leave without the children. The doctor explained he was better equipped to bring them back to Dodge and could give them religious comfort, but Checker ignored his plea. Redmond said that he was standing close by when Checker shot Dr. Gambree in the back as he helped the children into his wagon.

The report included the fact that Checker and his friends had returned with the medicine wagon and team, which were now in one of the town stables. Redmond's assessment of this act was: "Checker said he wanted to bring back the wagon to sell and make a few dollars for his trouble."

One long paragraph described the young, blond medicine salesman in terms of his proficiency in quoting Bible scripture, as well as his claim of being an "ordained minister of faith" and his wide assortment of nostrums. It was noted Dr. Gambree had brought his touring act of entertainment, gospel, and medicine to Dodge twice; most recently, this fall. Nowhere did the news story mention Checker was a former Texas Ranger captain—or the medicine man's assistant, Salome.

Redmond further asserted that Star McCallister wasn't involved in the rustling operation and had been arrested under false pretenses by John Checker. He said the gang had escaped on their own and had taken McCallister as a hostage, then the children, too, but he had escaped. The story included Redmond's statement that McCallister had tried to convince the gang to take only him and leave the children. Redmond's reasoning for Star's initial arrest, along with the rustlers, was: "The Texans wanted to show Dodge who was really in control of the town and they considered Star McCallister one of the true civic leaders."

Redmond also affirmed that he had not personally harmed Mrs. Hedrickson or been involved in the shooting of Mr. Hedrickson; those committing these awful crimes had been shot or hanged by the Triple C riders. The newspaper ended with the acknowledgment that this was only one version of the events and that neither Checker nor any of the Triple C men had been available for an interview. Dr. Howard Tremons had not permitted an interview with Mrs. Hedrickson, claiming she was not well enough.

Sonny snarled, "Damn, that's one big windy. How the hell could anybody believe that bastard Big Tom?" He turned toward Sarah Ann and apologized for his language.

His face taut, Checker looked up from reading. Sonny had seen that intense expression before. When he was an outlaw. When the rustlers took their herd. And when they were closing in on the kidnappers. It was the look of attack.

"You—and Jackson—were right. Star is here." The fromer Ranger took a deep breath to inhale the new reality. "At least, now we know his plan. Have me arrested for murder, then get his conviction overturned." He glanced away. "I didn't see it. Guess I didn't want to see it. I wanted to believe he would ride on."

Sarah Ann's face whitened. "Star? Star McCallister? In Dodge?"

Sonny explained that it was likely the outlaw leader had returned and was orchestrating this arousal. He avoided Checker's pained stare as he talked.

"Where do you think he is?" she asked, breathing unevenly. "Certainly he's not in town. We would've known by now."

Checker folded his arms, partially to hide his bandaged right hand. "No, he won't show himself until he's good and ready." A calmness had returned to his countenance.

"When's that? When you're arrested for murder?" Her voice was trembling.

"That's a good guess."

She began sharing her worries about what was happening in town. Talk about Checker murdering the medicine peddler and the need for justice had swelled this morning. Sentiment in Dodge was also growing in favor of the idea that Star McCallister had been wrongly accused. Even the mayor had begun expressing those feelings. She pointed to a quotation in the story: "Mayor Stanton appraised the situation, 'The good citizens of Dodge City will not stand for this kind of violence against those have graced us with their healing words and ways. We will not stand for an innocent citizen wrongly accused. Justice must be served.'"

"Violet Kensington, that awful woman," Sarah Ann said excitedly. "She's been telling everyone in town that you're . . . you're a murderer."

To ease her mind, Checker showed her the telegram received from the Nebraska marshal; it calmed her somewhat and she held it against her bosom.

"Well, that certainly changes everything. I'll take this to Mr. Allen and get him to write the truth, for a change," she declared. "Dad felt awful that he kept Amelia from telling what really happened."

"He shouldn't," Checker said. "They would've said it was the ravings of a woman in distress."

Sonny's expression was a question about the second wire; Checker shook his head to indicate he didn't want to mention it.

"Maybe you and Sonny should stay away from town for a few weeks. Let things settle." She looked at the barn, where Johnny was carrying a full bucket from the nearby rain barrel, then back into Checker's eyes. "Dad thinks you should ride to Topeka and talk with the U.S. marshal. Get him to send somebody here to clear up all this awfulness."

Sonny eyed his tall friend. "Prob'ly a good idea. What do you think, John?"

That Checker had made up his mind was obvious. "No, that would take too long—even if the marshal had someone to send. This is going down fast. Star's got to take advantage of the town's attitude. Thank your father for me, please—but I don't want either of you getting involved."

"Why not, John?" Her expression was a mixture of surprise and hurt.

Checker attempted a smile but it only got halfway across his mouth. "Because I don't want you two taking that kind of risk. It's my fight. I'm the one Star wants."

She couldn't stop the runaway tear that slid down her cheek. Words that wanted out only reached her mouth and turned into a trembling lower lip.

Checker watched the barn for the returning children. "We'll head for town. Just like we planned. The kids want to see their mother. If Doc says it's all right, we'll bring her home."

Sarah Ann's eyes pleaded for Checker to reconsider.

He held out his hand for the telegram. "I'll need this before you do. Judge Buchanan should see it first. He'll be the next target, if they get me."

It was Sonny's turn to question him. "You think it's safe—for the kids? To come into town with us . . . right now? I could go lookin' for Star."

Checker folded the paper and returned it to his shirt pocket without comment.

Pulling on the brim of his derby, Sonny leaned forward to make sure Checker was listening. "If he's hidin' out somewhere near Dodge, somebody's gotta be bringin' him food—an' news. That means a trail. I found him before."

"Yeah, you did, following a gang and a herd of horses in a hurry," Checker said firmly. "How many trails from town do you think there'd be? All kinds of folks come and go to Dodge." He curled the fingers of his left hand around his gun butt. "How long do you think it would take to find him? A week? A month? We haven't got that kind of time, Sonny. We've got to act now—before we're dealing with a mob."

Sonny looked at Sarah Ann and started to make a comment about Checker's injured hand, then decided against it.

"Nobody's going to bother those kids. We'll go right to Doc's. You'll stay with them while I go see Buchanan." Checker's eyes indicated it wasn't a matter for discussion.

From the barn, Johnny appeared, beaming. Rebecca skipped at his side.

"All right, then. I'm going with you," Sarah Ann declared. Her eyes were bright with determination; her fingers flicked away the remains of tears on her cheeks.

CHAPTER TWENTY-NINE

"Looks like the town's busy today," Checker observed as he popped the reins over the wagon horses to keep them in an even trot. Sarah Ann's horse followed the wagon with its reins tied to the rear.

It was the first comment since seeing Dodge itself by any of the three adults on the buckboard seat. Sarah Ann sat between Sonny and the former Ranger, each lost in thought. Johnny and Rebecca sat in the wagon bed, watching the land pass; both eager to get to town and see their mother.

"Mama an' Paw liked to come to town to trade on Saturdays, too," Johnny noted and elbowed his sister so she wouldn't lean on his shoulder.

"Can we buy some more chickens?" Rebecca asked.

"They don't sell chickens in town," Johnny said and folded his arms.

Imitating her brother, she folded her own arms and looked disgusted. "I don't believe you."

In front, Sarah Ann glanced at Checker and forced a

smile. "Chickens seem to be rather important to a certain young lady."

"Yeah, I guess."

Looking over his shoulder at the two children, Sonny muttered, "Be thankful she isn't fond of buffalo."

Both Sarah Ann and Checker laughed, in spite of the tenseness they felt.

Their mirth was short-lived as Checker pulled on the reins to keep the wagon from hitting a series of holes in the road. His mind was mostly on Sarah Ann, touching his leg with her own. The rest of his contemplation lay on what they might find in town.

The children were looking forward to seeing their mother, and Rebecca kept asking Johnny if her mother would like her dress. Both were also excited about visiting Wright's General Store later as Sonny had promised. Rebecca reminded her brother that she had helped Sonny put together a list of things they needed. More chickens were on the list.

Ahead the river was sweetened with sunlight as they rumbled over the bridge into town. Both Checker and Sonny were surprised at the busy sense of the town. Morning sun painted the buildings a bright bronze and orange as men and women bustled about, buying supplies and selling eggs and milk Dodge was surprisingly active, although not jammed like the summer when drovers lined the streets, and the bawling of beef at the rail pens and the saloon noise could nearly drown out conversation.

A black carriage passed on their right, followed by a wagon half loaded with lumber. Checker nodded greetings and was taken aback by the expressions of disgust. Neither Sonny nor Sarah Ann said anything about the reaction.

They rattled past the barbershop crowded with men for haircuts, gossip—and to read the latest *Police*

Gazette. Proprietor George Dieter professed to be "the eminent tonsorial artist of the Arkansas Valley" and was proud of his array of personalized shaving mugs for regular customers. And his ten-cent shaves and two-bit haircuts.

Earlier, Diverrouve had entered the shop, waving his folded copy of the newspaper, and issued a demand— to the rest of the barbershop's occupants—that Marshal Rand and his new deputies should be encouraged to arrest Checker and hang him for killing such a nice man. The room filled with positive responses, yet no one left to seek the lawmen about taking this action.

Instead, discussion followed about the new deputies being Indians. Diverrouve deftly deflected the racial concern by stating that there was evidence Checker was jealous of Star McCallister's success in Dodge, and had arranged for the innocent McCallister to be arrested along with the gang of rustlers. His story, laced with French words and expressions, included the idea—expressed in the newspaper accounting—that McCallister had been kidnapped by the gang when they broke out and taken with them into the Territory.

Several patrons supported the idea that the Texans were an arrogant bunch who only wanted to tear up the town. Another asserted Dodge should bar Texans from bringing in their herds. That comment drew looks of scorn and disbelief. A heavily bearded customer declared that he suspected Checker had killed Star McCallister, too, which brought on more vitriolic statements.

"Hey, there's that doctor killer now!" The announcement came from the customer closest to the opened front door.

"Sure 'nuff, that's him. Boy, he's got some nerve," the man next to him proclaimed.

"*Sacre bleu!*" Diverrouve rushed out the back door.

"Where's he going?" the man closest to the front door asked. "Thought he wanted a shave."

George Dieter shrugged his shoulders and said, "Next?"

Returning their attention to the passing wagon, one old-timer pondered that Amelia Hedrickson's brother looked familiar, but couldn't remember why. Another longtime Dodge resident related a wild tale of a boy named John Checker who had long ago tried to kill a saloon owner, but been chased out of town and wondered aloud if this was the same person. No one in the barbershop thought that was likely. A clerk with spectacles and plastered hair announced that he had heard from several Texas cowboys that John Checker had been a Texas Ranger. A well-dressed townsman refuted it as just one more lie from that uncouth bunch.

That led to the talk dominating the town. Whispered stories about Checker killing Dr. Gambree had spread through the town, set in motion earlier by Diverrouve as planned and fully flamed by the morning's newspaper story. It served to give black-ink credence to the rumors floating through the town.

On the street, Checker saw their furtive glances and more. He had lived by seeing things others missed. The difference between life and death was often a thin line for men like him. He wondered if he truly could become a rancher like he and Sonny planned. He was angry with himself for not suspecting something like this before. Would Judge Buchanan listen? Or would he be influenced by the town's apparent attitude? How soon would the Cherokee deputies move to arrest him? That would be the next step, he thought. Then they would kill him and announce that he had attempted a jail break.

Checker heard none of the comments, only seeing the disdainful stares, and knew Sarah Ann had again been accurate in her description. He didn't think anyone would be brave enough to bother them now; the presence of their weapons would be enough to keep the town at the talking stage. Their rifles lay in the back of the wagon. Both men also wore their belt guns, in spite of the town's ordinance against them. The newspaper story, and Sarah Ann's assessment of the town, had been enough to override their original idea of appearing as respectable citizens. Checker pushed away the wish that he had practiced using a gun in his left hand.

"Are we really going to see Mommy?" Rebecca asked as the wagon worked its way through along the busy street.

"We sure are," Sonny said.

Checker couldn't hold back a smile; his friend was freshly shaved and wearing a new shirt and clean pants. He wished they could concentrate on building the ranch—and making it a warm place for Johnny and Rebecca. He wished Star McCallister had gone away so they could focus on this new life. Where was he, anyway?

"Are ya gonna have Dr. Tremons look at your hand, Uncle John?" Johnny asked, watching two boys playing stickball in an alley.

"We'll see," Checker said in a distracted tone.

Sarah Ann nudged him with her elbow.

"Ah, thanks for asking, Johnny. That's very thoughtful," he quickly added.

"Sure."

Eager to see Amelia, Sonny knew it was foolish to think that way about her. It didn't matter; he did. Trying to sound offhand, he licked his lips. "Wonder if Doc will be surprised to see us."

Checker glanced in his direction. "Not as much as the town."

"He'll be happy to see you—and worried. All at the same time," Sarah Ann said.

They drove down the street, drawing sideways glances and muttered observations.

"*Och der lieber!* It is him!" came a shout from the sidewalk from an older German man.

Sarah Ann's quick look identified the voice. "Oh, that's Herman Gotts. He owns a small meat shop around the corner. I'm disappointed in him. He and Dad are good friends."

"He didn't say anything bad," Checker said and touched the medicine pouch beneath his tunic and shirt out of habit.

He understood the meaning of the eyes upon them. In a way, the German proprietor had expressed it well. It was more than curiosity; it was fear in some; anger in others; disgust in a few. McCallister's strategy was working; town sentiment would allow his next steps to manifest.

"Yeah, I see it." Sonny's whispered comment broke into Checker's mind. "Feel it actually. We ain't real welcome. Thought maybe it was the sweet water on my face."

"Thanks, Sonny," Checker said and clucked at the horses to keep up their trot.

Stiffening her back, Sarah Ann said, "It makes me disgusted to see how stupid people are. My goodness, this is insane."

Sonny set his jaw. "Yeah, looks like some folks think we're bringin' in a load of smallpox or somethin'."

"What did you say, Uncle Sonny?" Johnny leaned forward.

"Oh, I was tellin' your uncle John that the town's been lucky not to have trouble with smallpox or some other bad thing like that."

"There were a mess o' measles around hyar last winter," Johnny declared. "Me an' sis didn't git 'em, though."

"Well, that's good."

Rebecca grabbed his shoulder and said she didn't want to be sick. Turning in the seat, he patted her hand and told her that he didn't want her to be sick either.

"You have to realize, underneath the smiles, they really don't like Texans—and the way we come in and take over," Checker muttered.

"A lot don't, that's for damn sure." Sonny pulled on the brim of his derby. "Heard tell over in Missouri, they chased some Texas boys and tied 'em to trees, fence posts an' such. Horsewhipped 'em. Warned 'em they'd be shot if they came back with their beef."

As they passed by a dozen women clustered on the sideway, one particularly large woman in an oversized, starched bonnet turned toward their wagon, pointed a folded newspaper, and yelled, "Murderer!"

Sarah Ann glared at her; neither Checker nor Sonny looked.

"Murderer!" she called again and two other women joined her chant.

"Why are they calling you a 'murderer,' Uncle John?" Johnny asked, staring at the women.

"Guess they don't like me," Checker said and concentrated on maneuvering the wagon around a passing buggy whose driver clearly didn't want to be so close to him.

"That's not very nice, is it?" the boy asked.

Looking over his shoulder again, Sonny explained, "Son, there are some folks tryin' to make it look like your uncle did somethin' wrong—when we got you from the outlaws." A fleeting look at Sarah Ann preceded his continuing assessment. "Remember that yella-haired medicine peddler? Star McCallister's little brother? He and another man tried to ambush your uncle . . . and he had to kill them." The words came as if talking about cattle or horses.

Johnny's eyebrows twisted into new concern. The

corner of his mouth quivered. "T-Tyrel tolt me 'bout that. He heard it from J-Jackson."

"Don't scare him," Checker muttered.

"I don't think actin' like everythin's sweet is the way to treat him." Sonny's voice was sharp. "He deserves to know we're ridin' into trouble."

Sarah Ann frowned. "He's right, John."

Checker's only response was to snap the reins at the team.

"Uncle Sonny . . . I-I d-don't understand." Johnny's lips were pursed and he was trying hard to act brave.

Without hesitation, Sonny stood while the wagon banged along, awkwardly climbed over the seat, and sat down next to Johnny. Quietly, he explained the situation, leaving nothing out. Rebecca crawled into his lap, but, for once, was silent. Her large eyes studied Sonny's face. Agitated, Johnny swept the area as if expecting to see the gang of outlaws coming at them again. Bile was edging toward his throat and he swallowed to keep it down.

"Johnny, it's all right to be scared," Sonny said quietly. "We all are." He put one arm around the boy and cuddled the little girl closer with his other. "The only way to deal with evil is to face it down."

"B-but Uncle J-John didn't do anything w-wrong!"

"No, he didn't. He saved your life—an' Becky's. An' when the right folks learn the truth of it all, it'll be fine again. Trust me." Sonny attempted to sound more confident than he felt. He took a deep breath and added, "But that's gonna take us standin' up for ourselves first."

Johnny bit his lower lip as tears welled in his eyes. "I—I can fight."

"I know you can. You're a man—just like your father," Sonny said. "We're gonna need you to take care of your mother an' your sis when we get to Doc's."

Giggling, Rebecca joined in. "Are you going to have a party? I like parties, Uncle Sonny."

Sonny smiled. "Well, we're gonna go see your mom. How's that for a party?"

"I miss my mommy."

"I know you do, sugar. So do I." Sonny's face reddened and he looked away quickly.

Johnny turned in the seat and watched the snarling bunch of women as the wagon rounded a corner. He wanted to ask more about it, but felt a strange sense of pride at being treated like a man by Sonny. He had been trusted with the truth. He had been asked to stand with the two men he loved most.

Soon they were in front of the Tremons house and both Johnny and Rebecca were eager to get down and see their mother. The troublesome scene in town was forgotten for the moment. Checker and Sonny jumped down and the happy cowboy lifted the little girl to the ground, while Johnny crawled out the other side and raced toward the door. Checker lifted Sarah Ann from her seat. Both men retrieved their rifles.

The door swung open and a concerned Dr. Tremons stood.

"Look like you're gonna be a mite occupied for a piece, ol' friend." Sonny chuckled as he and Checker followed the children to the house. "Let me know when you're ready to go see the judge."

Checker growled a response and grinned.

Dr. Tremons stepped outside and told the children that their mother was waiting to see them. Both scrambled past him with Johnny well in the lead. Sonny tipped his hat and said he would stay with the children; his right fist held his Winchester at his side.

"Thanks. We'll be right behind you." Checker held out his injured hand for Sarah Ann, holding his rifle in his left.

"Sure you will." Sonny winked and entered the house.

Checker and Sarah Ann walked hand in hand toward the back where a small stable stood. Rounding the corner of the house, he laid the gun against it and turned to her. After a warm embrace and longer kiss, she told him that they should take Amelia and get out of town quickly before any trouble started.

Kissing her lightly on the lips, Checker promised a return to the ranch as soon as the issue of Blue McCallister's death was settled.

"John, I'm scared. What if—"

"Shhh."

Their lips met again and their bodies closed against each other, seeking more.

Minutes later, he retrieved his rifle and they walked hand in hand into the back door of the house. Inside, he stacked his Winchester next to Sonny's, resting a few feet from the opening. Upon entering Amelia's bedroom, she greeted them joyously, as her children gathered close to her in the bed. Eager to share her decision, she told him that Attorney Whitaker, at her request, had written up a partnership agreement for Checker, Sonny, and herself to own the ranch.

Holding his derby with both hands in front of him, Sonny stood next to the window in Amelia's bedroom. Checker thought he looked particularly happy and definitely red-faced, as he mumbled a thank-you for her generosity and said it wasn't necessary.

"Yes, it is," Amelia responded. "You both deserve it. I wouldn't have a ranch without you."

"Thanks, sis. That is very kind," Checker said and looked at Sarah Ann.

Embarrassed, Sonny glanced toward the window and stopped. "Four riders coming."

Checker was beside him in an instant. "One is Marshal Rand. Didn't think he'd have the nerve to show himself. Looks like Judge Buchanan is another. I can see that big beard of his." Checker squinted. "The one on the far right is Do'tsi. I wonder where his big brother is."

He sensed Sarah Ann beside him without looking. "That's Eklin Stanton next to that awful deputy," she said, staring out the window. "He's our mayor."

"He the owner o' that real fancy place? Delmonico's, like the New York restaurant?" Sonny asked.

"That's him. His mother and father started it, though. He just struts around all day." Her voice couldn't conceal the tremble. "They're coming for you, John. I knew it. You and Sonny have to go. You have to."

"No, just saves a trip to see Buchanan."

"John, please. You have to leave." She pulled on his arm. "Take our horses—in the barn."

Dr. Tremons licked his fingers and pushed on his lock of hair. "I told ya that somebody should'a ridden to get the U.S. marshal."

"I've got nothing to hide. Judge Buchanan is a reasonable man," Checker said calmly. "The rest don't matter."

"Please, John, if they put you in jail those awful deputies will kill you. That's what they want. You know that." Her voice was determined. "Get away now. The town's convinced you murdered Dr. Gambree. They're coming to arrest you. I'll stall them. John . . . I love you."

"I love you." Checker touched her arm. "But I'm not running. Blue tried to kill me. He helped murder some of our friends. I've got proof that he killed the real medicine man." He patted his shirt.

"Sonny, please. You will listen to me, won't you?"

"Thanks, ma'am, but runnin' just ain't in my nature either. Agree with John on that. Never saw much good come o' it." Sonny pulled his derby tight on his head and peeked at Amelia.

"I—I don't understand." Amelia held both children beside her in the bed.

Johnny whispered in her ear about the women yelling at Checker and she whimpered; then anger filled her face. He told her quietly to be brave, that he was there.

"Don't they know they're talking to a Texas Ranger? The best one—" She bit off her words and sat upright in her bed. "What is this nonsense? You're a lawman, John."

"Not anymore—and not here," Checker said. "This is Star's doing. An' it's time to end it."

Amelia straightened herself. "But you're outnumbered."

"I'll get my shotgun," Dr. Tremons said, immediately heading out of the room.

"This isn't about shooting. This is about the law," Checker said.

"The law seems to work better if'n a man's got a gun." Dr. Tremons licked his fingers and stroked his front hair.

"All right, then, all of you. I'm going out first. Let's see what they want for sure." With a deep breath to steady her nerves, Sarah Ann headed for the door without waiting for a response from either Checker or Sonny.

She stepped onto the front edge of the porch as the four riders reined up at the hitching rack alongside the Hedrickson wagon.

Smiling, Do'tsi noticed Kana'ti as he slipped into the shadows of the small barn behind the house and knelt there. He had gone ahead as his brother had directed. Beside Kana'ti was the ugly dog, Zoro. The older Cherokee brother wanted to kill the former Ranger with his bare hands; his younger brother had given him permission when the attempt to arrest Checker was made. Although he wanted the honor of killing the former Ranger himself, Do'tsi knew his brother wouldn't stand around and wait much longer. It would be easy; Checker would not be able to fight with his right hand.

However, Do'tsi planned to shoot Checker when he was preoccupied with fighting his brother. He would deal with Kana'ti's disappointment later. After all, immortality beckoned.

"Miss Tremons, good morning!" Mayor Stanton waved his hand and the motion continued to his short-brimmed hat, touching it in greeting.

His smile was one of his best and his blue eyes examined her for signs of attraction to him. He was a handsome man, well aware of his effect on many women. It hadn't occurred to him that Sarah Ann found him quite repulsive. He brushed an imaginary speck from the lapel of his velveteen suit and straightened the silk cravat, centered with a gold stickpin. He liked being mayor. It gave him ample opportunities to talk and act important. However, there were rumors that he was hard-pressed for money, even though his upscale restaurant was quite popular. A bad gambling habit was noted as the reason. Unfortunately, these stories were true.

Something about him always made Sarah Ann uncomfortable. Now she was mortified, but tried to hide it.

"Good morning, Mayor. How are you doing? Well, I trust." Her smile was slow reaching her face, and her lips shivered a little. "What brings your to our home this day?"

"I so wish this was a social call, Miss Tremons, but we're here on official business," Stanton said with a pious lilt to his voice.

"We're here to arrest a murderer," Do'tsi snarled and his eyes sparkled.

A nervous Marshal Rand looked over at him and snickered.

CHAPTER THIRTY

"No, we're here to get some answers," Judge Hiram Buchanan corrected, his tightly closed lips barely moving.

None of the other three liked the correction, but none responded.

To emphasize his statement, the judge pushed down on the brim of his too-small, flat-crowned black hat, making his head look even smaller in comparison to the vast world of his beard. His suit was wrinkled as usual and his string tie slightly off-center. He sat on his horse as if he would rather be elsewhere, having come only at the urging of his friend, the mayor.

From the outset, the short magistrate had an uneasy hunch that something wrong was going on. More than anything, that sense had propelled him into riding with the others. And to wear, under his coat, his shoulder-holstered P. Webley & Son Bulldog Pocket wheel gun. He had insisted—to the other three—this was an opportunity for the former Ranger to clear the air and he questioned the truthfulness of an outlaw like Tom Redmond. Only Do'tsi had expressed disagreement.

The judge's acquaintance with Checker had been brief, meeting him at the trial of the Star McCallister gang, but Judge Buchanan considered himself a good assessor of character—and he liked this former Ranger. Moreover, he trusted him. He couldn't, and wouldn't, say that about his companions, even Mayor Stanton. Earlier, the stern magistrate had spoken harshly to both the mayor and the marshal about the two deputies hired, but beyond his words there was little he could do. The marshal had the authority to hire support as he saw fit.

When he spoke with Jacob Allen about the inflammatory story, the *Times* editor explained that he had a duty to write the news; Judge Buchanan responded that the newspaper had a responsibility to be accurate. Allen said he would write another article about the concern, when and if there was something to say. He suggested the judge have Checker come and see him; Buchanan had smiled at the notion.

"I've got an arrest warrant right here," Do'tsi replied and patted his holstered gun, pulling the judge back to the moment.

"I don't understand. What has my father done?" Sarah Ann asked, sounding as innocent as her face appeared.

"Not your damn father," Do'tsi said. "It's Captain John Checker we want. He murdered an innocent man and stole his medicine wagon. We know he's here. This is his wagon. Came through town only a few minutes ago."

Shifting his weight in the saddle, Marshal Rand nodded his head enthusiastically in agreement and mouthed, "This is his wagon."

"There must be some mistake, gentlemen. Mr. Checker is a former captain of the Texas Rangers. A man of considerable reputation. He is here after saving his sister's children from the awful Star McCallister and his gang. You know that as well as I do."

"Shut up, lady." Do'tsi swirled down from his horse. "Hiding a murderer is a crime. I'll go in and drag him out."

"Stay right where you are, Deputy," Judge Buchanan said. "I'll handle this." His voice softened. "Miss Tremons, it is our duty to question Mr. Checker about Dr. Gambree's absence—since his wagon and horses are in Mr. Checker's possession. On the face of it, this is a troubling issue. As is the *Times*'s printed testimony of an arrested outlaw, although a man of highly questionable character." He cleared his throat. "Is Mr. Checker inside?"

Dr. Tremons burst through the door with a double-barreled shotgun in his hands. String pulls attached to a sack of extra shells were draped through his fingers. "What is this all about, Judge? I've got a very sick woman here—an' her children are visiting her, thanks to her brother, John Checker."

"Now, now, Doc. There's no need for getting riled up. We just need to talk with Mr. Checker." Mayor Stanton also dismounted and stood beside his horse. He would make a less prominent target this way and it allowed his suit to settle around his figure.

He stroked his well-groomed goatee and sought Sarah Ann's eyes. Partially to avoid looking at Do'tsi, who would be angry at his comment, and partially to assess her effortless beauty further. Maybe he would return later to console her. Marshal Rand had assured him this would go smoothly and that the Ranger would surrender peacefully in their presence. The gift of appreciation from Diverrouve had been substantial, expressed as a thank-you for the mayor's service to the community. It wouldn't cover his gambling debts, but it would be enough to give him some breathing room. Rand had hinted more would be coming if things went well.

Noting the action of the others, Marshal Rand started to dismount, then decided against it. Under his coat, the shoulder holster felt both comforting and inadequate at the same time. He, too, had been convinced by McCallister that Checker would surrender peacefully with Judge Buchanan present. His decision to carry a shotgun was rejected outright by the magistrate.

Cocking his head to the side, Dr. Tremons waved his gun in Do'tsi's direction. "Now just who in the world is accusing Ranger Captain John Checker? I'd really like to meet the fella. Must be somebody who spends a lot of time in a saloon. Or couldn't be trusted with nothin'."

"That's not important at the moment," Mayor Stanton declared. "There is a charge against him that must be answered." He liked the sound of the phrasing and smiled.

"The hell it ain't important." Dr. Tremons released one hand from his shotgun and raised his fingers to deal with his wayward gray lock. "Or are you tellin' me this town is bein' run by the likes of that?" Realizing his fingers were wrapped around the sack strings, he stopped and pointed at Do'tsi with the sack dangling from his hand.

"This is wasting time. We'll arrest you, too, sawbones," Do'tsi snapped, "for hiding a killer."

"You'll do nothing of the kind," Judge Buchanan warned. "We just need to talk with him, Doc. I'm sure he can clear this up. We're all aware of Mr. Checker's fine record as a lawman in Texas."

Do'tsi whispered something to Rand, who swallowed hard, looked away, and finally said, "What he did in Texas is of no matter here. This concerns the murder of an innocent man."

Movement at the doorway startled the three men, and Do'tsi's gun appeared in his fist. Moving slowly with his rifle aimed at Do'tsi, Sonny cleared the entrance. Peeking out from the edge of the door frame were

Johnny and Rebecca. The cowboy had told them to stay inside. He did so again without looking around.

"Well, well, Deputy, where's that ugly dog o' yours?" Sonny said. "Or did it eat somebody's cow?"

Do'tsi's eyes tightened. "Judge, this one's also under arrest. He's wanted in Texas. Cole Dillon is his name." Under his breath, he muttered, "These two will be for you, my grandmother—and Captain John Checker will be for my immortality. Just like you."

"Sorry, Deputy. My name is Sonny. Sonny Jones." The cowboy folded his arms with his Winchester within them. "Sounds like you boys are full o' bad information today. Kinda like that joke of a newspaper." The presence of the gun was reassuring. He wasn't as confident as Checker that this wouldn't become a gunfight.

Judge Buchanan cleared his throat again. "Mr. Jones, there is a witness who says otherwise. He also claims to have witnessed Mr. Checker killing Dr. Gambree. We'll need to take you in, too—until both matters can be cleared up. You're not wanted for anything here, but if Texas wants you, we're obligated to keep you for them."

Sonny frowned and turned toward Sarah Ann. "Will you take care of . . . the kids until we get this straightened out?"

"Of course, Sonny."

Dr. Tremons took another step closer and waved his shotgun. "This is even more silliness. I can't believe you, Buchanan. You either, Stanton. This fine man is taking care of Mrs. Hedrickson's children. He's—"

"Judge, wire Texas Ranger Captain Hershell Poe in Waco. He'll confirm Cole Dillon is dead. So will I. I was there when Cole Dillon died." The voice came from the side of the house as John Checker walked into the front yard.

Sarah Ann's face was white. She turned toward him and her eyes asked him to be careful. Without thinking about it, she took the shotgun from her surprised father's hands. He frowned, but resisted only slightly.

Only Do'tsi appeared to notice. "*Osiyo*, Captain John Checker."

"I heard your request, Judge." Checker spoke slowly with his rifle at his side in his left hand. "I understand the confusion. Contrary to what you've been hearing, Dr. Gambree was a wanted killer. He killed the real doctor and owner of that medicine wagon." Deliberately, he propped his Winchester against the house and stepped away from it.

Do'tsi lifted his revolver. It would only take a second to gain immortality. The hell with what Star McCallister wanted. Or his brother.

"Put that gun away," Sarah Ann yelled. The shotgun in her hands was pointed at Do'tsi. "Mr. Checker is explaining his innocence. If they wanted, they could've shot all of you down already. Listen to him—or I promise I will shoot you."

The Cherokee killer's eyes flickered. Was this woman capable of that? The signs indicated she might be. Slowly he holstered the gun.

Marshal Rand's arms rose slightly away from his body to make it clear he wasn't going to do anything.

Startled by her aggressiveness, Mayor Stanton studied her once more, deciding he liked that in a woman. He considered telling her so; women loved to be complimented, he knew. A stroke of his goatee gave him a moment to reconsider and he chose to wait until a better moment.

Checker smiled and continued, "His real name was Blue McCallister. He was Star's younger brother, masquerading as a medicine peddler while he hired out his gun. He was wanted for murder and larceny in Nebraska." He stared at both the mayor and judge. "Check around with some old-timers and you'll find out about their relationship. Not that it matters. He killed two Triple C riders when he broke out Star and his gang. With the help of Rand here." Checker's eyes locked on to Marshal Rand's face. "Blue killed the real doctor who owned the wagon, a fellow from Nebraska named Ivan Janiskowski. Went by 'Dr. January.'" Checker looped his thumbs inside his gun belt. "Blue and a man named Tiller tried to ambush me at Star McCallister's hideout. After my friends got my sister's kids away from those bastards. Neither one was good enough."

Do'tsi screamed, "*Siyo!* See! I told you. He's admitted it. He murdered Dr. Gambree."

"No, Do'tsi, I shot them when they came at me with their guns—and gave me no choice. I read that ridiculous newspaper story. Tom Redmond wasn't even in sight of the gunfight. He lied—to save his neck. Or do you deny promising him that?"

His neck reddening, Marshal Rand blurted, "I had nothing to do with that escape. *You* are the one lying—to save *your* neck." He smiled triumphantly at his forceful declaration and smoothed his thick mustache.

"Ah, the whole world is covered in illusion. That's Sikhism, a religion from India." Do'tsi touched two fingers to his mouth.

"I'll keep that in mind, Do'tsi," Checker said. "There won't be any illusion in my evidence. Just facts." He turned toward the frightened marshal. "As for you, Rand, I told you to leave town before I got back or face the consequences. That still stands."

"See, Judge, see! He's threatening me!" Rand pointed at Checker and looked at Judge Buchanan. "I am the law in Dodge, the only law."

Do'tsi's narrowed eyes flashed and he screamed something in Cherokee that no one understood.

Looking down at himself, Stanton wondered if he should have worn a dark blue suit, instead of this gray one. He always thought the blue made him look more mayoral.

A soft sound behind Checker caught his attention and he spun around, expecting trouble. His left hand curled around the butt of his Colt. Kana'ti rushed at him with his massive arms outstretched. His top hat flew in the other direction and his quivered machete bounced off his back. Seeking to end his quest in one blow, the Cherokee drove a haymaker into Checker's chest, just as the former Ranger drew his Colt.

The gun flew from Checker's hand and he staggered backward, fighting for breath and balance. His own hat sought the air and fluttered a few feet from the weapon. With the quickness of a wild animal, Checker recovered and swung at Kana'ti with his left fist and missed.

Stutter-stepping, Kana'ti caught Checker's cheek with a powerful right. But the former Ranger was ducking and moving himself, and the blow was only a glancing one. Still, it carried enough wallop to stun him momentarily.

Snarling and snapping its great teeth, the brothers' dog lunged at Checker, only a few steps behind Kana'ti. Shaking off Kana'ti's partially landed haymaker, Checker stepped aside at the last moment and slammed his left fist down on its large, flat head. Zoro whimpered, hit the ground awkwardly, and spun around to attack again.

No one saw Sonny aim and fire twice as Zoro came at Checker from the rear. Gun smoke trailed the lead that drove into the dog's head and chest and jammed it sideways.

In the instant of Sonny's distraction, Do'tsi redrew his gun, cocked, and aimed at Checker's back. "*Wado*," he muttered. "My destiny."

Ka-boom! Ka-boom!

Twin barrels of Dr. Tremons's shotgun exploded, jumping in Sarah Ann's hands.

Do'tsi jerked and flew against the wagon. His gun fired, clipping the top edge of Checker's tunic along his left shoulder.

Crossing his arms in front of his face, Marshal Rand cried out and ducked, nearly falling out of the saddle. Mayor Stanton whimpered and hoped it wasn't heard.

Another right from Kana'ti followed, catching Checker again full in the chest and taking his wind. A sweeping left cross trailed it to finish him. Checker slid under the great swing and backed away, gasping for air. He had no time to worry about what might be happening behind him. Or to look for his Colt. Kana'ti came for him, hungry for victory; his eyes glittered with the lust of battle. His fistfighting was raw and slow compared to Checker's, but Kana'ti's strength more than compensated for the lack of skill. That, and the fact his victims were usually terrified.

Checker was not. He had fought often in Texas, too often. An older Ranger had taught him how to box years ago, and the experience had been put to good use. But his wrapped right hand would not be of much help; Kana'ti knew that; he was fighting a one-armed man.

Kana'ti slammed a right haymaker hard into Checker's body and it staggered him. The big Cherokee pushed through Checker's off-balanced left jabs to try to reach the former Ranger. Still struggling for new wind, Checker countered with a left, then a right into the bigger man's ribs. The impact of the last punch drove pain through his right fist and up Checker's arm, stunning him more than the blow itself had done to Kana'ti.

As he slumped against the wagon wheel, Do'tsi's face was half crimson and his clothes dotted with shot. Red was transforming part of his midsection. He raised himself to a kneeling position and cocked his gun again.

"For you, Owl Watcher. *Wado*. It is good . . . I will be . . . forever."

CHAPTER THIRTY-ONE

Orange flame spat from Sonny's Winchester, and Do'tsi's head thudded against the wheel. The roar was loud, as if there were two shots. The gun in Do'tsi's hand spun out of his control and went off as it hit the ground.

Forcing himself through the extreme throbbing in his right hand and seemingly oblivious to the gunfight behind him, Checker followed with a left uppercut to Kana'ti's exposed chin. The Cherokee's face snapped sideways as he tried to grab Checker, tearing his shirt-sleeve from its binding. The tall gunfighter hit Kana'ti twice more, so fast the blows appeared continuous. His right hand burst again with bright pain, but he forced himself to ignore it. Showing he could use both fists was vital to keeping the bigger man aware of that possibility.

Kana'ti's face was painted in blood and his right eyelid was cut open, as he windmilled his fists to drive away Checker's onslaught.

Checker slipped under another powerful right, letting it hit his shoulder, and countered with blows delivered with both hands to Kana'ti's body. His entire right arm felt numb and he couldn't lift it for another strike at the moment. One shirtsleeve hung from his wrist, held by a single remaining button. Ignoring the searing ache, he went under a rushed left, tore into Kana'ti's stomach with his full body behind a left jab. His right hand was almost useless, but he managed to use it to push away as Kana'ti grabbed at his Comanche tunic, ripping it slightly at the neck. His torn shirtsleeve fluttered like a handheld flag.

Sonny rushed over to the dying Do'tsi and kicked away his pistol.

"*O-osiyo*, C-Cole Dillon . . . I—I . . . will . . . meet . . . you again . . . on the . . . Pathway of Souls."

"Sonny Jones to you," Sonny growled.

"The woman, is . . . she . . . a raven mocker?" His bloody fingers reached for the derringer strapped to his left wrist under his shirt cuff. "You don't . . . think she . . . is my . . . grandmother?" Blood oozed from his mouth and decorated his teeth.

Holding his rifle in one hand, Sonny grabbed Do'tsi's hand with the other, stopping the advance. He yanked the small weapon free. "No, she's a woman in love. You wouldn't understand that power, Do'tsi."

Frantically, Do'tsi's freed hand grabbed for Sonny's shirt. "How could she keep me from my destiny . . . from being the man who killed Captain John Checker? How . . . ?" Do'tsi's chin fell to his chest.

Sonny pulled the still hand from his shirt, felt for Do'tsi's pulse, and stepped away. "Your destiny is . . . dirt." He tossed the derringer into the yard, several feet from the mayor, and picked up Do'tsi's Smith & Wesson.

"You have killed a lawman," Mayor Stanton protested, his eyes wide with fright.

"No, I shot a killer who was trying to shoot my friend in the back," Sonny said, shoving Do'tsi's revolver into his gun belt. "Or don't you know the difference?" He swung his Winchester in the fearful marshal's direction. "How 'bout you, Rand? You hired 'em."

"I don't see that you had any choice," Judge Buchanan responded. "This was to seek answers, not to murder."

For the first time, everyone saw that the judge held a short-barreled, British double-action revolver in his fist. It was smoking.

Sonny's eyes went to the gun, then back to the judge's face. "Thanks for the help."

"I had no choice."

Both Mayor Stanton and Marshal Rand studied the short, bearded magistrate, seeing him in a different light. Rand visibly shivered and wished he had stayed at home.

Stroking his goatee, Stanton muttered, "Oh God."

Nodding, Sonny jammed new cartridges into his Winchester.

In the middle of the yard, Checker and Kana'ti grappled, but Checker broke free with a furious series of punches to the man's midsection and face, all lefts, but the last was a powerful slam with the heel of his opened right hand against Kana'ti's nose. For an instant, Checker thought of running to get his Winchester leaning against the house. He had no idea where his Colt had landed and dared not look around for it now.

The big Cherokee made the decision for him as he charged. Kana'ti's face was split between pain and anger; blood was streaming from the opened eyelid, as well as his nose. Checker feinted with his half-closed right hand and landed another blow to the man's ribs with a thunderous left, then rocked Kana'ti's face with another left thrown as fast as he could recock his fist.

Sarah Ann stood shaking, the empty weapon at her side. Taking it from her, Dr. Tremons reloaded from the sack of shells wagging back and forth from his left hand. "Put a stop to it, Stanton. Or you, Judge. I've had enough of this. Always thought you were above this kinda crap. Stanton, you, I don't know—but you're sure paintin' a clear picture for me—and it isn't very pretty."

Mayor Stanton acted like he was not paying attention, straightening the silk handkerchief in his coat breast pocket.

Judge Buchanan blinked, but said nothing. His gun had been returned to its shoulder holster under his coat. He looked over at Rand, expecting him to respond.

"Tell your deputy to stop, Marshal," Judge Buchanan said.

"He is performing his duty, Judge," Mayor Stanton stated without looking up.

Marshal Rand's expression was that of a man who couldn't make up his mind.

"Says who?" Judge Buchanan snorted and yelled, "Deputy, stop this instant. Stop, I say!" He drew his gun and fired twice into the air.

Checker heard the exchange—and the shots—but didn't dare take his attention from Kana'ti.

Sputtering a Cherokee curse, Kana'ti spat a red stream as blood spewed from the corner of his mouth. He roared at Checker and swung a massive right fist at his head. Pushing the blow aside with his left arm, Checker stepped inside the rush and kicked at the Indian's groin, hitting his right thigh instead. As Kana'ti twisted sideways, Checker snapped the Indian's head back with a left uppercut that showered both men with blood, as the blow split Kana'ti's cheek.

The strike seemed only to anger the powerful Cherokee, while agony tore up Checker's right arm and gripped his entire body. With his arm held against his stomach to slow the pain, he ducked another vicious blow and countered with a ferocious left hook that cracked Kana'ti's ribs.

His mouth wide open, Kana'ti didn't understand what was happening to him. Blind fury took over and he charged again. Standing wide-legged, Checker drove at Kana'ti's head with a left hook, managed to lift his right arm quickly enough to parry the Cherokee's wild swing, then broke Kana'ti's nose with a smashing left that was as hard as Checker could throw a punch.

The gasping Cherokee staggered, but didn't fall.

Checker knew he couldn't let the bigger man get close enough to grab him. That would end in a broken back or neck. An agonizing death. He couldn't let the fight go much longer either because the Cherokee's greater strength would eventually wear him down. His only advantage was that Kana'ti had never fought a man who knew how to fight and had not been frozen in fear. Having only one good fist made him even more vulnerable, but he couldn't think about that now.

Now was about only finding breath and the opportunity to live. And stopping this brute before it could kill him.

"Don't let him grab ya, son!" Dr. Tremons yelled.

Accepting Checker's blow to his rib cage in order to get close, Kana'ti managed to grab his tunic again and reached desperately with his right hand to gouge out the Ranger's eyes. His fingernails dug into Checker's cheek. Savagely, Checker slammed his left fist into Kana'ti's throat and shoved him away. The Cherokee released his grip on the tunic, gagging and fighting for air. The rip at Checker's neck was longer. In the Cherokee's hand was Checker's small medicine pouch; the torn-apart rawhide strings hung through his fingers. Without looking, he released the pouch and let it fall.

As if strengthened by that act, Checker swarmed at him and smashed two vicious lefts into Kana'ti's stomach. Checker's right arm countered a feeble swing and he hit Kana'ti again in the stomach with a left, tried to hit him with an opened right hand but missed.

Judge Buchanan screamed again for the fight to end and fired into the air once more.

Neither combatant heard him. Or cared.

In a concentrated half crouch, Dr. Tremons inched closer, hoping to get a clear shot at the Cherokee thug. His tight grip on the shotgun mirrored the intensity of his gaze.

From the other direction, Sonny advanced a few steps. The two fighters were so entangled, or moving so swiftly, that any shot risked hitting the wrong man.

Gasping for air, Kana'ti swung wildly. Yet powerfully. The brutal blow connected, knocking Checker backward. He lost his balance and landed on his back. The big Cherokee pounced, but Checker was already on his knees. The former Ranger's rising left cross to Kana'ti's face shattered the momentum and gave Checker time to fully restand.

Sarah Ann turned toward her father, but he was ready this time and held his shotgun away. Wild-eyed, she ran to Sonny and told him to do something. The happy-go-lucky cowboy responded by muttering that he didn't have a shot. She gasped as the staggering Cherokee attempted to draw the machete from his quiver.

"My God!" Judge Buchanan yelled. "Someone stop him." He fired in the air another time.

"Look out, son!" Dr. Tremons yelled and swung his shotgun toward the bloody Kana'ti.

Sonny stepped closer to the fight, aiming down his rifle barrel.

"Don't shoot," Checker yelled. "Don't shoot."

Checker drove his right boot again at Kana'ti's groin, this time almost lifting the Cherokee off the ground as it smashed into his manhood. A searing cry burst into the air as Kana'ti bent over, grabbing himself with both hands. His unsheathed machete sailed in the air, then thudded to the earth, handle-first.

With his fists held together, Checker slammed down into the back of Kana'ti's neck and the Cherokee collapsed. His head wobbled against the earth and was still.

A wave of weakness slid through Checker's body, taking with it the last of his energy. He took a step and wobbled, caught himself, and gasped for air. There was no breath to let him move. His head was dull and his entire body ached. His own mouth and cheek were bleeding; his shirt was torn. His right arm hung at his side like it didn't belong to his body. The knuckles of Checker's left hand were bloody and raw. He glanced at the wrapping on his right hand, mostly covered with blood, but he didn't think it was his. Or, at least, not all of it. The throbbing was a constant beat, matching his thundering heart. His torn sleeve was a rag spotted with blood; the tunic sagged at his neckline. His body was soaked in sweat, his face splattered with blood. Some of it was his.

It didn't matter. He was standing; Kana'ti was not. He didn't hear the voices behind him. The only thing he saw was the torn medicine bundle lying a few feet from Kana'ti's still frame.

After picking up the tiny tribute, he pronounced through his gasping for breath, "My brother . . . the wolf . . . would not like . . . you using . . . his name."

He shoved the pouch into his pocket, then saw his Colt lying a few feet farther. He staggered toward the gun, awkwardly lifted it, and placed it in his holster. He saw his hat but didn't attempt to retrieve it.

Sarah Ann ran for the heaving Checker and held him to her. He couldn't speak any more words.

"Well, how about that, Mayor? You, too, Rand?" Sonny barked. "Even when your big boy comes at a man from behind, he isn't good enough. A man with only one good hand." He glared at the trembling marshal and the white-faced mayor, then back to the dead Do'tsi. "Looks like you boys guessed wrong. Real wrong."

His sculpted face recharging with hate, Mayor Stanton slowly studied Sonny, unnerved by the realization that the cowboy's gun was aimed at his midsection.

Sonny cocked his head to the side and stared at the mayor. "When this is over—an' the good folks of Dodge know who Dr. Gambree really is—and what he really did, then we're gonna dig Star McCallister out of his hole. An' we're gonna find out what he paid you to take up his banner."

Mayor Stanton's face couldn't hold the surprise of hearing McCallister was suspected of being behind this strategy—or his acceptance of a bribe.

"Didn't think we knew, did you?" Sonny grinned at the obvious accuracy of his hunch.

"I don't know what you're talking about. Both of you are under arrest," Mayor Stanton snarled haughtily. "Do your duty, Marshal."

"Duty? Rand? That's two things that don't go together none at all," Sonny barked. "Speakin' of money, how much did Star pay *you*, Rand? Was it worth the lives of Tex an' Harry—an' your two deputies? Was it?"

Swallowing and licking his lower lip with his tongue, the marshal heaved his shoulders up and down. His eyes sought the mayor for support. None came.

"Interesting." Sonny smiled, but kept his eyes nailed to Rand's face. "Judge, I'm guessin' you didn't know Rand was in on the breakout of the McCallister gang. Or the murder of our friends—an' his own deputies. Don't know what *you* knew, Mayor. Don't care." Sonny glanced at Judge Buchanan, then quickly back to Mayor Stanton, who was eyeing the derringer five feet from his polished boots. "If I was a judge, I'd be wondering why the mayor suddenly decided to call my friend a criminal. Why would he take the word of an outlaw who's a killer, a woman beater, an' who kidnapped some wonderful kids? Over one of Texas's finest lawmen. Of course, that's just me." His eyes narrowed. "Go ahead an' try for that gun, Mayor. It's only a lifetime away. Yours."

Taking a long, deep gasp, Checker took several steps toward the men at the hitching post. Sarah Ann was holding him up now. In her hand was his hat.

"Now . . . where were we . . . Judge?" Checker said, heaving for air. He took the battered Stetson from her hand and shoved it onto his head.

Judge Buchanan frowned, holstered his gun, and glanced at the dead Do'tsi, then at Mayor Stanton and Marshal Rand.

Behind them, Dr. Tremons snarled, "You go ahead with your business, I'll keep Betsy here on this mad dog." He waved his shotgun at the unmoving Kana'ti.

"I'd like you . . . to read this." Checker reached into his pocket to retrieve the telegram from Nebraska. "If you gentlemen would join me . . . we can go to the medicine wagon . . . I'll show you more," Checker said. "Then we can go to the telegraph office—if you'd like to double-check what it says here."

"Changed my mind," Dr. Tremons announced. "Sonny, you watch this Injun while I get something for John's hands," he urged and immediately headed for the house. He stopped and turned back to Sarah Ann.

Checker, mumbling, stepped away and wobbled toward the judge.

The wiry doctor handed her the weapon and sack of ammunition and twirled his straying lock of hair. "You keep an eye on him, too, sis."

"Where do you think you're going, Doc?" Mayor Stanton asked, trying to sound more in control than he felt. He didn't like the sweat beading on his forehead; no gentleman ever sweated.

Standing beside the judge's horse, Checker handed him the folded telegraph.

"I'm getting some hot water and Epsom salts for this brave man." Dr. Tremons stopped on the porch and turned toward the street. "By the way, Mayor, I will expect these pitiful excuses for constables . . . to be stripped of their authority right now." He pointed at Rand. "All three of them. Dodge City is a better town than this."

Chuckling to himself, Sonny stepped toward the downed Kana'ti, who was barely moving. "If you try to stand, it'll be your last. Hope you understand my words, big boy. Don't know any o' that Cherokee stuff."

"I will shoot, too." Sarah Ann's voice was firm.

Kana'ti was still once more.

Holding the telegram in one hand at his side, Judge Buchanan cleared his throat and withdrew reading glasses from his breast coat pocket. "You may count on proper action, Dr. Tremons. There was no certainly call for these attacks. None."

With a reaffirming nod, Dr. Tremons disappeared inside the house.

"Now wait, Hiram." Mayor Stanton waved his hands. "You can't blame these men for trying to do their duty. How was Deputy, ah, Kana'ti to know Mr. Checker wasn't going to shoot?" He pointed at the downed Cherokee.

"I'll say it again, Mayor. We came for answers. That's what I agreed to. Not attempted murder. That man attacked Mr. Checker without provocation. And Deputy Do'tsi attempted to shoot him in the back," Judge Buchanan stated evenly. "We've received the answers we came for. Read this. It is exactly as Mr. Checker said."

"True, Judge, but John Checker is a known gunman. m sure Kana'ti thought he was doing the right thing." layor Stanton stared at his feet as he spoke. His tongue long his parched lips offered only momentary relief.

"I truly hope you don't believe that, Eklin." Judge uchanan shifted his weight in the saddle and contin-ed to hold out the telegram. "I said, read this. After e're through here, I have some questions for you. And ɔu too, Jubal."

"Me too, Stanton." Checker's stare cut at the man's re-aining courage. "Like why you let Rand hire two nown killers as deputies? Did anyone wonder why the ame day a medicine wagon came to town Star and his en escaped? Has anyone wired the U.S. marshal bout Dr. Gambree—or these two?" He stopped and ɔok a deep breath. "Like my good friend, I'd also like to now how much Star paid you."

Squinting to hold in the emotion, Mayor Stanton bit is lower lip. "I have not done anything wrong, Mr. hecker. I was acting in my official capacity as the ɔwn's leading officer."

Checker smiled and pointed at the judge's out-retched hand holding the wire from the federal law-en in Nebraska. It was a long smile that made the olitician squirm and look away. Finally, Stanton went ver to the judge and reluctantly read the telegram. His ɔouth was a thin line as he handed it back with no ɔmment.

Meanwhile, Sonny told Checker what had happened uring the fight, including Sarah Ann's role and Judge uchanan's. Checker nodded his appreciation toward e judge and turned to comfort Sarah Ann, who was embling. The shotgun in her hands was equally shak-g. He spoke quietly, reassuring her that she had done hat had to be done.

Dr. Tremons reappeared with a large tin bowl filled

with water and salts, placed it on the porch, and told
Checker to sit there and soak his hands.

With Sarah Ann's encouragement, Checker complied.

"Keep 'em down in there, son," Dr. Tremons advised.
"It'll take the soreness out. Don't worry about getting
that wrappin' wet. I'm gonna change it anyhow." He
took Checker's right hand in his. "Figure you broke it
again?"

"Don't know, Doc. Stung something fierce."

"I'll bet. Didn't help those bones heal none banging
into that mountain. Sure wouldn't have missed it for the
world, though. Never had a doubt you'd whip that big
thing." Dr. Tremons grinned and stared back inside the
door. "Now, kids, you go stay with your mama." He listened for a moment. "Yes, sir, your uncle is going to be
fine. But you stay inside." He placed Checker's right
hand into the bowl.

"Thanks for your help, Doc." Checker placed his left
hand into the soothing water, beside his right, and
looked at Sarah Ann.

She mouthed, "I love you."

He chuckled. "Me too. Will you marry me?"

"Yes."

Sonny used the wait to walk over to the stirring
Kana'ti. After examining the dead dog, Sonny pulled
the scalp knife from the Cherokee's knee-high moc-
casin, then picked up the machete and tossed both toward the wagon. He continued on to retrieve Checker's
rifle and walked away, holding it with his own Winchester. Ceremoniously, he propped both guns against the
buckboard, then gathered the two blades and Do'tsi's
derringer and tossed them into the wagon bed. Afterward, Checker's rifle was carefully placed there.

That security step taken, Sonny's mind-set changed. It
showed first in his eyes.

"You don't even remember Tex and Harry Clanahan

do you, Rand?" Sonny looked up with his own rifle in his fists. "They were my friends. Good men livin' good lives. You have a debt to pay. Maybe I oughta collect it now."

Rand's face was white. "Y-you wouldn't dare." A wet spot blossomed at his groin.

Across Sonny's mouth emerged a smile that didn't match his eyes. "You know, I'd be real careful about dares. You accused me of bein' some Texas outlaw. If I am, what've I got to lose by puttin' a bullet through your miserable head?"

Ignoring Sonny's threat, Judge Buchanan looked at Checker. "Mr. Checker, sir, are you able to go with us to review this other evidence you mentioned? Or do you need more time? It isn't necessary. I am quite convinced of your innocence. Aren't you, Mayor?"

Stanton swallowed, took a deep breath, and rattled it through his teeth coming out again. "Ah, y-yes. S-sure."

Worry decorated the judge's expression; he should have known something like this would happen. Earlier, he had expressed his concern about Rand hiring the two deputies to the mayor, but Stanton had assured him that it was a good move that would pay off next year during the cattle drives. Buchanan was angry at himself for letting that reasoning pass unchallenged, even though he had no authority to change the hiring.

"Yes . . . I am." Checker lifted his hands from the bowl and stood.

"At least let Dad put on a new wrap, John," Sarah Ann said.

"He can do that later." Checker pulled off the soaked bandage and dropped it. "Please watch the kids for us until we get back."

"Of course." Her frown was deep. "Be careful, John."

CHAPTER THIRTY-TWO

"Your rifle's in the wagon, John," Sonny said.

"Thanks. I'll head your way." Walking slowly, but steadily, Checker reached the buckboard, took the gun, and levered it with his left hand. His knuckles were raw and bloody, but his left hand wasn't stiff. His right arm and hand were numb and it was difficult to hold the gun while readying it.

"You realize you're in violation of our town's ordinance against carrying guns," Mayor Stanton snarled.

Revitalized by the mayor's bravado, Marshal Rand thrust out his lower lip and nodded agreement.

Ignoring the comment, Checker looked at Judge Buchanan, still mounted on his horse. "Judge, Sonny and I will take our buckboard." He glanced at Mayor Stanton, who was fiddling with his horse's bridle. "Mayor, you may ride along if you wish. Rand, I want you in front of me, where I can watch you." His stare cut into the mayor's whitened face. "Oh, and we'll keep our guns, Mayor."

From behind them, Dr. Tremons hollered, "Hey, who's

going to get this big thing outta my yard?" Dr. Tremons pointed at Kana'ti lying on the ground. "Somebody's got to do something with him."

Sonny chuckled. "I'll get him movin'. All right, Kana'ti, get up now. John, how do you say that in Cherokee?"

Checker repeated Sonny's directions in Cherokee.

Nodding his approval, Sonny walked toward Kana'ti and stopped. The big Cherokee was standing, holding the back of his head with his right hand and his groin with his left. His coat was streaked with blood, sweat, and dirt and his bare legs were skinned and soiled.

"Well, big boy, you're gonna walk ahead of us. We're gonna see a medicine wagon," Sonny said. "Oh, by the way, your baby brother is dead. He tried to back-shoot the wrong man."

Kana'ti's bleary eyes took in his dead brother; a twinge at the corner of his mouth was the only sign of emotion.

"You go right over there. Don't move till I tell you—or I'll blow a big hole in your middle." He motioned with his rifle in the direction of the wagon.

Checker said something in Cherokee.

Grunting, Kana'ti shuffled forward, holding himself. He stopped beside the wheel and stared at his unmoving brother. No one understood his words that followed, not even Checker. Without saying anything more, Sonny tied Kana'ti's puffed and bloody hands behind him. The huge Indian snarled every imaginable curse in Cherokee, but made no attempt to resist, his eyes never leaving Checker.

Sonny glanced past the beaten killer and saw a lone rider silhouetted in the distance. Was he headed toward the Tremons house? It looked that way. More trouble? "John, rider comin'." He stared at the beaten Cherokee. "Kana'ti, got any more nasty excuses for brothers?"

Checker had already seen the advancing horseman.

"Somethin' about that rider looks familiar, Sonny, but I'm not sure."

Sonny held his left hand to his forehead, shielding the sunlight. "Nobody I know. Can't see his face. He's one-armed, got his right sleeve pinned to his coat. Might be an ex–soldier boy. The way he's ridin', I'd say he's been at a saloon way too long." He turned back to Kana'ti, who shifted his weight and lost his balance, fell and slowly got up again.

With a long creak, the front door swung open and Johnny rushed outside and ran to stand beside Checker. The boy's right hand was a fist. His expression was determined; Sonny saw a shade of Amelia in the set jaw. Must run in the family, he mused to himself.

"Here, Uncle John, I thought you might need this." Johnny opened his fist and revealed the small white pebble. "I asked Mama for it. Got it off her table by the bed."

"Well, thank you, Johnny. I appreciate that." Checker smiled and held out his left hand for Johnny to place the stone in it. He tightened his fingers around the stone as best he could. "I'll keep this—until it's over, if that's all right." He shoved it into his pants pocket, trying not to let the stiffness show.

"You bet. I told Mama you'd likely be givin' it back to her."

"Johnny, you get back in the house now," Checker said. "I don't know who this rider is—but it might be more trouble. Take Miss Tremons inside with you. All right, bud?"

As all the men watched, the mysterious rider ambled closer. A black hat was pulled low, nearly covering his eyes; a long gray trail coat showed much wear even from a distance. His empty right sleeve was pinned to his coat.

"Uncle John, that's Tyrel." Johnny waved. "He's in Jackson's coat. What's happened to his arm?

The lone rider laid the reins across the saddle horn,

raised his hand in a similar greeting, and grabbed the leather again.

"Tyrel? What the . . . ?" Checker stared again, then glanced back toward Kana'ti.

The Cherokee killer's face was swelling around his nose and mouth; his right eye had already closed. His slight movements were those of a man hurting badly.

Tyrel Bannon kicked his horse into a gallop to close the distance and reined up behind the buckboard. As the farm boy pulled to a stop, his right hand popped through the opening between the buttons of his trail coat; his new Colt was in his fist.

Johnny face broke into a wide smile. "He was foolin', Uncle John. He was foolin'. Tyrel's arm's all right."

"It sure is," Checker said and stepped toward the disguised rider. "Tyrel, what brings you here—and all dressed up like that?"

Jumping down from the horse, Bannon held the reins and pushed back his hat. "It was Jackson's idea. This be his coat. It's the boss's hat. There's gun trouble waitin'— in town." He gulped to hold down the excitement in his young voice. "When we brought Salome to the jail . . . the McCallister boys was gone. Jackson and the boss figure they're hidin' in town somewhars, a-waitin' for you to ride through. They figure Star let 'em out. Yes, sir, that's what they be thinkin'."

In between gulps of air, Bannon told them Jackson had been worrying about leaving town with the two Cherokee killers showing up, and when they found Salome on the trail, half starved, they decided to turn around.

"Jackson said this were a sign—findin' Salome—an' we should go back. Yessir, them's his exact words," Bannon continued. "She's at the jail now—with the boss and Jackson." He licked his lower lip and took another deep breath. "Tug an' Randy are with the horses an' the chuck. 'Bout two days out. Waitin' for us. They're fine."

He said they didn't know what else to do with Salome and asked what was going on here. Checker explained and Johnny excitedly told about the fight.

"Jackson figured Star had sprung his men while Rand was away so the marshal'd have an excuse," Bannon said, glancing at Rand. "We heard the stirrin' 'bout that phony medicine peddler an' all when we came to town. Some lady tolt us whar you were." He twisted his face into a sour expression. "She don't care much for you, John. Anyways, Jackson thought I should be a-bringin' you the word—an' look like somebody they wouldn't'a suspect. He had me leave by the back door o' the jail. An' wander down to a saloon first. Didn't drink nothin', o' course."

Checker studied Rand's face for signs of advance knowledge, but the look was one of genuine surprise. A glance at Kana'ti told him nothing; the big Indian was barely standing. Mayor Stanton was trying to look indignant, achieving only a look of a soured, tan jack-o'-lantern.

"Jackson figured it were Star doin' the plannin'—and gettin' that story around town to set you up. He done read the newspaper to us 'bout you." He stopped and looked at Buchanan, then Stanton. "Back home, we call that skunk talk." He stared at Judge Buchanan. "Ya can't really think John Checker is a murderer, can ya? In Texas, he was the lawman everybody wanted when there was trouble. I can't believe such . . . skunk talk."

Judge Buchanan glared at Mayor Stanton, but said nothing.

"Jackson was right about Star. Paid the mayor here to try to make things worse," Sonny announced over his shoulder, not allowing Kana'ti to be out of his focus.

"He . . . I . . . did no such thing, cowboy. I don't have the faintest idea where Star McCallister is. You are the ones who saw him last, I presume. Or did you kill him, too?" Mayor Stanton straightened himself and pulled on his coat.

Fiddling with the reins of his horse, Marshal Rand looked like he was going to vomit.

Sonny laughed out loud. "Now, that's true skunk talkin', Tyrel—an' from a true skunk." He pushed back his derby with the nose of his rifle. "How come you didn't get to stay in the jail, Tyrel—with Salome?" He grinned.

Bannon's face flashed crimson, and then he, too, grinned. "Don't think she's gonna run away no more, Sonny. She can barely walk. Hungrier than all git out. Didn't look so purty neither. Reckon we saved her life. She said as much."

Unable to wait any longer, Johnny ran over to the farm boy and greeted him warmly. Bannon was equally happy to see his young friend and asked about the ranch. Johnny began a nonstop description of everything that had happened since the Triple C riders left. Bannon interrupted the presentation long enough to tell Checker that Jackson and Dan Mitchell planned to wait in the jail until they knew what the former Ranger wanted done. Likely, Mitchell would remain in the jail and Jackson would sneak out and find another spot to shoot from. There were no signs of the McCallister gang, but Jackson was certain they were waiting.

Judge Buchanan eased his horse next to the tall gunfighter. "Mr. Checker, looks to me like we've got more pressing issues to settle—before we go to the medicine wagon. Do you agree?"

"Yeah, looks that way, Judge," Checker said. "You and the mayor—and Rand—can stay here. Keep an eye on Kana'ti, if you will. Or let him go, he's your man."

"He goes nowhere. But I intend to ride with you," Judge Buchanan said. "Nobody can play hob with the law like this." He looked toward the house where Dr.

Tremons stood. "Doc, I'd be obliged if you let me borrow your shotgun and some loads."

Dr. Tremons nodded with approval. "Wish I could." He stroked the straying lock of hair. "But I'm goin' along too. This here has gone far enough."

"All right, I'll use my own." Judge Buchanan patted the coat covering his shoulder-holstered gun. "I could use some additional cartridges, however. Seems I've used most already."

Checker said, "Doc, I'd appreciate it if you would stay here and keep that shotgun on Kana'ti. Sonny, tie his feet together, will you? Sarah Ann, will you watch the kids?"

Dr. Tremons's mouth slid into the start of an argument, but he chose silence instead. Holding Rebecca in her arms, Sarah Ann mouthed agreement. Sonny immediately went to Kana'ti, told him to get down on the ground, and began lacing his legs together.

"The hell you say. I'll decide what and where I'm about." Rand's eyebrows arched wildly. "I am the top lawman around here." He yanked angrily on the reins he held, without realizing it. His horse snorted and jerked its head to avoid more pressure.

"Actually you're not." Checker rubbed his chin as if to relieve some soreness, nodded as if agreeing with some silent decison, and withdrew a second folded paper from his pocket.

Defiantly, Rand raised his chin. "I'm not afraid of you, Ranger. You don't have any authority here. Or are you going to kill me like you did that peddler?" He stepped backward, pulling his horse with him as an instinctive wall of protection.

Checker offered the paper over to the judge mounted a few feet away. Buchanan took out his glasses again and studied the printed telegram. He looked up with the hint of a smile dancing on his usually stoic face.

"Are you prepared to do this?" Judge Buchanan asked.

"I don't have a choice."

The judge chuckled at the repeated use of the phrase.

Mayor Stanton demanded to know what was going on. Marshal Rand felt the revolver under his coat, looked up, and saw Sonny staring at him. He swallowed and checked his bridle.

"With your permission, Mr. Checker, I'll share this aloud," Judge Buchanan said, his smile now readily apparent.

"That's fine."

"This wire is addressed to John Checker, Captain—Texas Rangers, Retired." Judge Buchanan cleared his throat and read, holding the paper at arm's length from his spectacled eyes. "'Understand situation in Dodge and agree with you—stop—As of this date you are hereby appointed deputy U S marshal—stop—Take action as you find correct—Advise when appropriate—stop.'" He paused and concluded, "It's signed, Joseph F. Daniels, U.S. Marshal, Kansas District."

"What?" Mayor Stanton's face was a bloated purple balloon.

Sonny leaned his head back and roared, "Ya-hoo! Been wonderin' when you was gonna play that card."

Laughing, Dr. Tremons imitated the drover's yell and ended it with a cough.

Sliding his hand toward his shoulder holster, Marshal Rand took advantage of the outburst.

"Rand, your hand better come out with a congratulatory cigar for U.S. Deputy Marshal John Checker," Dr. Tremons growled. His shotgun was aimed at the unnerved lawman.

Checker walked over to Rand. He reached inside the lawman's coat and yanked free the revolver, then grabbed his lapel where his badge was pinned.

"I took this off you once before, Rand. This time it stays off," Checker growled and ripped the badge from the cloth and shoved it in his pocket.

Rand gagged, turned toward his horse, and regurgitated down his horse's neck. The animal whinnied and danced sideways.

"Before we go, I'd like to ask the boy a few questions, if you don't mind." Judge Buchanan leaned forward in the saddle.

"Go right ahead. Sonny and I need a few minutes to talk things over with our friend."

Judge Buchanan looked at Johnny and said, "Son, you were kidnapped by that gang, is that right?"

"Yes, sir, I was. Me an' my little sis."

"I'm mighty sorry about that—an' your—"

"My uncle is takin' care of us until my Mama can do it," Johnny interrupted. "Our friend, Sonny Jones, is helpin' too. We're gettin' along real fine. My sis doesn't have nightmares anymore. Leastwise, not much." He looked over at Sarah Ann. "Miss Tremons, she done got our neighbors to put back up our place after them bad men burned it." His chin rose defiantly. "They kilt my paw. I'm the man o' the house now."

"I'm sure you will be a fine one." Judge Buchanan's face was gentle. "Do you mind if I ask you a couple more questions?"

"No, sir. What do ya wanna know?"

"Was this fellow, Dr. Gambree, with them . . . with the gang?"

"Not right away, sir. He came later. With his wagon—and the lady."

Mayor Stanton wrestled with his stirrup and lurched into the saddle. "Judge, this is most uncalled for. This is a boy."

Judge Buchanan's countenance changed from gentle to furious. "Eklin, I don't know what's got into you, but I suggest you change your attitude. Fast. I want to hear this boy's story." He turned back to Johnny. "Please, son, I'd really like to know what went on, especially about this . . . Dr. Gambree."

CHAPTER THIRTY-THREE

Johnny hitched his pants and launched into a detailed dissertation about Star McCallister calling the medicine peddler "Blue" and "little brother" and the peddler saying that he hoped the boy's uncle would come so that he could kill him.

"Thank you, son. Did you see your uncle . . . ah, shoot this peddler?" Judge Buchanan sat in the saddle with his arms crossed.

"No, sir. No one did. My sis an' me, we were with Tyrel." He explained about Bannon taking him to safety while the others fought the gang. He included Sonny being wounded.

"Do you know an outlaw named Tom Redmond?" Judge Buchanan asked.

"Oh yes, sir. A big mean-lookin' fella. Wears Rebel trousers."

"Yes. That's the man. Where was he while your uncle fought this peddler?"

Johnny raised his chin. "Well, he was standin' with the

others—with their hands up. He didn't see it neither."

Studying the intense boy, the judge asked if he would lie to protect his uncle. Johnny set his chin and replied that his uncle wouldn't stand for it.

"Thank you, son, that's most helpful." Judge Buchanan started to rein his horse away, then stopped. "Did you hear any of them talk about . . . Marshal Rand?"

Johnny nodded and told him there was discussion among Blue and Star McCallister about the Dodge City lawman and how he had slipped away from his sleeping wife to help with the breakout. He said Star mentioned giving Rand money; he thought it was five hundred dollars, but more was owed; he wasn't sure of that amount, however. He concluded that the peddler said they should have killed the marshal too, that he would break under questioning and tell about his involvement in the escape. The judge thanked him and eased his horse into a walk toward the wagon.

Marshal Rand avoided the judge's glare.

The decision was quickly made for Checker and Sonny to take the wagon, leave it a few streets away from Front Street, and advance on foot. Bannon would ride out now, repeating his performance as a one-armed drunk; Checker told him to ride past the jail and only stop for a moment, like he was trying to decide where he was. He would alert Jackson and Mitchell that they were coming on foot. If he saw any of the McCallister gang en route, he was to immediately ride back and tell Checker and Sonny.

Pulling alongside the three men, Judge Buchanan declared again that he would go with them and Checker thanked him for the decision.

"Mr. Jones, please remove the badges of those two deputies. I take it you have no objection, Elkin." He turned in the saddle toward the mayor.

Frowning, Mayor Stanton muttered agreement.

Judge Buchanan motioned toward Checker and asked him to put on the marshal's badge in his pocket. After Sonny removed the badges from Kana'ti and Do'tsi, he asked the happy cowboy to put one on as well.

"Please, Mr. Jones, put on one of the badges." He looked again at the mayor. "You agree, don't you, Mayor?"

The mayor shrugged.

Placing the Winchester on the seat ahead of him, Checker climbed into the wagon and sat. Battle adrenaline was infusing his body with new strength. It always seemed to do so. He squeezed his hands to test their stiffness. Most of the soreness was gone from his left hand, but his right hand offered only slow resonse.

"Gentlemen, I trust you will uphold the laws of Dodge City. This is a temporary appointment until this . . . is over. Say 'I will.'"

"I will," Checker said as he pinned on the badge.

"I will." Sonny's reply was a bit slower.

After pinning on his badge, Sonny whispered, "Me, a lawman. Who would've bet that way?"

"Looks good on you," Checker said.

"Wait, John, I've got an idea." Sonny stopped in mid-climb into the wagon bed.

Checker turned in the seat. "I'm listening."

"Tyrel and Jackson have it right. We need a disguise."

Checker's eyebrows rose with interest.

"We'll dress up Do'tsi to look like you. Let him wear your tunic and hat. Bullets ain't gonna hurt him none now. We'll have to tie 'im in place, prop 'im up with something. A board. If Doc's got one."

"Where will I be?" Checker asked.

"In the back with me. One o' us can handle the leather from there. Crouched down so we aren't seen."

Minutes later, the dead Do'tsi was tied into place on

the seat wearing Checker's hat and Comanche tunic. Bannon helped the two gunfighters prepare the deception, then rode off again. A long board from Dr. Tremons's barn holding him upright was also tied in place.

In the meanwhile, Judge Buchanan had reloaded his pistol with cartridges from Do'tsi's gun belt. Sonny gave him the dead Cherokee's revolver as a backup weapon.

"Sonny, let's go one more," Checker suggested. "You handle the wagon—and I'll take the mayor's coat, hat—and horse. It'll give me a better view."

"Good idea. Right, Stanton?"

Receiving the stunned mayor's garments, Checker demanded, "You be right here when we come back. If I have to come looking, you'll be sorry."

"Are you threatening the mayor of Dodge City?"

"No. I'm a federal officer making a promise to a crooked politician." Checker put on the coat, shoved the hat on his head, and climbed into the mayor's saddle. "You're a lucky man, Stanton. In Texas, we tar and feather your kind." He rode over to the buckboard and retrieved his rifle with his left hand. The reins lay across his half-closed right fist.

With his arms folded across his chest, the mayor tried to look unperturbed. The beads of sweat lining his forehead were growing more pronounced.

After it was decided that Rand should ride with them, the wagon and three outriders rode out in a measured formation, moving through the quiet residential street and turning south onto First Avenue. Bannon was nowhere in sight as they eased through neighborhoods adjoining the main thoroughfare. Do'tsi's body bounced, but remained upright.

The peacefulness of the city's residential district belied what lay ahead.

"It's a pretty autumn day, isn' it?" Judge Buchanan

commented, almost to himself. His revolver was in his hand, resting on his thigh. "If it weren't for this."

"Yes, Judge, it is," Checker said and added, "Look, I don't think they'll shoot at any of the three of us. Unless they recognize me. But when we hit Front Street, you be ready to find cover, just in case."

"I can handle myself."

"I know that. Sonny told me."

"I had no choice."

Checker grinned at the continued use of the phrase. "Glad you saw it that way. Stanton has a different problem."

"I know. Hiram is an old friend, but I fear some bad habits may have gotten the best of him," Judge Buchanan said. "I trust you really do have the evidence you mentioned."

Checker looked over at the solemn magistrate and described what was in the wagon and painted on its sides. Buchanan indicated he would talk with the editor about printing a more accurate story.

When Checker didn't respond, Buchanan changed the subject. "And this outlaw Cole Dillon I've been hearing about?"

"He was a bad one. Died right next to his wife's grave. I was there," Checker said.

"My goodness! It would be difficult to imagine your friend being mistaken for him."

"I know." Checker glanced over at the sour former marshal who was looking straight ahead as he rode. A strange twisted smile was pasted on his pale face.

As they neared Front Street, the town appeared unaware of the jail breakout, with people and wagons crisscrossing the street.

Spotting the judge and the man she thought was the mayor, Violet Kensington strutted onto the street from the corner of Chestnut and First. From the weight of her shopping bag, she had been busy. Checker reined his horse so he wasn't in her direct line of sight and ducked his chin to let his hat hide most of his features.

"I'm glad to see you've arrested that awful murderer. The kindly doctor was a God-fearing man," the heavyset woman declared loudly without looking at Checker.

"Miss Kensington, you'd better get inside. The McCallister gang has broken out," Judge Buchanan said without taking his eyes off the surrounding buildings.

"What? Oh my gracious! Oh my gracious!" She spun and waddled away, spewing the news to anyone nearby.

From behind the judge, Checker said, "Well, that should help clear out folks."

A well-dressed man and woman darted ahead of them across the street. The man was pulling the woman's arm to make her walk faster. An older man in unkempt clothes stopped in the middle of the street to watch them pass.

"Better get off the street, Henry," Judge Buchanan said. "There might be trouble."

"You're not arrestin' that Ranger fella, are ya?" the old-timer asked. "I heard o' him down in Texas. He's not someone to mess with, Judge."

"Thanks, Henry. I'll keep that in mind," he said and added, "Don't get close, please. This is official business."

"You betcha. Lemme know if'n ya need he'p." The old man waved and limped away.

"See anythin'?" Sonny asked from his squatting position just behind the buckboard seats. He was guiding the wagon horses with the reins draped across the seat, beside the propped-up Do'tsi.

"Not yet. Keep your head down. We're almost to Kelley's Opera House on the corner. We'll turn right. I'll tell you when." Checker held his rifle with his left hand at his side, cocked and ready.

"Shouldn't be long now," Sonny said.

The only sound coming from Front Street was the rattle of dice in a saloon chuck-a-luck cage.

"Maybe they ran away," Judge Buchanan whispered. Sweat wouldn't leave his hands as he alternately wiped them on his pants and squeezed the revolver nervously.

"Rooftop! Opera house!" Checker saw the movement and swung his rifle into firing position in the same breath.

From the opera house roof, orange flame cracked apart the quiet. Dust popped from Checker's borrowed tunic on Do'tsi's body.

Checker snapped a shot. Sonny aimed and fired twice quickly from his prone position in the wagon bed. A dark figure half stood from the roof and collapsed behind the parapet.

Rand spun his horse and galloped back down the street. Judge Buchanan watched him go, but decided not to pursue. His two shots were deliberately high. Rand's only reaction was to slap the reins of his horse hard against its rear.

With rifle smoke encircling him, Sonny stood and jumped from the wagon, letting it continue down Front Street, paralleling the railroad tracks, without direction. He hit the ground and staggered several steps, trying to keep his balance. His rifle flew from his hands. Grabbing the gun, he ran toward the opera house building adjacent to the street.

Gunfire crashed into the disguised, dead Cherokee from two places inside the Alhambra Saloon and two more from a window of the Great Western Hotel. The wagon swung wildly in the direction of the railroad tracks, then straightened and followed them toward the cattle pens. Checker's hat on Do'tsi's head snapped to attention and flew off. The body slumped awkwardly against the seat as the supporting beam slid sideways.

Gradually, the wagon slowed as the front horses eased to a trot, then to a complete stop ten yards from the stock pens.

A rifle barked from the jail; another from somewhere low along the railroad track itself. Checker guessed the gunfire was from Mitchell and Jackson; he didn't know where Bannon was.

"There's gunfire from the Great Western!" Checker yelled at Sonny, who was standing against the front outside wall of the opera house, loading his gun. "I'm going there. Judge, you and Sonny help Jackson and Dan."

Behind him came the boom of a shotgun, followed by more rifle fire and the sudden yell of "Don't shoot. Don't shoot. We surrender." A command to disarm burst through the noise; Checker couldn't tell whose voice it was.

He swung his horse toward the hotel, jumped the railroad tracks, galloped past the stand-alone jail, and headed straight for the hotel, firing his Winchester at a second-story window. He didn't expect to hit anything, but it was important to keep the hidden gunmen, whoever they were, off-balance. His mind told him there were more shooters than just the jailed outlaws. He leaped from the saddle before his horse reached the hitching rack and charged through the front door. Bounding upstairs, two steps at a time, he levered the Winchester with his left hand. Pain in his right hand, from just holding the stock, trailed the action. Fatigue from the battle with Kana'ti wasn't allowed to manifest in his bruised body. Not now.

At the top of the stairway, he stopped to listen. He slid along the wallway to the side of door 24. If he had judged right, this was the room where the shots had come from.

"Come in, Mayor Stanton. I am alone. A grand day it is. *Sacre bleu*, we have killed ze great John Checker—an' *le ami*."

Checker recognized the French-flavored voice as that of McCallister's saloon manager, Diverrouve. His statement about being the only one in the room couldn't be. Checker was certain two men had fired from the window. But if he had counted right—and no one else was involved—the two other McCallister outlaws should be in the Alhambra Saloon. That left only Diverrouve.

Unless Star McCallister himself was inside.

The room door slammed open and, from his kneeling position by the window, Diverrouve fired three times gut-high into the doorway.

"*Au revoir*, John Checker."

CHAPTER THIRTY-FOUR

With smoke from his rifle encircling his head, Diverrouve stared at the empty doorway. There was no sign of Checker or his body.

"*Quoi?* There ist no heem!" he muttered. "*Qu'est-ce qui s'est?*"

Squinting at the door, he was startled to see the nose of a Winchester pointing back at him just above the bottom hinge between the door and the frame.

An invisible voice commanded that he drop his gun.

With no sign of emotion, Diverrouve complied and held up his arms. "*S'il vous plait*, don't shoot. *S'il vous plait*." His gold tooth sparkled as he spoke.

"Where's your boss?" Checker stood and stepped backward into the hallway, making it difficult for anyone hiding in the room to see him.

The room itself contained a bed, a nightstand with an oil lamp, and a small closet. Filmy curtains flirted with the open air dancing from the window. He could see most of the area, except for the nearest inside wall.

"Ah, *Monsieur* Checker, I know not where *Monsieur* McCallister would be." The slender French saloon keeper avoided connecting with Checker's intense stare. "Est he not in ze Territory of ze Indian? You went after him, did you not?"

"Tell you what," Checker said. "Either you tell me what I want to know—or I'm going to shoot you. It doesn't matter to me which. I just don't have time to mess with this."

"But you are ze great lawman, *Monsieur* Checker— an' you are wearing ze badge of ze city." Diverrouve's face was awash in sweat. His eyes flashed in the direction of the closet.

It was the glimpse Checker was waiting for.

"Star, if you don't come out of that closet now, I'll tear it apart with lead." Checker stepped forward and aimed his Winchester at the closet.

"Good day to you, brother." Star McCallister slowly opened the door. "Didn't recognize you when you came onto Front Street. Smart move." He tossed his Winchester ahead of him to the floor.

"Had a feeling you were close by. This was supposed to be your big day, wasn't it? Too bad it didn't work." Checker studied McCallister as the outlaw leader eased from the compartment.

"Oh, you had a feeling, did you? Did you get that clairvoyance from your slut of a mother?" McCallister's eyelids fluttered as he wiped imaginary dust from his lapels.

The outlaw leader looped both thumbs into his vest pockets. His tailored, dark blue suit was a bit wrinkled and his cravat was slightly askew. A strand of blond hair was pasted against his damp forehead.

Checker didn't answer as he stepped farther into the room. It was the first time he had seen his half brother since McCallister's arrest. An unexpected sensation passed through Checker, wanting him to recall that happy childhood exchange between them at the pond. The former Ranger pushed away the tremor; this wasn't the time—and there was only one such memory anyway. Star and Blue were always hateful to Checker and his sister—or was it just childish competition? Checker shook his head. No, Star McCallister would try to kill him if he could. He forced himself to see Amelia torn and battered. Anger seeped into his mind and he allowed it to enter.

McCallister's eyes fluttered again and he looked like a captured weasel trying to decide which way to run, yet there seemed a calmness about him that was troubling to Checker.

"It's been a long ride," Checker snarled. "Want to guess what I'd like you to do right now?" The mayor's coat was tight along his shoulders and made him even more irritated than he was already.

"You wouldn't be able to shoot your own brother, would you, John?" McCallister said with a smile that didn't reach his eyes. "Oh, wait a minute, you already did. You killed Blue, didn't you? How awful. Who could do such a terrible thing—murder his own brother?"

"You're through, Star," Checker said. "You're going to hang. Take that iron from your shoulder holster with your fingers and drop it. Move real slow."

McCallister ran his fingers through his blond hair, being careful to move deliberately. "Don't like that idea, John. Hanging." He motioned with the same hand toward Checker's grip on his Winchester. "Hmmm, you've done something nasty to your right hand—and your left hand looks worse." He smiled and rubbed his chin. "Have a *feeling* you had a little run-in with Kana'ti."

"I did."

McCallister's upper lip came out like a little kid's. "You're standing. Guess that tells me what I need to know." He cocked his head to the side. "Do'tsi told me his big brother had never been beaten."

"He has now," Checker said.

"You think you're really something, don't you? The great Texas Ranger. Hell, you're nothing, Checker, nothing at all," McCallister spat. "I'm smarter than you'll ever be. You may look like . . . our father . . . but I'm his real son."

"You know, it took me a long time, but I found my *real* father. His name was Stands-in-Thunder."

McCallister looked at him again. His face was twisted as he tried to find the right response. "So what did happen to the two new deputies—after you beat up Kana'ti?"

"You and your boys just shot Do'tsi full of holes."

The outlaw leader's eyes became slits and the corner of his mouth jerked.

"That was him in the wagon," Checker said. "Well, actually, Do'tsi was already dead. Kana'ti is tied up, back at Dr. Tremons's house. There's a shotgun on him. If he moves, he'll join his brother. Oh, Mayor Stanton's there, too. Ready to talk."

McCallister glanced in the direction of the window as if he could see what had happened on Front Street. "So you took care of both Cherokees. I'm impressed. Some said Do'tsi was the best."

"I didn't do anything. He tried to shoot me in the back while I was fighting Kana'ti. My friends—and the judge—shot him."

"I don't believe you."

"I don't care if you believe you or not, Star. Quit stalling and take out the gun." Checker glanced in the direction of Diverrouve. "You stay right where you are, Frenchie, I can see you just fine from there. I can see your rifle too."

After squeezing his hands together as if in prayer, McCallister pulled the silver-plated pistol from his hidden holster and ceremoniously laid it on the floor at his feet. Returning to a standing position, McCallister smirked and told Checker that Do'tsi thought he would be reincarnated and that killing the former Ranger would give him immortality. McCallister's voice was soft, almost gentle.

Checker motioned for both men to walk toward the hallway.

"You hated us, didn't you, Checker? You hated the fact we were legitimate and you and your sister were bastards," McCallister said, without moving. "Well, look at you now. Your sister's almost dead—or will be. You've got nothing. Nothing but old shirts with badge holes in them. An' they're going to arrest you for murdering . . . your own brother." His laugh bounced off the small room.

"Don't think so, Star," Checker said. "That was a nice try with the newspaper and the fat lady—and the mayor. Too bad the federal marshals in Nebraska have a different version. Or hadn't you noticed the badge? Judge Buchanan gave it to me. Oh, I forgot to tell you, I'm a deputy U.S. marshal now."

McCallister frowned and his right eye twitched. He hadn't noticed and wondered what Diverrouve was talking about when he mentioned the badge earlier.

"Don't think you paid the mayor enough either." Checker moved his right hand on the stock to get a better grip. "Have a feeling his term's about over. Rand's definitely is. He left town when the shooting started."

"There's that 'feeling' again," McCallister said. "You know, things might've been different between us . . . if it hadn't been for . . . our father. He was always lying to us that you weren't really his children . . . that it was the wild tale of a whore looking for money. I'm sorry it had to be this way, John."

Diverrouve dove for his rifle.

Quickened movement filled the hallway outside the room.

Checker's Winchester swung toward the Frenchman and spurted flame and lead. Diverrouve grabbed his shoulder and the gun rattled against the wooden floor.

In the same instant, McCallister grabbed for the pistol at his feet, cocking it as he took control of the weapon.

The former Ranger spun his gun toward McCallister, levering a smoking shell, but didn't fire.

Behind Checker, two guns barked.

McCallister grunted and pointed his revolver at Checker. The guns behind the former Ranger fired again, then again. McCallister's hand wouldn't hold the shiny weapon upright and he grabbed it with both hands. Blood was creating circles on his vest in three places and slipping beneath his shirt cuffs onto his hands. His bullet smashed into the wall to Checker's left.

Glancing over his shoulder, Checker stood with his Winchester only half raised, and seemed surprised to see Sonny and Jackson in the open doorway with smoking rifles.

McCallister stared at them and gurgled, "So John Checker has others do his killing these days. How nice." His revolver slid unheeded from his hands and thudded on the floor, sending a bullet into the nearest wall.

"I didn't want it this way, Star," Checker said.

McCallister slumped to his knees as if praying. "I know. That's your damn mother in you. Our dad would've shot me between the eyes." He chuckled and blood gushed from his mouth and lined his teeth.

Checker turned toward the doorway. "Thanks, my friends. I . . . was in trouble." He stared down at the Winchester in his own hands. "Don't know what happened. Guess it jammed."

"No, John, you just couldn't shoot," Sonny said. "We knew you wouldn't."

Jackson added, "It was ours to do. He killed our friends."

Checker looked into their calm faces without totally comprehending what had just happened. Jackson pushed his spectacles back on his nose. Checker thought it was the first time he'd ever seen the man without his gray long coat. Sonny stood with his weight on his right leg. His usually happy demeanor had evaporated in his worry that they wouldn't arrive in time.

Checker's mind raced toward an earlier moment, one he had forgotten, except for the ride to the ranch a few days ago.

"You all right, John?" Sonny asked.

"Yeah."

"Everything's under control on the street. Ham joined us. That was his shotgun," Jackson said. "Redmond and Wells surrendered. Salome's in jail already. You boys picked Venner off the roof. Do'tsi . . . is shot to pieces. Your tunic doesn't look so good either." He tried to smile but couldn't.

"Our boys?"

Jackson chuckled. "They're fine. Oh yeah, Tyrel tripped and fell in a mud puddle . . . somewhere in the alley. He's a mess. Not hurt, though."

"Good." Checker put his hand on the black cowboy's shoulder, then on Sonny's. "If you don't mind, I'd like a minute alone—with Star."

Sonny walked across the room, kicked Diverrouve's gun toward Jackson, yanked the shoulder-holstered gun from under his coat, and lifted the wounded Frenchman to his feet. With his rifle riding against Diverrouve's back, Sonny led him out.

"Take your time, John," Jackson said gently as they left.

With their footsteps in the hall as the only sound, Checker moved next to McCallister and knelt beside him. Laying his Winchester down, he picked up Star's silver-plated revolver and shoved it into his own waistband.

"Remember that day when we fought off those dogs? Damn, they looked big and vicious," Checker said softly. "We were just kids then. I thought we were going to be friends. Brothers."

McCallister's eyes tried to focus as the dying man spoke, spewing blood from his mouth. "I—is your sister g-going to make it?"

"Looks like she will. No thanks to you."

McCallister was silent, and for a moment, Checker thought he was dead.

"Wh-why did you come back, John? Th-there never was anything here for you."

Checker pushed up his hat. "I guess I came . . . to find out who I was."

Convulsions took control of McCallister's torn body. Checker put a hand on the outlaw leader's shoulder and McCallister managed to grab and hold it with his own.

"Did you . . . find out . . . who you were?" McCallister coughed, leaving more blood on the floor. A soft sigh followed and he was still.

Checker pulled McCallister's hand away, laid it against his side, and checked the dead man's pulse. "Yes. I'm your brother." He rose, picked up his rifle, and walked away. In the doorway, he turned back. "I'll bury you myself. Out by that pond. Where we really were brothers. Once."

COTTON SMITH

STANDS A RANGER

Time Carlow is a Texas Ranger with a mighty dangerous job to do. A half-crazy killer named Silver Mallow has escaped from the jail in Bennett, Texas, and it's up to young Carlow to bring him back. All by himself. The killer has a three-day lead on him, and everything from luck to the weather seems to be against Carlow. Silver Mallow will do whatever it takes to stay out of jail, and he won't hesitate to use his gun. But he never counted on one determined Ranger.

Dorchester Publishing Co., Inc.
P.O. Box 6640
Wayne, PA 19087-8640

_____5539-2
$5.99 US/$7.99 CAN

Name: _____

Address: _____

City: _____ State: _____ Zip: _____

E-mail: _____

I have enclosed $_____ in payment for the checked book(s).

CHECK OUT OUR WEBSITE! www.dorchesterpub.com
_____ *Please send me a free catalog.*